SCORPION GRASS

PETER KIESNERS

Black Rose Writing | Texas

This is a work of fiction. Names, characters, businesses, places, events, and incidents are either the products of the author's imagination or used in a fictitious manner. Any resemblance to actual persons, living or dead, or actual events is purely coincidental.

ISBN: 978-1-68513-264-4
PUBLISHED BY BLACK ROSE WRITING
www.blackrosewriting.com

Printed in the United States of America
Suggested Retail Price (SRP) $25.95

Scorpion Grass is printed in Book Antiqua

*As a planet-friendly publisher, Black Rose Writing does its best to eliminate unnecessary waste to reduce paper usage and energy costs, while never compromising the reading experience. As a result, the final word count vs. page count may not meet common expectations.

Contents

SCORPION GRASS

Prologue

February

A small crowd had amassed on the pebbled beach next to Brighton Pier. The winter sun was low in the sky on a near windless day as a diver and a paramedic carried the slim body of what was probably a boy or young teen up from the shushing surf. Even from a distance, as she broke into a run, Cassy was struck by the pasty white complexion which fluoresced as it popped into view from between onlookers. For a moment it seemed the diver had picked up a shiny, otherworldly body having arrived by sea, but failed to do so alive.

Where's Keller? Per the cams on the pier, it looked like he reacted to what's happening, even though he didn't see the boy fall or drown.

As she neared, the crowd had thickened so that her view of the boy was blocked. Despite that, she slowed to a walk to survey the situation. So far, one ambulance had arrived, and one police car. No media as of yet. A jogger slowed down and craned his neck, a woman with a stroller was contemplating leaving the boardwalk for a closer view and attention from passersby all over, was gravitating to the gathering. *People have a thing for death and sinister things.*

Then she saw him, walking across from the pier, in no rush, apprehensive. Cassy kept pace with a large man and his voluptuous wife or girlfriend, using them as a shield, keeping out of Keller's view if he were to look her way. But she could not understand what he was doing. *Is he waiting? Talking to himself again?* Then he picked up his pace in resolve and thrust his way through the crowd. *Go man.*

Cassy moved ahead and positioned herself a little back from the front, still not wanting to be noticed by Keller. Not that he knew who she was or had ever seen her before, Cassy preferred to keep her distance. She had been shadowing him on and off for the last few months, ever since a notable incident at the Emergency department of a London hospital. A man had swerved off the M25 highway, his truck rolling into the median. Keller had pulled over to help and found him in critical condition hemorrhaging. He followed the ambulance to the hospital, lurked there in the waiting room and then burst upon the scene when doctors were giving up resuscitation. The man was considered dead. Yet Keller, a medical student, made an awkward scene when he insisted they continue resuscitation and finally began yelling at the corpse. Not directly at the body, but at the man's ghost, whom he later explained to journalists he could sense to be somewhere above and behind the body. Keller simply challenged the man aggressively to 'Stop being such a wuss and give it all another go. Life is short as it is,' he had yelled. And, just as doctors began to lay hands on the apparently demented student, just as security guards swept the curtains aside to grab him, there was a blip on the monitor. While doctors and nurses froze, a suddenly quiet Keller was muscled away from the scene and later held for questioning.

The corpse, on the other hand, came back to life. It took another 3 hours or so of surveillance and treatment until he was stable, but he lived, no brain damage evident. While the doctor on duty had little to comment, the survivor went on to tell tabloids of his amazing recovery, thanks to a bloke who had screamed at him during his darkest moment. Dark as the devil's molasses, he had said. Keller became an overnight celebrity to some, and a bungling psychopath to others—a flukester who had lurked the halls of countless hospitals looking for a coincidence to manipulate. Cassy knew he had done no such thing.

Cassy could see and hear fragments of a heated discussion between paramedics, the diver, and Keller, who was insisting the boy could make it. *He's doing it again, this time saying he's a doctor… Oh, just let him work.* Cassy inched forward and yearned to break in, to tell the paramedics and diver that Keller was indeed a specialist in hypothermia and had been part of countless situations such as this. It maybe wasn't true, but Cassy felt he could bring back a freshly frozen man in a block of ice 10,000 years old if given the chance to do his thing. Cassy also felt the presence of the boy, a struggle nearby, an abstract cry for help.

"He's dead, let him be," an elderly man said, greyed with distinction, out for a jog no doubt. He brushed past Cassy, the corners of his mouth twitching, redness having crept up his neck and into his face. But most others stood and watched the discussion, curious.

Before long, Keller fell to his knees alongside the boy, speaking to him while beginning CPR once again. *He's talking about the boy's dog? Yes… but how did he know?* Moments later one of the paramedics yelled 'Clear!' and as Keller backed off, an electroshock surged the boy's chest. Keller's tone became more intense. One woman grabbed her head and turned. "I can't bear this. The boy is dead—that guy's playing God," she said, stepping past the second row. "The man thinks he's a necromancer is what," she said to Cassy, passing by.

"He's a psychic," Cassy muttered under her breath.

"What did you say?"

"He's very talented, let him work," Cassy said a little louder and turned back to the scene as Keller announced there was noticeable color in the boy's cheeks.

"Then you're a quack, just like him," the woman said from behind. Cassy ignored her, lurching forward now as she sensed a change in the crowd which had stiffened and stood very still, mesmerized, quiet. But as she made it to the front, she could see Keller was heatedly speaking to someone in the crowd… no… he wasn't focused on them at all. *He's talking to the boy.*

Moments further, a paramedic announced he felt something — the boy had twitched and seconds later, he indeed heaved. The second paramedic yanked the tube from his throat and prepared an oxygen mask while the first pushed the boy to his side. Gently at first, sputtering, and then harder as his skinny body wretched to eject water from his lungs much like a garden tap long unused. *He's coming alive!*

As if verbally echoing Cassy's thought, people broke out of their trance with cheers of disbelief. "I thought he was a goner, I thought!" one man exclaimed, while another slapped Keller on the back who stood back now as the two paramedics continued to stabilize the boy.

Cassy also moved to retreat, the blue sky bluer than before, the winter sea more turquoise than grey, lapping gently against the pebble beach. A rather enormous crowd had formed now as another ambulance and two police cars had stopped on Madeira drive 50m away. Cassy noted a journalist who seemed to have materialized from nowhere, talking with the diver who in turn pointed to Keller. Keller, overhearing, made a lavish gesture towards the paramedics and soon after melted into the crowd, people clamping his shoulders and arms in congratulations. The journalist pursued him.

Further down along the beach, Cassy caught the journalist catching up with Keller, who looked like he preferred to shrug him off. *Not one for spotlights, I guess.* She yanked her phone out and texted. *All good. He brought the boy back by talking about his bloody dog. It's like he knew where the kid was all along.* Cassy pressed send and pocketed the phone.

When she looked up to check, she could see the journalist taking a photo, exchanging more words with Keller, who, judging by his hand gestures and shoulders jumping up from time to time, seemed to be insisting he didn't know what had transpired. *Not good, don't blow it off, be specific…*

Once again, she wanted to run and catch up with them, entice Keller to a cab and whisk him away. *They'll make a meal out of him on the net and off.* But Cassy refrained and turned to walk back to her car the way she came. *No sense in meeting him just yet. Maybe next time.*

Chapter 1

The following May

Violet walked alongside Henrik as if it were a simple night on the town, and they a distinguished couple exploring the warren of streets and alleys known as The Lanes, in Brighton. Once a fishing village, it was now glossed over with pubs, restaurants, and tea houses buzzing with nightlife. Upon looking over the profile of the man next to her, Violet remarked with a spine-tickling chill how malevolent a perfectly intelligent and handsomeish man could be. He must have sensed her gaze or perhaps noted the lethargy in her step and offered an arm, which Violet accepted. *I feel like a whore. Less than one. A cadaver connected to a brain.*

"Where are we going?" Violet asked, a little ashamed she still didn't know.

Henrik paused to look at her, drawing a straight line with his lips. "To meet a friend."

"Beautiful night for it. Can you not actually tell me the name of the place? Or the friend's name?"

"It's a surprise."

"Let me guess, when you gave me something for my tummy ache, you took something yourself as well. And now you're just guessing how to get there. You've forgotten."

Henrik chuckled.

"Why are you doing what you're doing, Henrik?"

"And what might I be doing?"

"This. I'm tired and I'm groggy and I don't even have my purse."

"You don't need your purse."

You're so high tonight you forgot to check if my wallet was even in there.

"This friend of yours we're meeting, does he like to party?"

"I imagine so," he answered indifferently.

"Do you even know his name?" Violet began to laugh.

Henrik stopped and faced her, waiting until she calmed. "We're meeting Keller Mod."

"Keller? Oh, the guy, the son of the guy whom you blew up."

"I didn't blow anyone up. Violet please, keep it together," he said, clenching jowls.

"Can I pick the place?"

"Ed insisted on The Library," Henrik said, pointing ahead to a pub with emerald walls and bay windows.

"Oh, my, The Library indeed. You do everything Ed tells you?"

"Yes, unfortunately."

Violet didn't ask why. She knew he wouldn't tell her much. She felt like a little bug who had landed on a meaty red blossom one sunny afternoon, only to find it to close down on her. As a human, she knew the mansion where she stayed was a Venus Fly Trap of sorts, but on an insect level, didn't fathom the depth of it. Nor the consequences.

"So, Ed is like your excuse, your license to do everything you do, is that it?"

Henrik didn't answer, instead putting his arm around her waist as she miscalculated the curb, heels wobbling. Music tinged the air, weaving through purling voices as the outdoor tables at The Library neared.

"What's the plan then, are you going to kidnap him too?" she continued.

"You came to us out of your own free will," Henrik said, stopping again.

"You're such a bullshitter Henrik."

"You wish to leave, or do you prefer to see this thing out? Run if you want. But do it now. Take a bottle and smash it over my head. There's an empty wine bottle on the table behind you, and plenty of witnesses. Go on." They scanned each other's eyes for a moment until Violet looked away.

"I think you mean it," she said. *He needs the witnesses to show Ed.*

"I do. Or stay with me and help me convince Keller to come along. We need his help. One way or another, Ed will get him. So might as well be us, and tonight."

Violet nodded grimly. *You're corralling people because you're in over your head. No one should hack the human body like you, it ain't natural. Yet here I am, whoring to be young gain. How messed up is this all?*

They walked into The Library, indeed a library of sorts, in that there were shelves full of books, complete with ladders, sofas, and study lamps on the tables. There was also a grand pub presence established first and foremost by a circular bar, the nucleus from which everything flowed outward—the aisles, servers, drinks, and wide-screen TVs. Violet noticed they formed a heptagon.

She and Henrik sat down at a semi-private study table—while Henrik faced the outside windows, Violet the bar and entrance. Seconds later, their server arrived and minutes after that, a tray of drinks, appetizers, and coffee.

"You don't waste any time," Violet said, her hands clasped in front of her.

"We should take advantage. I'm really not sure how this night will pan out," Henrik replied as he glanced at his phone.

"How inspiring."

"Forgive me. I find coffee to be the most elegant of chasers, and, I'm hoping a Manhattan is alright for you."

"Ah. Yes, thank you. You remembered," she said, taking a sip, leaving the black olive on the side.

Feeling less tired after a stiff drink, Violet warmed up to Henrik, who eloquently explained almost every inquiry she had regarding the Jolly More Mansion where she fell prey to curious experiments and tests, and where Henrik ran things. The conversation led to paranormal activity as Henrik told of how the place had been renovated. Numerous entities had attempted to foil their progress with flooding, electrical disturbances, and shadowed apparitions, which he digested as hallucinations. Yet Violet could see a glint in his eyes, testing her boundaries and flogging his own.

"I assumed it may have been a lack of competence amongst the trades people—they were all from the island," Henrik mused.

You have no idea, do you? Violet smiled and made naïve comments. She was first and foremost an actor, born, bred and spent her fair share of time on the big screen. It was a relief to be away from the Mansion. While stories of 'disturbances' as Henrik had called them had not bothered her, the overall presence of someone alive and watching via security cams was creeping her out in a way that shucked oysters did—a delicatesse revered by some, despised, and ridiculed by others.

And though an actor, reality shows were not Violet's thing— the distorted speaker phone voice of Ed, the big boss, who never showed himself and the multiple cams throughout the mansion suggested surveillance and secrecy too extravagant for plain security.

As the evening wore on, Violet realized she and Henrik might be friends if things were different. Henrik was not an actor, though tricky, but rather the closest thing she had seen to a mad scientist in real life. If he were to lighten up on substance abuse, it might work in his favor.

While Henrik kept checking his phone, he didn't appear to get the answer he sought, or any.

"What do you need Keller for?" she began.

"Let's just say he has abilities. He's deeply troubled about it all, but very talented. Perhaps you remember a story from a year ago about a man who dies in a car crash and gets brought back in hospital, allegedly by a guy who yelled at the ceiling?"

"Yes, I know that one. And about the drowned boy. I'm sure there are others. But why do you specifically need him to be at the Jolly More?" Violet said, burping inwardly and feeling a little drunk.

Henrik began as if to answer, then reconsidered. "Let him explain when he arrives. Ed told me he'd come, but I don't get that impression," Henrik said, putting his phone on the table.

"Ed is full of surprises."

Violet noticed the bartender glancing her way at times. "I think you may have competition, Dr Poole."

"Not a doctor."

"But it suits you."

Then Henrik did something which delighted Violet. He got busy on his phone and by the end of the next drink, he showed her the screen. Surveillance cams revealed the bartender glancing over from time to time, then texting. "I think you're right," Henrik said as she laughed quietly.

But by the next drink, Violet got dizzy, and her sight blurred. Henrik appeared very attractive at this point and the man with a nice build and baffling tattoos who had sat down at the bar, even more so. *I've lost track, not like me…*

As if noticing her behavior, Henrik got busy once more. This time a small test strip of paper appeared in his nimble fingers, and he dipped it in Violet's remaining gin and tonic.

"What are you doing?"

"Just a test strip. Our barman looks like he's waiting for something, and you look flushed and ready to party hearty. With that guy at the bar."

"He's cute in an evil way, and a hard body — I like the tattoos. Harsh, but I don't mind," she said, as if reflecting.

"Better safe than sorry."

"You give me scopolamine without telling me and now you're worried?"

"It's one thing if I give you something for your stomach and so that you argue a little less, quite another if the bartender gives you something to knock you out without asking my permission."

"Excuse me?" Violet licked her lips and eyed the man at the bar once more.

Rolling his eyes, Henrik caught her by the chin. "Stop, let's keep this between us. The drink shows positive. Could be GHB. I'm going to give you something and then it will be time to go."

"Go where? I like it here," she said, her eyes narrowing.

"Violet, listen to me. We've been set up, and you need to vanish. This will give you a few minutes to get a cab while I talk to the bartender and his friend." In the next instant, a thin syringe appeared in Henrik's hand, which then disappeared under the table. Violet could feel him groping her thigh and let out a giggle.

"You have a way with chemicals," she said, pale now, feeling the prick.

Henrik said nothing until he finished the injection. "There's not an ingestible chemical known to man I don't know about," he said, placing the syringe back in his jacket breast pocket. But when his hand reappeared, it held something else, much smaller.

"Including this. I don't suggest swallowing it, mind you," he said, holding an ampule. "Put it in your mouth, its plastic, brittle and won't melt in there. Bite down on it and blow out. Hard. Don't breathe in. Then spit out the shell."

Violet took the ampule and slid it into her pocket. The injection made her feel brutally woken, horrifyingly alert. *WTF.* "I'm just not sure if I can stand up. What was that?"

"Never mind, just go. Now. When you feel like passing out again, hide. Sleep it off," he said, slipping her a wad of money.

Violet got up, steadied herself, flung her hair back and headed to the bar. *And, action.* Once close enough, she mustered a genuine smile, glancing at the bartender and then at the man sitting at the bar who had turned towards her. The bartender did an odd thing, Violet thought—he nodded towards Henrik. Violet paid no heed, but the other man spoke, a subtle, calm voice in the corner of her reality.

"Where you off to miss?"

I'm not a miss. "A girl's got to piss," was all she said, her world slowing down. The bartender's hand swung over what looked like a fob. His index finger daintily curled and tapped on one of the buttons. Then Violet was past them.

"Sure, your choice honey," the bartender said. Violet sniggered, but upon hearing a muted groan, turned to check Henrik in time to see him spasm. *The foam on his lips, that's superb, nice trick, old boy. What are you up to?* Next she heard the squeak of a bar stool and a sudden pad of footsteps on the carpet, guessing the man at the bar decided to follow her. She turned the corner as a bodily tremble overtook her and bounded towards the toilet door, the ampule in her fingers now. *Please don't drop it.* She pushed on the door while popping the ampule in her mouth and stopped just inside, behind the door, as it would no doubt open soon. Feeling the ampule at the back of her mouth, she feared swallowing it as it tickled her throat. Violet gagged, and it moved forward to her molars just as the man entered. She stood behind him as he paused for a second.

"I think you might have the wrong powder room, cowboy," she slurred. As he turned, Violet could see he wasn't paying her a visit to see how she was getting on. There was violence in his eyes, the kind a mind set forth when it had to convince oneself that what followed was necessary. Violet took it as a cue to step forward as she chomped down on the ampule. Instead of blowing outward, her rubbery face made a crude expulsion of air and spittle accompanied by the flapping of lips and cheeks, much like a baby when ejecting disagreeable food for a full splatter effect.

The man stood spellbound for an instant, then swatted the side of Violet's head with a meaty palm as he began to choke. It sent her slamming against the side of the open door, her head hitting something hard. Violet couldn't grasp what. Dazed, she made her way around him as he fell to his knees and grabbed one of her legs. Balance off-kilter and vision blurring, she crashed to the floor. Winded, she kicked at his arm with her free leg and barely withholding a scream, managed to wrench free as his grip relaxed, glimpsing a tattoo of 5 on a die there between thumb and forefinger—a simple, authoritative punctuation to the grotesque horrors mutilating the rest of his arm. *Maybe you're a little too hot for me.*

As the man lay choking, Violet scrambled up praying no one would come in, exited the toilet, and made her way into the kitchen, circumventing the staff who paid little attention. She body-checked an exit at the back which led to an alley, one of the little, cobblestoned quaint ones where garbage didn't smell, and druggies didn't shoot up. *Right.* Her ability to carry herself was rapidly deteriorating, though the fresh air plied her with hope. *Henrik was foaming. Was that for real? I'm not going back; he can die in his shit for all I care.* Violet noticed a cab sitting 100 yards or so away, engine off. Yet above the seat she could see the silhouette of a head and, knuckling down, she made her way there, swung open the door and thrust herself inside, allowing gravity to take over.

"Lady, you can't stay in my cab. I don't vant barf in here. Please get out," said the driver effectually, having twisted back to face her.

"I promise not to. Just drive. Just a few blocks," Violet slurred on, pulling out the wad of money. As she heard him turn the key, she kept babbling on automatic, all the while her mind grasping for a destination. *I'm not English, I don't know anyone here!* As Violet passed out, somewhere in the distance she could hear a man yelling.

Chapter 2

Having hoisted the bike to his shoulder, Keller went out the door and stood at the top of the long narrow steps. It had been roughly a year since he had hastily quit medical school, packed his things and left London. He stared down at the black and white patch of tiles at the bottom of the steps and wondered if he had moved far enough away. His mind couldn't settle on an answer once the idea of hacking identities crept in. He hadn't even changed his. 'You don't have to travel far to seek cover,' his mother once said. 'It's all about discretion.' *You're so full of crap, but I guess I'm the wiser for it.*

Keller had chosen to migrate to a lush life in the city of Brighton, which he was already familiar with, having visited many times. Here, few knew of him and his gloomy talent for perceiving the dead, and hopefully didn't care. It's what he liked to tell himself and took a stiff drink when it wasn't convincing or if someone brought it up.

The moment passed where he thought he might fly to Africa and disappear into the desert, and he made his way down the staircase where he rented a one-bedroom flat above Vincent Pizzeti's Pianos. The building neighbored Reptile Nation—a spacious establishment occupying the corner lot and housing every imaginable reptile from crocs to lizards, snakes to chameleons. On the street he adjusted his backpack, donned his Vuarnets and waved to Tara, nicknamed Tarzana, who owned said Nation and had completely renovated it by herself. She was tall, beastly attractive to a point where men were afraid of her, and could always muster an intrigued smile, regardless of the occasion, and say in a low, smoky voice, 'Well lookie here, what an odd little — .'

The sea was close by and fragrant; fresh winds peeled off it, cleansing the streets of toxic accents — exhaust, hair spray, urine, vomit, sweat, and garbage, amongst others. Keller hopped on his bike, already sailing on one foot, and made the morning peddle, keeping up with traffic. He swept past joggers, the previous night's stragglers, shopkeepers, students, and people walking to work — some glum, some indifferent and some content to be in a new day.

He was on his way to his own establishment — an American-style diner called Lucy's. Shaped like the edge of a 50s metal table and adorned with plenty of chrome, chequered tiles, glass and colorful neon lighting, the gleaming facade screamed 'Hot Rod' more than anything else and was a magnet for locals and tourists alike. The dishwasher, spying during his breaks, calculated that 5 people photographed the place per hour, on average. That included Tarzana, who parked her 67 Rolls Silver Shadow and posed in front of it wearing a gold mini, metallic purple top, and tall, black leather boots. The python who lived in her car posed on her shoulders and left arm.

Keller had modelled the restaurant after a fleeting and faded childhood memory. His parents were young and healthy back then, perhaps even still in love, if they ever were. Little boy leading, they entered the establishment. The chatter of flatware on micra set off a happy journey charmed by laughs, dancing and photos, which peaked with the thud of a tall, fat sundae glass packed full of 3 different ice creams, brownie chunks, lucky charms, and caramel sauce. Though the dreamy memories lacked luster since things for his parents hadn't exactly ended the way they started, Keller designed and opened his own anyway, as part of his new 'disguised and discreet' life. Any of his doubts had been vanquished by his financial partner, Bruno Emerson, who shared his vision. Bruno was into a lot of things, but since the man had rapidly invested, Keller rode the wave and didn't ask too many questions.

Taking a courtyard entrance from the back alley, he popped his bike in a shed and slammed the rusty door shut. The dishwasher who stood out back and smoked observed his arrival. Laurence, aka Lurch, named for his humorous austerity, made no greeting. "I'm almost done with the prep, meat truck hasn't been here yet though."

"If he doesn't come soon, I'll give him a ding. Ice-cream order here?" Keller asked, noting Lurch's eyes were fringed with red. *Worked late then party, party, party.*

"Should have yesterday, lemme check," he replied, flicking his butt in the mouth of a covered black ashtray. The smoking section for staff and customers alike comprised a worn leather sofa flanked by metal tables, and a few wooden lounge chairs. Across the yard, an outdoor BBQ area lay covered up, which often kicked in on overly busy holidays.

"Yeah, check please. Otherwise, I need to pester them too."

"What else is on the list?" Lurch asked, stretching the conversation. As with Tarzana, Lurch was one of the few people Keller hung out with and trusted. They often sat late at their own bar or went out. Lurch hated the institution and admired Keller for leaving it all behind. He was a surfer of sorts, at heart, stuck on dry land, Keller philosophized.

"The usual."

"Here, I'll check the ice cream right now and then we can recap."

Keller opened the back door and entered to the thunder of heavy metal blasting the house, a requiem of death pounding its message. Lurch detoured behind the bar to turn it down a decibel, then disappeared to the kitchen. Moments later, he burst back just as Keller flicked the switch on the espresso machine.

"There's a woman in the walk-in freezer. She looks, ah, deceased," he said, suddenly awkward and pinched.

"What?"

"Come see. We, we got to call 999," Lurch continued, with an unnatural tremble.

Keller ran to the freezer and through the plastic strip curtain. The temperature change was drastic, the music grew distant, and his breath billowed translucently in the air before dissipating.

"What are you talking about?"

"There, behind the new stock, there!"

Keller peeked around a stack of ice cream boxes. There she was, huddled on the floor, up against the wall, legs pulled in, arms folded on top, chin on forearm and eyes closed. No frosty breath emerged. Pale, motionless, with a calm yet troubled expression which suggested difficulty in falling asleep. A wax replica in a museum where the tag read: human frozen to death next to ice cream. Keller knelt and pressed her jugular vein, but felt no pulse. He slapped her cheek and shook her. She was not yet stiff, yet failed to give up so much as a grimace.

"Hey! Hey, hey, hey. Wake up!" No response. Keller shook her harder and yelled, but that didn't bother the mime deeply set in its role.

He rang 999 and after a few questions, the dispatch sent an ambulance. Seconds later, Keller and Lurch gently lifted the woman, plus minus fifty, light build and fit. They moved her deadweight to the hall near the dish pit and lay her down—she was not difficult to unfold. Lurch brought a space heater while Keller began chest compressions. Soon her face turned from frosted to wet glazed. Her expression lay set, yet there was a sign that someone had been home. *The light's still on, just no note.*

"Maybe we should spray her with warm water?" Lurch said, confused.

"Hospital's not far. The ambulance should be here soon. Let them take care of it. How the heck did she get in? Freezer was locked this morning?"

"No, doubt it, didn't pay attention; never really is. I mean, the front and back doors get locked, I don't think the guys bother. Maybe the night cleaner brought her and forgot."

"Forgot a person in the freezer?"

"She looks dead." Lurch let out a nervous laugh, "I told you, we need to install cams."

"We don't need cams. This isn't a bank. You want to be rec'd while you work?"

"No, jesus. She's not breathing, is she?"

"Nope." *You look bad, but you're not dead. Just need to warm you up first.* A flurry of studies regarding hypothermic cases flashed by. Keller had taken to them during medical school, curious about how people could die for hours yet still survive without noticeable brain damage. Six faces zipped by; six cases who lived to tell their story. Seven, including the boy who had fallen from Brighton Pier, slamming against a metal stilt on the way down.

Minutes later, two paramedics came in through the front door, pushing a stretcher along. Lurch led them to the back and, while one knelt by the victim and searched for vitals, the other proceeded to remove her jacket. Then Keller noticed a peculiar thing—the paramedic removing the jacket yanked something from her pocket. An object, a wallet perhaps. It was the sleight of hand which perplexed him, the speed of it. When Keller made to comment, the paramedic looked up firmly. "Stand back sir, we're doing all we can, please don't interrupt. This one's riding the edge."

"We just pulled her out of the freezer, must be hypothermic. Don't you need to heat her up first?" Keller responded.

"Are you a doctor?" he asked as they moved her to the lowered stretcher.

"No."

"Please let us work sir, we'll try to resuscitate and then take her in."

Riding the edge. No, she's not. She's alive. She needs to be warmed up!

"Keller attended the Imperial College School of..." Lurch blurted, but Keller motioned for silence.

The stillness in the woman didn't belong, nothing about her current condition did. *The damn door was unlocked. Who the heck waits around to see if they can freeze to death?*

Jacket off, the paramedic dispensed with her sweater as well. She lay on the stretcher in a tank top and jeans. A beautiful tattoo flowed around her right shoulder, back, and side and cascaded down her arm. It depicted the hull of an elegant old ship, complete with a captain. Beguiled with an ornate rendering and vintage letters, it jested from the smooth, feminine arm — perhaps she loved a sailor, a ship, or the idea of it all.

After CPR and a shot of adrenaline, with no reaction, they set her up for defibrillation and connected a monitor.

"Pads on!" the paramedic ordered, and for a forlorn split second, Delta's chest rose and held, trembling.

"Pads off," followed. Nothing. The line remained flat, so they continued.

One paramedic broke a mild sweat; the other expected the monitor to pop with life at any moment. They all did. Zapped repeatedly by an electrical dose delivered with just the precision a healthy fifty-something fallen on bad luck and a moment of darkness needed. Or not.

Her vacant face turned to one side as the charge eased.

In a tiny corner of Keller's mind, a thumbnail materialized and displayed a scene from his boyhood. It was his father's lab deep underground, beneath a town in the English countryside called Ironsmith. Nestled behind the intersection of two well-lit, paved, and white-walled tunnels, complete with signage denoting N57 and SW44, it was a mile from the computer center used by the government to control the Navy and Strategic Defense. The lab itself was a spacious, windowless, high-tech area. The location worked to keep things low-key. Very low. And for good reason. Father worked for the Ministry developing highly intelligent droids. Some were more human looking than others, but all were far beyond what the quaint world 60 meters above might imagine. It was Keller's introduction to the body.

That day after school, Keller entered the lift house, masked as a giant air vent above ground and circled by a tall, barbed fence. His iris did the job of getting him past the gate. As the elevator opened, he felt the musty tunnel air laced with ozone drifting into his face. The doors closed in silence, and he plummeted 20 stories down. It was the lab's private lift and had only one stop—the intersection of N57 and SW44, which father called Main and Queen.

As Keller entered the lab, smooth white and metallic lines enveloped him in its microcosm of minimalist tech. 7 meters away, he could see droids lined up on slanted ramps, each in their alcove surrounded by tools mimicking a techno-dentist's office. Some were well lit, others basking in a bluish, dim light. Each was in a stage of development. One had a half-unraveled leg—thin strips of activated silicone-titanium compound had unfurled on the floor, leaving a bare, friction-controlled ball joint visible. Another had numerous facial layers removed, giving away its indestructible mollusk interior. A third had no head at all—it sat on the alcove's counter connected to liquid coolant circulation extensions which hooked into simulated veins.

His father was busy at work testing the musculature of an eye—tiny ribbons of contraction nyflon activated by static which constricted and expanded upon charge and discharge many times per second. He paused when he heard Keller nearing, glanced over, then back at his work, and continued activating the hopeful spheroid.

"I want to mention something about people who appear to be dead," he said, out of the blue. Keller had come close now and watched as Tom used an almost microscopic ratchet to adjust the depth of the eyeball relative to its socket. "If a light was left on, you know they'll be back. Don't think of it as something you have to scrutinize, the light is either on, or off. It's obvious if you see it at all, which I *know* you do."

His father's analogy for the spirit world would beleaguer him for years to come, and it still did. Keller expanded the notion to include ethereal sticky notes, a kind of residue his perceptions snagged on. A light on or off. Someone at home, or not. A note left to say they'll be back. No note or no light on, meaning they were dead and gone.

Jane, it seemed to Keller, had left a light on.

The paramedics felt something similar, regardless of the vitals or lack of, as they swiftly packed her up and rushed her to the ambulance, promptly driving off. Keller and Lurch stood at the bar; the place was quiet. The other staff weren't due for another hour.

"That must suck," Lurch said, shifting his stance.

"What?"

"Going for ice cream and freezing to death."

"Lurch, we don't know she's dead. And I don't think she was back there just for the ice cream."

"I know, *I know*." Lurch walked to the kitchen without another word. Soon after the spray-gun shot against glassware and stainless, the door to the dishwashing machine slammed. "I bet the cops are on their way," he continued, louder than usual.

"No. If she were to die, they'll do an autopsy and then talk to us."

Lurch didn't reply. Instead, he cranked the volume and began chopping onions.

Keller spun around, expecting to see someone who had entered the dining room. Words escaped from nowhere, garbled and unclear, vocalized by an abstract voice. But there was no one there. It was Keller's turn to sweat. Not that he didn't like a healthy imagination, he did. But the voice had sounded detached from any thoughts in his mind. A distant gossamer specter, fleeting and scented, mocked his senses. A misty, lavender thing mixed with stale beer and flesh. *Not this again, no way, forget it.*

"I can't do anything for you or anybody else. Go with them," he spoke. "Or you're gonna be dead and departed if you aren't already!" Keller strode towards the center of the dining room, where he felt the emanation. Outside, he could see the usual morning traffic, oblivious. Inside all was still, the jukebox stood quiet. Then another faint message echoed from nowhere. *"Must I wait in vain for you?"* it asked.

How bloody appropriate. Keller stood where he was, picking up on something feminine, lonely, afraid. He chose his words carefully, but before speaking, 'she' launched a notional chuckle. *Confused? Surely not you.*

Growing enraged at what he considered his own delusion laying him open to a flippant hypothermia victim, Keller batted the air with a hand, discreetly, as one might in hiding cigarette smoke or the passing of wind.

"Really?" she intoned.

Feeling increasingly foolish, he quietly snapped and hissed a string of obscenities targeting the entity to cease any attempts at being the semblance of an apparition. *Not here, not now, you bloody curse!* "Go away, not gonna happen today!" slipped out of him quietly, his voice breaking.

"You okay boss?" Lurch asked, wiping hands on his apron.

"Yeah," Keller replied, suppressing surprise, wiping spittle from his lips. *Don't speak, his imagination's already in overdrive.* He clocked Lurches glance around, lips hinting at humor.

"Shame about that woman. And just to be clear on things, I know nothing."

"Okay Lurch."

"I just have love for you, my friend, and respect. Do what you must," Lurch said, returning to the back end once more, crooning *Highway to Hell*.

Chapter 3

Keller lived alone. He preferred it that way to balance the long hours spent mingling, directing and serving an eclectic crowd of staff and customers alike. He found the buzz tiresome and after all, he had moved to Brighton to remain low key and a popular restaurant was anything but. *Hiding in plain sight my mother would have approved. Not sure if I've pulled it off, despite Henrik's warnings.* While he was quick to join a group night out, that was it—no commitments and no family to speak of—they were either distant or dead.

Until age 8, Keller lived on the outskirts of Las Vegas, next to the Mojave Desert. The diner he originally became enamored with was in Vegas too. Back then, his father also worked in a lab which created experimental robots, ranging from crash test dummy types to not-so-dumb, realistic-looking synthetic humanoids. The lab was in the desert near Groom Lake, a dry salt flat. Tom was flown in and out daily, on a special shuttle designated for locals. Unlike the lab in England, Keller never visited that one.

At age 4, Keller first saw and spoke to a woman with antlers who walked out of the desert dressed in skins and corduroy. When the conversation was over, she disappeared. At the time, it seemed perfectly normal—she was quite pleasant and not bad looking. Years later when he mentioned it at school, trying to identify the tribe, his class and teacher howled. But what boosted the incident to wackodom was that the antler woman gave him a Forget-Me-Not blossom. The actual plant in real life, which didn't vaporize as she did. She called it Scorpion Grass, the old-fashioned way.

His father witnessed one of the incidents but didn't see the antler woman—he assumed the boy was playing make-believe. But when he saw the blossom, he got curious since Keller had not strayed from the backyard. Even if he had, there were no such plants in the area. So Tom, after questioning his own sanity, decided to believe the boy.

His mother thought little of it and saw it as a sort of 'Picking gum off the pavement and chewing it,' phase. "Probably got blown over by the wind. Remember, it doesn't have to come from the desert, we have garden centers, Tom. Or a girl threw them back in her boyfriend's face," she laughed.

"I asked the neighbors for at least two blocks around. No one has them in their garden, so the wind didn't blow it in. Keller was under my watch and I sure as hell know he didn't go wandering out. The nearest garden center is 7 miles away and they don't sell Forget-Me-Nots or Scorpion Grass as he calls it. It's a frickin' weed."

"It's not a weed, how dare you. They are hardy plants, good to cover a bald spot in your garden, but do like nice soil and water," his mother, Belinda, teased.

"Yeah, so where'd he get it? Get in my car and drive upstate? He's god-damn 4."

"You're telling me you believe a ghost gave our son a flower? How nice," Belinda fumed. "You been prescribed something I don't know about?"

Keller saw the antler woman numerous times over the next few years—she befriended him, and it broke up the long stretches he spent alone.

What Belinda considered nonsense, Tom wove into the fabric of his work. Something from the supernatural world had crossed a threshold and handed his son a physical object, a flower. No matter how small, it was a token of the paranormal; the spirit world was close by and in contact. It was where humans went when they died—if that was true, they could come back. *To a droid body.* Which meant a select group of willing astronauts could travel into deep space, he would tell Keller. While Keller thought it was cool, he couldn't imagine it leading to anywhere past a story. He believed in spirits but not so much Santa. The sheer logistics didn't make sense to him, even as a child.

Then trouble began to brew when Keller's aunt disowned his father after hearing through Belinda that he was trying to get a human into a robot. She felt such a 'hack' was a ghastly breach of the laws of nature and the good Lord would disapprove. Years later, Keller would see she was more right than wrong.

How this same idea then leaked at Groom Lake, no one knew—probably his mom again, at a party. Though very controlled and secretive, she knew how to plant a tidbit without being noticed, even by her husband. This also Keller picked up on as a kid but since he loved her (she let him shoot her guns even at a young age) he never told his dad.

Whether or not hers, the tidbit grew and left a precarious trail, creeping along and insinuating that Tom had *succumbed* to the paranormal as part of his experimentation. He sought answers in the supernatural for an alternate form of fighter pilot and space traveler. Management decided Tom was mentally unfit to continue in his line of work and made him redundant. 'Poltergeists and AIs do not mix,' they said, and 'Making such a fusion is not relevant, we have drones for that.' It was at this point his parents fought regularly and Keller could feel the antler woman, named Gouyen, didn't mind. He also realized he was a loner for a reason and didn't even want to trust anyone. Not even his parents. Keller was 8 by then and everything in his life was slowly becoming undone.

The irony was that the flower itself proved Tom's sanity and was kept in a safe. Tom didn't mention it. He also didn't tell them that the Atomic Force microscope he purchased was to look at the molecular structure of said blossom. It might have helped his case were Belinda to believe the story, but she did not, claiming both her and Tom's reputation would be further tarnished. That Keller claimed he got it from an apparition was naturally too much for anyone to grasp except for Keller himself and that set him apart once again, from everyone except maybe Gouyen the antler woman. His mother asserted he would outgrow her.

Tom uprooted the family, and they moved to England. The British were interested, one man in particular named Henrik Poole, a famous programmer in the obscure droid community, and they provided Tom with a new lab in an underground bunker. If it was the paranormal that inspired him then so be it — so long as droid development reached new plateaus, Tom had a green light. What exact result they expected, Keller could only imagine, and his mother played along, seething with pessimism.

It took them one night to leave the prodigious, wide-open spaces of a hard-baked Nevada coupled with the glitz of Vegas and land the following day somewhere near London in an entirely new world, green and rainy. As far as Keller was concerned, this was Kansas, except the tornadoes weren't as big.

They rented an SUV and drove on the wrong side of the road. When his father made detours into the local villages and stopped at a castle, Keller warmed up to the idea of staying. He loved the sheep, cows, and horses he saw in the lush fields hemmed by giant trees. And the ancient buildings — never mind the old ruins which he climbed and hugged. He had left few friends behind in Vegas, none really, aside from Gouyen, and there were things here to explore. Keller soon decided this would be an adventure. Tom had promised he could visit his lab after school, and that was the clincher.

Belinda, having grown accustomed to Las Vegas and the nightlife, loathed the move. Regardless, they settled in a small town called Ironsmith and that was that. Tom's new lab, hush-hush, was tucked in an out-of-the-way branch of Neufeld Bunker, beneath the town itself. When his father told him the people down there were all upside down, Keller believed him at first. But not really.

Allowed to show up in his father's part of the tunnel after school, Keller took the designated lift to the lab, a mile away from the active area used by the Ministry. Clever, quiet, and nimble, he adapted to the curious underground complex, explored it, and so grew up a tunnel rat. The scorching desert sun faded to damp and musty tunnel shadows.

To UFO seekers, Neufeld Bunker held a special potential—some claimed it was a place where the government stored UFOs. Keller didn't see any. What went down, as far as Keller could tell, was manufacture. Droid bodies which looked more human and less human. Skin, frame systems, brains/central control, perceptive systems, eloquent musculatures and even warmth with sweat in premium models. Just no tears as far as he could tell. Henrik Poole, the genius programmer who had convinced the Brits to hire father in the first place, worked alongside Tom and Uncle Alexey.

Alexey was a 'human engineer.' He developed the materials used to build the droids and designed the parts. A mechanic of sorts. While not a blood relative, he became a good friend of Tom's, and his daughter Katrina was a year older than Keller. Another tunnel rat and a tomboy at that, who liked to let Keller know who was boss—with a kick, a scratch, or a bite; or that she liked him—with more kicks, scratches, and bites. Keller couldn't tell which was which except that they were partners in crime. He learned to live with the rest, for he had a friend aside from Gouyen, whom he grew fond of. Whether Katrina believed in his desert apparition, he could never tell. She did then she didn't, depending on the situation at hand.

Aside from Katrina, Keller construed only one thing as being alien in Neufeld Bunker—father's invention, which he christened *The Cradle*. To Keller, it glowed with insanity—his own imagination fabricated a greenish, gemstone-like notion that pulsated quietly in the dark, waiting for the right time to unleash its fury.

When his father explained *The Cradle* to him, which in theory would allow a human to reside within a synthetic brain and forge a connection to a synth body, Keller worried his father might get fired again. This was no ordinary train of thought and not just talk. Tom had acted on his beliefs and brought the bloody thing to fruition.

The host synth looked human and possessed a mind—an artificially intelligent one with the possibility of an upgrade to sentience. The upgrade itself, an actual human, required a paranormal means by which to arrive. Keller thought of *Flatliners* and *Altered Carbon* and couldn't decide if what his father was doing should be happening. All supposedly possible because a ghost named Gouyen had handed Keller a real flower in the desert—a species that didn't grow there.

The Cradle was designed to connect to a human, a dead one, via a spectral plug-in area—a mystical socket. *And then this would make the synth be alive and more than just a machine.* Keller remembered the excitement blended with fear that this brought on him. *My dad is frickin' Frankenstein, thanks to Gouyen the antler woman. And me.*

All in all, his parents had fabricated the perfect backdrop for understanding the human condition—Keller had witnessed what frivolities the mind could concoct, despite belonging to a normal-looking person. The Forget-Me-Not blossom had caused his mother to fully lose her faith in his father. And his father, well, what Tom created was potentially crazy.

That he indulged the paranormal made people nervous — the green light the British had given him assumed he had learned his lesson. But Keller knew his father didn't waste time on things he didn't believe in, and he didn't get fired again either.

Tom perished in a lab explosion instead — a mysterious event as of yet unexplained. After his body and Katrina's were both extracted, charred to Picassoesque figurines, Keller was severely stricken, and life as he knew it was over.

Whether his parents initially met while his mother was still a spy, Keller didn't know. They wouldn't say and didn't talk much about her career. All he knew was that she liked to advise him on the oddest things and happily taught him to shoot, especially when they still had the Mojave behind their back yard — it was the happiest he'd ever seen her. And taught him to evade being shot at. Since she was supposedly retired, her loving collection of weapons remained in the US though she did manage to acquire a few discreet pieces in England.

But his father had behaved oddly when setting up Keller's future as if anticipating the outcome of his own life. The plan unfolded when a lawyer sat Keller and his mother down regarding the will. While her late husband had left her little, Keller was to move to London, where he would attend boarding school until he was 18. Then life was up to him. Belinda, somewhat inebriated, showed no signs other than contentment to begin a new chapter in her life. She signed the paperwork, and that was that.

Belinda spent a few years back in Vegas assuming her son was in good hands, having 'business' to attend to. Failing to recuperate from all that life had dealt her, she went insane, was dowsed by a barrage of correctional medications, and quickly deteriorated. In Keller's mind, the drugs showed up first, then she split. And after that, she went insane, finally losing her desire to live. He didn't know who or what tipped the scale, as she denied any fragility. Even a hairline crack.

After leaving Ironsmith behind, Keller buried his notions regarding the afterlife, the paranormal and ghosts in general. He didn't *see* either his father or Katrina after their deaths. Or hear from them. They were as gone as gone can be. In the ensuing grief which followed him for years to come, he obliterated all thoughts of things not of this earth.

After finishing boarding school, Keller attended university, majoring in biology. Bored, he fell into medicine and enjoyed its practical views minus any brilliant idea which prophesied a human could somehow be cajoled or coerced from a warm existence next to a pumping heart to a nyflon-alloy fabrication. And that humankind would somehow benefit.

But about this time, he had another encounter with the deceased. It happened when he witnessed his mother vacate any semblance of sense and die an untimely death. Her nurse told Keller that Belinda liked to talk about 'Her life as a spy and that her memories were backed-up safely.'

"Great imagination that Belinda has, God bless," the nurse had said, pointing out under her breath with wide-eyed nods that Belinda was a touch hallucinatory.

Once dead, he *knew* she was still around. He could almost see her, smell her. Keller was certain he glimpsed an ethereal distortion in the air, something that rearranged the photons to form a faint likeness. She came to check on him occasionally, and when he told her it made him uneasy, she left. As she departed, Keller's heart sank to a new depth and his chest remained heavy. It's how he knew the apparition was her.

If the mind did such a thing as devolve, Keller concluded his had done just that. He figured spirit sensing was a talent many people honed if they lost their marbles. So instead of embracing his temperamental talent as a mock medium or psychic, Keller bid farewell to his mother and moved on with his life. Aside from a man who died in a car accident and a boy who drowned beneath Brighton Pier, he ignored any supernatural experiences he encountered, much like a blind pedestrian who crosses paths with a homeless person—they could stop and talk but tend not to.

Alas, it was precisely memories of these last two incidents which paralleled the present situation with the woman from the freezer—something about her reeled him in, he couldn't entirely ignore her.

After Lurch returned to the kitchen, the ghost of Jane Doe spoke again, muffled and dispersed. Keller couldn't decipher the signal anymore, yet the feeling was unmistakable. It was a distress call.

"So, are you going to help me?" might have been the question, minus hideous interference.

"Help you with what?" Keller responded, playing the devil's advocate. *This isn't going to happen today, I've retired. Piss off.*

"Keller, I have news for you, a message, a warning," was the meaning he gathered, unsure, as a shiver drove up his spine and hot prickles patted the back of his head and neck. His mind spun upon hearing his name and so he took the obvious way out.

"I'm not your guy. You need a doctor. You'll be at the hospital soon, do your weird shit there. And when you wake up, call me, I'll come see you. Then you can tell me all about your message." Silence followed as Keller waited, keeping still, breathing faintly. *If she's talking to me, probably dead already, past a hope.*

Chapter 4

Plugged into the city surrounding it, lunch rushes at Lucy's were busy and the day Jane Doe showed up was no different. Local businesspeople and tourists alike poured in for a plate of starch, grease, and a kidding smile from one of the servers. The heartbeat emanated from the Jukebox which could spin every hit song known in the western hemisphere, past and present. Anyone could walk up to its magic arch, pop in 50 pence or a token, and pick something they loved. *Anyone.*

After the rush, Keller went to his office which he shared with his partner, Bruno Emerson, to see if he had arrived. The office was empty. Keller's morning espresso stood on his desk, abandoned five hours ago. A package for Bruno sat nearby — Keller noted the tiny gold logo on it with the word 'Morpheus' entwined. It contrasted the matte, black box, challenging an illegitimate recipient to peek inside.

During an afternoon lull, Keller had phoned the hospital claiming to be a relative who would identify Jane Doe. The receptionist told him she had indeed died from a drug overdose causing cardiac arrest. *What the hell were you doing last night? Pounding alcohol, GHB and ecstasy isn't you. Tat or no tat. Should have left you dead. Yet you waited — and no one warmed you up. And then I ditched you.*

Seconds later he handed the floor over to Stacey, a true barnacle and classic, like some songs in the jukebox. Then exited the diner through the dish pit, where Elvis cross faded to Metallica under Lurch's supervision.

"That was pretty messed up this morning," Lurch said, looking up.

Keller nodded.

"You're going to see her?"

"Yeah."

"My lips are sealed."

"I know. Thanks Lurch."

Keller stepped out back, pulled his bike from the shed and rode off, tirelessly playing through scenarios of what was possible, what wasn't, and was he himself losing it? After all, he had vowed not to fool with the paranormal, it only led to misery. Then the little drowned boy's wet, grey body popped up. The man from the car wreck too, heavily bruised and hemorrhaged after spinning off the highway and tumbling down a sloped median. Both were dead, yet both wanted to live, and Keller hadn't ignored them. Even though the media had ostracized him for the most part, he did it twice. *What's wrong this time?*

Upon arrival, he ventured through the buildings built on a slope and found floor 6 as another ground level. The reception was vacant, and entry was by key card only. Minutes later, a cheerful Spaniard dressed in hospital attire carrying two large rolls of toilet paper emerged.

"I understand the morgue is in this building, can you let me in?"

"Absolutely not, no visits to the morgue without an attendant, counsellor, or the coroner. I'm sorry sir," he said, shiny eyes betraying that he'd be fine to let him in, but rules are rules.

"Listen, I must be at the airport in a couple of hours, London, and I wanted to see this person before I go. For old-time's sake. I don't think her husband will want me at the funeral, we were in love in our university days." Keller mustered a moist eye. "I'll just tell the pathologist a counsellor is on their way. Please."

To his surprise, the man glanced around and seeing reception was still empty, swiped the card. "If you say anything, I could get fired. It's just to the left, down the hall, through the grey doors."

"Not a word, thank you." Keller slipped past him with a solemn nod.

As he turned the corner, taking quick, bold steps, Keller grew uneasy. The odor and texture of the air shifted; the weight of the dead pressed on his senses. The hall might as well have been adorned with sticky notes saying, 'Gone out, be back in 15.' Or 'See you tonight.' Or, 'Key is where it usually is, I'll see you soon.' The entrance stood at the very end—greyed-out windows with rounded corners mounted in bleak, heavy doors with large, playful handles. In seconds Keller passed through, matter-of-factly, ignoring the dull, sick hysteria welling up in his bosom.

Once inside, he slowed his pace, walking along the tall stainless steel refrigeration doors, guessing each housed 5 levels. The stark, spacious room of white baked enamel, eggshell-tiled walls and stainless-steel sinks, counters, tools, trolleys, and autopsy tables, was predominantly still. The space had an organized rhythm, an austere, utilitarian purpose that couldn't be masked. This was the grim last stop, lit up by rows of overhead fluorescent bulbs emulating flat daylight. A Pathologist, scalpel in hand, doted over the body of an elderly man with one leg, a whimsical melody by Bela Bartok floating in the air. She looked above her spectacles at him approaching, keeping her eyes on him as he scanned the fridge doors.

"Hey, can I help you? You really shouldn't be in here," she said, returning her focus to the body.

"Came to see, ah, Jane Doe," Keller said and stopped to face her. The Pathologist looked up again, her mouth a concerned line. "An attendant need be with you, or counsellor. I'm going to have to ask you to leave, sir," she said, matching his calmness.

At that moment Keller glitched when a familiarity about her struck him. *You wish. Ask her if she used to wear antlers and then watch your ass get kicked out.* "She's an old friend, if it's actually her, I was told at reception—"

"I don't care what you were told; they shouldn't have let you in."

"Please," he said, putting on his best solemn look, matching her straight lips.

"Tell you what, if you can guess which one she's in, I'll pull her out and you can take a look," she said, mischief in her tone.

Weird. "It's that one," Keller pointed almost instantly. "What's your name?"

"Nora," she said after a pause.

"Am I right or what? Interesting protocol," he said, squinting.

"Yeah," Nora replied, a faint smile possibly masking disbelief. "Lucky guess gets the corpse. And I can tell you're not here to grieve."

"And what'll I get if I bring her back?"

"If you even try it, I'll call security. No seances, understand?" Nora walked up to him, her eyes not leaving his, putting her hand on the latch. "I don't entertain resurrections on my shift."

"Yes ma'm." He wanted to spill the beans regarding the stolen wallet but didn't. Nora fascinated him. *What's not to fascinate. Something about her reminds me of Gouyen or I'm just desperately lonely.*

She swung the fridge door open, slid the loaded tray out and pulled back the zipper to reveal Jane Doe's head and part of her chest. Keller felt the hairs on his neck spike. She lay motionless yet the unsatisfied, *I can't fall asleep* look, still besieged her. The tattoo flowing from her shoulder sprayed seawater, incorporating 3 tiny birthmarks.

"Yeah, look, her cheeks aren't quite as bluish as when we found her," he began.

"What?" she responded, annoyed.

"Look closely, just *look*."

Nora did, blinked hard, then looked back at Keller. "You found her? Where?"

"Next to the ice cream delivery, walk-in freezer."

"That explains it, her temp has come up." Nora came closer still as if knowing that nothing was impossible. She had an air about her which dispelled with any fragility set forth by her spectacled, smooth oval face nestled in dark auburn high-lit waves. Punctuated with charcoal grey eyes, they injected finesse into the equation, and insight. She understands, Keller thought.

"You're a friend of hers, Mr ah..."

"Keller Mod," he answered, unsure if honesty was wise. "No, I'm not actually. But I do want her to live — she wants it herself."

A phone appeared in Nora's hand, and she speed-dialed Emergency. "Get me a doctor and ready a bay for deep hypothermia, I'm bringing one back — Jane Doe 3/5."

"Nora, are you joking me?" The voice on the other end of the line fluttered across the room, intermittently.

"Warm saline and warm oxygen, we're coming over now."

"You're serious..."

"C'mon, weirder things have happened."

Nora pushed a trolley underneath Delta's tray, adjusted the height, and slid her on. She wheeled it back towards a counter as Keller closed the fridge and took an interest in some tools. When Nora turned, a momentary grimace flashed over her face as she noticed Keller was at the body.

"Playing doctor — "

"17 degrees," he said, reading the temporal thermometer.

Her lips parted to speak. Instead, she took two strides to the trolley. "Let's get her to A&E," she said, tossing him blankets and yanking off the body bag.

As he wrapped the body in the first blanket, Keller got a better view of the large, somewhat faded, retro sailor's tattoo featuring a ship with sails up. The captain's face, distant, grinned back at him, the words 'Avast Ye' floated above in a banner. Keller put on the second blanket, nimbly tucking the edges.

Nora nodded to the exit, her lips compressed, as she pushed the trolley.

"I'm coming along," Keller asserted.

"She's been dead for hours. How did you know?" Nora asked with a shake in her voice, picking up the pace as Keller ran for the door.

"Anna Bågenholm* in Sweden and Audrey Shoeman** in Barcelona are a couple cases I know of. They both froze to death and returned after 5 or 6 hours. Or longer, don't quote me. There are numerous cases."

"You're joking, right? This is like a hobby of yours?"

"Relax..." he shot her a smile — Nora responded with widened eyes and firm lips.

For the next 3 minutes, they negotiated the back hallways connecting the morgue with Emergency. Once in the bay, a doctor appeared, a nurse and an assistant. Nora pulled Keller away as the group descended upon the body of Jane Doe and prepared to heat her intravenously. "Let them work," she said as the doctor glanced at her.

"It looks like a long shot, but we'll see what we can do," he said. "Who pronounced her dead?"

"I'd have to check," Nora nodded again and took Keller by the elbow, seeing he had something to say, "Not now," she said, under her breath.

While they both sat in the waiting room, Jane Doe was intricately defrosted in every way possible. They warmed her organs intravenously, her outer body with a circulation blanket and 37° oxygen sat waiting.

"It'll take some hours, they can't heat her up too fast, the shock would be too great. Kill her," Nora giggled. "And then they'll take a shot at resuscitation. In the meantime, I should get back to the morgue."

"The one-legged guy?"

"Yeah. Any prognosis I should know about?"

"No light on there, he's as dead as a brick."

"No light on, you're funny. Text me when she wakes up?" she said, phone in hand.

"Sure," he answered and recited his number.

Nora got up and left. As she did Keller felt his phone buzz and read the text: Nora. *Charcoal-eyed Nora who didn't have a problem believing me more than I believe in myself.*

Keller waited. When he peeked into the emergency bay a couple hours later, a nurse ushered him away. He texted Lurch instead and checked in with Stacey, who had corralled the staff and drove them with an iron fist. Then he searched what he could find on Morpheus and found nothing aside from references pointing to the Greek god. *Bruno must be investing in something suspicious, not even a site.* It didn't surprise him too much, Bruno often jumped into something he thought had potential. Like Lucy's Diner—he hailed it as one of a kind in Brighton though it wasn't really.

Late evening a nurse came out to talk to Keller. "She made it," she said, "Vitals are as good as expected. We've moved her to Intensive Care, you can pop by if you wish." The nurse led the way to the lift, and they got on. She turned to Keller as it went up. "Are you the gentleman who snuck into the morgue to check on her?"

"Guilty."

"Well, she owes you her life, unless of course you stuck her in the freezer."

"Ah, no."

"Do you mind if I take your photo? For our newsletter." Before he could answer the nurse stood next to him and snapped a shot with her phone.

"Sure, go ahead."

"Thanks," she said with a quick smile as the doors opened. "Come this way." After a few more steps the nurse indicated the room and then stopped. As Keller walked by her, she smiled again, the curvature of her lips and squint in her eyes riddled with mischief. Keller didn't react.

"Forget-me-not, Keller Mod."

At that, Keller jolted mid-turn, feeling the blood drain from his head. When he peered back, no one was there. No sound of footsteps, nothing down the hall. Keller checked the next bays, scanning, and around corners—the nurse was gone. He stood and looked at a wall, then the equipment on a trolley, finally clinging to the sensibility of a machine. He took a deep breath and spun once more to someone nearing him.

"Hey, Keller—oh, you look stressed, what happened?"

"Nothing, been a long day. She's this way, ah, you're still here…"

"Sure. It's rarely someone from the morgue makes it," she said, eyes alight, lips pursing wryly.

Now that the color was back in Jane Doe's face, fluids topped up, circulating and oxygen reaching her lungs, she had an undeniable presence. Jane filled the room and Keller was confident he had seen her before. They hung around a while, straightening Jane's blankets, deliberating whether to get flowers, trying to guess who she might be.

"I remember it now; I saw her in a movie. Not in a leading role, but I think she may have been one of the whores in *Unforgiven*," Keller said.

"Oh my god, she was in Avatar, I think. Look, her eyes are far apart, and I bet they're beautiful."

Keller looked at Nora and nodded a touch, "Avatar's an animation..."

Nora looked back at him. "*Unforgiven* I watched 3 times, I'm a sucker for old westerns. It ain't her," she said in her version of an American accent. Then she clutched his arm with a gentle squeeze. "You were a genius to catch her," she whispered.

"I was lucky. She caught *me* and didn't let go."

"Luck, Keller?" Nora said, squinting her eyes, a smile developing.

Their faces rotated towards the bed in unison as they both heard the light scuffing of fabric. With a soft touch, Keller put his hand on Jane's wrist, deciding whether to say something.

Jane Doe opened her eyes and whispered to him, "*You're being framed for murder*," she throated, her lips parting, wobbly on a plaster face.

Keller, paralyzed for the moment and blank, didn't respond. His eyes sharpened on her. He glanced at the EKG monitor — the heartbeat had picked up.

"Go to my house in Maine, the shipwreck... Captain Lee's, oh, you'll figure it out. Last and only house on Black Point, Deer Isle, the big one," she breathed. Her eyes closed. Keller darted a glance sideways to see if Nora had noticed. She looked beguiled, then cross faded to shock layered complacency.

"Keller, she spoke. Did she say murder?"

The EKG picked up further.

"So, you heard it too," he croaked, somewhat relieved.

"Is this a hoax?" she asked, her tensed neck yanking her lips. "Does she know you? You liar—"

"No. No, there's no way she knows me."

"Keller, why did she say what she did?" Nora asked, snatching up the alert button, still distraught.

"She's delusional, is what she said. There's always the chance of brain damage, isn't there?"

"Sounded pretty coherent to me, all considering."

"Put that down, wait 'till she wakes up fully and — what did you mean earlier when you said weirder things have happened?"

"They haven't."

Chapter 5

After lingering in silence, Keller suggested they let the woman rest. Perhaps a relative or friend might show up and clarify the situation. He planned to leave a note with his number next to the bed but decided against it. *I found your wife/daughter/friend frozen in my walk-in freezer, might not go over so well.*

They arrived at the atrium from behind the front desk, which faced the main entrance. The outer wall faced south, constructed of tall glass sheets and a metal framework. Sunshine drenched the space, casting grid-like shadows and spherical configurations on the floor and walls from sculptures looming mid-air above the quiet crowd passing through. From childhood, Keller had learned to sense when something in his environment didn't fit. Or fit in all too well for comfort—like a sidewinder in the desert—hidden and deadly. Amongst the visitors and staff, Keller picked out the media types, journalists whose mother ships sat parked just outside. *Oh crap, what's this? Who tipped them off?*

A young man with a camera lunged forward, snapping shots. "Keller Mod? I'd like to ask a few questions if I may."

Keller froze, a thought ricocheting through his mind, settling on a past moment much like a roulette ball on a number. *Henrik sat across from him in a pub and said sternly, "My reason for seeing you is twofold. One is to give you a warning — stay out of the spotlight. He's coming for you."*

"Keller, what's wrong?" Nora's voice tugged from a distance.

"How did the media catch on so fast?"

"Could have been any number of people, it's a big place and hours have gone by. Keller, when someone's returned to the A&E department from the morgue, that's quite remarkable."

"I don't like spotlights and I didn't save her. Sitting this one out, long story. It was nice meeting you," Keller said backing away.

"Here, this way," she said, grabbing him by the arm. Keller swam in her eyes for a moment, endless, dusky grey pools. She waved for him to follow, her eyes not wavering, and they darted out of the atrium towards an off-limits hall. Nora flashed her card, the sliding doors parted, and they ran inside, losing their tail.

"Exit one of the disposal areas, you won't be noticed. It's an old part of the hospital leading to a side street," she continued, pointing. "I'll ah, if you don't mind, I'll go back and talk to them if they're interested."

"Knock yourself out."

"If anything, just text," she said as they parted.

"Thanks, really." *It's like she lives for this sort of thing.*

Once outside, Keller paid little attention to what passed by. He sought a quiet place, a random open door where he could enter and pause in the shadows to compose himself, reflect on what had occurred and determine next steps. Jane Doe's comment was more than his mind could explain. It was a blatant anomaly. *What murder was she talking about?*

The more he walked, the more his head cleared, and the fatigue of the day dissipated. The back of his neck prickled as he realized that there could be some truth to what Jane Doe said — she hadn't awoken fully, though coherent enough, as Nora said. Keller felt relieved and even glad to have Nora's number.

Then he stopped and stood still. *The nurse who disappeared, who was that? Forget-me-not, Keller Mod, she said.* Those were words only his childhood friend Gouyen had ever used and luckily Nora had missed all that. *It would be nice to get to know her…*

Taking up long strides and eventually breaking into a light jog, Keller soon found himself by the sea. But as he walked out onto the pier his nervous system signaled once again. He took a quick look backward and noted a figure suddenly pause at *Brighton's Best Rock Shop.* She glanced his way then quickly back. 40 meters later, he came to an old vintage pavilion housing a seafood place, *Palm Court.* He rounded the outdoor seating but then stopped and peered back along the wooden wall as if checking the trueness of the construction. She continued walking toward him.

Keller spotted *Planet Of The Crêpes* and headed there. Any other day it would have drawn a chuckle, he had planned to visit. Now was the time.

As he turned to open the door, he could see his stalker reflected in the glass, dressed in jeans and a jumper. He pulled the door open and turned towards her, like an old friend before a lunch date. *Journalist probably, cute. Is this my lucky day or something?*

The woman quickened her pace. "So, he's the doorman, great. Just needed to have a quick word if you don't mind," she said.

Her gait had a symmetry Keller recognized but couldn't place, as did a quality in her voice — it irked him to not remember a person. As she drew near a spray of freckles crossing her cheeks and nose besieged her eye contact, leaving plain lips to pull a smile.

"A quick word about what?"

"I'm not doing a story about you, just wanted to talk."

"Let's go inside for a coffee. So, you're not a journalist?"

"No. Were you fleeing me just now?" she said, her eyes smiling, flirting.

"Yeah, you looked rough from a distance."

"Well, I am." Another smile flashed and vaporized. Despite the artsy scarf, bulky sweater, worn leather shoes, and unkempt hair, there was a cool precision about her Keller clocked as she strode past and through the door.

Echoing the Pier, *Planet Of The Crêpes* was in a time warp all its own. The place seemed to give itself up, moody and vacant, aside from the cook who mumbled a greeting before telling them to sit where they pleased. 'She' would return in a few minutes to take their order. 'Special is on the board.'

The woman sat down on a wooden chair next to a round, veneered, pedestal table near the back. Keller sat down across from her. He could see a walkway through windows with people passing by for an evening thrill. He imagined what was further on—rides, gambling, a nightclub, and Horror Hotel, amongst others. Beyond that was the sky and somewhere beneath, the sea, where a diver had pulled out the little boy.

Behind an opening in the wall, the cook ladled crepe batter on a low, black cylindrical surface and spread it. Keller turned his gaze back to see the woman staring at him. He stared back; he didn't mind. "So, you wanted to talk to me, ah…?"

"Cassy, just call me Cassy."

"Cassy." He nodded slightly, glancing once again at her freckles.

"We got a table, get in here," said the cook to someone in the back.

"I wanted to ask you about your father. I've been researching him, tried to find you in London. You're not easy to locate."

"Well, you found me now. As far as my father goes, I rarely discuss him or his work with anyone."

"I respect that," she said, as if anticipating the answer.

"But if you just have a few simple questions…"

His phone buzzed, and he looked down at it. "Hang on, let me check this." It was Bruno. 'Where are you?' the text read. Next Keller put the phone face down on the table, ringtone off, without replying.

"Sorry, it's been a crazy day, still is," he said.

"No matter, I can wait."

"I'm done, go ahead, shoot."

"You have a partial English accent, where are you from?"

"American originally, been here, oh, 19 years now. I tend to turn my accents on and off."

"Ok, so you grew up over there?" she said, looking down at a napkin, then raising her crystalline eyes.

"Got here when I was 8."

"Right," Cassy paused, looking him in the eye. "Is it true your father had a method of getting a person into a synthetic, droid body?"

"Few people know about that," said Keller, his lips forming an annoyed line.

"I have my connections in Ironsmith, in Neufeld bunker. So I've heard a few things."

"Really, and they couldn't help you more?" Keller looked at the passers by outside for a moment, keeping himself calm.

"No, they couldn't. God knows I've tried. The paranormal, supernatural, ghost stuff doesn't fly down there. They don't like to talk about it much, probably because of the incident."

"And what incident is that?"

She paused to just look at him, then continued. "Your father was doing some testing, stumbled on to something phenomenal, and decided to try it out for himself, not wanting to harm anyone else. If successful, meaning he himself could infuse the body of a droid, he didn't want the lab to fall into the wrong hands, so had the place self-detonate afterwards. It also suited if he, ah, died."

"And was he successful?" Keller eyed her, pessimism gnawing. *Except that suicide wasn't a hobby of his.*

"I was hoping you might shed some light. Please excuse me if I'm being too bold or trampling on a sensitive subject, but I don't like to beat around the bush."

"That's fair. Why do you need to know?"

"Research," she said abruptly, anticipating again.

"Ah. For whom?" *Research my ass.*

"All in good time. Now that Henrik Poole has been released from prison, I wanted to know what you think. What you know," she said in earnest. Cassy clasped her hands in a bridge. "Please, I could really use some help on this. Your father—"

"I was a kid back then. Those aren't simple questions, and I don't have answers for them."

"Ok. How about you then? Do you believe in ghosts? Spirits? I mean as actual live entities who come back from the dead or exist somewhere in between?" she said, perking up.

Keller looked at her a moment, feeling outgunned. Most people circumvented such issues, but this one was direct. "How do I know this isn't for some creepy tabloid?"

"It's not."

"I strictly deal with what I sense and what people tell me. No one has ever said they thought they were a ghost, hung around as one and then *came back*. While I find ghost stories intriguing, they are covered more effectively, albeit ineffectively, by theories on paranormal activity, and I'm not into that. I'm not my father."

"So, what happened 3 months ago on the beach here by the pier?"

"I got lucky. Do you work for Henrik?"

"No. And what about the guy from the truck wreck a year ago?"

Cassy pensively watched as the waitress came by, added two place settings, and gave them menus, pretending not to hear their conversation. She balanced just enough courtesy, with a quick hint that she was the boss. Wearing a youthful bob, she was aging, yet not old. "Come back tonight at 3am and I'll show you a ghost."

Keller stared at his menu and Cassy giggled, looking from one to the other.

"With all due respect to the Holy Ghost, I'd say there're tons of 'em," she continued, a specialist at heart, "And I dear say we've had our share here on the pier. Including the boy who drowned," she winked at Keller. "Mind you he's back where he should be."

He glanced at the waitress, then back to Cassy, who commented and smiled as the woman continued to speak. He drifted off to the lock of light brown hair arcing her entire face, and deep brown eyes. Though her smooth, worry-free skin and restlessness suggested youth and nothing more, there was a shrewd manner about her. Her frame was rather broad, and her clothing masked athletic alertness.

Returning to the conversation, Keller found Cassy waiting for an answer. The waitress had walked off. As if noticing his vague composure, she asked again, "And what about today?" She brushed her hair back, eyebrow flashing.

"Why, what happened today?"

"Keller... ok, I got contacted as it happened. Dead Jane Doe comes back to life. I got a call."

"That's more like it. Call from who?"

"A guy I work with. Is it so shocking that there are people out there who are interested in psychics?" she said, holding her hands palms up.

"All right. Today was incredible, to be honest." Keller explained at leisure what occurred regarding Jane Doe and Cassy seemed to enjoy the story, laughing at points. The waitress came and went, hovering a little at times. While he ate crêpes and drank coffee, Cassy hadn't ordered a thing.

"What exactly are you researching?" Keller asked.

"Possibilities."

"That's not vague at all."

Verging on a tongue-in-cheek vein she continued about paranormal behavior in people, how it related to high-end security and how intricate and professional breaches could be foreseen. "If we study people on a paranormal level, we might better predict what they will do once given the opportunity, self-generated or suggested, to commit a crime."

Keller asked if she was undercover, and Cassy replied, "What do you think?"

"I wouldn't have asked," he said. "Sounds like a farce, an excuse to explore transhumanism."

"But I know what you're thinking. You're curious," she said with a smirk.

She's difficult.

A suited figure appeared at the door and came in. It was Bruno Emerson, Keller's partner from Lucy's. Bruno was average height, greyed, and distinct. His shoes and gait spoke for themselves—he bound towards the back of the establishment, not pausing at the counter or to talk to the waitress when she offered a greeting, instead just nodding. *He's pissed.*

"Hey Bruno, you found me," Keller said, offering him a chair. But when Bruno noticed Cassy, he solidified into a mannequin, inorganic, and plastic. Likewise, Cassy glanced at him and then spun back to Keller, her eyes a touch fearful. She swallowed and continued to ignore the man who made as if to speak. Instead, Bruno faced Keller, who stood up and shook his hand.

"Just wanted to make sure you were okay. You disappeared, Stacey says." He was genuine enough, but something was off. *Why the hell would you come and find me? And how?*

"Keller, it was nice meeting you. We'll catch up later," Cassy spoke up and stood, shuffling out to the aisle. As she neared it,

Keller caught the moment in full—while Bruno reached to grab her arm, Cassy appeared to pause then shifted to the side with sudden adeptness, making Bruno grope thin air. Embarrassed, he tried again, this time faster. She eloquently deflected his arm. In the next instant, she had turned and was heading towards the door. When Cassy stopped to look back at Bruno, the expression in her eyes was not ballroom. *Stay*, it said. Bruno did, flashing an angry countenance, then recomposed.

A memory stirred in Keller. It was something he hadn't seen for years, never in something so attractive. "How about a crepe, Bruno?"

The man turned back to him, reddish, a fine sweat smeared on his brow. *He's freaking.*

"Yeah, sure. And a beer if they have it. How do you know her?"

"I don't. Just showed up, wanted to chat restaurants. How did you know I was here?"

"Tracing a phone isn't a big deal these days. Friend of mine," Bruno said, glancing around.

"Why go through the trouble? You look riled up."

Bruno didn't answer, waving it off, and Keller left it alone. He would enquire about the 'Morpheus' package another time.

After a few minutes, drinks and more crêpes arrived. Keller insisted on shots to accompany the beers. The man was high strung and needed to chill. Keller brought up the restaurant, new staff, and any small talk he could think of. A few more people filtered in and as Bruno relaxed, the conversation traversed to the events of the day and Jane Doe. Keller recounted the story, but Bruno took little interest and didn't break a chuckle. Rather, he looked concerned and when Keller finished, they sat in silence, sipping beer.

"Quite a tattoo on that woman, Avast Ye. She carries it well," Bruno said absent-mindedly. Keller, daunted, made nothing of the comment outwardly. *He may have heard of Jane through Lurch.*

Doubtful. He could never have seen Avast Ye unless he saw the patient undressed.

"Keller, I best be heading out as well. It's been a tiresome day. If there's anything you need, just let me know."

"Sure Bruno, thanks." *WTF?*

"Get home yourself and get some rest, you deserve it."

"Yeah, sure."

Chapter 6

The walk from the Palace Pier to Keller's apartment on Rock St was a mile. After deliberating whether to check on his restaurant or fetch his bike from the hospital, Keller decided against both. He took Bruno's advice, no matter how odd, and went home. Most of the way, he walked along Madeira Drive, next to the beach. Parallel the street were little tracks belonging to the world's oldest, functioning electric train. Had it passed by Keller would have jumped on. He turned north, and after a couple of side streets and alleys, he found himself on Rock. The road was void of media vans. *The guy knew my name, but that won't lead him here unless he visits Lucy's and Stacey wouldn't give out personal info.*

While the piano store was dark, Reptile nation boasted a neon sign which hummed and crackled. The chameleon who often stood tableau in a window display had been transferred to his night digs. Tarzana considered her store a hotel, a temporary dwelling for her guests, where comfort and security were of utmost importance.

Keller walked up the narrow staircase to his apartment without the bike. He wondered if the journalists would find it still locked up outside of Emergency or use his escape to frost the rest of the story. He thought of Nora and how she mitigated the situation with the doctors and when the chase began. *You're like my hero for today.* And then he thought of Cassy. *Nut job.* And finally, Bruno. *Maybe I was too quick to accept his investment. That guy has a sinister something about him. Morpheus…*

Keller sat down on the side of his bed and then flopped back. Minutes later, his feet followed. His mind lulled to a trance as the moonlight faded behind invading clouds, slowly turning off a gridded shadow traversing the room. Again, Nora popped to mind, and how she minded little when he showed up, and her tongue-in-cheek request to identify the correct fridge. Then she merged with blossoming fatigue as his thoughts drifted and he found himself elsewhere.

It was a bright, scorching, sunny day, as most days in Vegas were. Aside from when it rained. He was busy creating a fort from sticks, stones and gravel when he decided to get up and survey the situation out in the desert. He walked over to the low concrete block wall, which separated his haven from the cruel yet beckoning vastness beyond. He was just tall enough to see over it. Across the desert were mountains. Not far away, a woman had gotten down on her knees and planted a bushy bundle of thin stems with short narrow leaves and tiny blue blossoms. There were antlers sticking out of her hair. She looked at him, got up, and walked over.

"I'm planting Scorpion Grass," she said in a dusty voice, "See the tail?" She jiggled a new bunch, and the cluster of blossoms and uppermost leaves moved as one. "They're curled like the tail of a scorpion. Your mother might call them Forget-Me-Nots; that's the new name. Started maybe a hundred years ago."

Keller didn't know what she was talking about. But he liked her and the antlers too.

"The Scorpion Grass is a lot like people," she said. "It's pretty yet can survive almost anywhere. I'm seeing if it'll grow here, in the hard, dusty dirt and amongst the stones."

Keller smiled and waved. He was 4.

"As long as it has some water, it'll survive. They say it likes the shade, but it will learn to like the sun. You'll see."

A telephone rang in the distance. There was no phone booth in the backyard. Keller searched for a phone outside but when he turned back to the antler woman, she was gone. Then the ringing plagued his ear. Keller awoke and answered the smartphone on his bedside table.

"You awake?" said Bruno. "It's your wake-up call."

Keller didn't recall asking for one but told Bruno he was awake, that it was 5am, and what did he want?

"Just checking on you, mate."

Considering it a prank, Keller hung up. Bruno's sudden interest in his well-being felt absurd. Nausea welled as the world around him lay in dawn tranquility, the urgency was clear: *something's off.* The Morpheus logo on the package popped into mind alongside the half-conscious Jane Dow muttering, "You're being framed for murder." Her decisive manner and effort to speak suggested a clarity far beyond what could be expected from a person who had survived a death of numerous hours. *Assume she's right and that she carried that torch for a reason. Don't ignore it.*

His phone buzzed and rang once more. Bruno. "What this time?"

"Keller, Lurch can't make it in this morning. He called *me* because it's technically your day off. Can you come in, just to open, deliveries and such?"

"Yeah, I suppose. I'll be in at 7 or so." With those words followed a realization and once more Keller hung up. *He's corralling me.* He refrained from texting Lurch, not wanting to complicate matters. *Yep, something's really off.*

Keller dragged himself out of bed, made his morning espresso and took a shower. A half-hour later, his phone rang again. *Sussex Police.* Keller didn't answer. He quickly got dressed, grabbed his shoulder bag and threw a few things inside. He thought of how Jane Doe woke up to say what she did. Her brief mention of directions to a house in Maine lit up like a beacon, and he tossed *two* passports into the bag. Instead of heading to work, Keller strode to the hospital a few blocks away.

The receptionist, who sat in a geometric configuration framed in a tall, gridded glass wall, was hair-lit by warm halogen spots—another night shift was near completion. She bid him a good morning—her eyes echoing two bulbous, black security cams sitting in the protrusion 2 m above. Keller muttered something in return not pausing in his stride to the lift for Critical Care on the 7th.

The ward was quiet; the patients were asleep by and large. As Keller walked past the darkened bay areas, monitors glowed, showing most were occupied and stable. When he reached 703, door partially ajar, he first noted the monitor was dark. He opened it further and walked in. The bed was empty.

Must have moved her. He walked back to the nurse on duty and enquired about Jane Doe.

"They transferred her earlier this morning, at 3:27am," the nurse said, checking her system. "That's odd, it doesn't say to where. But she's definitely not with us." The nurse typed, made a few clicks, and stared. Her brow was knit and while her head turned towards Keller, her eyes remained riveted on the screen. Then they followed, large and concerned. "She doesn't seem to be in here, maybe... no, it also doesn't say she was released. Not that we release patients at that hour."

"You're telling me she's vanished?"

"I'm sure there's an explanation, I just don't have it."

"It's fine, which doctor?" Keller paused. *Someone took her out.*

"The schedule says Dr Adams, also odd, I've never heard of him."

Keller drew a blank. *Never heard of him.* "Someone might have provided her real name at least?" Keller noticed his phone buzzing—*Bruno again. Not this time.*

"Not in the system, I'm sorry. You're the man who was here with her, yesterday..." she said, brightening up.

"Yes, and thanks."

Keller back-pedaled to the lift, took it down one floor, and crossed a small laneway over to Pathology. An ambulance stood silent in the early dawn, spotted with reflections. Two paramedics stood outside talking and Keller took care to pass them quickly, unnoticed. *Probably a stupid hunch.*

Once again, he faced the door requiring an access card. Realizing he was on camera and not skipping a beat, he sat down at reception. *I just need a few minutes in there.* He searched the desktop, underneath, its drawers and sure enough a remote revealed itself. The doors slid open, and he headed down the stifling corridor to the grey door with inviting handles.

"Can I help you?" a man's voice bit the air with a slight echo. Keller turned to see a sixty-something, greyed and spectacled figure, messy beard, neat attire—pressed from the top down. *Henrik Poole. Why am I not surprised?* He wore gloves, an apron and was mid-process. Keller glanced at the table, and it became clear who lay there stripped of clothing. Captain Lee greeted him from Jane's naked bodice once more, the text 'Avast ye' visible and more ironic than ever. *Pay attention. Ironic.* But it wasn't the bruises, cuts and smell of garbage that shot adrenaline into his bloodstream. That was upsetting, yes, and that she was dead with no light on or sticky notes. It was the blatant inconsistency of the ink on the tattoo which set Keller off—it had become more vibrant overnight, more saturated. *Impossible. Greasy?* No little birthmarks either—where they had continued the sea spray on her chest had been replaced by black ink dots. *Not her. Hair, not her. Skin too smooth. Not bloody her!*

Keller suppressed his initial reaction, while his vision jiggled, and hid it behind a smile that erupted on all its own. "I came to see Jane. Can't say I expected to see you here," he said, placed his shoulder bag on a counter and donned latex gloves to divert Henrik's attention.

"I told you to stay away. So instead, you went and raised a woman from the dead. Now get out of here."

Keller began snapping photos with his phone.

"I'm afraid you can't do that. I'm performing an autopsy and she's under police investigation. You're a suspect by the way," Henrik paused and lowered his voice, "This is *him* coming for *you.*"

"So I hear." Keller didn't pause in his pace. "You called 2 nights ago and texted that you wanted to meet. What was that about? A reminder to stay away?"

Henrik behaved as if intervening, but Keller kept snapping, watching him through the corner of his eye, nullifying his threatening remarks with quick, senseless answers. "It's all right, this can be part of the police report."

"Keller, you need to go."

"You didn't answer my question."

"You've been set up, we both have. I'm giving you a head start," Henrik hissed quietly.

Keller and Henrik stood face to face. The old man's eyes were troubled, and callous, meaning what he said. "Did you kill him?"

"Your father? Of course I killed him. Just so I could spend the rest of my life paying for it!"

"I never thought you the victim type. Who's doing all of this?" *Who's bloody coming for me?*

Henrik continued to meet his gaze. "I'm obliged to call the police. Soon, there will be a city-wide warrant. National by tomorrow. You get a ten-minute head start Keller. Punch me as hard as you can and run. For the camera. This is one nightmare you don't want to investigate."

Peeved to be cornered by delusional activity, Keller threw a sudden, vengeful roundhouse that sent Henrik crashing into a trolley and bodily slapping the floor. After getting a quick shot of Jane's teeth, Keller was off. *Too perfect.*

Minutes later, the semi-conscious Henrik collected his cracked spectacles, then crawled further to what was left of his phone, splattered against the wall. Ignoring the plastic parts he took a pillbox from his lab coat pocket instead, flipped the lid open, and selected 2 painkillers. *Tramadol will do.*

Chapter 7

Keller was relieved. He had never asked Henrik if he had blown up Tom's lab, killing both Tom and Katrina, for which he was originally sentenced to life in prison. When he met him a year ago a free man, he didn't have the nerve because Keller *knew* Henrik hadn't done it. But now that he was entangled in a new crime, it had made sense to ask. Whether the old drug addict told the truth was another matter but Keller had a feeling he might have.

After cutting through the A&E Department, he hopped on his bike, and rode downtown, stopping at a hardware store to pick up a tube of GripDog and a new phone. The credit card had never been used—the name on it was Stan Williams. After, he stopped at the bus depot, chose a bus that wasn't scheduled to leave just yet and got on. Knowing that Bruno had tracked him the previous evening, he backed up the phone, reformatted, then glued it under a seat. As the driver started the engine, Keller jumped off.

Next, he called Tarzana.

"Keller? Well, if it isn't Keller. Cops were around, looking for you dear."

"I can explain. Can you give me a lift to the airport?"

"Sudden holiday? This I must hear."

15 minutes later Tarzana arrived and popped the boot. Keller assumed she would get something out but instead motioned for

him to come closer, much as an old man might to a kid. "If you're messing with me, I need to know now. And then I shall turn you in," she said, putting a big hand on Keller's shoulder.

"There's no time to explain, I'll do it on the way. I'm good to go, I have an alibi," he spoke, not wavering.

"Who?"

"You."

"What?"

"I know you see me coming home at night. C'mon, I've seen the street view from your place, and I know you like to watch. Everybody. So, you know I came home alone."

"You did, as usual."

"So, there was a murder last night, real ugly type. Body was found in a dumpster. Somebody somehow decided it might be me because the victim looks like Jane Doe. Did I tell you about her yet?"

"Nope, but I heard. Quite a story," she said. "But as for the murder, you could have done it on your way home."

"Jane Doe was still in the hospital then. She was murdered after 3:30am. I mean, a look-alike was, I saw the body, it's not her."

"Sounds complicated, ill-contrived."

"Very contrived."

"I was asleep by then; you could have slipped out. But you saved her in the first place. Well done by the way."

"It wasn't so much me, but thanks," he said as Tarzana gave him a side hug with one long arm.

"So, who was it then? Who told them she's alive? That was a bloody resurrection if you ask me."

Keller nodded and shrugged.

"Get in. I'll drive, and you tell me all about it," she said, indicating the open boot with a long finger and curved, gold fingernail.

"You're kidding me."

"Quick, this is becoming a scene. A fugitive is a fugitive."

"I'm not—" Keller did as she asked and when the boot door slammed down a little light came on. Tarzana and Keller talked by phone, he into his and she put hers on speaker.

"There's a snake in here!" Keller yelped, moving to avoid touching the head and serpentine body emerging from the back seat partition with ease. Helplessness and claustrophobia knocked and pinged messages of horror, spiking the blood pressure in Keller's brain.

"Take it easy, she's friendly. Mia is my security. She lives in the car, so I don't need to use an alarm. People see her and leave it alone. As you notice, I've fitted the boot with a night light. Her food is in the compartment beneath, with the tire."

"Poisonous?"

"Nope. Piss her off all you want."

The engine erupted, and the car surged forward. In a couple turns it felt like Tarzana drove out of the bus depot and merged with traffic. The trip to the airport just south of London took over an hour and during that time Keller told Tarzana the full story, including how he met Nora.

"You like her don't you..." she finally said.

"Nothing like that."

"The story you just told me was one-fifth necromancy and murder and four-fifths Nora."

"She even covered for me, I admire that."

"M-hmm. Maybe it's time to let someone in. Don't get me wrong, I enjoy our late-night talks but there's something amiss I'd say."

Keller didn't answer, instead eyeing the python who eyed him back.

Tarzana dropped Keller off in the multi-level airport car park; anyone who may have seen him get out didn't let on. *Cams. Security won't be interested yet.*

"Take it easy," she said, giving him a hug. "Not a word out of me, except that I know you were home last night," she said with a wink.

"Thanks Tarzana. And thank Mia for not biting me," he said, walking backwards and then turned to jog towards the elevators.

Soon after, he approached the counter to buy a ticket for Bangor, Maine. The only Black Point Road on Deer Isle he could find, the big one, was on the coast, 60 miles south of Bangor. The airline attendant asked for his passport, and Keller handed it over—Stan Williams it said inside, English nationality. *Thanks dad, came in handy after all, even got a credit card to match. Is it a buddy of yours who's framing me? Henrik's in on it too, so…*

"You remind me of someone I saw in the morning news," the attendant said.

Keller kept staring at her hands as she passed back the passport, then glanced up, hoisting his bag further on his shoulder as if it were necessary. "Really?"

"Yeah, a restaurant guy they say, in Brighton," she smiled and let go as he took the passport from her. Upon glancing again, he noted a slight blush. "He brought some woman back to life in a morgue of all places. Whatever does it for some. Dual personality they say."

"Amphibious," Keller added.

"Pardon me?"

"I'm ambidextrous."

She gave him a mild look soured by distaste.

Huh… Keller thanked her and moved on. The genuine test would be at customs. If he were a wanted man, there could be an alert. *There's no way legally the police can decide and move that fast.* Keller thought of the paramedics, Bruno, and Henrik. The paramedic who swiped the wallet must have known what he was coming for. Bruno had become a wild card and Henrik certainly knew everything and was even bold enough to give him a head start. He had always liked Henrik, but now things were weird. They had been weird ever since Henrik left prison, and they met in London.

There was no line at customs either. *Timing-wise, this is awesome.*

"Where to?"

"Bangor, Maine."

"How long?"

"A week or so, depends how the fishing is."

The officer did his thing, looked at the passport, and verified it on the computer. Keller simply looked at him, then away, then at the counter, then back at him for a second. *He's caught on something. This is longer than usual. Is there a notice?*

· · · · ·

Meanwhile, at his office desk in Lucy's, Bruno inspected a little black box, taken from a larger package, with a gold logo comprising two wings and a poppy blossom with a tiny inscription that read *Morpheus*. He speed-dialed a number on his smartphone. A voice answered. Bruno told him Keller had vanished, nowhere to be found in the hospital or elsewhere. "Security footage is being searched," he said.

A somewhat synthesized voice replied, "Don't worry, he'll be a wanted man shortly, he'll get picked up. I'll let the Police Chief know. He's a restaurant manager, not a spy and I don't care who his mother was."

· · · · ·

"All right, have a pleasant trip," the customs official said, handing back his passport. "You okay?"

"Yeah, just tired, worked late, up early," Keller replied.

The man nodded and waived Keller to move on. He did, covertly jubilant at this moment. *The news, whatever it is, must not yet be out. The battered corpse in the morgue wasn't Jane. Nor did it have a light on. Yet I run.*

Keller walked the short distance to the departure lounge and passed by a kiosk, just opened. A stack of newspapers sat on the floor, and Keller couldn't help noticing the front page. *Restaurant manager talks to the dead.* There was a small photo of Keller, but the hero shot showed Nora and her assistant standing in the morgue. He turned and continued to the lounge. *Wait 'till you hear the latest.*

He sat down to wait, bleary and exhausted. The airport was half empty and quiet, yet the bustle followed as more people rolled in. He looked at the flight timetable from time to time and watched as people passed by or lounged. A little boy, tired, pummeled his mother with questions. A trendy couple took their seats in unison, each with a coffee in their right. An elderly man scanned a newspaper.

Lulled by the surrounding rhythm, Keller flash-backed to when he walked down a central side street in London and noticed the pub he was looking for. His pace slowed and the people walking by him also seemed to lag, glitch a little. The sun bounced from window to window, glimmering from the uneven glass. He pulled on the heavy brass handle and the solid door gave way invitingly. *Let's get this over with.*

Once inside he shortly noticed a man sitting at a table with his back to him, an angular back he recognized. The man turned as Keller approached, stood up and smiled. They hugged. The sweet smell of wine-dipped cigars was the fourth thing Keller found familiar about Henrik Poole. The third was his messy beard, which had greyed. The second was his smile, which could be misunderstood.

They sat down. The scene forwarded to a segment in the conversation.

"We have clients who are very interested in our program," Henrik said, in earnest.

"What program? Drugs are us?" *You're on coke, I'd say, I noticed as soon as I walked in.*

"Not funny Keller. We specialize in revitalizing people in a wholeness never before seen."

"So, you've made a breakthrough on the anti-aging line. Big business these days. Always has been I suppose."

"Ten, twenty, thirty years younger. On a cellular level."

"Right."

"It's complicated Keller, but seeing you have a feel for *people, alive and dead...*"

"I don't do dead. I don't mess around with paranormal theories, I'm not my father, Henrik. Just a medical student."

"Of course not, course. But tell me then, what happened last week?"

"I witnessed a guy lose control of his truck and roll it into the median. He was taken to hospital and died there. I didn't believe it was over yet, and... The media likes to exaggerate for a better story; you of all people should know how it works."

"Yes, and I do," Henrik said and looked sideways, his jaw gesticulating. He looked back. "*We* aren't messing around either. Our technology can add many years to a person's life. As I said, decades. It was initially created by your father."

"Oh no, not interested. That's what this is about?"

Henrik took on a stern tone, "My reason for seeing you is twofold. One is to give you a warning. Stay out of the spotlight. He's coming for you. He's seeking your skill set which is quite rare and will go to great lengths to get it. *Especially from you.* Get out of London and vanish unless you prefer a much more complicated life, one which you may not survive."

"And?"

Henrik paused, pursing his lips. "To plant a seed of curiosity."

Henrik's eyes gave him up—there was no humor there. Keller investigated them and saw a hardened man. He saw the man he knew as a boy. But it was callous now, reckless, desperate. The wrinkles, bad teeth, unsureness in the shape of his lips—they were twitching as if trying to send a message on their own.

He was forced to see me, and he's not lying or joking.

"Seats one to twenty-five boarding now. Please have your passports ready," a woman's voice said through the speakers. Keller got up and joined the line.

Again, his nerves pecked at his sanity when it came time to hand over his passport. Keller relaxed his mind and enjoyed the flight attendant's mannerisms—an angular but soft face posed under a roundish dew, capped smartly above straight shoulders. Her gentle, manicured hand took the passport and flicked it open to the inside cover. She studied her screen for a moment. Her brow crinkled and eyes slit, much as the night nurses had in the critical care ward, seeing Jane was missing. Then she looked back at Keller. "I'm sorry, but the seat you've reserved is taken. Sometimes happens with last-minute bookings. Let me see what I have."

Keller smiled, nodded, and watched as she continued to study the screen in full seriousness. "That's fine," he said, "I'll take whatever you have."

Chapter 8

Cruising along a cracked and patched two-lane highway, Keller kept his eye on the shady evergreens racing by. When the trees grew sparse near a derelict farm, the sun strobed between the trunks. Blinded, he eased off the gas, fearing that if he missed his turnoff, there was no going back. *It's not here...* He checked the fuel gauge, three-quarters of a tank down, enough to greet fate in an entirely different fashion — cut loose for good this time. *Good luck with that.*

Being out in semi-wilderness on a beautiful spring day didn't exactly geyser inspiration, despite the panoramic view windscreen. That a pair of Vuarnets remained 3000 miles away next to a DIY lamp, artfully invented from scrap garbage by his neighbor who enjoyed gifting fire hazards, bit him in the butt. Having flown to Maine from England early that morning was a dark, curious impulse, more than anything else, propelled to outmaneuver a wicked situation.

They say you're wanted for murder, pulsed once more through his consciousness, a chilling shock wave resonating in his chest. The sun looked evil and bleak behind its paralyzing flashes for a moment, reporting a lie without scruples. *Heads off with the mock medium, the miserable freak! Henrik warned me not to do it anymore, it attracts too much attention.*

He's coming for you, Henrik said.

Traveling retro with a paper map had a quaintness about it. Folded down to a manageable size, it was no more dangerous than reading a book—Keller didn't mind, it went hand in hand with his already shot nerves.

Narrow, paved rock roadways spanning bays of water, distant fishing villages, stretches of forest, bush and vague signage leading to god knows what, filled the journey thus far. An obedient stream of telephone poles connected the many peculiar spots—a pit stop named *The Galaxy* with its peeling hand-painted placard, a deep woods hotel complete with a shrimping vessel planter, a designated hiking trail sign ripe with bullet holes, and an artist's studio gallery graced by a dog chewing on something, eyes bulging.

Keller pulled over into a shady pocket to scrutinize the map once more. He had taken a model without GPS—untraceable and rollable over a cliff with no qualms. As far as his new phone went, he had already smashed that and tossed it.

Almost 2 hours had passed since leaving the airport in Bangor, Maine, and presently he was close to the ocean and Jane Doe's house. *Not dead, and if she were, she would have said something by now. She would be freaking out.*

Engine off, a host of sounds materialized, seeping through peace. A light breeze pervaded the forest, pushing its way past millions of pine needles as one unified hush. A tree swayed and creaked, another bumped its branches high above, and something small, running and searching, created a rustle nearby. A flamboyant, lush roadside medley had popped out through last year's dead leaves. The bugs hadn't chomped into them yet, no grasshoppers buzzing in the air. Somewhere nearby, they were no doubt millions bursting out of their shells, en mass exodus, only to be intercepted by whatever was next on the food chain.

A snapping branch stirred Keller. *Need to find the house. No other reason for coming, no point in dawdling.* He turned the key, and the engine gurgled reassurance. Being apprehended, strung from a tree, and left to rot by a mob of bloodthirsty man hunters misled by the same intel which knew the whereabouts of his alive and breathing murder victim, was not on the itinerary. No, he would make it to Jane Doe's house—perhaps an ambush, a garden of answers, riddles, or all three.

A sudden grey-white splash of bird poo decorated the panoramic view as Keller pulled out and drove on. *Elegant.* According to map symbols, it couldn't be far now—the house closest to Black Point, evidently named after a ship, the Madame Noir. Her Captain, sailing by a late November moon, inebriated, cut too close to a point plagued with shallows. They presented themselves too late for a ship enjoying brisk, pre-swell winds and eager to reach its destination.

He miscalculated. Otherwise, we would have never known Captain Lee was running rum. Nor that some of the overloaded rowboats capsize, and even to this day, ethereal shrieks echo against the shore as precious barrels roll into the dark waters and bob away along with the men who scratch and claw them for one last rush before submitting to a hypothermic grave. Lame move Jane Doe, to try and die the same way your tattoo did.

Rows of pines gave way to a solid mass of timber and banished the sun—the cracked and pot-holed pavement ahead, veiled in shadow, turned a grim hue of grey, and the worn white lines, faded. Another mile crept by.

This must be it. Keller hit the brakes, and the car skidded easily on remnants of coarse winter sand, stopping in the intersection. He thought of driving past and running. The drive ahead looked tempting compared to the private trail which yawned helter-skelter—a vague passage flanked by a rotting mailbox, collapsed fencing and an overgrown ditch. Keller envisioned a plethora of inviting towns and harbors dotting the Maine coast should he not choose this way. He would arrive out on Route 1 in under an hour, heading northeast and into Nova

Scotia, Canada. His fake passport was good to go anywhere. *The old man knew I might need it, knew I would end up in trouble because that's the way he liked it. Loved it.*

Instead, Keller made the turn, which seemed to cross an unspoken boundary as it entered the gloom. Creeping forward at first, fiddling with the headlights, then slowly adding gas, the rental bumped ahead on the stones and ruts. The overlay of greenery looked unscathed; tracks camouflaged. Little bugs, tiny dark ones, gravitated to the beams. *Must be black flies.* Visions of past camping trips flashed in his mind, the little buggers crawling into his eyes, ears, nose, and tickling the back of his throat.

The road was narrow, and the sky above visible through cracks in the arcing branches, twisted and black. Keller found his mouth ajar, in aid of concentration, as if the house might be the size of a golf ball.

If it's an ambush, I should turn off the engine and walk. It's not an ambush.

Adding to the ominous view ahead, a shroud of mist befell the forested throat; the trees turned colorless and grew taller before him, behemoths passing judgment on the automobile pressing through. *It looks like their growing before my eyes.*

But just as one can arouse from a dream, the road following the next bend brightened. Following that along, a white structure emerged, shining from within the trees. *Must be the damn house.* Enveloped in a soft sheen, it was the last—the only thing beyond it was the ocean. As the old, proud Victorian came into full view, boasting an aggressive footprint for what appeared to be a wilderness outpost, a square tower jutted skyward from the long, steep, slate roof. *Dreamer.*

As he drove closer, he could see what looked like a fresh coat of paint on its wrap-around veranda. *Probably the 10th.* A double-seater hung motionless, harmonizing with the railings, ornate posts, hanging pots, fairy-tale windows, and the distinguished black door. A single light shone from a lamppost to the right of the turning circle, whose border was encroached by spring growth.

Keller glanced at the terrain past the house. The trees shrank and thinned, devolving to brush and ruddy grey stone. The land dropped off, and beyond the view flourished into an expanse of sky tinted with orange and pomegranate.

Being wanted, nibbled at his core. The last he had seen in the airport, on a bar's wide-screen, the UK manhunt was active. Though doubtful anyone would trace him to the US, his next actions were paramount to keeping it that way.

House looks in good shape, a classy hideaway. You're involved with the wrong guys, Jane Doe.

Keller pulled around and parked. The cool, salty sea air greeted him as he stepped out. Drawn to it, he kept his distance from the old Victorian and walked toward the shore, still hidden. A flock of gulls bantered afar, circling and yapping.

The rocky path between stunted trees and moss led out to the open. It ended abruptly, dropping a few yards to a sandy shore. A pattern of distant waves silently fanned outward and away, beyond the island's shadow and into the remaining glow.

Up along the coast, the cliffs varied. Barren blocks of ruddy stone piled high, made as if to crumble beneath the deep green forest above. Yet it jeeringly did not, suspended in motion for what could have been a million years.

These were the executioners after the verdict of the tall trees, Keller's imagination careened. His gaze dropped to the waves lapping the shore below. A turquoise hue toned the metallic waters, interspersed with dark blotches where submerged boulders broke up the sand.

His urban perceptions dulled and preoccupied missed the little cracks of breaking twigs, which blended in. It would have been filed as 'squirrel or chipmunk' if they registered at all. But the gentle sound pattern that followed he could not miss. They were the footsteps of a larger mammal. Keller whirled. A man in his seventies, thin but broad-chested, wearing a face that knew it had to do what it had to do, had arrived and was standing 30 feet inland. The shotgun he held like a prop tipped up to eye level. Keller could feel the crosshairs on him, a phantom insect, frantically deliberating where to bite.

A precious sliver crossed his thoughts, a shooting star. 'I'm gonna teach you something Keller,' his mother began, suddenly serious now. 'Don't be scared,' she said as she pointed her pistol at him. "It's loaded."

"Is there somethin' I can help you with? I mean, before I blow your head off?"

"That's very kind. I'm looking for a shipwreck," Keller said, making conversation.

"What makes you think there's one here?"

"I don't. I mean, there could be a shipwreck, but it's actually a house I'm looking for, the last one. Nearest the shipwreck. Legend mentions it was here, where shrieks can still —"

"And I suppose this is where I invite you for coffee, and we become best friends?"

"I could probably use a drink."

The phantom insect settled on his forehead, Keller guessed.

Chapter 9

3000 miles away, two men stood by a tall window facing east, overlooking the gently rolling English countryside. The window belonged to a mansion of the Baroque era. Created by an English architect, it lacked the flair present in its Italian cousins but made up for any deficit with its mysterious dignity. The mood extended to the two men who commented on the new dawn, paying particular attention to a falcon which swept across the view. The house stood on the Isle of Wight, off the southern coast of England.

Despite the gentlemanly repose of both, an older man held a bowl of breakfast cereal and passed a spoonful to the mouth of a younger man from time to time, in between comments of daybreak colors, dew, and the bird of prey.

"Can we keep the bird?" said the younger man, still chewing. They called him The Kid, after the famous baby-faced gunslinger he liked to emulate. He was tall, built, sandy-haired with robust features—the biggest of all were his ears. His childish expressions looked comical because they were set on a grown man's body.

"If you can catch him, sure. And if the neighbor doesn't mind," commented the older man, Henrik Poole. Next to the Kid, he looked shorter, wiry, crooked, and aged—an angular man of South African descent. His eyes shone in perpetual glee, caressed by wavy wrinkles beneath greying curls of brown perched high on his forehead. He glanced at the Kid and seeing his mouth empty, gave him another spoonful.

"I can feed myself, you know," the kid muttered.

"Yes, and I know what you can do with a spoon. Tell me, what do you know about Falcons?" Henrik asked, picking something from his unkempt goatee, then touching his thin spectacle frame on the edge to adjust the exact height.

"I think they are the coolest ever."

"Do you know how they survive, what they eat?"

The Kid stopped chewing and swallowed. "On a show I saw how they kill, how one swooped in, dove, and picked up a field mouse. They like little animals, that's what they like. The rest of the time they just cruise around and sit in dead trees."

"Does your wife like pets?"

"I told you before, I don't have a wife. I'm a kid. The Kid. I don't know why I'm so big. Please stop asking me trick questions."

"Very well. But if you remembered anything, you'd tell me, right?"

"Not if you bug me and give me cereal full of medications."

"I'm just making sure you eat. No harm in that." Henrik shoved another spoon up into the thick-lipped mouth. *And to think he's only a few months old.*

"Vernon said I was stoned yesterday when I told him I felt woozy. He said he could tell by my behavior and pupils."

"Vernon is a security guard, and no more. He can say what he wants, it doesn't mean it's true."

"He showed me how to do a handstand too."

"Nice. That's very good," Henrik replied, scraping the bottom now, feeding it to the Kid and letting him drink the rest of the milk from the bowl. In minutes, the boy became lethargic and flopped back on a sofa.

"I would like to show you some more pictures, okay?"

"Yeah sure, we've done this before I think."

Over the next hour, Henrik passed a series of prints across an ornate writing desk where they sat and the Kid looked at them, humoring Henrik. He obviously didn't mind. The scopolamine he had been given was doing its job—he was talking openly and would probably not remember much or anything. He said he was groggy, and that was it. He hardly remembered the previous time, and Henrik would speak with the guard not to complicate the boy's views on what was happening.

The boy had nothing revealing to say. Over the last few months, he repeatedly claimed he was not connected to the memories related to his body, much to the chagrin of his wife. The Kid insisted he was born someone else and died as a child. No matter how many memory pulls Henrik printed off and showed him, he denied them being his own and couldn't explain what had taken place beyond the obvious. The Kid considered them somebody else's life, confusing and at best entertaining. The owner of the memories, the original owner, Myron, was not him and he was not Myron.

Unlike Alzheimer's, which may have riddled Myron, the boy remembered everything that happened to him in his new life—people, names, bugs he had seen, and plants. He was intelligent and was continuing to learn. Yet he remembered little of what he considered his old life, blaming that on its abruptness and how many people don't remember their childhood much anyhow. Odd thing for a kid to say, Henrik thought.

So, it made him a 24-year-old 'childish imbecile' who had been injected with the memories of a dying 64-year-old. Until this was resolved, Henrik had failed. While the result was miraculous simply because the man/boy was alive, the wife refused to pay the balance and filed a lawsuit. Since the paperwork had been signed by Myron himself, the case would be a hard win for her. Publicity wise a circus might brew, and Ed, the phantom phone voice who ran things, was opposed to that.

"We're a private, secluded clinic on the Isle of Wight. We don't belong in the papers connected to some hogwash, it's not the attention we require," he had said, with sham innocence.

Meanwhile, the Kid behaved boyishly and enjoyed life as much as it allowed. He hadn't caught on to the scopolamine, sodium thiopental or rohypnol per se, but he knew something was up, so sought to defend his position. He knew that Myron's early memories were missing and those of his own life were vague. Yet he didn't go crazy. Memories were just memories. He giggled and blushed when he saw ones of the wife, naked and copulating. POV, he would say, blushing.

When Myron's wife visited a few days after the original procedure, the Kid recalled her face but did not regard her as anyone close or a person he had ever *met*. Henrik suspected brain damage and a host of mental travails, yet nothing he did or prescribed converted the boy to be the man he was expected to be. His personality was altogether different—hence The Kid.

The wife didn't know her husband when he was 7, 8 or 9 for that matter, but had heard stories. This couldn't possibly be him, personality shift or not. Henrik explained it could be a form of DID—that perhaps the procedure itself had been far more traumatic than anyone realized. She didn't buy it. The clinic was a hoax she believed but agreed her husband's look-alike shared some similarities with Myron. His features and build were one. She theorized he had been bombarded by plastic surgery to get him that way, after which 'this childish man' recited the memories familiar to her. Those had been forced out of Myron under threat, the influence of drugs, or both. Or Myron had agreed, wanting to disappear. She just couldn't prove it yet.

Henrik walked to the back of the study and poured himself a stiff drink. He looked at the little jar of scopolamine tablets he had in his lab coat pocket but decided against them. The boy had had enough. Instead, he pulled out an oval pillbox and took 2 Xanax from the middle partition for himself.

The boy had fallen asleep on a sofa facing the window. Henrik sat across from him, sipping whiskey. *He doesn't know a thing, he's not Myron, who am I kidding?*

Henrik's mobile phone buzzed; the screen displayed *unknown number*. He let it ring a few times and then picked it up off the glass coffee table between him and the boy. Just before pressing the answer button, Henrik glanced at the sofa again. The boy didn't stir.

"Yes," he breathed.

The voice on the other end was that of the unknown man who called himself 'Ed'.

"You need to check the memories of Violet."

"What for? You realize, it can kill her or make her crazy."

"Relax, just do a light scan. Apparently, she said something in the hospital yesterday — the security footage shows she opened her eyes. The pathologist present claims nothing could be heard but I'm looking at those lips and... Don't go deep and please don't get too attached to her Henrik."

"Deep or not, it's risky. But I'll take a look."

"That's it, buddy," Ed said and then, "Thanks for toughing it out the past few days. I think we got our man," and hung up.

Henrik stared at the speaker phone. *The bartender didn't need to zap me, that was cruel you bloody bastard.* Then he rose from his chair and peered once more out the window. He turned back to see the Kid staring back. "I fell asleep."

"Yes, you did. You're a growing boy, that's fine."

"What did you give me? And why are those pictures out?"

"I need you to remember your old life."

"I remember a life. Those are the memories in my head. I've told you a million times. Just it's not *my* life," he said, his eyes turning wet. "I know my mother, and the person in my memories is not her. None of them belong to me except the older ones, the faded ones. Where I am a boy. I died you know, from Leukemia."

It was Henrik's turn to stare back, the horror of being zapped echoing through his body.

"I feel like mushy peas and tired," the boy finally said.

"Tell you what, let's go visit Violet."

He suddenly looked up, surprised.

"You like Violet, don't you?"

The Kid blushed a little and smiled. "Yeah, I like all three," he said, blushing more deeply, "Even the old one."

Chapter 10

"Where did you say you're from? Don't sound local," said the geezer with the shotgun.

"I didn't, you haven't given me a chance to say anything," Keller replied.

"Well, if it's a house you're looking for you must have a name or an address," said the elderly man holding the shotgun. His faded jeans, old purple sweater and worn tennis shoes suggested a peaceful type, but his adept handling of the shotgun meant anything could happen.

"Not quite. I was just told its *nearest* the shipwreck. Yours I imagine," Keller said, chin indicating the old Victorian. "I came here on behalf of a woman who almost died yesterday. Is anyone you know staying in England?"

"You must mean Violet. She's my niece, is she all right?" he said, moving the elaborate shotgun a little higher. Keller took a small step back, keeping his hands in view, making a slightly calming gesture. Other than squinting, the man didn't move. *Nora should see this guy.*

"That's what I'm here to ascertain. She's in stable condition but I need to ask some questions since she's not able to speak herself, not yet, and it's a sensitive situation. She was considered dead, then alive, then dead again, but I'm sure she lives."

"Gimmie a break. You a cop? Scotland Yard?" he responded, his eyes slitting.

"No. The hospital board sent me. She arrived with no ID, and we really need to find out who she is."

"Hospital Board. Hmm. You look familiar. How do I know you didn't kill her and now wanna get rid of me?"

"You don't. I mean, why would I—"

"What's your name?" he said, taking a step forward. The blast from the double barrels could not miss. Keller swallowed and shot a glance up and sideways into mid-air.

"Stan, Stan Williams. I have my passport here if you want to see."

"Stan, hmm. You hang on to that passport, you'll probably need it again." The uncle paused to look at Keller. "Well Stan, I'd like you to come inside, I have something to show you. Strangely, you mention she cannot speak yet she told you where this place is."

"That was about it. Fell back asleep after." *How did he know?*

Taking a trodden earth path, they walked back up to the house which from the front loomed high against a dark forested background, glowing pink in the remaining sunset. The dirt path veered off and the walkway ahead was made of collected stones—grass and moss shared the spacing with cement. That in turn gave way to a sturdy, wide set of wooden steps, painted white some years ago, now worn and faded. They took the stairs up to the wrap-around veranda. Keller was instructed to enter the double French doors, also peeling in places, no doubt from whatever weather the sea brought on. Keller calmed himself, curious what came next. *I can talk to this guy. He's worried, but at least he hasn't lost it. Yet.*

"Sit down, over there," he motioned to a comfy chair. In front of it was a wide-screen TV mounted to the wall. To the right, a tall window revealed the sea. To the left of it, a large mantle crowned with an old, gleaming wood beam hung over the fireplace. Rustic but civilized was the theme of the living room, its central piece a long, massive wood table surrounded by sturdy, bulky chairs, designer padded. On it stood an open laptop and a few crumby dishes. Darkened doorways and narrow halls breathed mystery into the bluish grey and white wallpapered space.

"Pick up the remote and turn it on. I'd like to replay something for you."

Violet's Uncle remained standing, shotgun raised, a little behind and to the left of Keller as he instructed him to get the correct news clip. Then it played. Keller watched, not saying a word.

An astute BBC News anchorwoman sat on a long, curved, bright red sofa. The screen behind her played excerpts as she read off the headlines — including a shot of a covered body in front of a dumpster taped off for investigation.

The story involving Keller Mod was up first and a photo of him behind the bar of Lucy's, smiling right at the camera, filled the screen. *An old shot from last year.* While the uncle didn't say a word, Keller could sense the air stiffen and his head desensitize. Next followed the guts of the story — essentially, Keller had raped a woman and threw her in a dumpster miles away. His DNA was found on her, as well as his semen. The uncle rustled at this point.

"Now tell me that's not you, *Stan.*"

"The photo of the man was me, but —"

"*Stan!* What the hell is this? You say the board *suspects* foul play. The goddamn body was found in a dumpster, for christ' sake. My Violet! And you're a prime suspect!" There was spittle collecting on his lips, his face turned purplish red as the anger lashed through his body. Keller watched the man's fingers and while their white-knuckled grip made for little movement, he glimpsed the large index finger. As if it knew Keller was watching, it moved from behind the trigger to in front, ready to pull. Keller looked up into the uncle's eyes. They were far away, untrusting, bewildered.

"She's not dead. The corpse they found is not her—I have photos to prove it." He glanced back at the finger.

"I bet you do."

"Shoot if you want," Keller made a hoarse croak, his mind spinning now. *Semen, DNA, Violet was right, a setup. How did she know? This guy wasn't filled in.*

"I took some photos this morning at the morgue. You tell me if it's her. I just need a computer and internet. I can go get mine."

"What's internet?" he muttered, the forearm of the finger on the trigger twitching. He motioned the barrel to the laptop. "Violet1968."

Keller stood up without sudden moves, walked over, and sat at the long table. Despite the rustic build, the surface was smooth and had the pleasant touch of worn yet clean. It suggested a fine country mansion, and the windows beyond viewed the approach to the house where darkness had all but fallen and the solitary streetlamp warmed the scene. Keller noticed his rental and yearned to be inside.

While the laptop was dated, Keller found his way around, opened Google, and logged into iCloud as Stan. Meanwhile, the uncle took a comfy chair behind him, setting the shotgun on his lap. Keller could hear him inhale and sigh, sounding distraught. *He's nervous but not stupid.*

"How do I know you didn't retouch them?"

"Why would I show up here if I knew my photo had been plastered all over the news?" Keller blurted the words, tense gobs ringing through the room. He didn't recognize it as his own voice.

The uncle sat morose, opened his mouth, and flicked a tongue over his lower lip. His eyes widened in anticipation and his hands tightened their grip on the gun.

"Here, come and look. I'm a restaurant manager, I don't retouch photos, not even for marketing. I mean, I have someone do it. Forget it…"

"Stand over there, face the wall, hands where I can see 'um."

Keller complied, got up and walked to the wall, eyeing the watery blue, white, and grey paisley wallpaper up close now. It smelled a touch stale, resonating with the forest outside. He listened to the fine clicks of the mouse, under breath mutterings and more sighs. *He's a smart man.* The situation gnawed at him, the impossibility of it all, the reckless abandon of any common sense by the media and police. Keller let his skull tip forward and rest against the wall.

"This ain't her. No way. But she also doesn't have a twin. Are you conning me?"

"What the hell for? What could I possibly gain by showing you these or even showing up here?"

"A morbid sense of curiosity. Psycho. To kill me too, and tie up loose ends, *Stan Williams*. But they're not retouched, I can tell. No visible imperfections in the noise and metadata point to this morning."

Keller listened more as the uncle continued to click in between the hollow plastic swipes. *A competent hand, yet shy. He's no gamer.* Keller was jubilant the man could identify the integrity of the photos. The chances of that were almost nil. Especially out near a fabled shipwreck on the coast of Maine. But there he was, clicking away.

The next click was different, louder, more like a fingered shuffle. *Must be the safety. Please be the safety.*

"She looks foreign, too young, though death can do that. The tattoo — I never did like that thing, but I grew accustomed. It feels off, too colorful. The hair has a different flow, her birthmarks are missing in places." He continued to look and click. "Plus, there's no scar on her hand. Violet was bit by a dog real bad when she was a girl. Broke the bone in the ring finger, almost tore it clean off along with the little one. I remember it because she was on my watch, and I drove her to the hospital. She was 11, but I gave her a little whiskey and cranberry juice for the pain." His voice trailed off, and the sentence ended as if it were to himself. Then silence.

Keller looked over and spoke with caution. "Now open the folder next to that one. It's a shot from her yesterday when I visited."

A shuffle, some clicks, swoosh of the mouse, more clicks. Sigh. Then more silence. Then a sniffle and a quiet breath slid across the silent room. *He's crying... hang on, he's not, he's—* "That's Violet, that's my girl," said the uncle, squeezing air through his chest and throat in a manner of laughter and relief. "Is she alive, or isn't she? I mean now?"

"I'd say she is. After that photo, she opened her eyes and talked to me. We left her resting. She was taken out of the hospital during the night. Gone without a trace."

"So then tell me what happened before that," he said next, as Keller turned towards him. "I sense any crap, I shoot you in the head, simple."

"You like saying that don't you?"

He shook his head. "There's also no actual, physical wreck of a ship near here, though the story lives on. It was Violet's idea to name it 'Shipwreck', did it as a child. Later the name stuck like code, so journalists and media couldn't track her here. No one knows about this place. And it's how I know she *may* have sent you."

Chapter 11

By the time Keller had conveyed the story regarding Violet, aka Jane Doe, he and Violet's uncle had made their way through half a bottle of whiskey. The Uncle said little throughout, and Keller noticed he might be overwhelmed — there wasn't much sign he believed anything nor that he disbelieved. After a while they sat in quietude.

The Uncle mused to himself, then squinted at something imaginary up in the air above Keller. He wet his lips and spoke like a storyteller whose turn was up. "She's been dead twice before, and both times she came back. Made the headlines — like she was made to be an actress on stage, on set, and off. Always attracting attention. I'll take you up to her office later. The clippings are there. But this one, which happened yesterday, that's a crown trump."

Keller sighed a small breath as his nerves loosened up.

"The first time she was in a car accident, wasn't wearing her seatbelt, nor was her nanny. Car spun, skidded off the icy road and smashed into a parked digger — they were passing by a construction area at night — shortcut I guess, the road was open. The nanny at the wheel died when the shovel smashed through the windscreen, but Violet made it. Rough shape though, vitals weak and then none at all. The doctors were ready to give up but kept her hooked up to the system. Odd I'd say. Later, when she woke up and had no apparent brain damage, they were stunned."

"That's incredible."

"The second time, she was up camping in Canada with friends. Algonquin Park for a week—she drowns there after falling out of her canoe in white water. The current pinned her down, the waters were icy cold, it was October, not sure what possessed them to go up so late in the year. No bugs somebody said. Anyway, by the time they fished her out, she was dead. But she was lucky, got airlifted a couple hours later to a nearby town. Woke up the next day like she knew what she was doing. No brain damage again, nothing." As he continued the dissertation of Violet's past, a softness invaded his eyes and remained. He often looked up and out to a distant scene visible only to himself.

He was worried about her, sick with it.

Then silence again. Keller waited before commenting in case there was more. The whisky slowed them both down, but the uncle's sincerity had done much to relax his nerves. Nevertheless, he eyed the gun from time to time as a nervous tick. Catching on, the uncle grunted, got up, ejected the cartridges, and stood the shotgun up next to a windowsill.

They talked a while longer about hypothermic cases—the uncle matching Keller's case study examples with his own. Both had their views on the afterlife and in time the conversation veered to the uncle's favorite: the ancient Viking religions and Valhalla.

When Keller began nodding off, blatantly relieved, the uncle led him upstairs to one of the attic floors. "It's just an office but there's the couch, blankets are underneath. If the police show up in the morning, just stay up here, they can't search the house, I'll deal with them. After that, you'll have to leave though."

Keller sat down on the sofa, surveying the room, the little bay window and the darkness outside. He listened as the uncle's footsteps receded back down the creaky steps and along a short hallway. A door clicked shut, and that was that. Keller opened the window, and the sweet pine, cedar, and sea smell flooded in. He sat back and sighed, a chorus of insect nightlife telling him to stay indoors. He was glad for the screen.

The first thing he scrutinized was a large cork bulletin board, which ran along a wall next to Violet's desk. It was covered in photos, clippings, and notes, much like an open scrapbook waiting to be assembled. The theme was the life of an actress, Violet herself. From old ticket stubs to signed photos, script pieces, some marked with scribbles, to fancy programs and notes taken on café napkins. It was as if Violet had been dumping the contents from her purse here.

While he had seen her as a complete mess in the hospital, the snapshots in front of him now showed a unique beauty — the strawberry blond, streaked, wavy hair framing a v-shaped ovalish face belonging to a slender woman. Her light red lips, thin nose and wide, green eyes might have resembled an alien by structure alone but did not, rather achieving the opposite — a seductive, cartoon-like humanoid. *Nora was right, she could have been in Avatar...*

But as he followed the cork board along, Keller realized he was looking further and further into her past. He discovered clippings headlining her near-death experience in her early twenties, high school photos and then on to childhood. Postcards, letters from friends just learning to write and then a few clippings regarding the NDE as a child.

Why did you invite me to your home, Violet? What's in here? Your Uncle had much to say yet nothing at all, you've kept him out of the loop.

Next Keller opened the laptop. Violet1968 sufficed again, and he ventured through but found nothing relating to the events of late. Keller was tired. 'You're being framed for murder,' rang through his head. *I'm not here to check through your junk Violet, spit it out.*

Her browsing history showed a long list of insignificant searches from nearby restaurants, car repair, online clothing deals, banking, etc. Interspersed was the odd link leading to plastic surgery. One doctor, a plastic surgeon named Alan Neilham, repeatedly popped out — she was obviously interested in him more than the others. It led to nothing concrete as if the man had dropped out of business. No recent entries.

Then Keller checked emails as much as he didn't want to. *You give me no choice.* Exhausted and bored, Keller first glanced back at the sofa and imagined it with blankets before diving in. He clicked on the open envelope icon showing Outlook. As expected, hundreds of marketing emails appeared, amongst them the odd personal mail of little significance. *Maybe social will show something.* But before Keller returned to the net, one mail popped out, sent last September, 8 months ago. It was from *Dr Frank Adams. Henrik?*

Dear Ms Copeland, Thanks for your enquiry about our clinic. Unfortunately, Dr Neilham has recently retired, and we will miss him dearly. If there is anything else I can help you with, please let me know. Yours truly, Frank. PS The brochure you requested regarding our clinic has been posted.

Who posts stuff these days? Keller ran a search on the email but nothing else appeared, not even her original query. *Must have filled out a contact form. And if they asked for her name and contact info...*

Keller sat back to view the desk in its entirety, then began a new search by opening the drawers. He started with the top one; it was full of pens, pencils, liquid paper, and every imaginable office knick-knack. Attributing his *spy-like* tendencies to the whiskey, Keller humored himself and swept the sides and back of the drawer walls deep inside and out. Nothing but more junk. Nothing on the outside. No brochure relating to plastic surgery.

He repeated the action with the subsequent drawer and just as thoughts of going through all the books and piles of paper were overwhelmed by notions of a warm duvet, he felt a wobbly lump. A small, rectangular object quickly came free, fastened by used tape. Upon pulling it out, he saw it was a USB stick.

Keller plugged it into the laptop and opened the drive. Only one file appeared, called 'Step by step for me'. Keller opened it. It was a simple layman's route to the dark web, complete with passwords. Electrified and sobered, he read through it nimbly and within half an hour, Keller entered the dark web. He copied the long link he found at the very end of the instructions, pasted it into the browser and hit return.

The page opened with a quote: *In every real man a child is hidden that wants to play — Nietzsche.* It melted away to reveal close-up video footage of women's faces, procedure details, staff discussing important things, and elements of décor. Keller chuckled, wiped his mouth with the back of his hand, and scanned over the various pages and menus. In the header, he saw the name *Jolly More Mansion* written in classy type. The site looked like it belonged on the usual web, nothing threatening at first glance or worth hiding. *Jolly More.* If anything, the prevalent word was 'aesthetic' and the imagery beautiful.

Then he came upon a page which vaguely described a revolutionary, new procedure that could help reduce a person's age *markedly.* 20 or 30 years was not out of the question. *Like what Henrik was telling me about a year ago in London.* Keller skipped most of the marketing, scanning onward. It ended with a brief history, which Keller would have ignored were it not for a small photo of the lead research scientist and his family.

The family in the photo was his own. The lab scientist was his father, Tom. They were standing in front of their home in Ironsmith. Keller cupped one side of his face in his hand. Flitting over the photo, he realized how little time he had spent at home. He was either at school or in the bunker somewhere, exploring or making trouble. The photo in front of him looked like any family might. House with a yard… Then the scenario drifted out of the murk—they were soon off on a drive to London for a robotics show. Henrik took the photo. His mom protested, and father had to calm her down. Now here it was.

Keller recapped in his mind what had just occurred, rubbing his eyes. The site described a clinic that offered any kind of plastic surgery imaginable on a discreet level. Radical surgery for those who had the money. As the site progressed, it hinted at further advancement, far beyond surgery which treated the whole body, inside and out. Something revolutionary requiring DNA samples and thorough checkups. Contracts.

Keller clicked on another page and looked out the window as it loaded. *Way out here the net's slow.* The moon had long since arced overhead. Peepers chirped their nocturnal mating call and a few blackflies and a moth spun recklessly around the lamp. How did they get in? he thought, avoiding he present situation.

The page that opened contained what appeared to be technical gibberish.

Shock pulsed through him in a crescendo, hushing in his ears along with the added adrenaline as he strung the words together. *It was his father's research.* The version that didn't work, which he invented to mislead his superiors—for which he was labelled crazy in the US, label pending in the United Kingdom. It outlined how a human might be transferred to an alternate body, which might attract a casual, psycho observer searching for something on the dark web, something desperate. And didn't mind if it was grossly illegal or even lethal.

Henrik is screwed if he's trying to use this and attracting people who are falling prey in hopes of a flatlining joyride. Henrik!

Beads of sweat squeezed out of his pores as Keller clicked on the last menu item on the home page 'Join Your Future'. It opened on a simple page with a few more glamorous close-ups and décor details. One brief paragraph in the center read: *The procedures we do are revolutionary. At times, we venture beyond known science and require the help of volunteers to do so. Volunteering can be a very lucrative venture, and we graciously invite you to learn more.* Underneath that was a *Learn More* button. Keller clicked on it.

The site vanished and an error message appeared in the center of a blank page. VPN failed to connect.

Chapter 12

Keller awoke in foreign surroundings. The clock on the shelf stood silent, though it looked like the ticking kind, wooden and ornate. 11:20 something, it showed. Outside the morning had evaporated into midday, the culprit high above casting hard shadows. Distant waves massaged the shore, bubbling, soothing. Gulls chortled up above, diving randomly to fish, swim, and socialize.

He shifted his gaze from the window and noticed the open laptop on the desk. His heart crashed upon realizing it was real. The past 48 hours were all actual. While the uncle's hospitality buffered his taut nerves and allowed him to sleep, deadly currents of the unknown continued to tug.

The daylight revealed details hidden in the warmth and elegance of whiskey's light from the previous night, which made the walls and ceiling look plain and robust. The bulletin board looked dusty and abandoned, decorated with tiny, glistening cobwebs. *Might have been gone a lot longer than the uncle realizes, a year or more…*

•　　•　　•　　•　　•

Then he beheld something of his own past. It was a Saturday and Keller wasn't too keen on being in his father's lab. The sun shone outside, and he had been told by his mother he could walk through town with his friend and foe Katrina, alone. He was 11, and she was 12. They had spent many hours together in the tunnels over the years but rarely above ground, alone, so he was looking forward to it. His father had called him over to talk about eyes.

Father laid it on thick. "After your last eye check-up, I had a chat with the doctor—he's worried that your condition is worsening, you could even go blind. I've developed a solution I want to show you, you can go to town later, I promise. This is important…" his voice faded as Keller noticed something large and spherical he had never seen before and looked over the matte black, smooth surface—he missed half of what father said. He trusted his father and if he said he needed to have his eyes fixed, then he really did—he realized himself that his eyes had gone from a little blurry to very blurry in the past year. He also couldn't see around the sides so well—Katrina had an easier time of creeping up on him. It wasn't fair. The lenses in his glasses were coke bottle bottoms and comments from other kids popped out at school.

"I call it alien silk," his father continued, showing him what looked like a tiny, thin piece of translucent fabric. "Because the material I made it from is quite complex, there's nothing else like it." After explaining the procedure and aligning it with how actually Keller was going blind, Tom got into technical details. Keller suspected he was trying to calm him with boredom. He looked on as his father's kind fingers handled the thin, shiny substance which had been soaked in something father also explained, but Keller did not get. Keller kept quiet so his father continued. He ultimately wanted to go to town with Katrina. He didn't mind if she bit him. Or scratched. Though that was rare now a days.

So when Tom reached for the thing Keller had never seen before, he wasn't surprised. It reminded him of an ominous sea creature because of what hung beneath. First, his father put drops in his eyes. They felt strange and got blurrier. Next, he injected something with a needle, but Keller didn't mind. He could still see lightness but no longer move his eyes. Father carefully placed the silky material directly on top of them, leaving only a grey glow to penetrate.

Finally, the sphere went on Keller's head — he felt a seal close around his neck and fresh air gently hissing in. His entire world became his own breathing and heartbeat. At one point Katrina had popped in and stood, staring, eyes wide — Keller knew because he suddenly heard her breathe and start saying something, the standing and staring she always did first, it was pre-programed in his imagination. Tom asked her to wait outside, not to bother them. To give Keller 30 minutes or so, and he would be free.

"He'll need your help. Now run along."

"Why is there a ball on his head?" she asked, her voice receding.

"He'll tell you all about it later, hon."

Next, Keller felt a pinprick on his upper arm and started to relax. He couldn't tell if he had passed out because he was already in total blackness. But the weight of the sphere on his head disappeared, as did the feeling in his hands, seat and legs. So he must have been out because he couldn't perceive the chair. Yet he could hear the pumping of his heart, his own breathing, both up close yet remote. His father said something and sounded calm so Keller felt ok.

Instead of looking at blackness and all the funny shapes and splotches in his imagination, Keller beheld a widening light strip. It got brighter and brighter until it blinded him — except he didn't feel like he had any eyes to blind. So there he sat, timelessly. Eventually, the weight of his body returned, the rubber seam around his neck was released and the sphere was pulled off.

Afterwards, he felt his father's hands covering his eyes, shielding them from the darkness. "Here, keep 'em closed. I'm putting some gauze on now so keep them shut."

"I feel funny," was all Keller thought of saying.

"That's 'cause you are funny. It'll wear off."

Tom walked to the entrance and shouted for Katrina. Keller heard her reply and soon after, light footsteps as she walked in.

"That was over an hour. Why is it dark in here?"

"You can turn the lights back on." Keller heard her walk away, then a click and then the hum of the fluorescent bulbs. Minutes later, they took the elevator up and walked outside.

"You look like the English Patient," she said.

"I'm American, how do you figure? And I'm not a burn victim."

"I'm not French, but I'll take care of you and we can fall in love," she giggled.

"That doesn't sound like the storyline," he said, blushing. But he sensed a tone in her voice that he had never heard. Like she cared or something. Like she didn't have to win because Keller had indeed won this time. He wore bandages over his eyes, which was for a good reason.

"Keller, keep your eyes closed," she said while pressing on his temple, trying to keep the bandage in place. He perceived the light now, even vague shapes. "It's falling off. I'm gonna get some more gauze, just wait here."

· · · · ·

Keller revisited the little attic bathroom, yanked open the tap and drank gulps of water from fleeting pools held in his hands. *Someone is trying to catch up to you father, through me.*

Keller stared down at the little white sink for a while, then up at his face in the mirror. A stubbly reddish face with mildly bloodshot eyes looked back at him. He wore no glasses; he had always been thankful for that procedure with the black globe, though the price, the explosion, was a great one to pay. Where it not for Tom's research and discoveries, there might not be anything to destroy. But he still wondered what his father had done; medically speaking nothing traditional explained it since his eyes had wholly recovered to normal and beyond. And who wanted to blow him up? Henrik got the blame and spent years in prison until suddenly, he was out. Just after Keller's fiasco with the man who died rolling his truck and then came back to life.

After showering, Keller descended into the living room and walked on through to the kitchen. The smell of coffee was welcome, and the Uncle looked up from his breakfast and managed a wry smile. He offered Keller a plate.

"Can't eat now, I'll get something later. Need some space, haven't been out of the city in months. I think I'll drive up the coast a way, perhaps head back. Either way, I'll let you know. You've been a great help."

"I trust you, son. Not sure why, but I do. I hope you found what you were looking for."

"Yeah, it seems she came on to something in the dark web."

"Listen, you shouldn't go out like that. I'll help you get ready; we may need to touch you up a tad."

Chapter 13

After coloring Keller's hair and lending him a pair of ripped jeans, and a worn baseball cap, the uncle searched his kitchen drawer for one more thing—sunglasses. Keller recalled the pair he had left behind, did a quick recall of what else was lying around in his apartment, and decided it wasn't worth worrying. *If they search my place, it certainly won't lead them here.*

On his way out, Keller snuck the hat onto his head, keeping the bill slightly lower than he usually might. Realizing the humor in his allusion to being undercover, he straightened it. He wished for a moment his mother was alive, he would call her and get the golden pill on how to disappear and stay unnoticed in society. Surely it was training hard won, but he imagined it instead as motherly advice: *"If you see a policeman, make sure to say hello,"* she might say, *"If you hide in plain sight, they can look for you all they want. But it'll take some guts."*

Keller drove out the same shady trail he had driven in and was soon back on Sunshine Road. The seam, running along the length of the road where the tar layered on one side met the tar on the oncoming lane, wavered ahead. Overall, the tarmac had aged and turned a light color, often patched. As interest in the new surroundings waned, a hollowness harping in his chest grew. Despite finding an ally in Violet and her uncle, he knew very little of either. *Police might be on their way.*

Perhaps the thirst, the burning dry, scruffy back of his throat triggered a return to the scene with the gauze and Katrina. His throat was parched there too, but for an entirely different reason.

•   •   •   •   •

"Keller, keep your eyes closed," Katrina said while pressing on his temple, trying to keep the bandage in place. He could sense the light now, even vague shapes. "It's falling off. I'm gonna get some more gauze, just wait here."

"I'm not doing anything; it just seems like it's loose. And I'm thirsty."

"Stop poking at it. Just leave it where it is. Here, sit down under the tree, don't look at the sun, shut your eyes may be." She grabbed him by the elbow and led him over to a tree. He sensed the shade come on; it was cooler.

Keller heard the door of the lift house slam; Katrina was quick on her feet and didn't waste time walking. She kind of glided wherever she went, silently, like a graceful young spy, Keller thought. Even though there was nothing special about them, he couldn't help noticing her legs. He figured it was the female musculature which allowed her such grace.

The mottled pattern of sunlight slowly became apparent and formed areas of vague lightness bordered by darkness. While still abstract, Keller scoped the little building that housed the lift and the ventilation shaft. It was a typical house shape butting up to a large, wide brick cylinder. More time passed. Birds chirped. Keller took Katrina's advice as it was his father's too. To wait and be patient, not to look at anything bright. "Go up, get some fresh air," he said, "Wait for me, I'll be up in a while." The while had turned to what seemed like hours. Keller faced his eyes to the ground and saw nothing at all.

Then he felt a tremor in the ground and jumped to his feet. The tremor escalated. Suddenly the vague shapes of the lift and ventilation buildings burst open, and out of them billowed a cloud-like silhouette, so dark it blotted out the sun. A heat wave followed, striking him as the cloud grew instantly to engulf all that was around, including himself. *Katrina! Father?* Keller fell on his back notwithstanding the impact and instinctively rolled over, scampered to his feet, and sprinted away seeing almost nothing now, choking on smoke, winded.

Tripping on a low hedge by the curb, he wiped out on the paved laneway. Then, closing his eyes and yanking the gauze over his mouth, Keller sought to take a breath down by the ground where the air tasted cleaner. The birds had stopped chirping. Somewhere nearby, a car stopped, and its door opened, a voice calling. The acrid stench of explosion exhaust had pervaded all.

•　　•　　•　　•　　•

Keller hit the brakes and pulled onto the shoulder. A bright red sign up ahead caught his eye: Nellieville. Nervous Nellie's Jams and Jellies followed further down—a colorful, wooden montage of letters and shapes forming a forest cottage and rooster. The cluster of buildings and shacks constituted a village which looked like a movie set studded with characters—semi-abstract figures made of everything from clay to wood to metal, fabrics and found objects. It reminded him of the fire hazards his neighbor liked to gift people, except this was on a much grander scale. Perhaps this is where his neighbor was from, no doubt hatched from an egg. *The stuff people come up with is miraculous.* While he had thought Lucy's to be quite original, this was the godfather of originality, a shrine above and beyond. Another sign appeared in the distance, nailed to a vacant, crumbling outbuilding. It read *Forget-Me-Not Keller Mod.* Keller stared, dazed, as his adrenaline once again spiked, and a chill swathed the sides of his head. *Funny, because I don't feel crazy.*

Then a pickup appeared from around the bend. Black and beautiful and for some reason hinting 'out of place'. Sitting just south of the blind curve, Keller pulled the beak of his hat down and pretended to study the map he snatched up from the passenger seat. A pickup meant nothing at all he told himself, it was the most popular vehicle in the US. He felt foolish until he noted the windows were heavily tinted. *Even that's ok, dude.* Tarzana's windows were tinted so the lizards could look out the windows from shade when she transported them. But this pickup was unique because it was also slowing down. He watched as it neared and felt the two figures inside inspecting him. *Not gonna outrun that thing.* The truck stopped on the opposite side of the road; the engine continued to idle. *Damn.*

If you see a policeman, make sure to say hello. They were probably not cops but Keller waved and smiled as he got out and crossed Sunshine Rd, pointing to his map. "I'm lost," he yelped. He motioned for them to take the window down, but instead, the driver hit the gas and the pickup took off down the road. *Assholes.*

As he turned and glanced around, he was relieved to see no one else nearby. In the distance, the sculptures stood quietly; somewhere, a swing set squeaked rhythmically. The vacant outbuilding no longer had a sign on it. Keller massaged the corners of his mouth. *Is that you Gouyen, doing this? And last night at the hospital? It would have been so much simpler if you just showed yourself and said hi. I'm not into the ominous crap so much.*

He had lost his appetite for visiting quaint towns, a craving for lobster, bar-room folk and a boat tour. Instead, he drove a while to calm his nerves—hallucinations and a 'suspicious vehicle' reminded him he could be just losing it. On the one hand he was a *psychic* but on the other, the mere definition of the word suggested something utterly intangible. Which is how he felt now, adrift.

He decided to drive until he came across a convenience store. This turned out to be in the village of Stonington, where Keller bought a bottle of bourbon, some simple groceries, and headed back to Violet's.

The name 'Shipwreck' had grown on him, and he imagined a little girl, doll in hand, christening the house from the road. She walked past it and out to the shore to cast her hairless beauty into the water — a sacrifice to the gods she had no doubt heard of from the uncle. Or perhaps she set it afloat, burning, and off to Valhalla.

Soon enough, Keller pulled onto the shady lane of tall trees, forest, and sea breeze. He stopped in the turning circle and turned off the engine. The house lay still, basking in the watery sunlight filtering down from time to time. The wind had picked up, and the sea massaged the sand and rocky shoreline with long bubbly sweeps. *Too still, no one home. No note.*

The front door was unlocked and after Keller opened it, walked in and called out, silence replied from within the house, aside from drapes gently flopping against an open window frame.

He walked into the kitchen, put down the bottle and groceries. The kettle was still warm, the sink wet. *Perhaps he's just out front, doing chores or fishing or something.* Keller walked towards the open door to the living room and a meter from it, as the view opened up, he caught a fragment of the uncle's silvery head, poking out from behind the back of his comfy chair. *Must be napping, hung over. But still no note.*

In another second, he crossed over to the chair. The paleness of complexion confirmed the no note, no light on, no one home. The Uncle was dead. Keller rapidly checked his vitals, lungs, heart, pupils, anything which might suggest there was still a chance. Someone had paid the man a visit and killed him. *The fucking pickup truck. That was them.* Keller found a syringe on the floor, scanned the room further, and saw a piece of paper wedged between the shotgun and the windowsill it leaned against. He walked over to the note and picked it up, keeping away from the window.

Call me Keller. The offer which Henrik had most graciously extended to you still stands. I will call the manhunt off, all of them ha, ha. You simply need to show up. Or, I can tip off local police you have just murdered Violet's uncle as well. This is not interesting for me, Keller. +44 7463132455. How do you like our website? Well done for finding it.

Keller strode to the toilet and threw up. *Impossible to track me to the ID of the laptop, unless the cam was hacked. Or the uncle was hacked, or something was hacked!*

Otherwise, the living room was tidy, with no sign of struggle. Traces of sand left by shoes peppered the floor. After examining, Keller concluded the uncle had been wearing some sort of cap—there was a band-like impression on the forehead. *While I was out on my drive, they were blasting him with something. And then gave him a shot for the final push.*

Keller folded the note and slid it into his pocket.

First, he built a pyre over a firepit near the beach. Violet wouldn't mind, he decided. An investigation might suggest where the ash had come from, but a decomposing body was worse. And burying a man set in his Viking beliefs would be sacrilege.

He collected up a heap of dry wood from the shed and drove it to the shore in a wheelbarrow. A fresh body would be like lighting a pile of watermelons on fire—Keller heaped the wood high. Then he carted the body to the site using the same wheelbarrow and rolled it onto the heap. Next followed more wood. The ritual would take place that evening.

After, he walked to the side entrance of the garage and opened the door. The key to the ancient pickup was tucked away in an old cigar box along with a pile of miscellaneous keys fitting locks around the property, some still in use, some long gone or rusted shut. It was an extra key from the days the uncle needed to escape his wife and migrate to a pub in town. Keller wished he could hear him tell it again.

The truck popped to life. He turned the engine off and left the key in the ignition. Keller opened the garage door, doing a sweep of the property outside as he did so. He drove his rental into the garage, parked it next to the truck. He took his duffel bag from the boot and closed the garage door.

Keller returned to the house and stopped once more in the kitchen. Through the window the gulls circled and played in the waning afternoon as new clouds rolled in to accentuate the sun, ghosting it at times. He noticed the bottle on the counter and decided to open it without the uncle, taking a gulp straight from the neck. *They can wait a little longer.*

For the next couple of hours, Keller cleaned. If there was an investigation, Keller would not be a part of it. He would leave the place as free of his prints as possible. No doubt his assailant would think of something elaborate to lynch him with if it came to that, but it would not come from him personally.

"If you ever decide to steal a cookie and end up eating half the jar, don't try and hide it. Take them all but clean the jar afterwards. Then 'put it away'," his mother would joke. Keller, as a boy, missed the humor. She was intoxicated.

At sunset, the horizon lay ablaze with peach, crimson purples and rose. Keller moved about in darkening rooms now, not daring to use the lights.

If they want to kill me too, they'll do it later. Not here, not tonight. Keller took what he needed for his solo party by the sea. The rubbish he would bring along and dump on the way to the airport. To a casual eye, he thought it should seem as if the uncle was on vacation.

Keller walked out to the pyre with a shotgun in one hand and petrol in another. The gulls circled about and took an interest until they noted he hadn't any food. The bourbon wasn't of interest, nor was the dead man.

It was time to burn the body. As if second nature, Keller said a few words of departure, a few on behalf of Violet and a few to the Holy Ghost. Then a few more from himself. He dowsed the body in gas, lit a piece of kindling, and tossed it on. The fire caught quickly; the gas erupting in a frenzy, along with the sap in the wood, which added fierce crackles to the deep hum. In minutes a blaze rose a story high, sparks floating to the sky amidst a column of heavy smoke and steam.

When it had thoroughly caught on, the smoke subsided and the flames roared hot, incinerating the man lying within. Keller walked the shore for almost a kilometer, away from the stench of burning skin and hair, hoping he wouldn't attract partiers looking for a bonfire night. If they saw the distant flames, they didn't show up.

Within a half hour, the fire toned down. The body's meat was charred, having shrunken back to reveal bone. Keller heaped on more wood and gasoline. It all had to turn to ash, he thought, staring into the flames.

• • • • •

The desert was scorching hot during the day as the sun beat it relentlessly. Keller noticed that the antler woman, Gouyen, didn't mind. She just kept planting, and the flowers didn't mind either — if anything, they perked up before his eyes. The woman had said her part; she was finished speaking. She no longer awaited answers from Keller, who stood curiously leaning against the low concrete block wall separating their backyard from the desert. He liked how the flowers stood up and refused to turn limp.

"Who were you talkin' to bud?" a voice from behind said. His father walked up and stood next to him. Keller looked at his thigh and then up at his face, smiling down.

"Antler wom'n," he said, pointing out to the desert.

"Your friend is out there?"

"Yeh. She gave me a fower."

"Oh I see, flower... She still out there?"

"She's gone." Keller handed his father the little blossom she had given him. The look in his father's eyes was a mix of disbelief, shock and darkness. The look in father's eyes at that moment was what Keller remembered most about his childhood. Aside from the blast coming out of the bunker lift house.

•   •   •   •   •

After peeling his eyes from the flames, Keller walked back up to the house, all the while scanning the forest, the veranda, and the windows as each came into view.

Once in the living room, Keller scanned the turnabout lane from a window. Darkness met him there, the shapes of the trees and road barely visible. He stood a minute longer to let his eyes adjust, then he walked over to the phone mounted to the kitchen wall by the entrance and punched the number from the note into the retro keypad.

A man's voice answered, dry and matter-of-fact. It was a mixture of low tones and mids, synthesized, feathered with an electronic twang.

The voice gave no name when Keller mentioned who he was. There was a pause.

"OK, I'll come," said Keller, sensing this would be a simple, minimalist exchange.

"Very good. We have settled in Jolly More Mansion on the Isle of Wight, near Wroxall. Easy to find, can't miss it."

"The Jolly More Mansion."

"Yes, precisely."

"You're a confused man. Why did you kill him?"

"I think a little incentive was in order. I am getting bored waiting for you, Mr Mod. Quite simple, not confusing at all."

"Why didn't you just pick me up on the highway?"

"My boys preferred you get rid of the body. They almost passed you by, were it not for the dash cam. Nice quality that thing, really zooms in. And then of course, you got out…"

"Is Violet all right?"

"She's fine. You'll meet her when you get here. Quite groggy, but as you know, she can be groggier still."

"What is it you do there?"

"All in good time."

"The manhunt is off?"

"For now. But I would hurry, there is work to do and my offer won't stand forever. Although prison might be just the place for a man like you, I can outfit you there instead if you like," the voice said and popped a forced chuckle.

Keller hung up without answering and walked outside. Back on the beach, the fire was burning hot. The gulls had retired for the night as a steadfast breeze picked up, fueling the fire to burn faster. When only coals and ashes remained, Keller shoveled the glowing mass into the wheelbarrow and rolled it into the ocean until he was waist deep. The water boiled around him and the dark plumes of suffocating steam, rose into the starry night sky and dissipated. Keller made three more trips until the uncle's remains vanished. He filled in the pit with more sand and feathered his tracks with a broom. The next rain or high tide would do the rest.

Back at the house, Keller showered and changed. He exited the back way, leaving just his breath as any sign he'd been there. Even the rental was wiped down and clean. He left it in the garage in favor of the uncle's *escape* pickup. After setting the GPS for Portland Jetport, Keller closed the garage door and drove off.

Running was not an option. The voice on the phone was someone he had to track down and face. His life depended on it, probably Violet's and Henrik's too. If the man could kill just to gain attention, he was remorseless, the kind no one ever found as there was no guilt to give him away. It would be easy for him to burn down Lucy's on a Friday night, doors chained from the outside.

Keller headed to the airport, playing through scenarios, his mind racing to reach a conclusion for which none readily appeared. He was surprised at feeling drawn to face this man at his mansion, or was it sick curiosity? He knew the answer yet pretended to avoid its implication.

Violet was a stranger to him, no matter her infatuations. It was her choice to search the dark web and get involved. Or had they tracked her and picked her up? Didn't matter. Henrik was a ghost from the past, an ageing drug addict. Keller owed neither of them, he thought, as he crossed a bridge to the mainland on an empty, dark, two-lane highway bolstered on both sides by trees and the never-ending chorus of crickets.

Chapter 14

August the Ramp Agent packed his bag—a business suitcase complete with number locks. He had always kept those at zero, feeling that if someone wanted to rummage through his things at the airport or even take them, they were welcome to. It simply meant they were more desperate than he, and he was pretty desperate in a laid-back kind of way.

Packing reminded him of his childhood. He did things the way his mother might have, by putting his socks and underwear in a separate plastic bag, his extra shoes too. Although he hardly wore it, he packed a casual jacket, folding it how he knew best, just in case something semi-formal popped up. He doubted it would.

He placed his passport in a pocket on his shoulder bag—he wasn't leaving the country, but he also would not leave it behind. There was the chance he wouldn't be back. His credit card and bank card were in his wallet. He took his library card out and tossed it in a drawer, the one on the bottom of his dresser used for miscellaneous junk.

He knew his life meant little to anyone, yet he wanted boost it up. His trip to the mysterious Jolly More Mansion on the Isle of Wight he had stumbled upon in the dark web while looking for 'alternate' in lifestyle, might prove its worth. If not, at least his ex-wife and child would come into a good chunk of cash.

It was his life vs one million pounds, acting as a lab rat for some insane procedure that claimed to make people younger. While it sounded like a farce, here he was packing.

If he survived the procedure, he got a new lease on life, an alcohol-free body. If he did not survive, his ex-wife got the money. The way he saw it, his ex and child would be better off as he was dying, anyway. Better to die like this than in a useless accident or by a disease he was eventually sure to get. But he still had to go through with it.

After almost two hours of discussion on the phone with an English gentleman whom he swore was high, August had agreed to visit a specific doctor in London for a physical exam, blood work, CT scan and DNA sampling. When his results proved adequate, he was invited for a personal visit three months later. Now the time had come, and if he passed the interview, the procedure was his. If not, he was free to leave or remain as a volunteer for something else, not as experimental. The man had sounded so pragmatic that August couldn't pinpoint exactly what the procedure entailed. They would explain when August arrived, he had said, cheering him on. Then August wasn't sure. He balked at people cheering him on, leery of one hidden agenda or another.

While surfing the dark web was not normal behavior for an average human being, August considered himself above average. A failure, worthless, but certainly above average. He had simply played his cards wrong in life, took too many chances and got hung up on the sauce. He was a boozer. At best a happy drunk, at worst a maniac who belonged on Mad Max's Fury Road instead of the small city he lived in, despite all the nut cases there.

And so, after many years of taking it, his wife finally left him, bringing along their daughter, 3. It made little sense to her they would survive if she stayed. When she left, 'You can kill yourself if you want to,' were her last words.

The Jolly More was a chance at something new, he told himself, having begun his second bottle of 'packing' wine. A case of beer lay in the boot for hydration purposes later—he wanted to remain reasonably fresh at the wheel.

Car loaded, August sat inside, engine off. He watched as a light rain fell on the windscreen, then fiddled with the radio. After settling on a song, he looked at his row house for the last time. It was rundown looking, just like him, but no worse than the neighbor's. Hadn't they once bitterly argued over who had a leakier roof? He picked up the bottle of coke sitting next to him and took a slug. It had rum mixed in with it, a perfect blend for driving. He put the cap on and placed the bottle back in the cup holder. A coke was a coke. No one would care unless the color got too light.

He hesitated until the warmth of the rum filled his body and mind. Now he was ready to drive. Now the streets wouldn't be so hectic, so aggressive. He started up the engine, pulled out, and drove off. He would mail the key and deed to his ex from the Jolly More Mansion if it came to that, they said it wouldn't be a problem.

August headed south on the A264. Traffic was light, so he kept on the speed limit and did nothing to attract attention. He drank no more rum for the time being and even stopped on the way for coffee and a beer. The hour-and-a-half trip became a saga for August, and he took it as such. He reveled in every town along the way, every village. Travelling to the south was exciting—it was a beautiful part of England to be alive in that day.

The town he had departed was called Ipsworth. Named after a clearing in the woods first inhabited by an ancient called Ip, from what he understood. Moving to Ipsworth had made sense once he started working at the airport nearby. Later, he met his wife at a pub. They mortgaged themselves to the teeth buying the row house and had a child. Life was complete. Or so it seemed. He filled the cracks and holes with a little pot here, a few stiff drinks there.

August had gone through the motions of life despite feeling dead, leading him to the Jolly More. What kind of person ventures into the dark web and signs up for a procedure which might end their life? He was an alcoholic, yes, but not terminal, not yet.

Once aboard the ferry, he eyed the expanse of water and tried desperately to build wonder into it. None evolved. The trip was a bore, and he resorted to his third rum and coke to rectify. It remained a bore.

On the Isle of Wight, August drove to Wroxall but then passed through, not stopping at the Jolly More Mansion just outside of town. They were expecting him, but he drove to a hotel on the coast instead and checked in. Relieved that he had arrived in one piece, August needed a rest.

He awoke in the middle of the night and found himself in trepidation. He was thirsty and downed a beer remembering he still had a fourth rum and coke hidden in his suitcase, mixed half and half. August choked some of that back too, and reminisced, as coziness swamped the foreign surroundings. It was a hotel, not the clinic. The clinic would wait until morning. It was okay, he didn't need to see anyone just yet.

They would understand; everyone always did. Or they just ignored that August liked to drink and paid little attention. As long as he did his job, he was all right. August had to call work and let them know he had the flu. He might get fired for doing it so many times, but it didn't matter; life was about to change.

The nurse at the clinic sounded nice. He talked to her after the stoned guy. Chinese, he guessed, though her accent was primarily English. He would meet her soon—she had closed him, it wasn't the stoned guy's bleating that had done it. She insinuated the physical might be waived if he looked all right and that common sense was common sense. With such a woman, arriving drunk would taint her first impression. Perhaps he would spend a day by the sea; a little tan wouldn't hurt. It was only May—did he dare take a dip in the English Channel so early? The cold water didn't bother him, not with a shot of whiskey beforehand, or three.

August watched a movie until it became too confusing to follow. After 3 am, he lay back again to pass out. Ah, vacation, he thought.

He knew this was all wrong, always had.

Chapter 15

"I don't recall ordering a cab," Keller said to the front desk lady of the little hotel which was just 4 miles from the Jolly More Mansion. He had spent a few hours there after an uneventful flight and boat ride which landed him in the coastal town of Ventnor. He was tired, hung over and needed to recharge before reaching his final destination.

"I don't think it's a cab, just a woman in a car. She mentioned your name, so I assumed it was for you. There, that little red one over there," she pointed out the window.

Keller had seen it earlier thinking nothing of it but now noticed the driver. *Cassy.* He took a second to digest, then smiled, exhausted a rush of air which tapered into a chuckle. *Why?*

The front desk lady looked at him a second longer before resuming her research on the screen to her left, projecting a look as she did, *'Not my problem.'*

Keller thanked her and walked outside. When Cassy waved and smiled at him, he was more alert than relieved.

"Hi Keller, did you have a pleasant trip?"

"How did you know I'd be here?" The black pickup with darkened windows flicked by in his mind.

"I like to do my research. The only other person you look like is Stan Williams."

He walked up to the driver's side and stood. "C'mon, how did you know?"

Her eyes stopped smiling and turned serious but gentle. "I'm keeping tabs on the situation at the hospital. Big security breach, I'd say. I knew you needed to leave town until things cooled off. And they did, right? Then I checked airports for people arriving in the United Kingdom. You weren't on any airport list, so I figured you got leery. Paris was the answer. Or maybe Brussels. Then you needed a boat..." She noticed a car parking not far away. Then she looked back at him. "I'm on your side, Keller. Get in."

"So, you're a hacker. Why does this interest you? Why make sure I get there?"

"Long story and there's no time now. But I promise, I'll—, and I certainly don't think you raped and killed her. I imagine you to do a lot of things, but not that. I have all the dirt on you, which means I know there really isn't any except for speeding tickets and you pay someone to look after your mum's grave instead of going yourself. And you were wanted for murder and now you're not. And you sometimes go on one-night stands."

"Who set me up?"

"I don't actually know. Someone quite clever. Well connected, good amount of clout. Perhaps someone obvious, hard to tell at this point. He must have a hacker working for him, or even a team. Could be a she I suppose, if the voice is digital as you say."

"I didn't say."

"Police are searching for someone new. There's been 'tampering with evidence.' The guy's creative, that's for sure."

"Vague. Means he could turn them back on me."

"Yeah, so get in. Either you sail back to France and on to Africa to disappear in the Gobi or show up. I don't know where he gets his reach, but he's got long arms. My gut tells me he's connected within the Ministry of Defense, but I have nothing on him."

"What is it you exactly do for a living?"

"Who says I'm alive? Okay, like I said, I'm in security. And like you said, I'm also a hacker."

If she's delivering me, I'll know by the time we get there. Keller got in. Upon doing so he wanted to reach out and touch her. Something was off. A wave of tiny prickles plagued the back of his neck. Her skin reminded him of the coating he had seen on a high-end droid over 22 years ago. But much finer. He left it alone, too weird. The pattern of hairs on her forearm was very perfect. They were tiny, but almost aligned. *Even the imperfections look perfect.* Animal skin had a flow which was hard to duplicate, and Keller remembered Alexey cussing about it. The number of oddities and wrinkles in a normal healthy forearm ran in the thousands. Teaching synthetic skin to emulate the original was an undertaking all on its own.

Realizing he had paused his gaze on her arm, Keller looked up. She had blushed a touch, and that was a positive sign. Or just cutting edge. Rather than take up the matter, Keller looked her in the eye a moment longer and then out through the windscreen at the sea. Cassy put the engine in gear and off they drove.

There were questions Keller wanted to ask her but did not. Complicating matters with the only person who knew where he was, didn't make sense. *For some reason I feel I can trust her. Desperate, Keller?*

Cassy surpassed the limit most of the time and soon enough they pulled up to an elaborate, wrought-iron gate, beyond which a little house stood, matching in period. Keller got out of the car as the gate slowly swung inward. A guard emerged from the house to greet him, with the swank of a car mechanic who worked on classics.

While Keller was no expert, the number 5 on a die tattoo, between thumb and forefinger, suggested he had been in prison. The pock-marked, scarred face, ruddy skin and dark, aggressive tats unravelling from under short sleeves to wrists suggested too much to imagine. When he spoke, the effort he made to be polite was obvious.

"Hello sir, we have been expecting you."

"That's nice to hear, always good to be expected."

"Does the young lady wish to park her car?"

Keller had to pause as he measured him up some more. *Unreal.* "Ah, no, she's heading back." He turned and waved. Cassy smiled and waved back, "Have a delightful time Keller." *Not sure if she delivered me or not.*

Keller nodded sheepishly and turned back to the badass. "Do I need to sign in or something?"

"You can do that at reception. Just go through the main entrance, it'll be at the front of the house, to the left, there. The road curves around, sir," he said, pointing and nodding.

Keller thanked him under his breath. Sir was a funny word. It meant respect but might also mean hollow respect, cynicism. Keller chose the latter for this guy — he had a boss and that was it. The clean-cut appearance was part of the job and as he turned to walk back towards the house, Keller noticed another scar, a short thin vertical one on the back of his neck, too perfect to be a wound. When it totally healed, it would be hard to notice. The work was neat.

The Jolly More Mansion was about 100 m away. Gorgeous yet forlorn, it dominated the countryside with its elaborate stonework which shone off-white; the even pattern of tall, gridded windows reflected the sky. The main entrance, punctuated by a circular window above, entertained a tiled, inset terrace which spilled outward into the lawns and engulfed a fountain where a flutist serenaded his mermaid. While the trees surrounding it swayed gently, inspired by the sea, the vacant stare of the house swept the lawns. There was no sign of activity anywhere aside from the gurgling flute song, adding sparkle to the breeze.

Keller approached the front entrance resolutely and emptied his mind of any thoughts. No turning back. The guard would probably not 'sir' him if he tried to leave. The door swung open smoothly and, as Keller stepped inside, he experienced an uncanny grace envelop and beckon him further. Once inside, he stopped and digested the under-lit, glass and marble reception area framed by the flow of a two-story stone wall behind. Oversized dome lights suspended above appeared as two black, shiny planets which had split from one and perpetuated the cool daylight percolating in from skylights higher up.

A woman occupied the front desk and stood without looking up, eyes riveted at one of the 2 large monitors before her. "Mr Mod, you made it," she said in a smoky voice, finally meeting his gaze with a calm yet forced professionalism. *She works for the same guy the guard does.* "Yes, here I am," Keller replied, walking forward, his nose not placing the faint odor suspended in veins across the room. A metallic, leafy fragrance which didn't belong.

"I'm here to see Henrik," he volunteered.

"He will be along shortly, please, have a seat," she said, briefly indicating a divan. She noticed her beckoning screen and sat down.

"This place has been beautifully restored," he said.

The receptionist didn't so much as look up. The ages-old room laced with high-tech installations begged to be questioned, commented on, and complimented. Keller saw no point. He had already interrupted the woman, probably a closed book with few pages. The Hugo glasses, perky, angled bob, and diligent make-up didn't help.

But it relieved him to hear no distant screams for help, or otherwise, no grim caretaker doing things caretakers don't do, and no waiting room lined with unsuspecting victims. Keller had the great hall to himself until at one end, a door opened. Henrik walked in, striding like a man of importance one step from defeat. The incident at the hospital evidently forgotten.

"I'm truly excited to see you Keller," Henrik said from 3 meters away. Then the distance vanished, and squeezing each other's hand they collided in a quick hug. Henrik was sincere. Worn, bruised cheek, but still a possible ally.

"What the hell is going on?" Keller asked quietly in Henrik's ear, searching for the man who gave him a head start.

"Come, you have much to see," Henrik said, ignoring any pretense. "I'm glad you could make it. Ed has an abrupt coarseness about him when he doesn't get what he wants, you'll get used to it," he said walking across reception, pointing to another exit. He said no more, signaling with rolling eyes and firm lips towards the receptionist. Keller glanced at her too, with a small nod which was not seen or acknowledged and followed Henrik out.

"Ed, is that the guy on the phone?"

"Precisely."

The next room was no less impressive and possessed pockets of the same delicate odor Keller couldn't place. While the ceiling did not extend to the roof, it was spacious and bathed in the same cloudy, cool light pouring through the tall vertical, gridded windows, appearing much larger from the inside. Unlike many historic buildings which ebbed coats of paint on uneven surfaces, these were all new—fresh ornate parts, gleaming, joined with great precision. Keller presumed it was merely a lounge, a library, a place to sit and sip coffee. Low flat sofas, tufted, some with scrolled arm rests contrasted the mansion's age. Long glass and tile coffee tables littered with magazines sprawled between them. A chessboard with oversized pieces sat mid-game in the center of it all, inviting passers-by to crack the next move.

"She may see us on cam but doesn't need to hear any details," Henrik turned and muttered as if they weren't alone. "This is the lounge, in case you haven't noticed," he continued. Henrik was at home, Keller sensed. But he had nothing to ask just yet, as this wasn't a friendly visit. Instead, he focused on the next doorway — the sudden yet tasteful shift from latches and knobs to a sleek, quiet, electronic sliding door suggested it led to something more technological. Had to be the host of the swamp aroma.

"It will all make sense soon enough, dear boy, if I may still call you that."

"Sure, go ahead," Keller said casually, leaving it at that. The questions would answer themselves beyond the next entrance unless he had already been drugged at reception and was now dreaming.

The air in the next room was ionized. Upon passing through the sleek entranceway, it was clear this was where the action took place. A very high-tech lab. Exceptionally stylish, it was not unlike a piece of continuous line art which had given birth to dimension carved out by flows of glass, marble, and LED edge lighting. The antithesis of Nervous Nellies. Tall windows stood veiled with blinds — the kind with one-way vision. A blue sky and swaying trees looked like they played on partitioned screens, projections of an imaginary backdrop.

"This is it. This is where it all takes place."

"What exactly?" Keller buried any interest he had. *He knows I'm curious.*

"I might as well get to the point, and then we shall progress in reverse. If you simply wish to dive right in, prologues have no place." Henrik was losing his patience.

"That's what I'm here for. My route here wasn't exactly void of shocks. And I like your security guy, a friend of yours?"

"Come this way, one more door," Henrik said flatly.

Keller followed, caution rising as he measured up the exit/entrance. It was stainless steel. Massive and accessed by keypad, card, iris or fingerprint. *Hysterical.* Henrik swiped casually and turned to face Keller. "We endeavored to vote, but I ended up installing them all. Did you have breakfast?"

"Usually do, why?"

Henrik didn't answer. He turned on his heels and walked through the widening space between the door and wall—another silent slider. The room beyond was dim, illuminated by what floated down from the high cathedral ceiling. Keller followed, letting his eyes adjust. As he took in what lay a few meters in front, his face turned rubbery, unfeeling. Henrik wore a look of concern and rekindled patience. Keller glanced at him, then at the spectacle, then at the ceiling, hoping a storm would tear it off. Then at the floor. Stepping slowly ahead, soaking it in, his pulse quickened next to a chilled spine.

Chapter 16

Keller stopped walking. What appeared before him was the source of the pungent smell. The reason for the ionized air. While studying medicine, Keller had seen many dead bodies in the dissection room and had worked on a few himself. He experienced no queasy stomach or faintness and had no problem pulling out an assorted sub and having lunch. He had also witnessed apparitions, ghosts, and poltergeists, which tried his nerves, as did the fire hazard living room lamp, crackling and fizzing.

Now this. After the few seconds it took for his eyes to adjust and confirm what was kept in the massive aquarium tanks, Keller panicked. *Humans. Not dead, not alive.*

Separated by aisles, the tanks were roughly 3 m high and about 2 m in diameter. Made of thick glass with ventilated lids, there was little to set them apart from their amusement park counterparts. Keller noted 2 rows of 3. The first row contained adult humans standing up as if waiting in line. Except there was no line. Each one had its eyes closed. *Asleep?* Each had an umbilical cord which arced to a loose coil exiting the floor. They did not breathe, yet the bodies wavered and swayed perceptibly to a mild current, indicating they weren't stiff. They reminded Keller of vegetation in a lake or ocean. The liquid possessed a turquoise tinge and was littered with gossamer patterns. *No lights on yet not entirely off.*

As Keller walked past them, he saw 2 more adults and then a darkened aquarium; it was impossible to see inside. Beyond them was a set of what appeared to be three high-tech baths, perhaps a meter high, shaped and opaque. They all had rounded, streamlined lids equipped with slanted panels of digital touch controls and dials. *How very spa, and more.*

He walked back through the middle aisle, fingering glass, breathing consciously, then paused at Violet's body. *Hardly any wrinkles, smoothed out by the liquid.* He fought the desire to vomit and returned to where Henrik scrutinized content percentages on a series of monitors. *The phoney priest in his nave.*

"You did this? This is your idea of anti-ageing? They look dead—just they're not stiff yet. I can see Violet in there," the words came tumbling out. Keller stood close to Henrik now, thoughts of violence germinating in his blood.

"Yes, *I made them.* They are not dead, they are very much alive and well, Keller. And *young.*" Henrik said promptly, stepping back. "Just never conscious, nor in coma. You can see the systems are intact here," he said with a wave of his hand towards a row of monitors showing heartbeat, oxygen levels and a host of other data. "*They are clones.* The Violet you are thinking of is upstairs in bed. That's her clone there, what you saw. The tattoo was added recently."

The direct statement blew through Keller on a molecular level. Steadying himself inwardly, he walked past Henrik to survey the monitors, noting how they were labelled by name, pushing himself to take interest and bury his emotions. *This hasn't happened, not yet. Violet plus two.*

"And how do you know they're never conscious?"

"They remain as they are, aside from an exercise regimen."

"Exercise?"

"The body is given precise data which allows it to run, for example, involuntarily."

"Not freaky at all. Why do you say not comatose?"

"They were never alive. Consider them unborn, fully developed humans in a fetus-like state."

"Ever had kids? No, I imagine not. Or maybe you got some whore pregnant back in the day."

"Keller..."

"You came up with all of this?"

"I had help, a great deal. Yuri Vasiliev for one, perhaps you remember him."

"Yes, a fanatic—claimed he could not only clone a man but fast track its development. I thought he was imprisoned."

"Precisely. He not only set us up here but turned over the reins. Quite a gentleman. Oh, and not imprisoned, out now."

Keller slid a finger along the second screen, Violet's, as if testing to see if it was really there. Thousands of times he had viewed computer monitors, yet this time he had to check it— smooth, solid and very thin. The screens appeared to float in the dimness, their data fluctuating in space, wavelengths fleeing suspicion. He noted a window containing amniotic fluid levels and breakdowns. *Could be.*

"How long does one of these take? Not exactly mamma's womb, is it?"

"6 months, give or take. They actually start in the baths at the back. Those are quite cozy."

Cozy for a corpse. Explains the cobwebs in Violet's office. "What part aren't you telling me?"

"You haven't asked me much; please do clarify," Henrik held fast.

"Why are you doing this? At what point did you dig deep into that trashed brain of yours and signal your mouth to answer yes, to this?"

"When it occurred to me that if I don't do it, someone else will. And when I decided I wished to remain alive. Curiosity played a slight part, I have to admit. Once you've calmed down and gotten accustomed to your new workplace, we can discuss it further."

"New workplace," Keller scoffed. "I run a restaurant... Why here? Why on this island?"

"Ah, excellent question. Ghosts Keller. This island is supposed to be infested with them. We are studying the afterlife so that we may make those people who visit the lab and die, return to live as their clone. Once someone passes on, I need to channel them to—."

"And how is that going for you?" Keller asked, a surge of rage coming over him. He quelled it.

"Mixed views on that. On the one hand, I have sensed an intense presence here, a woman I believe. Following that, I had my success with the Kid."

"You built a wicked droid, Henrik; what happened?"

Henrik made as if to speak but stopped.

"You're behaving as if this is somehow ethical. *Who is asking you to do this?*"

"Our common friend, you've already spoken to him."

"A synthesized phantom caller. Who is he? Where does he get his edge?"

Henrik again didn't respond but pointed instead. Keller followed the finger, taking a few steps forward, and noticed a tank containing an adult male clone he had paid no attention to. It was a handsome man, well-built. It was a younger version of Bruno Emerson. Keller walked up to it slowly, speechless. He touched the glass wall as if mesmerized by a school of baby dolphins. Then he looked back at Henrik.

"That's just one. Don't underestimate Ed," Henrik said in a lowered voice. "I've seen some pretty strange things in my life, but none as twisted as this fellow. Technically, if you succeed, if we succeed, he'll be able to play God. I mean, on a human level."

"If Bruno is backing him, then—."

"Oh, he is. And if it works on Bruno, there will undoubtedly be more. Investors are showing interest." Henrik looked into thin air, then back at Keller. "Your father tried to transfer a human to a droid but failed. I have been asked to continue his work so that it might apply to a live human body. There are many—"

"My father was crazy, and I'm not sure if you've correctly understood what he was trying to accomplish and how."

"That may be true, but he *was* a phenomenon. And he confided in you Keller, not in me."

"He didn't trust you, Henrik, nor do I, anymore."

They both stood silent. Keller glanced over the aquariums, once more noting the one in the back corner. "What's in the darkened one?"

"Food for nightmares, Keller, food for nightmares."

Chapter 17

Henrik smiled a thin, brittle line, his eyes betraying black humor. "Come, this has been enough for today. Let's visit Violet. She could use a check-up, and our resident doctor is on vacation."

"Vacation? Why do I doubt that?"

They walked back through the central lounge area, past reception, and took a lift to the second floor. While Henrik attempted a few questions, Keller did not answer. Visions of aquariums plagued him—bodies suspended between life and death. Uninhabited, unneeded, grown like vegetables minus the sunshine.

Dotted with skylights and classic decor, the upper hall oozed mirth, suggesting life was a pleasing, amicable illusion masking horror beneath. Henrik insisted they go out on a balcony which ran the length of the building, hemmed by pillars. Keller obliged, the fresh air diluting the weight in his chest. Henrik smoked while they stood in silence. The early afternoon was upon them, and the wind had picked up.

Keller imagined the two Frenchmen who had given him a ride to the Isle of Wight in their old trawler, the Elle, arriving back at their home port. He wished he had stayed with them and hired the captain to take him as far south as he would sail, as Cassy had said, sarcastic or not. Keller would have cut himself loose.

Violet's room appeared much like any private, upscale hospital room might when merged with a historical setting. Set against white walls framed by stonework and more strip lighting were accents of stainless steel in the surrounding equipment. A sleek, grey bed frame and lumpy duvet contrasted the polished black floor. The vision blinds were drawn.

Violet lay in bed comatose. After being transported in an ambulance, she had never woken. Keller didn't ask how either was possible; he didn't care. He took a few steps inside, scanning the vitals monitor, IV and Violet. When Henrik left him to it, to do a basic check up, she opened her eyes.

"Curiosity caught the cat, I gather," Violet spoke, awake, a sardonic smile gathering.

"Yeah, you could say that. How are you feeling?"

"Thanks to you, I'm alive. I'll make it."

"Yes, and I understand this wasn't your first time visiting the afterlife."

"No. You made it to the Shipwreck."

"I did. So you remember talking to me?"

"Vaguely. Took a lot of effort. How's he holding up?"

"He's ah—, the last time we spoke he said he misses you," Keller scrambled for words, trying to suppress the heat rising into his head. *Later, when she's better, I'll tell her.* He continued with the check-up the best he could—eyes, blood pressure, reflexes, organs, and asked tricky questions to test her wits. *Needs a CT scan but looks superbly recovered all considering.*

"Did he have an imprinted band across his forehead when you found him? Like mine?" She pointed to a reddish strand on her forehead skin, suggesting she had been wearing a tight rubber strip around her head, a cap of sorts, judging by the hair suffering from hat head.

"Yes. What's that from?"

"I thought so. They've developed a way of reading a person's memories. And copying them. I'm sure Henrik will demonstrate if he hasn't already. What they don't realize…" she said in a raised voice, nodding upward. Keller glanced to see a black globule, no doubt a cam.

Then Violet whispered, "That I was conscious the whole time, despite the anesthesia. It's a knack of mine. But it wasn't painful."

"You've lost me. Why did they need to see your memories, or your uncles?" he asked, seeing Violet was deeply agitated.

"Probably to help them find you. And now he's dead and you're here, trapped."

Keller said nothing, the influx of random info besieging his judgement.

"I sure muffed things up. All I wanted was a nip and tuck, you know, everyone in my line of business is doing it. Especially at my age. Then it all got perverted somehow, and I agreed to come and test the new procedure, thinking I could take it…"

He could see the tears welling and moved closer, putting his hand on hers. "You had no way of knowing. It was supposed to just be a posh country clinic."

"Never mind that now. As far as my uncle goes, he was quite ill, the timer was ticking. Did they drug him?" she said back in her usual voice.

"Yes, I'm sorry."

"They'll pay. Ed will pay! He may think he is clever meddling with the dead, but he will come to bear the horror, just like anyone else who walks death's lonely path and decimates it with crude behavior." At that moment, Keller didn't need extra perception to see what was about to happen. Her face flushed and the veins on her neck and skull gorged with blood. The heart monitor doubled in speed. She wept quiet tears, forceful, bitter. Keller pressed her unkempt head into his bosom, and she cried some more.

After a minute or two, Violet wiped her eyes and nose, calmed herself, and resumed her story on how she ended up at the Jolly More. As the monitors returned to a more peaceful rhythm, a nurse poked her head in, smiled per social reflex, and disappeared. *She reminds me of someone...*

Violet told of the obvious deceit she overlooked in her quest to be young again, the vanity of not growing old with dignity. Of craving the stage, the attention. "My uncle didn't know a thing, he thought I was just visiting the UK for vacation." She ended off with her near fatal episode in the freezer of Lucy's, only vaguely remembering being escorted by someone and talk of making Keller a prime suspect. Apparently she had walked in on her own steam, and they paid off the night cleaner to keep quiet or face having her fingers chopped off then and there with a cleaver.

"Thing is, when I realized they were thinking of killing me, by overdose, I slid into the freezer and crouched down behind the boxes, the ice-cream. I decided I could wait it out, freeze if I had to. Die on my own terms. The night cleaner slammed the door shut, perhaps she knew," Violet said, a scheming pride slipping in. "I don't recall the door opening again."

Keller noticed a sculpted chair in the corner, the kind with padding, and took a seat. *Nora would love this story.* Violet had survived her third near-death experience and lost someone close. While Keller felt he could relate, this was extreme. Violet was a hostage, a lab rat on an immensely criminal scale. Keller sat and stared out the window, all the while calming his own nerves. *But I don't believe she couldn't have escaped at some point — she's here to see this thing out.*

"And what exactly is keeping you here? I mean, if you could go—"

Violet began to laugh, a dry, comical eruption. "I'll let Henrik do the honors, see what you think firsthand and then we'll see how long your better judgement endures. Narcissism is a tricky affair."

Keller fell silent, sensing the woman could see his own motivations. His callous curiosity. Gathering thoughts, Keller realized no one had checked on him. *Probably just watching and listening. I don't care.*

"There's someone you should visit," she continued, in a low, drowsy voice. "He's just down the hall. Mind you, he said he'll be moving to a cottage, so I hope he's still there."

"Who's that?"

"Believe it or not, they call him The Kid."

"Henrik mentioned him."

"Nice boy, a little screwed up, but a good heart. Wrong body, I'd say. See, he behaves like a kid of 10 or something but looks like a man of 25. Good shape though, handsome."

"Sounds like a character. Which room?"

"Down at the end of the hall, I forget which side," she claimed, wiping her face with her hand.

Keller made his way down the hall towards the end. The doors had little windows and card-activated locks—retro compared to the lab. While most rooms were vacant, Keller came upon one which appeared well occupied. The window had evidently been replaced, and the door jamb had been tampered with. *Must be a powerful boy or just deranged.*

As he pressed gently on the door to test if it might open, a voice from behind spoke. It was Henrik. "I thought she might lead you here," he said, somewhat catching his breath.

"It's called security monitor, little to do with thought," Keller replied, glancing at the half dome in the middle of the ceiling.

"My patients aren't your concern, Keller. Remember that. Best prepare for the task at hand."

"I hear ya." Keller let his gaze rest on Henrik's. He was an old pothead; it was easy to do so. His hard eyes were that way from hallucinating, not wisdom. In seconds, Henrik backed down and glanced away.

"Come, I'll introduce you. He's an interesting one, it's as close as I've ever gotten."

"Close to what?"

"A transfer of consciousness, soul transfer, body infusion, whatever you want to call it. The reason we are here at all."

"Ah yes, that bullshit."

"You'll be expected to exercise more understanding than that. I gave you fair warning, but you showed up all the same. Now we have a job to do."

"Yeah, lets infuse some more bodies, like fruit with booze," Keller said, popping his eyes. At that moment, he wanted to bash Henrik's brains in. *Just take him down, drag him to the pantry and end it on the counter's edge.* "That's blasphemy, Henrik, to anyone alive."

"Easy Keller—solutions won't materialize this way. If you'd like to meet the Kid, we can go say hello," said the animate carcass of what used to be Henrik, concern spreading over his face.

"Yeah, let's say hi." *He's hiding something.* "You've become an old fart, Henrik."

"And you so pretentious."

Chapter 18

Upon entering the room, it appeared void of any person. There was an unmade adjustable bed in the 'head up' position. The mattress cover had slid off, revealing the label and tufts. Next to it was a cart with dirty dishes, and the floor was strewn with clothing and comics. A fork stood poised, stabbed into a computer tablet—testament to a potentially violent disposition.

"Kid, this is Keller, the fellow I said was going to visit us. Come and say hello," Henrik addressed a heap of dirty laundry, sheets, and blankets on the floor. Rather like a chameleon, it showed itself and stood up. A grown man with a boyish air. He strode up to Keller. "You wanna fight? I'll punch your lights out, murderous perv!" Before Keller spoke, he blocked a punch a half second too late. The man-boy landed one broadside his face as Henrik yelled and attempted a rear hold. But to no avail—the boy cast him aside by spinning on his grip and slamming Henrik into the wall. Returning to Keller with momentum, his fist darted out in a powerful roundhouse. Dazed by the first hit, Keller prepared to duck. As he did, electricity crackled and snapped in the air. The boy slowed mid-swing and crumpled to the floor, tasered. The nurse had arrived just in time and took no scruples in zapping him.

She glanced at Keller and helped Henrik up. "You know not to barge in on him when he's in his *cocoon*. All he does is train when he plays. The boy is tough, Henrik."

"Have we met?" Keller asked. It was a legitimate question for him. The woman wore no makeup, her golden complexion contrasting the short black hair. But her soft, Asian features, large brown eyes, and small thin lips triggered recognition.

"Really? You're an idiot for getting caught like that. I was—"

"This is Emma, our head nurse," Henrik cut in, and she backed off. Emma left as Keller turned to her. A vague memory of a party swam in his mind. *Getting caught for what?*

"She's been with us a while, knows the patients better than me. You can talk to her later."

"So, what's up with this guy? You're right, like a boy in a man's body."

"First off, we built the memory machine, per your father's prototype, Keller. It hadn't been destroyed in the explosion—it was sitting next door with the droids. The documentation was vague and incomplete, but I must say it works. We can not only view memories but also transfer them—all part and parcel of the *Cradle*. I imagine you knew about that."

"The Cradle yes, memory machines, no. I don't believe in such nonsense. Most of his work was theoretical. Camouflage. You can't *see* another person's memories—imagine what that might lead to."

"Imagine, yes. You realize, of course, you were the primary inspiration for his research."

"I triggered a series of delusional quests. Besides, it's handy to have a scapegoat."

"Keller, how do you think we found you? I'm referring to Maine."

"You gave Violet truth serum, tasered her or something cruder. Or traced the ping from her laptop, that fruity voice over the phone even—"

"No Keller. But never mind, back to the Kid. His name was Myron Saltmarsh, a billionaire, made it big in real estate. He was terminal, had lung cancer and a host of other malignancies. He had the initial investment and was gung-ho to attempt something extreme. As I'll show you downstairs, I could transfer his memories to his clone, to its brain. Mother Nature's own *Cradle,* you might say. If we ask the Kid to recite a few things, they'll match up with what we have on file. Everything before he came into existence three months ago. But I don't think it's Myron because his childhood memories seem to conflict with a duplicate set, and his present behavior doesn't align. There's one hell of a lawsuit brewing from the wife."

Keller stared at him, unmoving. "Lawsuit. So why don't you pull my memories? Think of all the answers you might get. Throw me in a dumpster after."

"It doesn't work like that," Henrik sighed.

"Because it doesn't work. There's something you're not parting with."

"There are a lot of things I'm not telling you. All in good time."

"How about the other patients, as you call them, how many didn't make it?"

"A few. That's confidential. They volunteered, knowing what the outcome might be. Suicide cases, terminal some of them."

"You know it can't work. Ed must—"

"It can work and the Kid proves it. You can speak with him yourself. We must move to the lounge now to discuss your offer in full," Henrik said, checking his wristband.

As Henrik turned, Keller noted the vertical scar on his neck, too. The cut was quite vague, possibly weeks older than the security guy's, Keller thought as surgical training fluttered by. *Henrik is withholding something.*

"Let me guess, he won't be here himself."

"It's doubtful, never is."

Chapter 19

This time when he arrived, Keller studied the lounge more closely. Ed was not online yet. Henrik, reminiscing about his days in the droid lab, explained, "Back then, controllers were the ones who tested and trained our new androids, making them react and behave like humans as best they knew how. I've done it myself, quite remarkable how they develop."

"You mean quite remarkable how *you* developed them," Keller felt obliged to add.

Keller surveyed the library, coffee machine, sound system and the sculpture, which dominated a corner of the space. It was a plaster cast that displayed the Fates, he guessed, representing the cycle of existence — birth, life, and death. Usually, the thread of life was spun by Clotho, drawn out by Lachesis and cut by Atropos. In this case, the cord representing life was not cut. Instead, the head of Atropos, which had been sliced clean off, lay in her lap. *The décor and symbolism are exceptional, Ed is trying to prove himself worthy...*

"What's to the left of reception if you go the other way?" he asked Henrik as they sat and waited. "You came from there earlier today."

"Everything anti-ageing, aside from the *fruit infusion* as you call it. The other half of the business, so to speak. The front end. We have amassed a discerning clientele. And our products are world class, as I'm sure you can imagine."

"Just a little quiet it seems. So, you do a little nip and tuck, perhaps change a few parts, organic of course, then sell them on the 'whole body' down the road."

"Upselling and aftermarket sales work for me. For now, its plastic surgery and *synthetic* prosthetics, not organic. Keller, this isn't a horror show. We don't grow people in order to harvest them," Henrik spoke in earnest.

"Why? What's wrong with that? The people we *grow* are not conscious. I don't see any ethical reason we can't do it," a digitized voice, raspy but calm and low, came over the sound system. *Ed* had arrived.

Keller took a mental health breath. *Don't take it up. It'll be a long argument with no end. Keep it minimal, don't give this freak anything.*

"So, you got what you wanted. I'm here, at your service, Mr Ed," Keller said. A pause ensued, after which the voice cleared its throat.

"My dear friend, I appreciate your showing up but, you should have run while you still had the chance," Ed said, following with gentle yet cynical laughter. "You are here only because you agreed to be caught."

That pattern of laughing... Keller said nothing and waited.

"Let me get to the point if you are so ready. While there is more to show and discuss, I will leave that to Henrik."

"Yes, I feel in capable hands. Why did you call this place the Jolly More?"

Another pause. "Because there's *Jolly More to life*," his fuzzy chuckle morphed to a laugh, booming through the room. "We have clients who wish to have healthy, *new* bodies. So, as you see, we create clones for them. They are organically grown, and we can take them to an advanced stage of development in months."

"That's very impressive, to say the least."

"It will be much simpler if you don't talk anymore. I am not interested in your patronage, Mr Mod," the voice had deadened.

"Keller, call me Keller."

"The hurdle we find is the transfer itself. To live a new and healthy life, a person must be able to inhabit their new body, be accepted by it, and so forth. Kind of like a brain transplant, but minus the brain. We are having an interesting time transferring the client to their new host. I'd like you to have a go at it. Your father—"

"My father had theories, but they were just that. Fantasies which failed in the real world. He was considered insane by the Americans as well as the British. Trust me, it was catching up to him."

"Was he, though? Now I do ask your opinion. You see, Keller, you have an excellent track record so far, 3 for 3; I like that. A track record which on scrupulous examination, proves impossible, considering the technologies used today in medicine. You correctly diagnosed a perfectly dead corpse three times as *wanting* to be alive. And don't tell me it was just a hunch. In the car wreck incident, the footage shows you yelling at the victim, who had already passed away. Yelling at the ceiling, rather."

"So, you've been watching."

"Since the day you left Ironsmith."

"I think you missed what actually happened."

"Oh, you're wrong there. Imagine the bigger picture, my dear Keller. This is what's *next*. Did you think mankind would cease to evolve? Or that it might not influence the process?"

"So, it'll evolve itself now? By trans-humanist hacks?"

"It always has, I'd say, minus the hack part. We only want to speed it up a touch and supplement a few extra choices," Ed said, pausing. "The talented son takes up where his father left off and proves that a great man is not insane but rather the opposite."

"He died when I was 11."

"C'mon. We kill a guy, and his ghost remains, lingers at the incredulity of it all. Then you, just put him back where he belongs—in the new clone. It's what you do best, Keller, I mean, I haven't seen you in the news for anything else so it must be what you do best, right? Yeah, show-off."

Keller remained quiet.

"When you succeed, you'll also have to catch me and talk me into the same thing. Perhaps you've seen my body, though it looks nothing like I do now."

"I'd be happy to kill you."

Pause. "There is so much to do and so little time. I'm afraid this conversation has come to the part where we must discuss your contract."

"I won't sign any contract."

"You don't have to. I'm simply going to tell you how it is. After all, we don't want to go to court; you will fail and receive a life sentence—I won't accept anything less."

"I don't believe you've infiltrated the judicial system to such a degree, especially once evidence is brought forth—."

"This is not interesting, Keller, please don't talk anymore. You have two weeks to complete a successful transfer of a human *being* into their cloned body. After a few test runs, we have volunteers for that, you will perform the transfer on our second client. Should you fail with the volunteers or client, you will continue working for me from prison."

"Why two weeks?"

There was a longer pause this time. "Because I said so, Keller. After two weeks the manhunt will be resumed once fresh evidence is introduced."

The Uncle no doubt. Out of the corner of his eye, Keller noticed Emma enter the room, her footsteps silent on the carpeted floor, and arrive somewhere out of sight. He paid little attention. Ed continued, "The reasons for such details aren't important. Let's just call it incentive. As time passes, you will learn, but I assure you, two weeks is the limit in more ways than one."

Where do I know her from? He didn't reply to Ed; his mind racing to find a catch, a way to slow the process down. What he was asking was impossible; Keller knew it. He needed time to scope things out. Ed, for one.

"Not to be mundane, I require time for research. I could use three weeks simply to get to know this place and acquaint myself with my father's work. As I say, I was 11 when — ."

"Becoming a good little lab rat who can regurgitate the works of Tom Mod is not what I am looking for. You have a way with the afterlife. You simply need to make a person return from death like you have often done. Only not to the same old body. Another new, fresh one. The one lying right next to it. The clone. I refuse to believe you can't handle it."

"Right. Well, it doesn't work like that, and it's not my decision. If I say I need three weeks, I need at least three weeks."

"I think that the more you learn about our procedures here, the more you will see I am not the person to test, Mr Mod."

"So tell me this. Why did you stage the death of Violet? Why go to such great lengths when you could have simply picked me up? Like grabbing and forcing me into a van. Heck, Emma could have done it with her taser there." *Where is she?*

"You noticed our wonderful Emma stride in a minute ago. I can practically see your heart rate rise. I have no shortage of good people and I like to use them."

Keller was momentarily flung back to a party he had been at weeks ago, drunk. A woman came on to him, she was irresistible, a nurse, unique, Asian. They took a cab to his place, she was a riot and loved his company too. He saw the line of her neck against a street lit window, her hazel brown eyes which she closed, then her clavicle, her deltoids appearing as her top slid down, the buttons open, he blacked out later. Emma.

"I have contacts in the media, police, certain national agencies," Ed drilled on, "The morgue scene was a wonderful bonus," he chuckled. "Dead the first time would have sufficed though that wasn't the plan."

"Forgive the complications."

"Why, you ask? Your life is a mess and now you owe me. I like that. If a couple of hoods drugged you and made the delivery, you'd be pissed off and not inspired. This way you are in deep. You are ruined no matter what you do. I am giving you a new life and you shall return the favor!"

In a moment, Keller felt brawny arms lock his neck from behind—a man's. The stale odor of cologne and tobacco struck at close range, as did the hard chest behind his head. Keys clanked. As he kicked and tried to wrestle free, the thick iron grip tightened, overtaking his efforts. A jab in his arm ensued. Fading fast, Keller strained to look up at the blurred face of a security guard and, of course, Emma. Her facial expression was neutral, her eyes deceitful, pleading. She had the same boss as everyone else—Ed.

Chapter 20

August hunched in his beaten-up car approximately two miles from the clinic, under a tree in a muddy cove. He liked the shade; his eyes were sensitive that afternoon. *It's time to go in.* He stared at a field of horses and couldn't decide whether to quench his thirst with water or beer. The beer would lead him one way, the water, to the clinic. He needed the money if for nothing else, then to save face. He was not proud of his life, his deeds, the places he had worked, nor his unkept promises.

One horse ran in a wide arc, slowed down, shook its head, and neared another horse. Probably a mare. She ignored him at first, then took a few steps away. He got closer still; she backed off again. Then he really got close and muzzled her neck. She stayed.

Animals can be quite direct, August decided. It's how life worked best. Be direct, take what you want. At least try, and you might get it. He pondered over his own life, and all the times he backed off, took a drink instead and entered oblivion. Oblivion built on moments of delusional euphoria. Cares and worries were suddenly masked by fake hope. Fake hope because there was nothing to back it up, no matter how amazing the party or how fast the rush of alcohol in the brain.

His daughter flashed through his mind. Positive moments, closeness, she had often reached for him. She didn't understand that there was something wrong. To her, he was all right. Better than all right. The funny odor didn't bother her much until it did. Then she knew. Then she knew because it coincided with his behavior. He got aggressive; he hurt her. August hurt his wife too. She could usually lick him or call the police, but he managed to hurt her, many times.

Now he had to pay. It was all that was left. He got out of the car, grabbed the remaining bottles of beer and set them at the side of the road in a row beneath the greening brush. Some lucky passers-by, on foot no doubt, would have a few beers. He laid a bottle of vodka next to them. That would be the landslide bonus. Especially if they were walking because money was tight. They could get shit-faced for the next leg of the trip.

August got back in the car, started the engine and was off. No stopping at variety stores, no walks along the beach to clear his head. No hotels. He would drive straight there and see what this Jolly More was all about. He didn't have to stay if he didn't want to. The choice was his; he hadn't signed anything. Yet.

His GPS took him straight there — it was a no-brainer. As the gate opened, he observed the house next to it — unusual for a clinic. Especially one so small. Prisons had gatehouses, companies with private manufacturing premises, places people weren't supposed to loiter but might want to, had gatehouses. Places you had to check in and out of with a guard. This was weird, but security was security. *Unless this is a hotspot for celebrities...*

The receptionist was a prune; he expected as much in such an upscale establishment. He waited a few minutes for the nurse. When she arrived, August was surprised at what lay behind the light, Asian accent. A babe, not so young but seriously hot, he thought and stared. She smiled and asked him to follow her. He did. Ann, Emma, Evie, something like that. He couldn't believe she had let him walk behind her. He remembered the horse, though he wasn't sure if that was a good idea.

She gave him a quick tour of the plastic surgery wing, ending with, "It's quiet today."

He nodded and said, "Yeah. Looks deserted."

"Let me show you to your room, and I have a few things for you to read over. I'll help you with that, okay?"

"Sure. If you have time, that's great."

"I have time," she said and shot him a smile. No make-up, he guessed, an all-natural woman. Fit, healthy, funny, friendly. They walked past a room; the door was ajar. August had seen little that made sense on the website and had questions, so he stopped. "Hang on a minute," he said to her in a lowered voice. "Is that the procedure?"

"No. That patient has a problem with his memory; we're simply implanting something that will help." Henrik looked up and smiled a wry U shape. His brows arced. Emma closed the door. "Privacy is one of our policies here. Please excuse me."

"No problem. The patient looks familiar, like I saw him on the news or something."

She led him to an upstairs room in the middle of the hall between Violet and the Kid. The room was fresh, blinds up and windows open. A bowl of fruit stood on the table, and a bar fridge was full of every healthy drink imaginable. No beer, mini bottles of hard liquor or wine. Not even a soda.

The paperwork was lengthy. August knew he wouldn't read it, so he paid attention to the parts that the nurse, Anna, Emma or something, pointed out. Even those passed by in a blur, and August couldn't help noticing her perfume. It wasn't strong, just a hint. He sat patiently and hardly moved, darting a glance at her forearms from time to time but seldom much higher.

"Did you get the part about your ex-wife?"

"Ah, yeah, I think."

"August, she won't receive the full amount unless the procedure is a success."

"So if I die, she gets nothing."

"You won't die. Only your suitability is in question."

"What happens if I'm not suitable?"

Emma moved closer to him, her finger leaving the page and returning to the exact text. She smiled a little and put a hand on his. "I think you are suitable. This is legalese, so the company is protected, and so are you. A screening of sorts. We sit for a while, sign papers and chat. I get a feeling for who you are. August, it takes a lot of guts to do what you are doing. This is unknown territory and you are choosing to venture there. Those that follow can only have respect for those who lead the way. Your wife will have to respect you too, despite what has happened in the past."

"Seriously, what happens if I'm not suitable?" he said, fear caressing his mind. Or was it withdrawal from his daily dosages of booze? August was cautious. She was beautiful, but she was not here for him. That was clear, and he needn't kid himself. *Get it together, man.*

"You end up in critical condition from which we will nurse you back. You may remain comatose for a while, and we continue to nurse you. Or you die. It says right here."

"I should get paid for my suffering, don't you think?"

"Yes, and you will. 40%. But to get paid the full amount, be a winner and go all the way. Stick it out. I know you're able. August, if you can drink umpteen bottles of liquor a day and still function in a semi-normal life, you can do this. Most people in your condition would already be dead," she said, moving a little closer. "I'm being earnest now," she added with a quick, broad smile. Her eyes were moist, he observed. A hint of her breath caressed his arm; her cleavage heaved noticeably in his lower peripheral vision.

He took the pen and signed. Next, he leaned in towards her. Be the horse, he thought. Emma leaned as well, and as her lips came close to his, her left hand positioned itself over his leg. It held a syringe. She kissed him once, then again as she drove the needle into his thigh, pressing the liquid out as he squirmed.

August shook, but instead of pushing her away, he looked down and put his hand on her wrist. "What are you doing?" he said, nervous, caught in a dilemma.

"Relax, August, I like you," she said. Warmth washed over him, and he did relax. She stood him up, walked him over to the bed, sat him down, and laid him back. August didn't protest. He felt good.

Emma pressed the buzzer next to his bed. "I need some help in 202."

"Right away," replied the orderly. By the time he arrived, August had passed out.

"Get him ready for bed. He'll sleep awhile, hopefully through the night. Call me if he wakes up and makes trouble. Just dress him in his gown in the morning and sedate him if you need, but keep him conscious, please."

"Of course. Is he being tested?"

"If that's what you want to call it, then yes."

Chapter 21

Keller awoke with a start and took in his surroundings. He couldn't recall arriving or falling asleep. It dawned on him that the security guard had held him fast, the one with the sensational, harsh tattoos, while Emma shoved a needle into his arm. He recalled her matter-of-fact face; the responsible kind people make when hard at work. As he sat up, pain flashed through the back of his neck. His right hand gingerly inspected the area, a classic enough move except that this was not muscle soreness. *Stitches.* The back of the guard's neck flashed by him too, then Henrik's. *It's not like I didn't expect any glitches.*

Realizing he was alone in a small cottage, Keller stood up. It was centuries old, quaint, cozy. Exposed beams and uneven, whitewashed plaster defined the low ceiling. The floor comprised wide, worn boards bordered by trim. The only other rooms were a kitchenette and toilet. He gazed out the window after pushing back sheers, greeted by woods and a low stone wall dividing two fields. A falcon soared in the distance. He followed the lane which led to the gate and guardhouse, all but hidden by trees. An ornate clay bowl of fruit sat on a table in front of the window with a note. 'Welcome to your new digs and sorry for any inconvenience. This is the procedure for all senior staff.' *Senior staff, what crap.*

Keller showered and dressed. He didn't shave but combed his hair and was out the door. The route to the house took him behind the guardhouse and back onto the long lane. The green world around him was alight with dew, receding wisps of fog and articulate chirping birds. Instead of entering through the terrace, he took the back, buzzing until the receptionist unlocked the door. The entrance had obviously been lavish once but as few guests arrived by horse, it served a more practical purpose of accepting deliveries and trades people.

He made his way through to reception, where the receptionist stood up to protest. Keller stopped and pointed an angry finger at her. "Sit," he said. She did. "Where's Henrik?"

"Mr Mod, please have a seat and I will—."

"Where is Henrik!" Keller uttered an intimidating shout, then calmed himself, his eyes on her not wavering. Her left hand slid under the desk.

"In the lab, I'll let him know you have arrived. He actually—."

"Thank you." Keller walked on to the lounge as the receptionist picked up the phone and called Henrik. Seconds later, he was at the lab entrance. Keller saw it was closed and noted the keypad next to it and the iris reader above that. Next, the door slid open. Henrik sighed as Keller strode past and into the lab, not saying a word.

Henrik closed the door and signaled with his eyes into space.

"I don't give a crap, record me. What the hell is in my neck?"

"Come Keller, sit, I will explain."

Keller did so. While it was not an operating theatre, Keller noted parallels and that it had been prepped. He walked about the lab, briefly inspecting an odd apparatus he had never seen. Henrik watched him, a patient half-smile emerging.

"So, talk," Keller said, reiterating with his hand.

"We all have it, Keller, I had no choice. It's protocol around this place, and pissing him off just sped things up. I told you—"

"Have what? A chip?"

"Yes. A Morpheus prison chip."

"Morpheus..." Keller quieted. *Bruno is in on this... the package on his desk...*

"It's actually worse than that. We all have special editions installed. It's a death chip, Keller. Let me explain how it works."

"Explain, yes, I'm listening. It just might be the last thing you ever say if you don't yank it." Keller was surprised at his own chill, as a desolate plateau settled on his mind.

"That's not possible. It's sitting on and plugged into the central nervous system. So pain is in the game. Little tentacles have been programmed to make contact points. The chip is a simple AI instrument. If you extract, the tentacles remain as they get torn off. They proceed to wreak havoc on your entire body. We have such a case in a psychiatric ward on this very island." Henrik went to a broad white chest and opened a drawer containing the schematic diagram. "Have a look if you like, but I kid you not. Emma can hit the switch if you wish a demo. I don't suggest it."

Keller studied the drawing, and while he wasn't a specialist with computers or chips, he could see how it connected to the body, and the exact points at which it did, were key in a person's ability to feel pain and function. While his mind raced, there was no calculation to be had. No maneuver appeared which would remedy the situation. A surgeon had to inspect it, via x-ray. For now, he would humor them, and play along. *This changes things.*

Moments later, Emma entered the room, looked at them both silently, and nodded. She walked up to the table and stood between them. "I heard my name being mentioned. Keller, you seem upset. Henrik, you have that *look* in your eyes. What's up?"

"I just told him."

"Ah," was all she said and turned towards Keller, resting her right hand on her hip, like a server in a restaurant dealing with a disgruntled customer. "What did you think, that we were all happy showing up to work as criminals?"

Keller looked at her, noting the vitriol shade in her voice. *The upset is definitely real.* Then he dropped his gaze to the table and let his eyes wander over the articles. Books on the afterlife, odd-looking electrical devices, an audio recorder and a camera with a unique lens.

"You got me, Emma, that was slick back there in the bar."

"I do what I must. I enjoy staying alive, despite all. You were given plenty of hints. But I think you know what got the best of you," she said, turning and raising her hair to reveal a slender neck with a vertical scar one inch long. "See it? Same thing Henrik has and now you too." Keller looked up at her, quiet. His eyes moved down along her uniform, noting what natural selection had bestowed.

Emma smiled thinly, her lips flat. "Was I worth it?"

Keller looked in her eyes, then swung his gaze to Henrik. "Jesus, how can you work like this?"

"It's not easy. We make do. Need to keep a sense of humor about you. And don't do anything which can trigger your chip," Henrik replied, glancing at Emma.

"And some coke, I take it," Keller added.

"Comes in handy."

"Suck it up, Keller; the next volunteer is ready to go," Emma said.

"Ready to go for what?"

"Remember, it's what you do best, Keller," Henrik spoke, "I believe in you."

Keller felt rage flicker across his thoughts. "It's one thing to pull someone out of a car wreck, a tough, strong person, one with willpower and a desire to live, and bring them back, even when it looks like they've croaked. It's another to—to perform some seance hoping a miracle will happen. This needs some research." *No, it needs to end.*

Henrik motioned for Emma to keep quiet. "It's really quite simple. We kill the guy and you bring him back. Like Ed said, not to his old body but to his new one. All of his memories will be awaiting him. That machine there, I was going to demo it—"

"That thing?"

"Yes Keller, it works."

"Go on." His mind raced in overdrive, scanning a pile of coal for one gold nugget. *Some might say it's all gold.*

"We need to get him into his new clone in one piece. You saw how the Kid turned out. We need this guy August, to wake up as *himself.* And judging by your track record, we think this is something you can do. No backing out. Research might take forever. I know you Keller, if anyone can do this, you can. Consider it an emergency. *Yours.*"

Keller shuddered at the idea that an ageing drug addict, no matter how genius, had given him a pep talk. It reeked fake— Henrik was covering himself. He looked at Emma, who stood still, poker-faced. They were both past caring what happened to anyone. A chip meant death or serious torture prevailed at any moment, should they slip up.

The personality of Ed suggested he had abandoned all good sense and honed a case of insanity which propagated itself on the idea of a maybe, a narcissistic *maybe me and only me except for a few others I can control.* The may-be of immortality which had always been destined to remain just that. An idea above others, a hope of grandeur. Or that which was reserved for a higher entity others followed, believed in, and turned to in their darkest hour. This entity was not Ed.

"So what happens next, we sit in a seance? Is that what the lounge is for?"

"We do whatever you suggest, Keller."

Chapter 22

Keller looked at himself in the bathroom mirror. Set against whitewash, a single light bulb in the ceiling cast a dark shadow past an ornate, dented, faux gold frame. Slapping water on one's face, was the classic mode of behavior enacted by anyone about to engage in a risky endeavor. Or murder. Or was waking up from something, a long dismal part of life. It's him or me, Keller thought, trying to justify what he was about to do. Thanks to the Morpheus Terminal Chip, there was no circumventing the situation at hand.

The key word in the name was *terminal*. Regardless of the interpretation, the chip was a killer. It was the fear factor in knowing one could die a slow, torturous death, were it to be activated. The activation had potential on many levels, starting with a painful zap to severe, writhing pain merged with insanity. There was no way out. Once installed, the chip remained active until death. Even after that, it remained active until its power source was disconnected, which could only be done by smashing it to bits.

What he saw in the mirror was an angry, threatening face, laced with fear. He worked much of his adult life to entertain people, not harm, or kill. No matter the calculations or what his good sense said, it shriveled compared to the reality of the moment. He was going to play along with Henrik and Emma and pretend that it was possible to help a man by first killing him. *That this is somehow evolution.*

Keller threw up, violently retching whatever breakfast he had eaten that morning. *This is becoming a habit.*

After returning to the mirror, Keller brushed his teeth. He changed into scrubs whilst watching a falcon soar in the distance. He momentarily thought of running, but cast the idea aside. If someone had to kill August, it would be him. Because if there was the slightest chance August could be brought back, he would catch it.

•   •   •   •   •

"Looks like he's about to flip the light switch," his father said. "Probably the whole power box."

Keller stood next to his father in front of his dying grandfather who mustered a grimacing smile. He had stayed alive a bit longer just for him. Grandpa passed minutes later — he simply stopped breathing and closed his eyes. Classic death, Keller recalled himself thinking, even then.

•   •   •   •   •

A sharp knock on the door jolted him from reverie. It was Emma. "Keller, you there? We're waiting for you."

"And what if I don't show up?"

"Not thinking of running, are you? Curly and Mo are at the guardhouse."

"No, I mean, what if I don't do this?"

"What do you think? He'll zap you and make one of us do it. A good jolt of pain works well as a warning. But trust me, you don't want it. C'mon, there's no way out of this. Not today. Just do your best," Emma said coolly.

"Do my best, huh? We're gonna kill that guy. After that, it's his choice whether he comes back. Not mine or yours. And if he did decide to live, he might consider his old body if he's not entirely blacked out. You people don't know half of what you're talking about. This is murder, pure and simple."

"That's why you're here. Keller, I've read about you."

"That's nonsense."

Keller finished changing and walked up to the mansion with Emma, two prisoners on a long, effective leash. The day was cloudy, sunny, and still. A goldcrest dove into a blossoming cherry as they passed and dove out again ahead. A typical sight belonging to a not-so-normal day, Keller thought. Curly and Mo gave a slight nod as they passed. They were out for a smoke. When Keller looked back, he could see the gate was closed, bathed in a patch of sunshine. *The neighbors probably don't suspect a damn thing—no one ever does with something like this. It's beyond comprehension.*

Minutes later, Keller watched as Emma approached the lab door ahead. She chose keypad over iris, print or card, and the door slid open with an innocent swoosh. Keller walked in. Henrik was preparing the memory machine behind the patient August, who lay on an operating table, torso and head angled upward. After noticing Emma stride in, he turned his head back to Keller, and recognition flooded his face. It rattled him, and Keller saw he was withdrawing—eyes, pulse, heart rate, they all played the same theme song.

"Are you able to remember better now?" he asked Keller, who barely paused before replying, noticing a wink of Henrik's. "Yes, of course, my memory is most excellent."

"Good. I'd hate for you to forget what you're doing or how to do it."

"Excellent point. Rest assured, I'm about as sharp as they get."

"Hey, you look a lot like the guy who was wanted for murder," August continued as Keller clasped his bare forearm. *Clammy, sweaty.*

"Yeah, that was me," Keller said, smiling, "But you also know it was all a big mistake."

"So you didn't do it?"

"No," Keller said while feeling the man's forehead. He looked over at Henrik, standing behind the chuckling patient, who shook his head. Keller didn't say what was on his mind: August needed to rest a few days without booze and come out of withdrawal. *Alcoholic, fresh from a bar.*

"No time, Keller," was all Henrik muttered.

Keller noted August's shaved head.

"Not for glue," Henrik said quietly, "Emma did it for the cap."

"We'll start with induced hypothermia mixed with anesthesia," Keller finally said to August. "You'll get cold, then drowsy until you're asleep. Then we do the procedure. And no matter what happens, you just listen to me. That's all, and do as I say. Even and especially if you feel separated from your body." August looked at him blankly, opened his mouth to speak but stopped himself.

Emma administered a sedative, propofol, and as August calmed down, his other self was rolled in. He was lying in a similar up position on an identical table. His eyes were closed, and he wore an oxygen mask. A monitor displayed his vitals were all stable. Calm. An IV followed along. His head was also shaved clean.

"He's ready for action in the same way you are," Keller continued.

August looked at the clone, his eyes darting about its body then pausing higher up. *He's noticing the clone's head. He sees that it's him and isn't too happy...*

Next, August burst into whatever action he could, struggling to get out of his ergonomic surgical table, trying to wrestle free of his strapped wrists, chest and ankles. His veins were bulging, his skin red. He tried to yell, the muted throaty sounds hysterical. Urine escaped the suit he wore. August eventually slowed down and stopped lurching, the propofol taking effect. Seconds later, he tired some more, his eyes betraying his actual state until they too became droopy.

"I still think we should do a lethal injection and get it over with," Henrik mused.

"No, we may need him to return to his old body. You saw how he reacted. Did you not show him the clone earlier?"

"No. He didn't strike me as the type who could handle it," Henrik said.

"So how is he supposed to do this?"

"You're the expert."

"Yeah, and I say hypothermia. It buys us time."

Henrik rolled forth the memory machine, which he positioned between and behind the two patients. He gelled August's shaved head and pushed a clear silicone cap onto it. It held dozens of fine contact wires, multicolored, which ran into a bundle in the back much like a streamlined, synthetic pigtail. Two meters along, the bundle entered the side of the machine.

He placed a cap on the freshly shaved head of the clone in precisely the same way—the twins with colorful, futuristic hairdos did not stir. Henrik entered a string of code into the memory machine. Without a whir or start-up note, the bundles twitched during configuration. A flat green LED signaled the machine was ready. Henrik typed a second line of code, touched return, and the machine paused.

They took August's temp down until his vitals were barely visible. The process was lengthy and dull except that a man lay before them who was on his way out. Then August flatlined. Keller realized he would have a few hours if they kept lowering the temp. Had it been an emergency room, Keller would have insisted the man could live, that he was still around. This was not a hospital, and they were not saving him. They had murdered a man, and Keller knew it. But his sense of curiosity prevailed. He stood and demanded with his hands that Henrik and Emma not move. He knew the camera was rolling, and he had to show them he was doing what he could. So, he played the role.

"Begin the memory transfer," he said.

Henrik typed more code; the bundles of colored wire twitched once more and relaxed. Keller studied the monitor next to the memory machine and watched as images flew by. Some paused longer, others challenging to see, faded, obscured by deformation, fog, abstract shapes, confusion. Still others shone crystal clear. This was the recording of a life, the life of August Burl, Ramp Agent.

"Now that's impressive if those are them," Keller muttered. *That is actually impressive.*

"They are," Henrik answered, a man in his element.

Keller's mind heaved forward as he sought the next step, fearing there was none. Then he thought of Violet in the morgue, Lesley, the car wreck victim who died in Emerg, and Torrance, who drowned when he fell off the pier, smashing his body on the way down. While the boy died, he was a breeze to bring back. A few words of encouragement and mention of how lonely his dog would be, and poof, there he was again, pink creeping into his cheeks. The paramedics were confused but thanked Keller, not entirely sure why. The boy had quite a story, and that, along with a few words Keller had given a journalist, exploded into sensational headlines on and off the net—Boy Drowns and Talks to Bystander While Dead. *Ed must read those.*

Keller looked for any sign of life in August, anything perceivable. There was nothing. In the moment's gruesomeness, he could not tell if a light had been left on or not.

Keller blinked, wiped the sweat from his forehead, and searched for August again, simply closing his eyes and concentrating on nothingness. He forced himself to see as if his eyes were open, projecting his perception to circulate. *Who am I kidding?* But Keller sensed the panic from where Emma stood while confusion emanated from Henrik's position. *Or is it a guess... touched up by imagination?*

Then he saw him. By the counter, next to the sink. A vague distortion hanging like a mist. Hallucination or not, Keller kept himself calm, concentrating on the vision. He opened his eyes. August was still there, a waning after-image yet obviously him, just bored looking. *Can't be, he was just freaking out.* Shaking his head from side to side, he pointed to his clone. His open mouth moved, but there was no sound. August faded and vanished.

"No, no, no... come back," Keller spoke quietly, compassion spilling out. "I need you here. We all do, stay with me. This can totally work. August!"

August vaguely materialized an inch from his face. He yelled something, enraged, which Keller couldn't hear. *But I can smell him… booze, sweat and bad breath.* August went out like a dimming hologram once more.

Keller was tall enough to see over the concrete block wall, so he had a good view. The woman in the desert behind their yard talked to him as she walked along. The palms of her hands brushed the scorpion grass, which grew in abundance as far as Keller could see. Yet the sun was hot, and the thin blossoms showed no sign of wilting. Keller was surprised, and wasn't sure why. He liked Gouyen even though he couldn't always hear what she was saying. And then he could. She said, looking him in the eyes, 'You can see me, just like I see you.'

Keller snapped out of it, wiping his brow once more, his mind racing back to August, who had faded in again as if giving him another chance. *Ghost, apparition? Why wasn't the antler woman transparent?* He glanced at Henrik, then at Emma. They were staring back at him and had stopped doing what they were doing as if suspended. Henrik had been about to pull off the cap from the clone. And Emma was increasing its oxygen. Instead, both looked ashen and dazed.

Confusion washed over Keller, and he trembled inwardly. He had just killed a guy and pretended like something more was happening. *The perception of August is real. Go with it, take it and run.*

"Ok," he said to August. "You can come back to the old one." Keller motioned emphatically with both hands towards the original body. August stood still, saying nothing, expressionless, only his eyes moving about. Then a grin broke out, shy. *He's having a bloody epiphany.*

"Warm up his body. Warm it up! He won't take the new one. Just warm the damn thing up." Keller said to Henrik and Emma.

"Not possible, Keller. He can only wake up over there or not at all. Strict orders," Henrik replied, dryly.

"He bailed; he doesn't want to do it!"

"How do you know?"

"Screw both of you."

As Keller went to August's body and set the temp to reverse, he caught Henrik nodding to Emma with apprehension, in the corner of his eye. She had retreated to the control room with a window facing the theatre. A few seconds later, Keller screamed in a manner of self exorcism—the pain which ran through him was none like any he had felt. In moments he crumpled to the floor, paralyzed, muted, saliva dribbling from his open mouth. He lay in horror, thinking only about how to stay alive. Next, he became languid. He was free from the pain but couldn't move. While Keller rejoiced, urine ran out onto the floor; he trembled and couldn't move to get up, his muscle controls confused. *Not fucking cool.* He blacked out, melting into aftershock, jolts of horror dancing in his mind as mangled faces and burnt body parts.

After receiving a call from Henrik, the orderly arrived to mop up the urine. Keller was otherwise left alone. He helped Henrik roll Clone August away and return him to his tank.

The orderly knew his duties and did them promptly. It was a fairly simple job for the pay, and he was sworn to secrecy on the level of national security. His line manager was Emma, and she kept him chill. Besides, there was not much to say. August had not made the grade and now, well, it was all part of a contract. No need to keep him around. Henrik had verified his condition and would later take care of him. All was in order so far as the orderly could see — he had to move the body down to the basement morgue and leave it there. It wasn't to be refrigerated.

It was the end of the day and with other jobs complete, he fed garbage and roadkill to a blackened conveyor and switched it on. As it rolled into the iron cavern set in stone, the flames burst in and flooded it. The orderly slammed the door shut, stood back, and had a smoke. This was the ritual. It would take about fifteen minutes to complete the incineration. After, he would turn the flames off, lock up, and leave for the day.

For now he'd keep his mouth shut and see how things developed.

Chapter 23

It was dark outside when Keller opened his eyes—the windows rose up along the wall stately and somber. He heard a fat bug hit a windowpane with a tap. The room lighting was low, a few lines on a dark monitor shone along with an exit sign. The first thing which struck him was the smell of rancid mop water mixed with sanitizer. Then it followed he was actually on the tiled lab floor, lying on his side. He saw shoes dangling from legs nearby. His entire body felt sore as he struggled to raise himself to sit. He was groggy. The fleeting memory of what had transpired left him relieved it was over. And stunned. He rubbed the cold side of his face and felt the burning thirst in his throat.

"That was your initiation. Welcome to the club, Keller," Henrik spoke. He sat nearby on one of the contoured chairs, making short partial turns as he spoke.

"Did that come from the chip? Really thirsty..."

"Yep. Experienced the magnificence a few times myself. Though yours was brief, thanks to Emma's gentle touch."

"I've been tasered, but this was worse."

"Yes, where?"

"After a party, a friend wanted to buy some pot. We were both hammered. I think they thought I was a cop. Nut job pulled a taser."

"I see. Well, I don't suggest getting zapped often. The soreness will be gone soon, but the memory might linger awhile."

"How was it so powerful?"

"You saw the design. And, like the rest of us, you had to experience it for yourself."

"How clever of me."

"Well, don't protest, do what's needed. That zap can be a lot worse, and total termination is just another button on the remote. There are witty combinations as well."

"Charming." Keller hauled himself up and walked over to a sink. He spotted a dirty coffee cup and filled it with water. He guzzled 3 cupfuls, letting the overflow dribble onto his neck and chest. Keller breathed. "What was needed was to keep that guy alive. If you want me to figure out how to do the impossible, checking on 'failed transfers' can be very enlightening. He could have told me what happened and made it the next time. This way, you wasted a human life for nothing and lost the information. Gone."

Henrik eyed him, and Keller sensed he did not like to be told by a newbie how things should roll. "And after he awakens, he reports to the authorities and tells them we attempted to murder him. As you know, a near-death experience can inspire a person to live. It's a big second chance. We would be stuck killing a live, conscious man to avoid much trouble. Would you pull the trigger then?"

"No, I'd keep him here and do it again. At some point, he'll go over." *I'd tell him to run.*

"And if he asks to use the phone? After they arrive, the volunteers are taken by surprise for a reason. This isn't exactly natural," Henrik said blandly.

"That's because you don't have the right guy. And you're lying to them. Being taken by surprise and shocked, jesus."

Henrik gave Keller a ponderous look but said nothing.

"No more outright killing. You do that again, I toss in the towel, prison or no prison. In case you haven't noticed, Ed's a lunatic, he'll take us all down regardless of what happens."

"It's not so easy to just toss—" Henrik was cut short when a hand slammed down over the speaker phone.

"Very well Keller, have it your way, the next one will get warmed up. The lunatic agrees with you," Ed's voice crackled, fuzzy with filters.

The man is here, after all. Probably curious. Keller played through several scenarios and took a second to search for a common denominator, something impressive. Ed wanted a show; he was going to get one. "People see things when they die, things you wouldn't expect. I believe that's where the answer lies. We need to reach them during this time, which I actually did, and maybe we can turn them around if they have chosen otherwise."

"That's murder two if we don't count the uncle, Keller," Ed declared.

Keller did not answer this time. *Play along.*

"It's okay, you don't have to speak. I prefer it that way, and I must say, I'm happy to see you are alive. But you are going to give me a solution, Keller. One way or another. Not a philosophy. We haven't much time and I'd hate to experiment with *you*."

"I could really use an extra week. Zapping me and killing my patient didn't exactly speed things up. You lost a lot, right there—seems to me you're not very serious about getting a result."

"No. I believe in tough deadlines," Ed chuckled. "You'll make up the time. And I'm not very serious about anything, including your life."

"I should visit my father's lab in Ironsmith, in the Bunker."

"Ah. A sudden interest in crazy father. Actually, we've done that, all the relevant materials are here. Copies and some originals. The lab itself is a charred hole and no more."

So, he's seen it. "I know. But I still need to go. Can you get me in?"

"Of course, but why? What do you need in there? If you think there's someone who'll remove your chip, there isn't. I'll zap you if you try or even bring it up."

"Well connected in the tunnels, I take it?"

"Irrelevant. I can get you in; that is all you need to know. Answer the question, Keller. What are you looking for?"

Keller paused, swallowed, and donned his best grave face. "Henrik was blamed by some that he caused the explosion. They may not trust him enough to allow access to *everything*. Not sure about you and what you saw down there."

"Carry on."

"My father liked to work in layers and often created misleading dead ends. What might appear to be theories for transferring people to droid bodies might have been a ploy to make himself look insane. Don't ask. I'd like to poke around and see if there's something you missed." Keller could feel Henrik boring down on him. *You like it screwed up, here you go.*

No one spoke for the next few seconds.

"Fine, you will go to Ironsmith. Alone. I agree, people there don't entirely look favorably upon Henrik. Remember, the chip can be located anywhere, even a deep bunker."

"Right. How about the back part of Neufeld?"

Ed didn't comment though Keller thought he picked up a slight inhale, a cut-off reaction. *What is his connection to Neufeld Bunker?*

Emma, who had been in the lounge, entered the lab. "He can use August's car. It's a wreck but should make it."

"Good, we need to get rid of that thing," Ed said, "And have the orderly clean and sterilize the room."

"Of course."

"Keller, you will be accompanied wherever you go—*even the deserted backside of Neufeld Bunker.*" The line clicked off.

Chapter 24

Keller yearned for a point in his desolate life to hang on to, a home-free card, even if temporary. Driving became ethereal—he travelled in a fiberglass and metal container propelled by a petrol engine speeding on tarmac leading to nowhere. Anything worrisome from the past didn't compare to now, mere trivialities, shrunken dust by comparison. *Except for the explosion which killed my father and Katrina. That equated. That's how it began, and this is how it plays out, unbeknownst to anyone.*

He couldn't call Lurch or Tarzana; it would only endanger them. Cassy was a wild card—at worst, an agent for Ed in the field. Bruno was in up to his eyeballs in lies. Then there was Nora. He could write her letters from prison if he got out of this alive. Keller imagined her keeping them in a shoe box, never replying and then one day tossing them by mistake. *I don't recall ever writing to a woman by hand, why would I start? Last ditch effort to be romantic? A romantic psychopath…*

He hadn't been back in Ironsmith for almost 20 years. A little town tucked away in the southwest, straight north from the Isle of Wight. Its location had no bearing on anything except that the Romans, and later the Britons, had once quarried the stone there. And iron. That lead to a vast tunnel system which, as a millennium passed, expanded to become miles of roadway flanked by habitable quarters of every kind—in essence, a second town underneath Ironsmith itself. A hidden, technologically advanced existence heavily contrasting its counterpart above. Secretive and purposed for the advancement of something Keller had yet to figure out. There were the usual excuses of war, homeland security and technology to keep up or get ahead with, but he didn't believe in those. They were too easy to follow along and get absorbed in. Or perhaps he just considered himself more inciteful than others. Knowing. Licensed to do what he wanted.

"You're in control of your life, only you," his mother said, handing him a loaded piece. It was smooth, heavy, solid. His hand was awkward as it trembled a little, he didn't want to touch the trigger yet. "You have to know that baby, in your soul. No one can take that from you but they'll sure as hell might try." Keller glanced at her, her confident face looking back at him through sunglasses, the hot desert breeze tousling her hair and silk scarf.

As the ferry ride to the mainland had been uneventful, Keller was happy to speed recklessly. Or else, he kept to the limit— hoping to happen across the golden answer, the solution to the impossible, written in the leaves or sung by the breeze along the way. Hidden amongst the sheep in the fields, carried under oath by cyclists, a man walking his dog or even protected by the unlucky Magpies in the wood. The scent in the air told him he wasn't far off, but he couldn't pinpoint what that meant. *Whatever the answer is, it's under my nose.*

As in Maine, the lushness and fresh air were welcome. Not that the Jolly More wasn't situated in a beautiful part of the countryside, it was. But it was also home to the lab floor where he had crumpled the previous day. The entire house, contents and property had become stifling to him; chemical and reactive—inspiring raw, dark emotions. An inner battle ignited as he knew he did his part to kill a man while excuses surged to undermine the truth. He could still feel the cool clay tiles on his shoulder, hip, leg and face, the state of utter uselessness, even to control his own bladder. The body had become a paralyzed putty for what felt like hours, though it had only been minutes until he blacked out. But he hadn't paid the price for the life of August, not a fraction. *We literally wasted him, and the precious time he had left. No life is worth that little.*

Ed had degraded him thoroughly. Emma and Henrik had set him up. *I lost control. Sure — what choice did they have? Henrik warned me, I ignored him, righteous me.* In moments of weakness, he'd given up key information regarding his father's work. Not that it was accepted or understood or that he could think of anything else to say and not hang up the situation.

And now he was heading to the place he least wanted to visit. Yet his boyhood years were spent in Ironsmith. He had, after all, grown up a tunnel rat like Katrina. A dull loss surged in his chest — she and father had charred to a crisp while he lived. She died. She paid. Tunnel rats were supposed to be hard to catch, let alone find, and tough to kill. Unless they were trapped or poisoned. Or blown up unexpectedly.

If what he needed to achieve with this visit was even possible, or the place he wished to see even existed, the tunnels were it. *And why do I think I know this? Ed understood what the back end of Neufeld was, an abandoned part few knew of. Nothing there, only places we used to explore, which led to more places coalescing with darkness.*

Keller noticed a small parking area, most likely a trailhead. He drove in, parked under a shady tree and turned off the engine as a breeze scurried by and a bird began a glassy melody stuck on repeat. It was now ironic to think that he had felt trapped in Maine. But he also wasn't content to believe that the chip couldn't be removed. A high risk, yes, but it had to be possible. He would reach out to Arnold at the right time if he still worked in the Neufeld. Something might slip out. Arnold liked to talk and tell stories. They often had some truth to them or carried an inside scoop.

Arnold was the Maintenance Chief in the bunker. He was a friend of his mother's while Tom didn't pay him much attention. Dreamy, quiet, and enjoyed tinkering with computers in his spare time. No one took him seriously, in fact father and Alexey liked to mock him — all in good fun but Keller could see it was wounding; perhaps that was why his mum had such a thing for him. She liked to befriend the underdog, flirt, and hang around his office. Keller could sometimes hear them laughing — Arnold liked to pour her a glass of wine, which he always had around. While he was not much to look at, he had a boldness about him, especially when he joked. Belinda fell for that, funny or not.

After his father died, Arnold consoled Belinda, and they hung out in town above ground. A coffee here, a walk there. They often drove to Bath. Keller remembered his mum being happy, which was rare for her, aside from when they went to shoot at targets in the desert. Then, after Keller settled in London, she and Arnold took off to Vegas together, only returning a couple of years later. In the months following their return, Keller found his mum had distinctly changed, grown distant, and waxed a disconnect seriousness unlike her.

Only I'm in control, there's nobody else.

He gazed across the fields, as if something had altered and the hidden answer might materialize after all. He called Bruno but got his voicemail. Keller didn't leave a message, instead looked at the phone. *Bruno, you'll have to explain a few things.*

The situation at hand was grim — a slow mental assassination of knowing that at any instant, his persecution might erupt. Akin to burning alive. Keller chuckled, triggered by the memory of cooked meat on the uncle's bare bones. *Could be me.* The chuckle rose to laughter, which reached a hysterical pitch and then subsided. He wiped tears of glee from his eyes, leaving his sight blurry.

•   •   •   •   •

After a vein of fresh air met him at the ground beneath the smoke, Keller regained his breath, scrambled up from the pavement and opened his eyes gingerly, the gauze in his hand still covering his mouth and nose. The shrouded daylight was painful to behold and Keller shut his eyes. Seconds later, he tested them again, squinting. Still blinded, he moved towards the lift house, engulfed in smoke. He put the bandage back over his eyes, the tape still holding, but barely. He could hear people yelling nearby, questioning each other, cars stopping, doors opening, and slamming. He kept moving forward.

Before he knew it, a man's hand was on his shoulder, asking if his face was bandaged because it had been burned. Keller didn't reply; he knew it was Arnold, thinking him a simple caretaker who was so stupid that he thought Keller walked around with gauze, waiting to be blown up. Thinking that the man was involved with his mother, like adults sometimes do, secretly. He hated him for it but was glad at least someone he knew was around.

Tears forced their way to the surface around his eyes, but Keller beat them down. He let the hand on his shoulder be, and that would do. He wasn't going to tell him a thing or cry in front of him. The gauze unstuck from his hair and Keller stole a squinted glance up at Arnold who looked back at him. His face looked weird. Keller hated the weird look, the look of paleness, strain and conjured disbelief which didn't match up properly with the situation at hand.

"My father, is he all right? And Katrina?" his voice shook as if he hadn't spoken in a hundred years. The scene felt bad. He couldn't see hardly; the whole bloody situation was evil. And how come Arnold was above ground, he wondered.

"I don't know. The fire trucks are on their way, ambulances too. What happened to your eyes? Are you okay?"

"Yeah," he said quietly, bending his head forward so he could snap a glance above the gauze at the lift house. Black smoke billowed from it; he could tell by the silhouette, the reek.

•　　•　　•　　•　　•

Keller opened his eyes which had never been closed. He shifted his focus from a distant tree to a tiny bird which had landed on the hood of the blue-grey BMW. Time for lunch and strong coffee. *I know just the place. Ironsmith can wait.*

As he pulled back onto the roadway, he tried to remember if he had seen the back of Cassy's neck and if she had a faint scar. She usually stood or sat facing him, or her hair covered the back of her neck. Then he remembered the pattern of little hairs on her arms and realized the cut mark might not apply. *Human or synth. Now I'm losing it.*

Chapter 25

As he continued to head northeast, skipping his turnoff to Ironsmith, Keller heard the first few notes of Thunderstruck seep from his new phone, a ringtone of Lurch's he restored from the cloud. When Keller ignored it a text appeared. 'You have proceeded on A6, should be A350' Keller read and pulled over in a small, muddy alcove next to a tall hedge. He answered the text. 'Detour. If you zap me, I'll kill you and incinerate.'

There was no reply and Keller knew Henrik could hit the switch anytime. They had digressed to a brutal animal existence. *You hurt me, I'll make my revenge worse.* It felt like second nature, beckoning. Yet distant and implausible, rather an old instinct fermented from the dregs of evolution.

Leaning on the car, facing a garbage bin and a hedge beyond which was another field, Keller called Alexey. He was a good friend of his father's and an engineer who also worked on the droids in the Bunker. The father of Katrina who had blown up along with Tom. Keller hadn't met or spoken to him in years, unsure where the man stood on the explosion. While kind and decent, Katrina was the brightest star in his universe.

He's probably still got the same number. It rang a few times and then kept ringing. Keller didn't hang up. A garbled scuffle ensued, then a pause, and a voice which stirred his memories spoke, 'Hallo.'

"Hey Alexey, it's Keller Mod."

"Who?"

"Keller. *Your* Keller."

"My Keller. Yes of course, Mod! You all right?"

"Yeah, not bad." Keller paused and looked at the ground. "How have you been keeping?"

"Ah, all right..."

"That's real good."

"What's wrong? Boy, with you, I could always tell and still can. Spill it."

"I'm just outside of Bath; I'd like to pop by for a visit."

"Sure thing." They chatted a while longer and Alexey gave him his postcode.

No doubt Henrik would suspect where he went. Ed was more intelligent, so he probably didn't care where Keller went if he thought it addressed the question of immortality. The man was an authentic nut case. A classic. And loved himself for it.

Alexey lived in a house with a large garden at the end of a lane. The neighborhood was blandly picturesque, a definite cul-de-sac as far as country villages went — cars ranging from small to mid-size, well-kept gardens, roofs fixed, gates level, windows clean. Keller noted that Alexey's place deviated. His garden was overgrown but fresh looking, wild. On his driveway stood a black shiny RAM pickup with an extra-large cab and a short bed. It was jacked, and the tires of heavy tread. Next to it, the house looked smallish, overlooking the valley of River Avon.

A shrunken Alexey met him at the door, noticing Keller's arrival from between the drapes. Never tall but always sturdy, the man had thinned and greyed. *Wife dead, daughter dead, would make anyone sallow.*

Keller followed him into the living room, where he noted a little bar stood in the corner, open for business. Though the curtains were parted and only sheers covered the back window, which looked onto a long backyard, the room was dim in the late day. A sizeable ornate gold lamp was lit; Keller grinned at the red and gold tassels hanging from the lampshade edge. Majestic patterns adorned the area rug on the floor, and a similar carpet hung on the wall. Three high-back chairs occupied the living room, along with an ornate divan. The walls were painted blue and mustard. There was little chance for the light to bounce around, so it lingered in the weaves, tapestries, and robust, oak coffee table.

They caught up a while and flipped through a few family albums where Keller sometimes appeared with Katrina. Solemn moments passed, mixed with laughter, tears and chuckles. *To think I was somewhat normal back then. I probably even loved your scrawny lass. Still do I guess.*

"So then tell me about the news stories. Obviously, you didn't kill the woman or else you wouldn't be here, right?" and then quietly, "Or are you on the run?"

"No, I didn't kill her. Long story," Keller said, slowly, looked out the window then back at Alexey. *I need to tell him.*

"I got time."

Alexey poured two shots and then two more again as he listened. After introducing the restaurant where he worked after quitting medicine, Keller recounted the events of late, up until the manhunt for him was called off. *Thanks to Ed. Everything courtesy of Ed.*

"I couldn't believe my eyes and ears when I saw it on the news. I'm glad you came; this is an enormous relief," he said, eyes glazed.

Next, Keller described his flight back from Maine and on to the Isle of Wight, the stay at the hotel and his ride from Cassy to the Jolly More Mansion, which the clinic had purchased and renovated.

"Jolly More, what a name. Yeah, he's a psycho, no doubt there," Alexey added, thoughtfully.

Then Keller told of his attempt at transferring August to his living clone. "So you see, technically, I did murder someone. But

I didn't intend to, they zapped me when I tried to bring him back. The plan was to heat him up, so he had a choice and could tell me what happened."

"Choice has power. Zapped you, how?"

Keller explained and showed Alexey the back of his neck. Alexey gawked. "This is no joke. Who gave it to you and why? Were you in prison after all?"

"Henrik. And for no good reason."

"Putting you in such danger doesn't sound like him. I don't care what they said after the explosion." Alexey's eyes moistened further, "I don't believe any of it."

"He's got one himself. He and this nurse are simply doing what it takes to make it through another day. It's routine. Henrik's been ground down to practically nothing," Keller continued, "Just like I'm getting to be. Might be all for the best."

"So you're here for the letter."

"I don't follow."

"Doesn't matter—people always do things for a reason, whether or not they know it. Here, let me dig it up." Alexey got down on his knees to search for something in a cupboard beneath a tall bookshelf crammed to total capacity. With another dusty album in one hand, he got up, his face red with effort, grey locks crossing his left eye and revealing large ears. His skin was taught over his bony features, and he smiled, perhaps from back pain—his hand shot out to clutch one of the high backs as he stood.

"Got it, I was keeping it tucked away. Not sure why it got sent here, though I imagine you are hard to track down." He promptly pulled out an envelope from within the album cover and handed over to Keller who pulled out the letter. It had an air of antiquity about it, the writing had panache.

Dear Keller,

Hope you are well, despite all. I don't have an address for you, so I sent this to Alexey. I figured you would show up there eventually. Katrina is well — things aren't always as they seem. And I'm sorry for the horror you had to witness but see, it turned out for the best. There's a reason why I didn't leave a light on, and I hope you'll come to forgive me.

The pressure to perform was immense, from forces I can't explain. Even voices in my head, which, if we ever talk again, I'm hoping you might shed light on. Gouyen she calls herself, or perhaps that's just another name for insanity.

I don't expect you to believe anything immediately, though I know it's in you. I know that in time you will see the truth.

Yours truly,

Tom

Next to the signature was a green smiley face stamp. To Keller, it all looked like his father's handwriting. *Not vague at all.* The smiley face was created by the same stamp he used as a boy — one eye had been gauged by a pocketknife, and instead of looking like a wink, it had come out possessed.

"There's no date, when did you get this?"

"A few months ago. What does it say?"

"It's a prank," Keller said, tossing it down on Alexey's lap. *Must be a prank. If not, then I'm truly screwed. If he made it into the Cradle, he could be anybody with how synths have evolved.*

"You used to put those smiley faces all over the place," Alexey said, having become pale. "What kind of bastard… Keller, what are you wrapped up in, son? I mean, this is getting downright obscene!" When he picked up a lighter to burn the letter, Keller yanked it from his fingers. "No, wait, I'll keep it as evidence."

"Are you buying into this crap, Keller!?"

"No, I'm not. You don't understand, I was set up for *murder*, and I still could be wanted—it's like this guy Ed dictates how the party rolls. Whatever pathetic life I had is gone with nowhere to turn; I started running a year ago. A flick of the switch, and I go down. I pissed myself, for christ sake."

The two men stood silent as Keller folded the letter along with the envelope and stuffed it in his pocket. Alexey walked over to the bar and poured a couple more shots. "Your father and I were keen on robots and synths since we were kids. Both of us. You've heard my stories and some of his no doubt. I even remember Katrina telling me some of Tom's stories to see if I had something that could trump it. It's the way she was," he paused to toss back a shot and eat a small wedge of lemon dipped in sugar. "But with the Cradle, I told him not to go there. It wouldn't work I said, it mustn't work, not on this earth! Besides, he could get fired again, institutionalized. He didn't listen, and I did nothing to stop him. Now look at us today. Katrina is dead," Alexey pause, "Keller if something happens to you—"

"It won't. Over my dead body," Keller smiled wryly. "They are expecting me in Ironsmith, in Neufeld Bunker, today. *Ed* organized it. Could have been him who sent the letter, just to mess with us in case I visit you. He knows about my family so why not you."

"Screw Ed. You will go first thing in the morning with a clear head, there's no other way. I doubt Ironsmith holds any answers, but it will buy you time."

"If I get zapped, promise you'll shoot me. I mean if it doesn't stop," Keller said, the whisky talking.

"Ya, okay, but then I go to jail," Alexey replied, palms out and lifting.

"You don't have a silencer? I thought all Russian spies did."

"Russian spy? No, I'm an engineer. You've seen me work," he said, hands falling back on thighs.

"Yeah, but I never paid attention to what you actually did. I noticed what you didn't do."

"Like what?"

"Like be at home in the evenings, or even at night."

"My wife died long ago. Keller, it's not funny," he said with a serious face, like he was offended. Then they both cracked up laughing, pressure dissipating into the air. "I don't know what you've gotten yourself into, but in my heart, I know you'll pull out of it. Alive I hope."

"Yeah, well, I feel genuinely cursed."

Alexey didn't reply, instead poured two more shots.

"I'll tell you something, Keller. Your mother was a spy, the real thing. Someone could have been after her too…"

Keller nodded and looked down. "Arnold? She became a serious lush after she met that guy. He really took her mind off things," Keller began to laugh giddily.

"She always liked her liquor. We all do, comes with the territory. He was kind to her after your father died. Give him a break. You never really know who someone is until you know. And even then—"

Keller sat back on the sofa and looked over again at a photo of Katrina on the bookshelf. *Yep, if I allow myself, I miss you a whole lot.*

"Keller, look at me. You realize what this Ed fellow trying to do, what he's asking *you* to do for him?"

"I do, yes. And he's got me cornered."

"Cornered? There is no such thing Keller."

Chapter 26

Driving into the town of Ironsmith, where Keller had lived from age 8 to 11, was like cruising through a movie set. Little had changed, and even that blended in well. The Peacock Arms stood kitty-corner to the Curiosity Shop and Chen's Fish & Chips. Sometimes his mother would leave Katrina and him in Chen's while she popped into the Peacock. Then they would browse through odds, ends and antiques in the Curiosity Shop. It's where Keller found the smiley face stamp.

Further down the high street, with an ornate metal sign hanging from a rusty chain was the army surplus store where Keller bought his first pocketknife and Katrina, a pistol that played realistic animal sounds—another tool for her repertoire of intimidation. *I had such a crush on that girl, even when she spit in my mouth.*

Despite quaint appearances, secure and friendly, he knew part of the reason the town survived well was because of what lay underneath. The people on the surface had an inkling but didn't question things and certainly talked little. Most of the people employed underneath lived on the surface and were sworn to secrecy. It all worked out—things appeared relaxed above and below much like any conservative society living a lie.

Keller entered the parking lot of the Neufeld Underground Security Centre—he couldn't help but grin at the complication of the word *bunker.* There were plenty of empty spaces and the lot was surrounded by a green belt. Keller parked at the far side. He recognized some of the trees he had climbed, the trunks and branches much thicker now and higher. The parking lot had been re-paved some years ago and was fresh looking, the white lines crisp.

There was no building or lift house. The earth formed a large mound covered in grass, patchy in places and surrounded by a cleared perimeter and high fence. Nothing dramatic. Next to the mound was a short street, which ended at a windowless brick structure. Beyond the street, a narrow perimeter, and the fence were more woods. Keller headed for the gated entrance and mound area. It was unmanned, but there were cameras — Keller pressed the button on the intercom. It crackled, and underneath the interference, a distant voice said something.

"Keller Mod here to see Simon Ekstrom."

More crackling followed, and the gate slid open.

Next, he approached the entrance to the mound itself, a wedge-shaped concrete walkway flanked by concrete walls. The deeper into the mound, the higher the walls — essentially, he was walking into the cross-section of a dome. And at the narrow and deepest end of the wedge, stood the entrance, a glass and metal door. A few more cameras hung, retro style, but towards the entrance and in the wedge and above it, was a black, shiny, bulbous protrusion. *The eye no doubt.*

Once at the door, three options presented themselves: A back-lit keypad, retinal scanner and intercom. For a joke, Keller tried the retinal. No sound, only the wind on the trees and a few birds chirping nearby. Then a buzz came from the door; Keller opened it and walked in.

The space surprisingly expanded, much like a movie theatre's atrium. Up ahead the gridded floor appeared to drop off into the darkness. Before his eyes adjusted, Keller felt something hard in his side. *What, gun barrel?* The man holding it calmly told him to get down on his knees while another stood a few meters away. A bag was promptly thrown on his head and his hands cuffed. Keller cooperated, realizing he hadn't even noticed them when he walked in. Once stood up, he was patted down.

"I was actually expected," his voice deadened by the thick, smelly canvass.

"You set off an alert from the parking lot—the retinal confirmed it. Come with us please."

"You must have IDed me long before I arrived; why all of this?" The guard didn't reply, and Keller said nothing further. His contact was the Head of Security, so he let things play out. The trip down the escalator was around two minutes. At the bottom, they walked straight ahead, a card swiped, and more doors opened. Double by the sound of it, metal he guessed, yet smooth and quiet. They passed through, walked a while and Keller was jerked one way and then another as they came to turns in the hallway. Then another door swoosh. Keller was pushed in and guided to sit down. His hands were uncuffed and then re-cuffed to a metal table where he sat.

Next, he waited. Someone remained in the room with him; he could hear low breathing and shuffles from behind. They didn't speak, and Keller didn't want to talk, content to wait. For the time being, he was in the right place. Compared to the paralyzing, convulsive shock of the chip, the rubber and canvas odor of the bag over his head was welcome.

The ratcheting noise of the door handle was followed by someone entering, treading softly.

"Leave us," a woman said. Keller was instantly alerted by the voice. *WTF.* The rubber around his neck was released, and the bag lifted off. As the woman dressed in a Military Police uniform walked to the other side of the table and sat down, Keller sat dumbfounded, eyes adjusting to the room's lights, lips parted. *It was Cassy.*

"Hey, Keller."

"So, you really do work in security."

"I am Cassandra Version 23 and am pleased to make your acquaintance," Cassy said with a childish smile.

Keller finally recognized what *it* was—a synth. A true-to-life synthetic human replica, something he never knew even existed. The droids of his youth in his father's lab were human-looking but *obviously* robots. *This one was human-like.* Keller couldn't understand for a moment what kind of *human* he meant.

"Don't look so shocked; I'm still *real*."

"Yeah, so were your boys."

"My apologies. They don't know you like I do, and I don't want them to; you're all mine."

"Right."

"Plus, it doesn't help matters you're wearing a very advanced monitored chip, quite deadly. That was a surprise for all of us."

"You don't say. I must have been scanned at the door."

"That's classified." Cassy smiled before her demeanor shifted to a seriousness Keller had never seen.

The face relaxed, pure machine now.

"This room is private, off the record, no mirror as you can see. I'm simply submitting that you are here on a request to see the research of Tom Mod and have arrived. The materials are to be used by Jolly More Mansion Inc to aid in the development of an advanced anti-ageing procedure. Correct?" Cassy rattled off.

"I suppose."

"Keller..."

"Yes."

"During their last visit, your company snooped around the paranormal stuff, made a lot of copies and borrowed prototypes. Why is that?"

"Why didn't you ask them? I mean, someone must have authorized it."

"Back then I wasn't assigned to this task, I'm asking now."

"They've told me almost nothing. I'm here by my own suggestion." And then more quietly, "Off the record, I'm buying time."

Cassy paused, then continued through a multitude of formalities and after wrapping them up, she sat back.

"What you got there is about it. Tom was my father, and I'd like to look over what was left after the explosion. For me, there's a dual purpose," Keller began.

"Nonsense. You've stayed clear of this place for 19 years. And now you show up wearing a prison chip which I doubt you requested."

"Then enlighten me, why am I here?"

"You're here by force." When Keller didn't comment, Cassy continued, "This is the second time someone has shown up to investigate Tom Mod's work from the Jolly More. First, it was Henrik, also tagged. But we have no idea who authorized these visits and why—you're both potential criminals yet your chips don't trace back to anything. C'mon, Tom Mod's work is extremely controversial, experimental and dangerous. If I entertain it as a possible addition to science, it would potentially change life as we know it.

"Sure... And is that why you've been following me around?"

"Yes. Keller, the real question is, can we work together?"

He took a moment, looking at the droid, noting its imploring stare. *She's on to something... a Tom Mod buff... a fricking machine seeking life or something, consciousness.*

"No Keller, not seeking any more sentience than I already have," she said.

Keller paused to look at her. "Yeah, I'm in. And your interest is in utilizing the paranormal to predict criminal behavior?"

"Nope, asking a ghost if he did it doesn't help. It's just a cover project, staying on topic. I want to know what happened to Tom and why the Jolly More scooped up most of his work."

Keller didn't respond. *Cover project. You'd lock me up if I told you…*

"We can talk later," she said, as if seeing it in his eyes. "Time to see Simon; just need to check in, then I'm all yours, and so is the Neufeld."

"And what does Simon know about this?"

"Like me, he suspects the Jolly More is venturing into something questionable, potent, based on Tom's work, but it's not in our jurisdiction to investigate. So, he's just cutting me slack; I visit the field, as you know," she said, sitting up straighter, glancing at her paperwork as she did.

"Yeah, and you seem quite eager to do your job. Or is that programming?"

It was Cassy's turn to pause and look at him. "Thanks for the complement."

Sarcasm?

They walked down a few halls, passed by a mess area and then out into a wider tunnel, a proper road. Upon rounding the corner, old memories gushed in as Keller noted a partially open, metal door. Inside was an even older man dressed in overalls, spectacled, white stubble, a big nose and tiny eyes. He was surrounded by motors, contraptions, ventilator parts, generator segments, spools of wire, and everything mechanical or electrical related to tunnel life. The man was inspecting a console, Keller guessed as he slowed his pace, glimpsing what appeared to be a portal into his past. Keller could see a few old baseball posters on the wall and suddenly remembered Arnold was a fan. As a boy, he had found it odd for a Brit when football was sacred.

"He's getting senile now, inefficient, going to retire soon," Cassy said as they stopped. "You wanna say hi?"

"Ah, yeah," Keller said, surprised the synth brought on a tender moment.

"He may not remember you. Diagnosed with Alzheimer's a few months ago. At first, we thought he was playing a prank, and later, we see he's got it. Hence the retirement. He's like an installation. Still does good work though, despite all."

Keller returned to the open door and stood for a few seconds. The man, Arnold, didn't notice him. Then he turned, and Keller saw a slight semblance of recognition in his eyes, a flicker. He was sure of it.

"Yes, can I help you?" the man asked.

"It's me, Keller, Arnold. Been a few years since I last saw you."

"Are you lost? I don't know any Keller."

"He's with me, Arnold," Cassy said from behind.

"And who are you? Security?"

"Yes Arnold, it's Cassy."

"Get him out; I'm busy."

"We'll let you alone. See you later, Arnold," she said.

He didn't reply. Keller studied him a second longer and turned to join Cassy. *There was a flicker and then disconnection, a termination Arnold instigated.* To go back and shake him to see if that was true wasn't wise for the time being. *He's either a sly bugger or doesn't want to see me.* They continued around the corner and veered off the main roadway into a new labyrinth of hallways which Keller recognized all too well.

•　　•　　•　　•　　•

Keller moved the gauze from his eyes to his mouth again. The explosion had shaken the ground, and the billowing smoke bothered him—way down in the bunker, it had to be much worse, and his father's lab was near the lift. Keller ran forward, not knowing what to do; his vision heavily occluded. But closer to the lift house the smoke grew thicker and he began to choke. Not far away, someone called him. Arnold again.

As Keller turned, the man grabbed him by the arm and pulled him further away. "It could blow again; stay clear boy," Arnold said, upset in his voice yet calm. Calculated.

"How did you get out?" Keller asked.

"I'm not working today, just came to pick something up."

Keller looked at Arnold, squinting, tears welling up even though he had decided that wouldn't happen at any cost. Arnold looked back at him. Though blurry, Keller could see the look on his face, one of *adult concern*, one teacher might use when a student couldn't answer a question which should be easy.

"Stay here, don't go any closer. I've called for help; the fire department should be here in a few minutes. No one from the bunker hears me; the reception must be knocked out."

Keller looked down at Arnold's hand. It had a phone in it, but the screen was dark.

"So try again. The hub is nowhere near here. Are you saying the entire bunker blew up?"

"No, of course not. Yeah, lemme try again."

Keller looked back into the smoke, tears taunting.

•   •   •   •   •

"In here, Keller," Cassy said as they neared the end of a hall which flowed seamlessly into a stark, minimalist reception area. Curved glass and matted lumex panels morphed into a silhouetted counter and seating area. Sleeker, meaner and far more technologically elegant than Keller remembered. *New décor.* Hidden strip lights led the way, interspersed with powerful LED spots which splashed the walls.

"Welcome to the Hub Mr Mod. Perhaps you remember it," said a sturdy man with a brush cut, wearing the same uniform as Cassy. Keller noticed him put his hand behind her back which seemed to stay there for too long. *Old friends? Involved?*

"Keller, this is Lieutenant Evstrom," Cassy said, stepping sideways and indicating him.

"Call me Simon," he said as they shook.

"Hi Simon, pleased to meet you," issued Keller.

"I'm going to make things clear right from the start. Five days ago, you were still wanted for murder. I'm a little apprehensive about having you here today. No one is searching for you anymore, you're off the hook, and I understand. But I don't believe people become wanted criminals for no reason. See, I've also been ordered to let you go where you want, within the relevance of your research. No reasons given; despite the tag you're wearing." Evstrom stepped closer, Keller could smell his breath. "Covert ops don't interest me, Mr Mod, but the safety of my staff down here does. Pull any shit in here, anything resembling trouble, and you're out. Get it?"

"Yeah, it's all clear to me. Who approved my visit?"

Simon sent him a stern gaze.

"I won't be any trouble; I simply—"

"Good. The Cassandra V23 will escort you and has been instructed to apprehend you whenever she sees fit. Any sign of struggle or non-duplication will be taken as a threat to the Ministry. So, the leniency for her to use force is great. Understand?"

"Yes."

"Very well, I'll leave you to it then." With that, Simon walked out.

"Come, have a look," she began, waving him to the next room. As they moved towards the open doorway, Keller could see it was the hub. Gigantic wall-sized screens backdropped rows of desk monitors and men. Anything anyone could imagine looking at on the planet could be accessed, provided a cam covered it—from outer space to ground level and everything in between. Continents and oceans down to unidentifiable street corners.

"It's this one here," she added.

There, on a wall of its own, was the Neufeld bunker system. As Keller walked up to it, he saw similarities to the old paper version dancing in his mind.

"Oh, now that brings back memories," he said.

"I thought it might," she said like she meant it.

Keller noted the off-limits area where his father's lab was located. Seeing the lift nearby stirred up a sick feeling. Keller turned blank as he searched for all the places he had been, now defined on screen with thin, glowing, color-coded lines, precise and ready to burst into 3D at a touch. Once satisfied he had seen what he needed, or at least pretended to, they walked out into the tunnel system.

"As Simon said, I'll be with you at all times."

"Good, I can use the help."

"Who said anything about help?" she said, a faint smile manifesting.

Simulated sense of humor with a touch of flirt, nice. For a moment, Keller forgot about the dark task which awaited him at the Jolly More and the terminal chip plugged into his nervous system.

Chapter 27

They walked the first leg of the tunnel in silence. Keller sensed Cassy glance at him once and then again as Tom's lab drew near.

"Despite all, I think its great you decided to pay us a visit. It takes nerve. Especially with whatever you've got going on there."

Keller remained silent, only nodding. The sight of the closed lift, the walkways, the intersection of Main and Queen, while it had been unsuccessfully scrubbed and whitewashed anew, he could see, feel and smell what it was covering up.

"I've been through the area myself to ensure that what we see on the scans is actually there. The hub map doesn't show details in the closed-off areas and outer parts."

"Is it all there?"

"Pretty much. There will be another large monitor in the Archives, covering the uninhabited and off-limits areas; I'll log us in. Mind you, some things are best left alone."

"What do you mean?"

"Your father's lab and the surrounding areas, including below, have been investigated thoroughly. Sabotage was suspected, yet the intricacy suggests an inside job. Because of their whereabouts that day, Tom himself still remains a suspect and, unfortunately, Henrik."

"So I've heard." *Keep your mouth shut about the letter.* "Why do you say, unfortunately?"

"He served the Ministry well, and while his file contains incidents of drug abuse, it does not contain any acts of hostility or something that would suggest criminal behavior. He was part of the team that created my predecessors, and they all found him agreeable. Aside from the drugs."

"But you've never met him."

"No, at least I don't think so," Cassy hesitated.

Don't think so?

Ahead lay the entrance to Tom's lab. Without skipping a beat, Keller walked straight for the newish door, no doubt installed after the blast, pulled the handle and swung it open. *No use in stretching things out; god, it stinks in here.* He stood in the doorway for a few seconds, his eyes pervading the demolished and stripped-down room. Not a piece of furniture or equipment was left inside. *Ed was right, a charred hole.* While parts of the outer wall had been replaced and patched, the inner walls had been left as was—charred and melted pieces of framework sagging from within gashes where pieces of drywall had been torn from the blast.

"Where is the recovered stuff?"

"Archives, with the Data Droid. Data May we call her."

Keller slowly passed through as if admiring a property, looking at it for potential following a good gutting. He sought something obvious, a sign, a link to his past. He found one and stopped by the doorway leading to a storage room. Only hinge sockets remained. A succession of thin scratches on the metal door jamb showed his height from ages 8 to 11. Keller swallowed.

•   •   •   •   •

After the fire trucks arrived, the lift house was dowsed. Keller was assured that other firemen had approached the blasted area via the tunnels. No one answered questions he had about his father and Katrina. His sight returned, ironically, to a dark, black and chaotic world. Eventually, his mother arrived and squeezed him as hard as she ever had, upset. She pulled herself together and asked him about the gauze.

"I'll tell you later," he said, still holding the tears back. She spoke with Arnold for a while and questioned the police. Keller had never seen her so distraught; it was as if she had woken up. And then, there was news that 2 bodies were recovered from the lab and moved to the bunker medical area. Keller wasn't told directly; he overheard a policeman telling his mother. Fresh tears trickling, she knelt and hugged him hard once more. Then he knew it was bad — it was the first and last time he saw his mother cry.

Keller never saw the bodies which had been charred beyond recognition.

•　　　•　　　•　　　•　　　•

"Keller?" Cassy bumped his elbow with hers. "Stay with me, pal."

'Stay with me pal' resonated through his mind. Keller snapped back and noticed the lighting had been replaced and rewired.

"Why bother rewiring? Why not use portable lights?"

"It's not like I remember. But blasts like this rarely happen, if ever. So someone rewired, perhaps even Arnold."

An AI-operated synth that doesn't remember... "He was thorough; I'll give him that. Slow but thorough. Like everything he did was a chess game," Keller mused.

"Yeah. I mean, he's still like that, in a way."

"Now he just forgets stuff, eh?"

"Yeah. Thoroughly," she said, enticing a smile.

Keller searched the place a while longer and decided there was not much point.

"So let's go see Data May I guess," he finally said.

"Sure. I mean, she doesn't have much. Henrik took what was useable."

"What do you suggest then? I mean, unless your scans show hidden vaults…"

"They don't but… A guy doesn't spend years working on something and then blows it up without a backup. Just doesn't sound like the Tom I've been researching."

Keller remained silent.

"If we do this, I'd like you to share with me everything you know."

"Do what exactly?"

"Track down Tom's storage dump. I came across some notes which allude to a location, and when I went to check it out, it definitely looks suspicious."

"So…" The folded letter from Tom felt hot in his pocket. *Not now.*

"What goes on in the Jolly More? I need to know," Cassy said, crossing her arms on her chest. "Is Henrik trying to reconstruct the Cradle?"

"No. But why do you need to know?"

"I may have something that can help you. Stop you from getting fried—I know what your chip can do. But I don't want to hand over what I have, to a bunch of maniacs. This isn't for mass consumption. Tell me Keller."

Keller paused to just look at her. *An ethical synth? What does she want?* "Henrik has switched to organic."

"What do you mean, organic? Organic prosthetics, organic organs? Organic… oh my god…"

"He transplants the whole bloody thing or is trying to. He makes clones for some mystery guy they call Ed by using a technology originally developed by a Yuri Vasiliev. Vasiliev could create clones and grow them, but they were mindless beasts who eventually had to be put down. Henrik is trying to take it to an entirely new level—the ultimate in looking *and feeling* younger—using Tom's technology behind the Cradle. Except..."

Cassy stared. "Except what?"

Keller shook his head.

"I suspected more than skin creme and lipo. I just didn't think it was all so advanced. Your father worked solely on droids. There was no plan to transfer a human to a human so far as I could tell."

"Henrik has taken it over the top. Only he can't figure out how to get a person into their own, new body. So we end up just killing them."

Cassy said nothing at first but Keller could feel something stirring, welling up within her. "That's not the Keller I know," she said quietly.

"You don't know me. And I'm stuck in this now so if you have something to show me, then show me. It doesn't have to go to Henrik or Ed."

"If it does get to them, it won't be a bite or a scratch. I'll snap your neck," Cassy said and walked out of the room.

Chapter 28

After pouring over notes and deliberating for two hours, Cassie and Keller exited the archive area leaving Data May piqued. According to a survey she ran some months ago, Cassy was convinced of a particular location where Tom may have stashed his things—marked by a large patch of plaster which slightly differed in color and was less dense.

"These walls have not been smoothed out with household plaster; it's usually marine grade concrete due to the moisture," she insisted. "And his notes indicate SW59."

Keller thought of the letter in his pocket. *If Tom is around, he could have just told Cassy where it is. Or maybe he did and Data May... or I'm just losing it.*

"First, we get a cart and then a few supplies," Cassy said, once outside the Archive.

"A tunnel rocket, haven't seen one in ages."

"We get as close to SW59 as possible, then we walk," she continued with a chuckle.

"An adventure. I like it." *Almost too simple.*

They picked up oxygen, excavation tools, a generator, and headlamps at the utility station. After packing it into the cart, Cassy spun out for take-off, soon enough reaching a top speed of 25mph. In about 20 minutes, they crossed the border of the Neufeld tunnel system and entered its back end, where the road became rougher and strewn with debris. She pressed on, the cart swaying and shaking, as the lighting became sparse until it ceased altogether. Cassy slowed down and continued with headlights on. Neither one spoke.

What followed was a venture into history. The particular area they entered had been readied during the end of World War 2, in case of a nuclear attack on Britain. Though 40s style décor prevailed in the backside of Neufeld, it had never been inhabited. As the call center, cafeteria, bakery, living quarters, offices, a hospital area, storage rooms and a host of other areas, halls and dark corners floated by, a quiet nostalgia pervaded the vacant charm—they all breathed mystery into the stark LED spots gushing from the cart. Fine dust rose all about as they slid forward, disrupting the still air. The beams, igniting the specter of nuclear war, searched for an end. But as corridors crammed with silent ventilation and water purification systems passed by, civilization's buffer dissipated and ahead lay a barren tunnel trail, growing cracked and bumpy.

As rubble in the way of loose boulders and heaps of debris appeared in their path, Cassy slowed down and stopped. The cart was no 4x4. So they got out, turning on their headlamps and grabbing their gear. Neufeld was done. Ahead and into the darkness was Sector SW59—Southwest five to nine. Five roughly mapped out areas of the tunnel, a few of them extensive warehouses once used in the manufacture of fighter jet engines. The others housed a canteen, toilets, supply chambers and a munitions dump. All empty now—shells of dilapidated and eroded spaces, testaments of might.

"You sure you want to do this? It's only a hunch, but I'm rarely wrong. You with me?" Cassy asked.

"You keep asking that, yes."

"Like old times."

Keller didn't respond. *You're not old.*

They walked the remaining half mile towards the lonesome place that contained the suspect patch of plaster. The rooms and spaces connected to the tunnel became fewer still as they moved on, giving way to a stretch of empty wall. While the back end of Neufeld had been historic, SW59 was plain desolate. The odd rusted installations on the way suggested a junkyard—no amount of ingenuity or restoration would ever bring it back. The rusted rivulets, rotten edges, and collapsed structures were doomed.

"You must be off the grid, I mean, as far as Simon goes. He doesn't mind?" Keller began.

"That guy has such a crush on me he lets me do what I want. But yeah, no one can pinpoint where we are, not even Ed. Don't worry about your device."

They walked a while longer, side by side, head beams dancing on the walls, ground and ceiling, far and close. The odd rat scurried and squeaked along a rusted duo of pipes, following the forgotten shaft into an abyss of darkness. As far as they could see, the wall looked uniform.

"And how did you happen on the patch? There must be dozens of tunnels back here."

"Luck. I paid little attention, thinking the scans would show a sealed-off area but they don't."

Cassy stopped and stood facing the wall.

"This must be it," she said, making a circular motion with her beam. "See, it's different here. We need more light."

Keller inspected a line of lighting, no doubt connected to a defunct power station further along but not beyond hope—the odd socket still held a bulb.

"Yeah, lemme start the generator."

"Hang on," Keller said, pulling out a hammer. He tapped on the wall and sure enough the coating crumbled to reveal a white, powdery interior.

"Yes, that's it!" Cassy squealed, touching the brittle plaster.

"Certainly not rock or cement," Keller noted, turning to Cassy as he did. Her face was wildly lit up from the LED headlamp, afire against the dreary backdrop. The pattern in her irises popped as did the spray of freckles, sliced by a blade of brown hair cutting across. Her lips parted a touch as she looked at him. In the moment's excitement, Keller ran a test on the synth he told himself—he leaned in and kissed her. What he didn't expect, was that she let him, her synthetic lips kissed back.

"I couldn't help it," he began, a few seconds later. A fragility passed over her face he didn't expect to see, distant, hurt.

"Oh, so just seeing how a chunk of plastic would react," she said, turning. "Don't do that again."

"I meant it though," he said, seeing the upset linger. *You just tested positive, I'm just not sure to what.* Again, he thought of the letter in his pocket. *'Katrina is well—things aren't always as they seem.' Not going there, no way.*

"We have work to do," she said, cutting off any emotion. Cassy went to the generator she had been lugging, squeezed the choke and yanked the chord to start it up. The engine sputtered to life and stabilized to a welcome purr. Keller set his pack on the ground and pulled out a handheld mining drill.

"Do you even know how to use it?"

"I drill holes, we put in charges and blow a hole in the wall. Then, when the dust clears, we look inside."

"Let's say for some reason there was a lift inside. It's what the notes suggest. You'd destroy it. Let's try this first, then you drill." She turned on a sonar device, and sure enough, a hollow area registered, roughly four feet across and deep, similar to an elevator.

"Okay, hotshot, maybe you're right; it's definitely hollow," Keller said.

Keller drilled while Cassy walked further into the tunnel to look for an old power generator marked on the map. The tunnel lights came on, and minutes later, Cassy returned.

When Keller finished, they broke up the wall segment with pickaxes. A while later, Cassy struck what sounded like a metal drum and when they uncovered it—a lift door presented itself.

"A bloody elevator door, built to take a beating," Keller announced the obvious.

"To where is the question."

Taking care not to smash the control buttons, they cleared the remaining plaster. Cassy walked back to the generator room to investigate the power box further. Lights flickered on in the distance, and a machine started up somewhere. Next, the giant ventilator engaged, protesting with shrill squeaks. When black dust surged in the air, she cut it and tested still other switches but to no avail.

But as Keller continued to clean around the lift, wiping plaster dust out of the crevices, he noticed a tiny flash of light that pulsed every 10 seconds. *Iris lock.* He turned his eye to the tiny monitor, and it scanned a moment later. Next, the control lights turned on, little pins in the buttons, and deep down, a whir erupted as the lift mechanism engaged.

"What did you do?"

"Iris. The energy source is from within I'd say."

"Lucky guess," she said as the door opened, quiet and steady. They got on.

It dropped steadily for 6 seconds before the lift came to a halt. The door opened into darkness. Keller switched his headset back on, which illuminated a short hallway, dusty but well finished. Nothing to remind of the 40s, this was modern. At the end was a metal door and Keller proceeded towards it, smelling the cool stagnant air. He yanked on the door handle, excitement churning beneath his thoughts. It gave way smoothly, surely and Keller headed into the opening.

"Aren't *we* on a role." Cassy commented from behind.

But Cassy's voice was distant now as she also remarked something about low oxygen. A wash of even cooler musty air greeted Keller as he shrugged off Cassy's words and continued inside. It was a library and sitting room of sorts, gloomy in the headlamp. Confusion returned as he searched the walls for a light switch. Cassy was nearby, but her voice sounded muffled and muted.

"You need the oxygen tank," he heard her say and turned so that she could slip the harness and tank on him. Afterwards, she handed him the mouthpiece.

"Put it on and breathe." He did so, suddenly realizing he was short of breath, all the while searching the room, still shocked at its existence. His headlamp sporadically crisscrossed books, a stylish desk, lamps even what looked like curtains. *What was that?*

Keller cast the light back towards the desk. A figure appeared in the gloom, sitting behind it. It was a rough-looking synth crossed with a robot, a hybrid. It sat quietly, parked in hideous repose—scratched, worn, and beaten. Appearing robust and armored, with large hands tapering into fine, retractable tips Keller decided it had a functional purpose. *Sitting in storage.* The shortness of breath became a wheeze as the man nodded to someone behind him. *He moved, nodded to Cassy.* A small desk lamp clicked on and lit up the immediate area. And then Keller saw it, his own eyes picking it out from amongst an organized line of fine tools. *The smiley face stamp...*

As giddy laughter welled in his chest, he felt both arms pulled behind his back, both wrists suddenly bound by one rugged grip. *Cassy.* He breathed from the mouthpiece, but it didn't make a difference. Quite the contrary, he was getting weak and slowly passing out. The mask wouldn't shake off. The man at the desk said nothing, his mouth which could double for an excavator, brutal and emotionless. The eyes were tiny black beads sunk deep into a callous, metallic face. He blinked but didn't move.

Keller slipped into oblivion, feeling strong hands hold him up as his legs gave way. *Oxygen, my ass... who the crap is sitting there... fucking blinkey.*

Chapter 29

Although Katrina was a little taller than him and a year older, Keller was a fair bit stronger. He held off the brunt of the crumbling rock, slowly piling up, rolling, and sliding into the alcove they had retreated to, with an old wooden lunch table. Suddenly Katrina disappeared from his side.

While exploring an old mining tunnel branching from the backside of Neufeld Bunker, it had collapsed after Keller forced a rusted old shaft door mechanism by jumping on it. While not major, the crumbling rock had trapped them in an alcove mess area. Keller trembled with effort as bits of stone piled up against the table. He repositioned to use his back, facing Katrina just in time to see her remove her jacket, whip off her t-shirt and put the jacket back on. Aside from the skin on her torso and the t-shirt, all else was coated in dust.

"You didn't look, did you?" she said, catching him stare.

"No. I mean, you're only three feet away."

"Why not?"

Katrina was impossible. Keller had learned to live with it.

"Okay, I looked a bit. You're nice. Real nice."

"Nice? Nicer than your fantasy antler lady? You should be drooling."

"I'm 11. Her name is Gouyen, and she isn't a fantasy, she's a friend."

"So. I'm 12. And I know the antler lady was a ghost. I believe you. Not."

"What are you doing?"

"Making masks, for the dust."

She used a little, dull pocketknife to cut into the t-shirt and rip it apart. She tied one piece over his mouth and nose and did the same for herself. But with the next wave, more chunks of tunnel wall fell beyond the alcove and the ensuing dust poured in thick, coating them completely. Smaller rocks bounced about. A somber grey murk hung in the air, they could hardly see. It became increasingly difficult to move as the table had shifted before stopping, shoved by heavy rubble. While the collapse ceased, Keller could hear Katrina sniffle, she was on the verge of crying. "I can't breathe hardly, Keller, get us out," she said, and that was it. He found her hand and held it. "Just hang on, someone will find us," he said, confused, finding it hard to breathe himself. "Probably tracking our phones now. Calm yourself, take shallow breaths, keep your mouth shut and don't choke."

"Phones can't be tracked down here, silly."

•　　•　　•　　•　　•

"Are you in love with me, Keller?"

"Ah, what?" Keller rubbed his eyes, waking, recalling snippets from the dream. He was certain he had been in the bunker both in his dream and recently in actuality. He glanced at the clock on his bedside table. *Must have been yesterday she drove me back.*

"You were muttering my name. Are you in love with me Keller?"

"Huh?"

"I bet you wanna know what happened," she began quietly, moving closer. "I mean after you kissed me."

"No. I'd like to wake up first," he said, feeling groggy. "What the hell did you do? Who the heck was that thing, sitting there?"

Keller recalled passing out. Then he realized the back of his neck was very sore. He touched it and noticed staples instead of stitches.

Cassy tossed something onto the blanket covering his chest. Keller picked it up and looked closely. The tiny metallic device reminded him of a futuristic insect.

"You took out my chip. And I feel all right, I mean, *I'm alive.*"

"Nice to hear," Cassy let off a lopsided grin.

"Tentacles?"

"Think I got 'em all. I'm a droid Keller, in case you didn't notice," she said playfully smirking. "I can sustain extreme precision when I operate. If I want to. While the chip is as elusive as they say, taking it out only sounds impossible to scare you into not trying."

"Like a DIY project for prisoners on parole."

"Yeah. Just remember to keep it with you at all times."

"I'll hang it around my neck after embedding it in epoxy," he said, placing it against his chest.

"Never thought you for the jewelry type."

"A nice amber medallion with a bug inside on a leather cord never hurts." Keller paused, looking at her. "Thank you."

"You're welcome. Please don't let it happen again."

"No. I… so you did this in…"

"Yes."

"You sure have a great bedside manner. I mean the tranquillizer and not turning on the O2 were interesting elements of medical practice," he said looking beyond her and out the window. A falconer was out by the stone fence. *Now he's gone.*

"Keller, I did what I had to do. You might not have agreed once we got in there."

"Was that Ed?"

Cassy began to laugh, her synth voice reaching its limits with unearthly twangs and distortions. "You really don't get it do you. I'm on your side honey."

Keller just looked at her. She looked back.

"Keller, I didn't expect him in there."

"Bullshit, he nodded to you."

"He thought I knew he was there, he recognized me; your father probably planted him for security after the construction. If they have a power source there's no limit, or they just shut off."

"Never mind. Tell me about the, ah—"

"I was shocked. The lab was impeccable—ludicrous equipment, some I've never seen before. He really went all out."

Keller studied her once more. "I need to see it."

"Keller, relax. I'll show you once this is all over. Too risky now."

In the following instant, he perceived a peregrine falcon on the windowsill just outside, looking in. Then it was gone too. He shook his head and rubbed his eyes. *I missed it taking off.*

"What else happened down there? There's something you haven't told me."

"What do you mean?"

"There's no way all you did was take out a chip. All I should do is feel better, not worse. And looks like we were down there an extra day," he muttered his eyes rivetted to the bedside digital clock. Under the large glowing numerals was the date. "Must have been quite an operation."

"Maybe it's infected."

"You stapled it up yourself or did Bob the Builder do it?"

"It was me. The incision looks like its healing fine, I've been checking it."

"Ok. But I'm hallucinating."

"You are?"

"Cassy, what else did you do?"

Again, they looked at each other, eyes locked. Cassy attempted to drain her face of any emotion but failed—the telltale signs lingered.

"Don't act like you were born yesterday, Keller. You knew what you might find down there. I just took things one step further. Machines are very A to B, remember? And I get the feeling it's you who's not telling me something."

She's nervous. You'd think she'd turn that off too if she was hiding something. He was in awe of the programming, seeing the droid as a real woman, concerned, vulnerable. Cassy had pushed her sleeves up and Keller noticed a gash on her forearm, scratches, and scrapes on her hands too. *More happened down there than she's letting on.* Noticing his glance, she pulled the sleeves back down.

"You're right, I ought to tell you."

Their eyes clashed.

"So?"

"Remember the story about the alien tourists who can perceive, ah, tell apart life forms from convincing synths like me? It notified them what ammunition to use."

"I do. How did you know about that story?"

"It was in Tom's notes, something I bet he made up to tell you when you were little."

"Yeah, he did. I believed him too." *What notes?*

"He claims to have back engineered a translucent skin, containing a web of nanotechnology, that fits snugly over the eye and programs extra functions into it. Organically, it teaches the cells some new things. It would allow someone to detect life forms with or without a body. Ghosts, spirits. Some children can do it naturally as you know—this nanotech gives others the chance."

Keller flashed to the antler woman in the desert behind their backyard wall.

"Well, two days ago, it all looked quite compelling, so I decided to go ahead," she said and paused. "Hello, Keller?"

"You could have asked me first before massacring my brain."

"There was no time—I was shocked to find the lab, the equipment. And Tom had—I had to make a fast decision. After I took out your chip, I went up. I had to check-in. Simon was getting nervous, suspicious. You took a long time waking, so I put 2 and 2 together and went ahead with the nanotech. It's what you were searching for, right?"

Eyes intense, Keller looked away, then back. "Yeah, maybe," he answered. "So, it's back to the perception of sight, must be. What specifically did you do?"

"Must be, yes, I followed explicit instructions. And then, to cover our tracks I hauled you over to another abandoned lift shaft and caved it in. If anyone needs to investigate, they can go there."

She's being difficult, bloody difficult. "And how will I know if it worked?"

"You'll know. May be those aren't hallucinations you're seeing. Besides, I'm a machine, remember?" Cassy said, searching his eyes for understanding and empathy.

Keller looked into hers and glitched himself a little. She felt human at that moment. *Brilliant, absolutely brilliant.*

Chapter 30

"It's Vernon, right?" Keller took a moment to address the guard with the dice symbol on his hand and a host of atrocities raging on his arms. Cassy had finally dragged him outside and now they made their way from Keller's cottage to the Jolly More Mansion.

"Yeah, says so on my badge. Sorry about the other day, Mr Mod. It's protocol, and I—"

"You have to do what you have to do, I understand. Wearing one yourself, I presume."

"I am."

"Does wonders for morale, doesn't it?"

"Sure does. Like an electric poker up your ass."

"Right. And this is Cassy; perhaps you already met. She'll be staying with us a while."

"Cassandra V23. They say you're retro, but you look not bad."

"You look not too bad yourself. A little worn around the edges, but I bet you keep this place safe. And as long as there are no blood tests, you're good to go," Cassy retorted.

Leaving the guard behind, they headed along the lane towards the mansion, side by side, pretending to enjoy the scenery. "What a beautiful place," she said. "Oh, and what a handsome, fit man, must be a patient. He looks lost."

"That's the Kid. Henrik's *almost* transfer. Only the wrong guy showed up inside."

"Wrong guy… so you're saying that over there is a clone of someone, and it's alive and well?"

"I suppose. Only not the right guy."

"Right guy or not, it's bloody alive! Keller, you never told me this," she said in a shrill voice, with a distorted buzz edging it. Keller could hear upset, jumbled with disbelief and joy. *That looks like an emotional machine.*

"It's not the expected result."

"But it's still a miracle."

"Just doesn't feel like one, feels like murder. The right guy is gone. Dead."

"Crime or not, I was right. It's possible. *Henrik Poole has altered evolution*," Cassy uttered, a tremor present in her voice. She stepped back from Keller.

"Okay, calm down. It was a leap for science, yes, but more Tom actually. Though I hope it never goes so far as to affect evolution. Kind of bogus, coming from you."

"I'm glad you said that about Tom."

"What difference does it make?"

Keller watched as she collected herself, ignoring him. Behind her, in the distance, the Kid had stopped too, noticing the two of them and Cassy's raised voice.

"Mind you, the wife is trying to launch a lawsuit. Ironic," Keller added.

"Who cares? I want to meet him."

"Be careful; he can be aggressive."

"Why, did he punch your lights out? Probably what you needed," she said, a little smile cracking.

They strolled over to the edge where the grass met the wood, and the Kid continued to play. He ducked behind trees, pretending to be shot at, rolled along the ground and took shots himself. When they were 3 m or so away, they stopped walking and watched. The Kid did a few more rolls, leaping further and falling harder than before. He got up from one particularly heroic move, looked at them directly and came forward, breathing with his mouth open, serious eyes soaking in the audience.

"Bravo," Cassy shouted, clapping. "You could work as a stuntman anytime."

"You'll need to talk to my agent."

"I'll keep that in mind."

"So you must be the bot," he said, walking up to them.

"I am. You've heard of me?"

"Not directly, but I overheard of you. Cassy V23. You look not bad."

"Thank you. I seem to 'look not bad' to a few of you here," she said, glancing at Keller.

"No, I mean, you're beautiful. If you were my girlfriend, I'd build a fort with my bare hands for you."

"How very kind. I must add, you're quite handsome yourself."

"Yeah, I know, I rock."

The Kid blushed, looked down and back up, a mischievous smile appearing.

Cassy began walking away from Keller, and the Kid joined her. "I've heard you can be quite a fearsome lot if you wish," she began. The Kid responded, laughing.

Keller left them to it and they strolled towards the low stone wall bordering a falconry. He could see they were horsing around and laughing, then talking freely — the late afternoon sun haloed their heads and shoulders, tiny bugs darted about. *They've made an instant connection, like a long-lost brother and sister.* He entered his phone to find numerous messages from Henrik, some of which had already been answered by Cassy during the 'emergency evac'. Keller also read her request to return with his own unconscious self, insisting she had approval from Simon.

Keller noted Simon's number had been called, and they had talked for 3 minutes. Henrik had agreed. *Henrik is certainly not afraid of synths.*

After a further, furtive exchange, Cassy and the Kid parted. The Kid headed for the guardhouse, and Cassy turned back. *She looks more relaxed. Is that even possible?*

"He's a good kid," she said, brushing a wavy lock from her face.

"Looks like he cheered you up."

"Yeah, he did," she said and left it at that. They continued their walk to the mansion.

Henrik appeared at an open lounge window when they rounded the corner and motioned for them to hurry and come in. As they walked in through the front entrance, Cassy gasped. Keller noticed and asked, "Did you really mean that or was that elite programming?" A fleeting expression of surprise crossed her face, hurtful, smothered by a smile.

"Programming most likely. I don't keep track, Keller. Do I have permission to enjoy myself?"

"Yes, of course. Well said." *The perturbed face, that was slick.*

They walked past reception and into the lounge area. Emma sat reading, and Henrik sipped his tea. Keller noted the dilated pupils, nodded to him and introduced the Cassandra V23.

"What the hell happened to you?" Henrik cut to the chase.

"An old lift shaft collapsed," Cassy replied. "I called you, remember?"

"It did. Oh, and I'm fine. Cassy pulled me out. We were investigating an older part, on a hunch," Keller interjected, his aggravation for Henrik apparent.

"What older part? You find anything?" Ed's voice came over the loudspeaker with a bit of added bass.

"No. I mean, not in the tunnel. But I did find Cassy," Keller continued, unfrazzled.

"Yes, and now here she is. Why? Why was I not consulted?"

"Didn't she already tell you?" Keller said, seeing a sudden jolt on Cassy's face.

"Why?!" Ed thundered.

"Because she proves that my father's theories work and that a human can be transferred to an android body, a synth as some call it," Keller spat out.

Even Emma looked up. Ed remained quiet, and Henrik sipped his tea, commenting to himself. Cassy shot a glance at Keller but also said nothing. Keller studied her every facial expression. The personality under the face knew what mistrust was, he thought.

"Tell them who programmed you, Cassy."

Cassy did not speak and then, "That's classified information; I don't get to know that."

"She's right, she doesn't," Henrik chimed in.

"I bet she does. So, we keep her here, ask questions, study her. I have been inspired by this synthetic person to think that this is all possible. Because someone like her, a synth, was the original target of Tom's work. Considering he was successful, it's most likely that a transfer, an infusion, can be achieved with a *blank*, organic human body, in a similar fashion," Keller announced.

"Blank? I put memories in it. It has food for consciousness," Henrik retorted. "And there's absolutely no basis for assuming she used to be human."

"Yes, of course. Except that she behaves like one. Too many imperfections for a synth. And why did you choose this island Henrik? Enlighten us once more."

Silence.

"Your stunt with the Kid proves a clone can have anyone's memories and still live and not go crazy. I imagine it varies from person to person," Keller continued.

"I disagree about the Kid, he's not exactly Myron Saltmarsh, is he? Our next volunteer, Francine, is on her way Keller, do you think you'll make it work this time? With Cassy at your side?" Ed jested.

"Perhaps. It's up to Francine herself. If she wants it. And she still has to want it after she's dead, or else... You can't expect someone who died against their will to be friends with their murderer after the fact. Perfect bod or not."

"Allow me to reiterate. We *won't* kill anyone. Make sure she knows that there's a choice. Especially if she tries to flee after flatlining," Ed said.

"Death is a very emotional moment. It's not so cut and dry, but I'll do my best."

"As long as you get the job done. And I like the term 'infusion', like vegetable infusion. You take a human vegetable, someone stupid enough to try this, and infuse them with themselves," he said with a moaning laugh.

The conversation continued on into details and timing. Even Ed took part with interest, having been given hope, his convoluted guard slipping momentarily. The group congealed like a festering wound after a sound cleaning—at least the puss was no longer visible. Whether it relapsed or survived was another matter.

Keller realized he had been squinting to keep focus. The room had been pulsing somewhat, which might have borne an odd facial expression. Presently he reached to pick up his cup of coffee, but his index finger missed the handle loop. The cup tipped as he bumped it, and coffee spilt. Keller retracted his hand.

"Did something happen to your eyesight? Dexterity?" Ed asked.

"My sight is fine. I'm tired is all."

"After a day of rest? Emma can provide you with a sedative if you wish."

"No, I can provide myself with whatever I need. Bring on Francine, I'm ready," Keller announced as he left the lounge. His vision was distorted; it was annoying. On his way out from the lounge his hand missed the door latch. He grabbed hold of it on his second try, wrenched the door open and bumped the jamb with his shoulder upon exiting.

"What's up with you?" Cassy said, having followed him out. "I thought things were going well; even the crack about me got them thinking. Then you start behaving like you're on something."

"Ed's a coward. If I behave boldly, he gets confused. He's used to Henrik obliging his every wish," Keller replied, massaging his eyes.

"Don't rub so hard, it's like scratching a wound. Let them heal," Cassy said, gently taking his hand away from his face.

"Where are you staying?" Keller said, dropping his hand to his side.

"Emma has me upstairs, down the hall from Violet and the Kid."

"Okay, a good place to charge up from. It's been a long day."

"Please, no more stupid comments."

Back in the lounge, Henrik remained for tea and as he collected his cup and saucer, Ed spoke, his line still live. "What actually happened in the bunker?"

"It's hard to say, I'll question him tomorrow. But he sounds convinced, despite his somewhat fragmented focus."

"I'm not sure I believe him. We would have known if there had been such a success by Tom. I've been hacking the Neufeld for years. Unless the system is holding her as a decoy. Keller is buying time; the required rest and bad eyes says a lot."

"He left a lamb and returned a lion. The part about Cassy, that was ah, probably a joke," Henrik added cynically.

"Precisely. There's a reason for it—he's unstable both psychologically and physically. Kill the next volunteer if you

have to, Keller may be better off in prison. It'll make life simpler;
I won't have to worry about him wandering off."

"We agreed we wouldn't do that."

"He has a week left. Let's keep him to it, especially now that
he has his assistant. Why did you let her in? Simon doesn't need
to know details."

"And he won't, I've spoken with him. I also have the codes
for her debilitation and shut down. Oldish model, right down
my alley," Henrik illustrated smugly.

"Fine, then give her a go. If she acts up, slam the off switch,
and ship her back, current memory erased."

Henrik had nothing to add, his thumb rubbing the little
medicine box in his pocket. *Ed the contradiction. Our synth visitor
left with a book, bet you missed that.*

Chapter 31

A woman drove along the road from Wroxall to the Jolly More Mansion, pulled over a few meters from the gate, turned off the engine, and waited. She was much too far from the intercom to buzz and decided she wouldn't get out of her car to walk over to it. She tried spotting the clinic down the lane and saw a fragment of the beautiful mansion. A security guard appeared through a side gate and approached the car. He was holding a clipboard.

"Good morning, madam. Are we expecting you today?" he said through the closed window, noticing her finger arced over the opener but hadn't pressed it yet.

Judging by his tattoos and ruddy face, she felt he was an ex-con. Or a murderer out on parole. Or not caught yet. Now was her chance to say: No, just looking. What house is that? Just passing by, had to check my phone, sorry to block, am I in the way? She surprised herself by pressing the window opener instead. "Yes, I believe you are. This is The Jolly More, right?" *He is dashing in a twisted kind of muscle memory sense.*

"Sure is," he said, pressing a remote; the gate opened. "Is it Mrs Sanders?"

"Yes, call me Francine."

"Drive straight ahead, parking is to the right, Francine. Walk to the main entrance around the other side of the house, opposite the fountain."

"Fountain, sounds nice. Are the people here crazy?"

"No madam, there is an entire staff of medical personnel ready to deliver your procedure, whatever that may be."

"Right, okay. See you later." *Christ, please don't say madam again.*

Francine drove in and over to the parking lot, where she again procrastinated in her car. She could see the side of the house; it was beautiful. Beyond there was a field and indeed she could make out the side of a fountain. *What am I doing?*

Tears streamed down her cheeks as her life's failures ganged up on her at once. *This could be the end, a total dud.* A few minutes later, she exhaled deeply, grabbed her things from the boot and headed for the entrance. Upon entering, relief flooded in as her first impression measured up to what she saw on the site. Then she noted the receptionist.

"I know she's here; what do you want me to say, Vernon, that I copy that?" the receptionist purred into the telephone, a period piece from the last century which was quite large compared to her head. She stood up as Francine came forward, pulling along her suitcase, the little wheels clicking at each tile space.

"Hello dear, we were expecting you. I'll call a nurse to take her up to your room."

"Room?"

"Yes, let's drop off your things and get settled," Emma said, entering from the lounge with Cassy right behind. "And then if —."

"How very dear of you," Francine interrupted, her gaze settling on Cassy, then back to Emma. "And I know my clone has been created, so I'm quite committed, but let's do the tour first, shall we?"

The receptionist mustered a smile, which uncovered an array of crooked and chipped teeth stained by cigarette smoking. Emma introduced herself and engaged Francine, answering her questions, giving a little history on the Jolly More and gearing up for a tour.

While listening, Francine leaned back a few inches and looked over at Cassy, as if testing to see if she could entice a reaction. Cassy looked back at her directly, with a small nod, raising her lips at the corners benevolently, calmness radiating from her hazel eyes. The woman breathed deeply, a sigh of steeling herself. She walked up to Cassy and looked some more. "What the fuck are you?" She turned back to Emma and the receptionist. "What is this? Is that a clone? Is that how I'll end up?"

"No, honey, she's not human, not a clone. Purely synthetic. Good eye for noticing; most people just see a pretty face."

"I'm a lawyer. Been looking into people's faces all my life, seeing if they're telling the truth. You get a feeling for it after a while."

"I see. That won't be you, unless you want to go for it," Emma continued as she guided Francine out of reception and into the lounge.

"Nope, I'm fine with organic."

"So, let me give you the tour. This is our lounge."

"It's beautiful, spacious."

"Would you like some tea or coffee?"

They sat and talked a while. Emma showed her the transfer room but insisted it was best to see her clone in the morning. And only once a contract was fully signed could a person enter the Clone Hall. While Francine feigned awe, she also became gravely disturbed. Though she was terminally ill, her upbringing frowned on intervening with God's work, as she put it. She wasn't sure and doubted her ability to make the jump. Then, with a slip of the tongue, Emma mentioned Keller Mod. Francine turned a lighter shade and looked over her cup at Emma.

"The man who is wanted for murder, for raping and killing that woman?"

"*Was* falsely accused. I mean, c'mon."

"You don't know that, the news is full of crap."

"That's what I mean. How about you meet him and judge for yourself?"

"Yes, I'd like that. What's he doing here? Working in the kitchen?"

"Mr Mod is our transfer specialist. He's a psychic. He has spent years working with the government on projects like this and now he is an acting consultant. He'll be helping with your transfer. Remember, he's brought many a poor soul back in the past, so this makes it a fabulous fit. I'm sure *He* won't mind either," Emma boasted, rolling her eyes upward.

Francine said nothing but looked out of the window, sipping her tea and enjoying a truffle. As her thoughts reached for the edge of the wood, Emma's voice became distant. She felt a warmth expand in her chest and brightness creep into her mind. The décor in the lounge perked up, and she noticed sunshine flooding the window, having escaped a barrage of clouds. *The truffles are a touch bitter and it's not the dark chocolate. She's given me Alprazolam, just in time.*

Out at reception, Cassy flipped through the woman's file the receptionist had reluctantly handed over. "She doesn't want to stay; she's freaked out."

"She's freaked out at you, dear, not the rest of us," the receptionist countered.

"I'm not sure of that. I'm actually surprised she could tell."

"You've been underground too long. This is the real world dear; better keep your wits about you."

Cassy studied the facial expression that the receptionist's semi-transparent skin made over top of her lean facial muscles and bone. Noticing herself gawk, Cassy looked away, then back to Francine's folder. It was patchy at best. During her preliminary visits and tests at a dodgy clinic in London, she had expressed caution. If things went wrong and the woman survived, she could bring on a lawsuit. *Herself.* Cassy searched for her online, tapping into the modem nearby. Francine was on the net, showcased along with numerous cases where she had triumphed, some of them long shots. *She's a fighter. The bitch might be just the one to do this.*

Keller stood by a window in the lounge, looking out behind the house, watching the Kid engage in a make-believe duel with a forest monster. A light fog had settled, adding an aura of mystery to the scene. He made out the falcon circling in the white soup further on and looked below to see a couple standing and talking by a low stone wall, a surreal sight. He thought one looked like the falconer; judging by the leather on his forearm — it must be his bird. The other, a woman, was dressed in traditional English garb from the last century as if she had walked off of a movie set. His eyes moved back to the Kid as he made a particularly grand stab, holding, then thrusting further. *Must be killing it.* When he looked back at the couple and falcon, they had vanished. His concentration was sporadic as of late; had they entered the mirk of the fog? The falcon was a bird of prey, after all, elusive and elegant. But the people had been standing.

Keller checked his watch. It was 6:15. The new arrival, Francine, was upstairs. She had agreed to stay after all. Tomorrow, he would attempt to infuse a clone with her ghost. Tonight, he would go for a walk, see the falconer and his lady perhaps, if they were out. *Is a film being shot?*

Chapter 32

When Keller arrived in the infusion room the following morning, Emma, Henrik, the orderly and Cassy were preparing. Two operating tables were set up, side by side, with matching shape settings. Both well-endowed with straps. IVs and monitors were off to their respective sides adding symmetry to the view—the memory machine itself remained central, a focal point, an indifferent host with an unearthly purpose.

A hoist, operated from a steel rail 2 m above the clone tanks, was positioned over Clone Francine, which stood peacefully, eyes closed. Its complexion and lean, firm build were more healthy, smooth and fuller than its original's. The clone was seated in a harness and hoisted vertically out of its tank. It remained unconscious while swung over, dripping softly onto the marble floor, and lowered to a trolley.

The orderly wheeled her to the left operating table and, together with Cassy, transferred her on with a quick lift and swing. The body remained relaxed.

After being re-hooked to a monitor, its heartbeat proved steady and robust. Clone Francine did not breathe. Instead of reconnecting the synthetic embryonic tube to its stomach as an oxygen supply, the clone was resuscitated much like a drowning victim. After being triggered, the preprogrammed and duplicate genetic memories injected by Henrik lead it to fight and survive.

In another five minutes, it coughed up the liquid not yet absorbed by its lungs, sputtered and breathed on its own.

Francine arrived at the lab, head shaved, along with the orderly. She was still apprehensive but in admirable spirits, commenting on the excellent coffee and breakfast. She stopped as she noticed the younger version of herself, laying calmly on the table, also shaved.

"Good morning Francine," Emma began.

"Morning," she replied, her eyes riveted to the body.

"Come and have a look," Emma continued, "It's okay. She's asleep."

"But breathing. This is no joke," Francine countered.

"No joke. Color's good too, wouldn't you say?"

"Ahem, yeah, better than mine right now," she let out a nervous, broken chuckle.

"You can touch her; she's warm. No need to be afraid; it's human. A big baby, you might say."

"Real big," Francine said as her fingers lightly ran along the clone's forearm. "You've gone with a tiny bit of hair; I would have just had none."

"It was created using your own DNA, as we discussed in the beginning. Not necessary to change anything at this point. All you have to do is pick up the reigns."

Francine took the clone by its hand gingerly and giggled.

"She's not gonna suddenly wake up, is she?"

"No, you'll have to do the waking up, sweetheart."

From Francine's point of view, the clone's face was blank, not yet infused with the tribulations and joys of life. It hadn't worked, worried, felt pain to any degree or failure. It hadn't laughed, cried, loved or hated. Francine's own life randomly passed before her eyes as she strove to grasp what was missing from the expression of the unconscious clone. She saw her mother sleeping when she was a child, her dog jumping on her, feeling afraid to swim, falling off her bike, then loving swimming, working at a part-time job she hated, her first kiss, driving too fast, her father scolding her, sitting with her cousin by a fire, losing her virginity, skipping class, university, mom dying, her professor a friend, an enemy, her first case, her job, marriage, giving birth, twice — she paused there, blank. Then her doctor telling her she had cancer, the cancer receding, the cancer benign, then not, then depression, searching the dark web, her son hugging her. The other one standing back, crying. My sons... Then the incident of her lying to her husband about the business trip she was on. 'My client wants to sue a clinic on the Isle of Wight,' she had told him.

"You'll be inside of it, and it should feel similar to how you do now," Keller said. "You will have fresh organs and a new musculature, skin — it should arguably feel better. Just needs to be worn in."

"Like a shoe, nice. New nervous system, I hope," Francine added, "Mine is shot."

"That too," he said, "And afterwards, you can live here a while as you get used to things."

"All right," Francine became resolute. "Let's do this. If we wait any longer, I'm afraid I'm gonna run. Drugs or no drugs. I already don't know how to explain looking like that to my husband. He's Christian and —"

"One step at a time. We'll deal with it when we get there. Think of it as a succession of nips and tucks."

Emma and Cassy helped Francine lay down on the table and strapped her in snuggly. Both bodies were in a zero-gravity position, much like cradled babies.

Keller explained the procedure, including the silicone caps and transferring of memories. Her temp would get taken down to 12°C. The table itself had a refrigeration system winding through it, and she was to be injected with coolant. The bodysuit she wore doubled as a cooling jacket. She could be warmed up at any time, but would in fact, be flatlining soon enough.

Francine darted a look at him while Emma administered the first dose of anesthetic, which calmed her in the following seconds. Keller nodded to Henrik, who readied the memory machine, Cassy assisting.

Francine gazed over at the clone, following its profile, watching its chest rise a touch and then fall. Then Francine panicked. She fought as fear unleashed upon her body and soul. Angry veins popped out on her face and body as she struggled to wrestle free of the wide, soft touch straps. Finding it hopeless, she shouted orders instead.

"This is insane; let me out!" she gargled from her numb throat, her popped-open wild eyes painfully spilling the turmoil raging within.

Chapter 33

"Your eyesight OK today, Keller?" Henrik asked.

"Yeah, peachy," Keller answered, realizing he was squinting again. "I squint from time to time, doesn't mean much, just some irritation."

"Keller, you know whom you're talking to, right? If I thought it was a minor irritation, I wouldn't ask. Or I'd suggest drops. Your facial expressions suggest you're seeing something we're not. Like you're in your head, watching something. And your eyes look much younger, very white sclerae, clean irises. The opposite of mine. Except that before you ventured to Ironsmith, your eyes were also bloodshot and stressed."

"My, aren't we chipper today."

"Keller, there's something you're not telling me."

"And there's a whole lot you're not telling *me*."

Henrik continued setting up the memory machine after glancing at Cassy. He prepared the skull caps made of transparent silicone rubber and filled with a multitudinous network of fine wires, creating a pattern throughout. At every millimeter, a wire left the network and descended to touch the skin of the skull.

"She didn't mind being shaved?" Henrik asked.

"She did, even teared up. Then finally gave in," said Emma.

Francine, who had received the rest of her anesthetic dose and had been considerably cooled off both mentally and physically, headed quickly to her body core destination temp of 12°. She lay next to her clone, who appeared relaxed and asleep. At the front of the room tall windows with vision blinds revealed tree shapes and fluffy clouds.

Behind the bodies and in front of an empty counter, the memory machine stood silent, bundles of colored wires gushing from its sides. Both heads were illustrated in 3D on a monitor. Henrik wiggled the cap onto Francine's lubricated head. He stood back to double-check the alignment to the delicate markings on her skin. A duplicate cap was placed on to the clone's head. Finally, he typed a string of code into a field below the 3D heads and hit return. The heads began revolving as each initialized its cap, ensuring a connection. The bundles of wires twitched slightly as the initialization was completed. Henrik typed more code.

Soon, the monitor revealed flickering images being transferred at an alarming rate. Aside from random glitching, thousands passed by each second. A lifetime for Francine, 46, would take approximately one to two hours to complete, depending on the density of the images. In essence, on her past ability to capture detail using all of her perceptions.

Complete after an hour and twenty, the screen ran blank. Henrik typed in more code, and the machine stopped. He pulled the caps from the bodies' heads. A few minutes later, Francine flatlined. Her shallow breathing and faint heartbeat were no more.

Keller had been standing next to Francine in her final hour. The memories didn't interest him; instead, her soul did. Gouyen flashed before him, as did his lunatic mother, his grandfather's death and the various signs left behind at the morgue, the notes. Nora's face and then Augusts—irate before he walked a way to join the dead. *Why Nora's face in all of that morass? Because it doesn't bother her…*

Keller walked away from the body and over to the windows. He turned back towards the room. Behind the machine and to the right, sitting on the counter, was the terminally ill lawyer. Watching. Instead of denying the monochromatic, translucent hallucination, Keller decided this time he would play it through, making the 'vision' easier to iterate and describe later. The data which came forth was meant for *him* and difficult to transcribe into language. Then he decided *he* was just *him* talking to himself and discarded thought altogether, as best he could. *Let loose, don't try.* He observed what he saw as fact and treated the situation like it were *real*. The woman was dead; the monitor she was hooked up to proved it. *This is real. So don't let it bother you as if it's not.*

As he walked up to a greyish Francine, she simply stared at him, a little shocked that he could see her.

"Easy does it, Francine. How are you doing?"

"Am I dead? Dumb question, I guess."

"Yep. As a doorknob."

"Funny. I didn't think it would be like this."

"So, you gonna stick around? Your choice."

"My choice, yes, I realize that. But no one else sees us, right? Just you and I here, Keller. I don't think the others even have a clue. I mean, look at the droid. Even she looks confused—can't compute why you're talking to yourself. And Henrik, amused. Emma, yeah, she believed in you. But even she doesn't know a god-damn thing," Francine spoke, aggression tinging her tone.

"It's basically a decision to live. Take the clone; try it. If you want, I'll shoot you later," Keller said, trying to keep up with her tough cool.

"You're joking, right?"

"Your husband and children are waiting for you at home; go for it."

"And what do you think will happen if I show up looking like that?" she said, nodding to her clone.

Keller noticed numerous *others* had joined them, watching to see the outcome. Keller froze. He hadn't expected company and since they all seemed to tune in and out like poor reception, it was overwhelming. Keller turned back to Francine, who proceeded to hop off the counter and walk toward him. "Enjoying the party? I actually feel pretty good, but I'm sure as hell not getting into that thing. It's not me," she said, evil replacing the mild aggression.

"It could be you. It's healthy, strong, it can wake up and live if you choose it."

"I doubt that Keller. Looks like Frankenstein to me. Worse, at least with Frankenstein, it was obvious he was a monster. This one is gorgeous, thanks to my genes. I'm not about to live a life of horror just so you can tell yourselves you've achieved fake immortality in a human. That's not my life, Keller. What I had before you killed it was my life. For better or for worse."

"I can bring the temp up, we resuscitate, and you can have your old self back. That's fine with me. Totally fine."

"Bullshit. Murder is murder, Keller, and you just committed it. I've left a very detailed outline of how my husband should bring this to court. It's only a matter of time before he figures things out. You're going to prison, and my family will live well without me. I had little time left, anyway."

"This isn't about court or documents or settlements; I'm not here for that."

"It is for me." She turned and faded.

"Francine!" Keller yelled after her. "This is beyond anything anyone can imagine. No one will believe him!" Her fleeting shadow taunted his perceptions, challenging him to make a move. Once more, Keller summoned the zeal he had in the past when people hung on the edge, but this time he felt fake. He could *see* she was indifferent. She wasn't struggling for her last breath or bleeding out. She had planned this, not trusting the outcome. Not trusting the empty voice of the receptionist, the smooth-talking manner of Emma or the rantings of a drug addict, Henrik, was not a surprise. *Did Ed talk to her?* Francine had already seen all manners of trickery in the courts and out. Void of vested interest, probably beneath her, she came after them instead. *Gutsy.*

Cassy had walked over to them and touched Keller on the elbow. "What's going on? Who are you looking at? You were talking to *her,* right?"

"Yeah, and she's gone."

Cassy stepped back rattled, an awkward expression for a synth, but she pulled it off.

"That's it, she's dead?"

"Looks like it."

"So do something!"

"I will, it won't matter."

"So we've just killed somebody!"

"Yeah. But take it down a notch, it's what we do here," Keller said, frigid.

Cassy retreated further, horrified. Her eyes glazed over, reddening in protest of impossible tears.

Keller turned to Henrik and Emma. "Heat Francine back up," he said, not knowing if what he had witnessed was real. *It was bloody real.* Cassy looked petrified, Henrik appeared dubious, and Emma perplexed. He would check the video footage later. Many After Life enthusiasts had claimed to capture spirits on camera when the eye could not see them. His father's research was full of it. Keller didn't believe in such.

Now he scrambled about Francine's body, his own losing sensitivity, adjusting dials in the table to bring her core temperature back up to normal. Emma reversed the suit's temp and Henrik, the intravenous. Cassy stood clear. Ed remained silent; no one had checked to see if he was online.

The inquisitive souls lingered and gathered around the clone. But sensing it would need assistance to live, didn't make a move—taking a fully grown, inexperienced body for a spin meant someone had to start it up and keep it that way; there were no parents to help. While a few commented, Keller ignored them. He could feel some and see shadows of others. A few tuned in quite well—none were Francine.

This is where the Kid must have been brave, Keller thought, as his own fear subsided. It was like taking a life-threatening risk, only far more intense, an unexpected dimension added. The dead surrounded him, and he hated them and what they stood for—failures to move on or even care. Failures to admit it was over. Like anyone who hangs on to how it was, no matter the cost or whom they were burning.

The idea of ghosts and spirits led his father to go insane or appear convincingly so, and even worked to inspire. While his own fear had melted, Keller felt cold. He had killed what had been a live person, someone's wife, mother, friend. Confusion blasted him as he searched once more for Francine amongst the old, watery spirits who were also fading. He wanted to deliver an appeal from the heart, but she was nowhere to be seen.

It took about 3 hours to heat her body back up. It lay on the table without so much as a flinch, the entire time. The calm expression of death on her face—peaceful, smooth, nothing to suggest any struggle or change of mind had evolved. Despite all, she had lived her life and chosen a good time to leave.

Meanwhile, the clone was returned to the tank, lungs filled with liquid and connected to the umbilical cord once more. Keller ignored Henrik, who wore a stony look of concern. Perhaps he saw or felt something too, Keller wouldn't put it past him. But this was ludicrous. It was murder no matter the reason. Had the woman pulled the plug herself, it would have been different. That would have been assisted suicide, also illegal. Illegal for a reason.

When the body's temp reached 36, Keller didn't see or feel anyone return. Or anyone hover or make any comments to him.

The vitals were totally flat, and no amount of resuscitation helped. Adrenaline, electric shocks, it didn't matter, and Keller knew it. *She told me so herself, I heard her say it and I saw her go. No light on here.*

Keller left the Transfer Theatre. He strode through the lounge, gaining speed as he entered the reception area where the receptionist was missing. Late afternoon May light drifted in through the tall windows. The woman in the period costume whom he had seen by the stone wall entered just as Keller headed out. She stopped to get his attention. Keller looked at her, washed over by warmth, then suddenly angered that the previous day he had been so stupid as to seek her out at a film shoot that didn't exist. He walked past. *That's another one. Lost.*

He stepped onto the terrace, paused, then spun around. She was gone. *I know that face, but it can't be.* Instead of awaiting her return, he walked down the lane, out the gate and down the road. The guards let him be. Confusion had taken hold, and Keller didn't fight the grip. He bathed in it—a madman swirling in a vortex of deceit.

Henrik and Cassy moved the body to a stretcher while Emma gave the orderly instructions. Ed, who had been silent the entire time, spoke up. "I take it she is dead."

"Yes," replied Henrik. Cassy squinted her eyes, turned and left to help the orderly.

"And Keller? Where did he rush off to? Not a convincing exhibit yet theatrical I must say."

"To get some fresh air, I imagine, he'll cool off and return. I'd like to know what happened—he sure played it like something did."

"Yes, let's sit down when he returns. His stay here is limited, only a few days left. Perhaps being relocated to prison will work out better for him," Ed muttered on.

"I'm not sure prison's inspiring for anyone. We need to find out what the antics were about, may lead to something."

"Henrik, is that droid getting emotional? I've never seen her quite like that."

Henrik glanced out the top of the window to ponder the clouds and had the good sense not to look at the camera. His blood pressure spiked, his hands revealed a tremble, so he subtly transferred them to his pockets. *This is someone who knows this particular synth.*

Chapter 34

Despite what Henrik told Ed, Keller did not return, at least not that evening. He walked to town, entered The Colonel Pub and ordered a whiskey straight up with a beer chaser. Then he had a second. Next, he thought of texting Nora, not that he expected her to reply. He wondered if she had seen the news and if she would ever meet him again. Instead, he ordered a cab and waited for it to arrive, with a third drink followed by one for the road.

His route was straightforward. First, he needed to catch a ferry to the mainland. Then he would drop by August's ex-wife, Jennifer, who still lived in Ipsworth.

Keller needed answers. Afterwards, he might visit Bruno at his home. If the police picked him up for questioning, so be it. If he exposed the clinic, his sentence might be reduced, but if he continued to murder people, it would get worse. He was not chipped. Henrik had reverted to complete animalism and could not be trusted nor counted upon for anything. Emma, well, she could take care of herself. Cassy would be returned to the bunker, perhaps reprogrammed, and the receptionist, the orderly and the others—he could not worry about them now.

The alcohol was taking effect. Nevertheless, the sensation of having killed someone scraped at the lining of his skull, reverberating dully through his mind.

Time was not on his side; Keller felt his inner clock nag. Life would get threateningly complicated if he didn't discover Ed and stop him. Pulling off a successful transfer didn't seem like a solution anymore, never was. *It's murderous curiosity.*

In a few hours Keller found himself on Highstreet in Ipswitch. To play along with his own game, Keller walked down to the memorial gardens with a spiked coffee and sat down on a park bench. He threw two pieces of breath gum in his mouth and chewed. After a while, he pulled his microchip from a compartment in his wallet and stuffed it into the gobby ball. He pressed that under the park bench seat and resumed drinking coffee. *I'll be gone an hour. If my chip remains on the radar, they won't track the phone. Like I should care.*

Next, Keller googled Jennifer's address. It would be a 15-minute walk, so off he went. On his way, he tossed the empty cup and felt at ease amongst the others who used the park as a living room or backyard.

The residence he sought was situated in a row house on a dead-end street. A few meters along the drive a sturdy door, befriended by a plain bay window and a tabby cat leering from between curtains, beckoned. Keller had rehearsed many scenarios, which now evaded him. Visions popped up here and there, and his eyesight was periodically fuzzy. He hadn't eaten since breakfast but decided it was better to visit now than miss the chance. Not that he knew she was home.

Keller rang the doorbell, and instantly a dog barked. It was a high-pitched, consecutive series of yelps which suggested a small, cute dog. The kind you might use as shark bait. Keller focused himself on the now. The woman who answered the door was attractive—a compulsive smiler who felt she had to cover her teeth. *Good natured.*

"Yes, can I help you?" she said, the door barely ajar.

"I'm looking for Jennifer Tulip, ex-wife of August Matthews."

"That's me. What does this concern? Are you a friend of August? You look like you've had a drink, and I don't tolerate that in my house, so I'm afraid you'll have to call back. Or don't bother," she let out in a tight string.

"I have a few questions regarding his latest endeavor at the Jolly More Mansion. I've had a rough day and need a little information."

"It's that guy who was in the news and who I met at the Jolly More," a hidden voice spoke. It sounded familiar, and Keller's mind spun to locate a match as the man appeared at the door, jolting it open. Keller shrunk back in disbelief; the vision didn't have the telltale signs of a hallucination; it was no ghost. His thoughts wove through the clone room, he personally saw Clone August there the other day, it wasn't that. *This is the dead August.* Keller wanted to punch the wall in front of him, grab the door latch and rip it off, anything to get himself down to earth. He sucked a breath, steadied himself, and looked at the man. *Can't be a duplicate. He's the original.*

"You have a lot of nerve coming here after all the papers I signed. I was told the clinic would never try to contact me, and now here you are. Smelling like whiskey, no less. What a joke," the man rattled off.

"The clinic didn't send me. I thought you were ah…"

"I'm not. Now this violates our agreement. I can call the police and have them investigate. Is that what you want because I can say for sure you're guilty as hell for attempted murder."

"Please don't, I was just checking up."

"To see if my wife's free? Mourning? Screw off, you bastard," he said; Jennifer pulled him back and sent him to sit in the living room.

"Keller Mod is it, am I correct?" she asked, returning to the door.

"Yes."

"It's not smart what you're doing. But I'd like to hear your side of the story. I have my husband back, and he's been sober since returning. We're still divorced, but he's a changed man. I think it was his 'near-death experience' which changed things around. Come in." *She cares, it shows in her eyes.*

Keller was suddenly thirsty. He rarely stopped to drink water but when he needed it, he just put his face under the tap and drank. He needed to do that now. The desert sun was high in the air and the antler woman had finished talking. She smiled at him and gave him two of the little blossoms. "Forget-Me-Not," she said, fading. Keller looked down at the blossoms but when he looked up, she was gone, along with the entire field of Scorpion Grass growing in the sand.

He could hear someone in the distance talking, it was Jennifer. He found himself in a living room, average, nicely done in pastels and worn around the edges.

"You okay? Really shouldn't drink."

"Probably right, just today I—"

"How did you decide to see us?"

"I'm trying to understand a few things and need answers. August being alive changes things, but not everything. Did you receive any money in the end?"

"20% for taking part but not succeeding. Was supposed to be 40. The nerve of those people," Jennifer said, but with little force.

"Who were you in contact with?"

"A lady, very abrupt, didn't give a name. Mansion administrator, she said, quite impersonal, all considering."

The receptionist. "I'd like to apologize for such rudeness at a time like this, when your ex-husband's life was almost taken."

"Don't bother. Keller, do you actually work there? I mean, I've heard about you in the press and aside from the murder story, which I understand it wasn't you, you don't seem the type.

August said he discovered the clinic on the dark web. Mind you, his frame of mind was different then."

"Yeah, I know. And no, I don't work there. I was invited to consult but I'm worried about the organization's integrity, and I'm trying to reach upper management."

"Let me guess," August had returned, "You probably don't know who that even is."

"No."

"I tried to do a search on them and found nothing. Though the medical office in London seemed legit—they were simply collecting samples and doing scans. When I got to the Jolly More, Nurse Emma overwhelmed me, used sedatives. I realize I let her though, my bad. Was pretty hungover that day," he said, shooting a glance at his ex.

"Well, a miracle did happen," Jenny took over again. "Albeit not quite how I might have expected things to pan out, but it did. Moments of crisis can catalyze such things."

They talked a while longer, August even explaining some things he remembered happening, seeing Keller for one who evidently *saw* him. "I'm still not sure if it was a dream or what. But I had croaked, I guess, for a few minutes. Or longer."

"More like hours. I saw it too," Keller added. *He explained my hallucination exactly. So, must not have been a hallucination. None of this is.* Keller's mind stopped thinking.

"Do you make a lot of money from this Mr Mod?"

"Not a pence."

"So why are you consulting for them and attempting to do something brutally impossible? What happened? Considering you almost took my ex-husband's life, I think we have a right to know." They both looked at him now, waiting for an answer. The delicacy of the situation suddenly dawned on Keller, he had to watch what he said. With Ed's creativity and reach, things could get dangerous.

At that moment, his cell rang. It was Cassy. Keller insisted he had to take it. "Yes?"

"Keller, where are you? I mean, Henrik thinks you're in Ipswitch, sitting in a park, but I'm not so sure."

"I'll call you back, can't talk now."

"Keller, there's something I have to tell you."

"Later."

"Watch yourself. Get back soon."

He hung up and turned to the couple. "The less I say right now, the better. Trust me on this; I'm not impervious to the horror. Going to the authorities now would be a mistake, especially since we don't know who Ed is. The voice. *He* set me up for murder in Brighton and since then I've met the woman I allegedly killed. She's alive and well and so are you."

The couple was shocked yet unsatisfied with the answer, flickering subtle grimaces as they eyed each other. The wife shook her head slightly. "Well, we'll just have to keep it low-key for now, won't we," August said resolutely.

They exchanged telephone numbers and shook on it. Minutes later, Keller walked down the street and kept straight ahead. As he hit Highstreet, an assortment of people passed by, no doubt drifting from the shops and mall. A gaggle of skateboarders, an elderly Indian man with his granddaughter and a pregnant Polish woman in a heated discussion over the phone were amongst them. *How simple life can be if you don't screw with it. We don't need to live forever; we need to live here and now.*

Henrik, you had me fooled old friend. It could only have been you who saved August's life.

Returning to memorial gardens, he found a family eating ice-cream on his bench. He lingered at a distance until they left and then sat down as a young, rollerblading couple arrived nearby, gleefully braking and twisting onto the grass. Their dog sniffed Keller and even licked his hand with the gum. Keller petted the dog, keeping the gum away by dropping it in his front chest pocket. When the dog tried to climb on him, he pushed it back, scratching its ears.

Keller got up and left. He felt eyes were on him, but a few minutes later, looking back, the couple and dog were gone too. He could see them further along—she was losing control while he helped her regain balance, howling with laughter, dog jumping and wiggling its behind.

Chapter 35

"You were quite rude earlier today," a woman's voice cut in. Keller had loosened up, half daydreaming, soaking in the dusky countryside sliding by as the train picked up speed. After the announcer had welcomed the passengers and listed the forthcoming stops, all that remained were purring wheels, the shudder of the swaying car, and the contented murmur of voices. Keller had planned to doze off — it was impossible to miss his stop, as Brighton was the last.

The voice which stirred him crackled and hummed like an old radio transmission, AM band, with reception wavering. Keller half expected an elderly person playing a small portable sitting across the aisle listening to radio theatre. Keller turned, curious. What he saw was an apparition of the woman in historic attire sitting next to him, looking straight ahead, beaming. The one he had seen at the Jolly More entrance earlier that day and by the stone wall the previous evening. Her faded self was experiencing the same poor reception as her voice. But she was there, up close. Keller followed the line of her forehead down over the bridge of her nose, the upper lip, the sturdy chin. Upon closer scrutiny, the lines in her leathery skin denoted deeper weathering, echoed in the high cheekbones and dark eyes.

Can't be. Dressed as an Englishwoman?

Keller retracted from the vision, sweat beading on his forehead, pretending he saw nothing and looked out the window the other way.

"I see the boy I once knew has his eyes back, those that were lost, and he is no longer a boy. As a man, does he hide behind the years, hoping to forget something etched in the very core of his being?"

Keller turned back. There she was, poised, confident of her existence, the reception much better now, but the blood drained from his own face he imagined. His lips twitched; he couldn't speak. *Maybe I've fallen asleep. I was curious about her. I wanted to meet her on a bloody movie set... but I never expected this.*

"Gouyen?" he said, glancing around the train car.

"Hey Keller."

"Why are you dressed as an Englishwoman, sitting on a train acting like bad reception?"

"Because I can. And I'm trying to impress upon you."

"This is really jacking my nerves."

"Is that what you say to an old friend?"

Keller took a deep breath and calmed himself. "Actually, it's a relief to see you. Didn't recognize you back at the Jolly More, nor in the fog when you were standing by the wall with the falconer. Looks like you've lost the antlers..."

"The antlers I wore because I thought you might like them as a boy, did it work?"

"Ah, yeah, I guess. What are you doing here?"

"I've dropped by for a visit. And was curious about the mess at the Jolly More."

"This mess all started with that flower you gave me, just so you know."

"My, my, what a pretty little blossom can do."

"So, you've seen the mess, what now? What's the solution?"

"You, my friend. I think you're in a tight spot and need a little push."

Keller laughed. He wasn't sure if it was a giddy reaction or if he had heard a joke. Tears soon streamed from his eyes, relief pouring out with them. *Saved in the nick of time by my childhood friend, the bloody apparition.*

As the overhead speaker came on to announce the next stop, he simmered down. Keller looked over at Gouyen; she was still there smiling a patient smile, parting her lips as if to speak, breathe or just pass judgement, but kept quiet and closed them instead. The slight confusion in her eyes incited him to burst again, but he quashed it, darting a glance backwards at the couple who had reduced their conversation to a murmur and stared back at him. Keller didn't care.

"To be honest, I see you as a delusion in myself."

"I wasn't when you were a boy, why would I be now?"

"Because little boys have awesome imaginations. Limitless. Little girls too."

"And when they grow up, all is lost," Gouyen added with lighthearted sarcasm.

Keller stared at her a while. *No sense in looping through that which I've been looping through a million times. I'm not talking to myself here. Francine and her death was real, August is alive, the blossom was real, Cassy is acting weird, the Kid is alive, a creation of Henrik's. So, humor Gouyen and see where it leads.* "Ok, let's just agree you're not in my mind and my father did, in fact, engineer a way to see the dead using nanotechnology—targeting people, psychics, who can perceive the dead. Those stuck in-between."

"Or let's just say you're gifted; why do you deny yourself that?" she said, turning towards him in earnest.

"Because it just doesn't mix with this world. I'm a miserable wreck."

"That's not the Keller I remember."

"He grew up and has probably gone mad. For one, I thought you were much older," he said, quickly glancing at her.

"Back then, you were a little boy with a crush."

Keller shrugged but said nothing.

Gouyen behaved as if she were alive, chatting casually about things he didn't know or could barely remember — stories about his father, lab, and research. She explained how she had tried to help him at times, to speed things up, but Tom couldn't see or hear her. *I even tried crawling into his head. And then he went and blew himself up.* Keller didn't comment, taking what she said in stride. He thought of the letter.

"From what I gather then, your interest in all of this is so that you can come back to the world of the living in style. And not lose your mind on the way," Keller said. "And maybe you'd rather be a synth vs organic."

Gouyen just smiled and eventually looked past him and out the window. Then she suddenly looked back at him, "Bingo. Life is only interesting if you can survive it. Well. And plastic doesn't rot."

"Have you met Cassy?"

"Have you?" Gouyen said with evident mischief.

"Yes, down in the Neufeld — ." He cut short when he saw her face tilt to the side, brow arch and lips purse. He glanced around the train again. The politely dressed couple walked by him to the exit doors, getting ready for the next stop. Curious glances shot his way, ravenous eyes feasting on what could be the remains of a feeble mind. *Who am I kidding, Gouyen is real, always was. And Cassy…*

"What is that in your shirt pocket? It's soaking through," she began, the teaching face replaced by distaste.

Keller looked down and pulled out the chip wrapped in gum. In his efforts to reach the train on time, he had forgotten about it. He unraveled the gum and held up the chip.

"A tiny gadget I presume," she commented.

"The Morpheus Prison chip. Ed's harrowing leash. Cassy took mine out."

"Cassy, of course. Does the Kid have one, my dear Leonard?"

"Dear Leonard? I thought he was supposed to be Myron."

"Leonard beat Myron to the body. Before that, he remained on the island and refused to move forward. Or get sucked up by the tunnel of light. I'm glad he's having so much fun now."

"Nice for him to have fun while the rest of us endure purgatory."

"Perhaps. But you mustn't give up. You see, if you don't pick up the blade, someone else will. Ed is already vying for it. And look at the good surgeon who attempted to blow the whistle on your clinic."

"Not my clinic; what about him?"

"You've killed patients, so I'd say that makes it your clinic too, Keller."

"One patient. And she was very welcome to not die and remain with us. Her choice."

"Very well. If you can, I would kill the surgeon—if you think you're suffering...."

"I shouldn't kill anyone. Do you realize what I do for a living? I run a restaurant."

"You're good at it; Lucy's is quite popular. Though I think medicine and psychic endeavors are more your style."

Keller shrugged again. "My medical and psychic endeavors don't explain what you are. And I need to know. Because it also doesn't strike me as hallucination anymore."

"A hallucination? How unimaginative. 10,000 years of history on this earth, and that's the best you can consider?"

"For now. So what's in it for you if I succeed?"

"In the world of the dead, the in-between, one can still engage in magic and have terrific force. But having a few friends 'alive and well' would be exciting, don't you think? You only really start to understand life when you're about 90, but by then, it's no fun. I find it odd that the man attempting to change evolution hasn't grasped something so simple."

"Evolution? I doubt I'm there yet," Keller muttered vacantly.

"Personally, I think we created evolution ourselves so that we could be together in the first place. Instead of being lonely spirits cast out in the middle of space. Natural selection or unnatural selection, it doesn't matter. We make our decisions and that leads to evolution," she said, elbowing him in the ribs.

"Then nothing needs to be changed."

"Concentrate. Make the infusion, then we'll go from there."

"So, you tossed me a flower so we could work things out for you?" Keller said with a skeptical grin.

"Maybe. Do you think these illusions are easy to manufacture? You must try it yourself sometime; try making a simple little flower," Gouyen said with a smile.

"I really wish you hadn't."

As the train filled up it became increasingly difficult to talk. After a few words of departure, Gouyen vanished. Keller sat back. The man across the aisle shook his head and chuckled. Keller looked out the window and thought of the Scorpion Grass growing in the desert. He missed the endless, gigantic spaces, the searing heat. The cold, crystal clear night sky, which harbored a gazillion stars, and showed off the Milky Way. Then he thought of the dead mounting synthetic bodies and flying off to explore the unknown, Gouyen leading the charge. *Keep it together, Keller.*

Chapter 36

Cassy stood alone in the lab. She had received an unusual yet thorough tour, demonstrating and explaining the clone tanks and their inhabitants. It had been odd seeing Violet in there, so young, although they had never met. The tall, well-built man belonged to Ed, whoever he was. The alcoholic, August, was there too, as was Francine, who stood stone-faced. Something didn't add up, and her calculations kept repeating, finding no answer, rerunning. *There's a reason I was allowed to stay and see all of this. Stay sharp.*

When Cassy had enquired about the darkened tank, Emma skirted the question, claiming she didn't know, perhaps a developing body. It was exclusively Henrik's domain — only his thumbprint or that of Ed could lift the tint.

She eyed the memory machine now while Emma went off to check on the living Violet. Cassy wanted to look at what Francine had seen in her life, who her husband was, her children, and how she talked to them. If she accessed directly, would she view the memories as if they came from herself? Cassy rarely ventured so far into human emotions; her security work in the tunnel allowed little time. *This is based on Tom's prototype, yet I don't recall having had my memories scanned.*

"You need to turn it on first," a man's voice said from behind as Cassy looked at the blank monitor. It was Henrik. She didn't answer him.

"I'm sure you know that. Human memories, I bet you've had a few loaded into your database."

"Yes, quite a few. Images, of course, not memories per se. Data."

"Images with data, memories, they are similar. I like to call them home video," he said, flashing a hesitant smile.

Cassy turned and looked at Henrik thoroughly. His eyes were not clear, his hair a little lopsided as if he had been napping. There was a stain on his lab coat, probably from something he ate. This is the resident genius, she thought. *He's gradually losing control; it used to be his greatest asset.*

"Come, I'll show you," he said and pressed the power button as they both sat down—a smooth circle, part of a multitudinous array of 2 dimensional, symbolic looking controls surrounding a central keyboard. Cassy recognized the *touch-grip* keys—designed for humans—a key could be felt when touched, yet visually nothing suggested it was there aside from the symbol. The monitor blinked and a password field appeared, empty. Cassy looked away, and Henrik typed. "You can see it; I don't care. Amaryllis."

"How sweet. So, if something goes missing, you can question me, is that it?"

"Yes, I'd like that very much," Henrik chuckled. "But here, let me do a demo."

He proceeded to play a man's past, stopping randomly in his childhood, his teenage years, and through to events in his adult life. While the images streamed by in a blur, some were tagged. An AI had searched through 46,714,060,800 images which equaled 24 per second for 64 years, which was the man's age at the time of flatlining. The AI had been given specific parameters to 'tag'. In this case, a sudden change in speed, environment or action. Those images paused on screen, and if Henrik hit return when they did, the picture was copied to a separate folder.

In the next set, Henrik typed in 'kiss and run', and the AI spit out several sequences at the age of 5 where Myron kissed an older woman, his mother no doubt, and ran. The images played like a fuzzy movie, where the mother laughed sporadically. As the viewpoint shifted, Cassy could see the voluptuous woman reaching for what looked like a beer bottle.

"Whose memories are those?" Cassy asked.

"Myron Saltmarsh's—the Kid whom you've met."

"The billionaire client."

"Yes. Only the Kid doesn't behave like he knows anything about Myron the adult but claims that some of the childhood pictures are his—I've pulled random shots and shown him. But let's keep moving—see if you can spot an anomaly. This thing runs too fast for my liking, and if I slow it down, it can take weeks to watch."

"Well, I can see the images just fine; keep it rolling." They continued to observe. The voluptuous woman appeared often, and the child rarely left the house except to attend school in an old two-story schoolhouse on a quaint downtown corner. On his way home, the boy liked to pause at a pawnbroker and stare in the window. The images played on, some in full motion, others stunted.

"Slow here," she blurted. Henrik did as they came to a part where the viewpoint received injections on the arm. Henrik slowed more, studying them, then continued at a faster pace. More injections and IV as well. An extended period in a hospital bed. Views of the ceiling, a door to the hall, nurses and a doctor coming and going.

"I certainly hadn't noticed these," Henrik muttered. "Odd, very odd. Why don't I have a record of this? Why didn't he tell me?"

"Record of what? He's obviously very ill."

Eventually, the memory footage came to a point where a woman was over the Kid, crying. His eyes went shut; a period of blackness ensued. Then the hospital room again, then being transferred back home. Then darkness. Then, what appeared to be a funeral. The boy was attending a funeral. The imagery was murky and ill-defined. None of the people at the funeral reminded Henrik of anyone he had seen later in Myron's life. But then, he hadn't studied these memories closely, having missed this part of the boy's life, he told Cassy.

Cassy watched Henrik looking at the screen and talk. She turned her head ever so slightly to take him in—though he appeared absorbed, she could tell he was looking at her too.

Henrik slowed down at a time when the viewer attended a posh upper school, sports training and kissed a girl. Then he fast-forwarded to recent years and slowed at a tag where Myron shook the hand of Bruno Emerson. She flinched, attracting Henrik's glance. Henrik fast-forwarded and slowed again when Myron was in the lab, dying. It was Cassy's turn to become absorbed, trance-like.

"I'd like to run a scan on your memories, Cassy," Henrik said, turning to face her.

"If you think you can log in, go for it," she said, still staring at the monitor. "Hang on, go back. The change must have been right back in childhood; I doubt the person from the beginning met Bruno. Even if Myron did. And the scenery so changed after the funeral."

Henrik obliged and returned to the end of the funeral, this time reducing the playback speed to normal. The viewpoint was from behind the coffin. Suddenly the perspective of the room changed drastically, including views from the ceiling. Seconds later, the recording went blank before picking up in a totally different place, a backyard of a new house, yet unseen.

"What was that?" Cassy asked, excitement tickling her voice ever so slightly. "I noticed it twice in what you showed me, like a runaway camera displaying weird angles. And now, a total change of scenery, which certainly isn't a holiday."

"Pausing and reversing can cause damage in a human mind, but you're not a human, are you?"

"No, yeah, I understand, but what happened in the end?"

"That's a good question. The boy continued to record after death, is what I think, and the machine picked it up," Henrik mused.

"Machine picked it up? Flying boy? What recorded it in the first place?"

Henrik remained silent.

"Those angles and speed aren't possible unless your machine picked up a bird," said Cassy.

"I've never run this system on a synth, so it would be fascinating if it found anything. I mean, the data you have recorded, I suppose I can review, anyway."

"Exactly, so no need to get complicated. I doubt my superiors would be keen to see me return a messed-up heap of junk."

"How true."

Next, Henrik muttered a string of code—quietly yet distinctly and rapidly, sweat beading on his nose. Cassy at first turned, surprised. It reminded her of Ts and Cs being read at the end of a radio advertisement. *The bastard can get in.* Moments later, she felt her facial expression turn blank. Uncontrollably. Her body became unresponsive, so she sat still and, after a few seconds, closed her eyes.

"But I'd like to try anyway," Henrik finished. He pulled her hair off and studied the skull. It was streamlined and smooth, a good fit for the transparent rubber cap he stretched on and adjusted to center the wires. The contact with the skin was excellent. Then he heard the door open, the quiet swish sound.

"Movie time, Henrik?" asked Emma, walking in with Violet on her arm. "Why would you try to run that thing on *her*?" Violet began.

"Need to run a diagnostic, which would cover a dual interest."

"You put that hat on me; I had band imprints. Is that how you found out where my house was?"

"Precisely."

"You did so without consulting me; that's a crime, Henrik."

"Violet, might I remind you that you came to us. Your clone is alive and well, waiting for your transfer. A real edge for an actress of your age and popularity. Or were you looking for a frozen face and overly forced features? I mean, I've studied the best, talked to them too, and what I've prepared for you blows it all clean out of the water, *young lady to be*."

"Just, it would be a shame to screw Cassy up," Violet backed off.

"I'm aware of exactly what will happen. Do you even realize whom you are talking to?"

"Henrik, she's one of our patients," Emma broke in. "She's taken enormous risks for us. Take it easy; she has a point. Keller brought the droid here to do a job and I happen to like her."

"It."

"It. I mean, we aren't trying to advise you in your area of expertise, but remember that guy who worked here as a security guard? It really messed with his head. Not to mention some of the others who came for the initial testing. Like the guy who sees a birthday sparkler whenever he needs to remember something?"

Henrik was at a loss. He needed a hit, and at the moment, he couldn't settle on what. The tests on the droid would get run later.

Once awake, Cassy felt she had blanked out and expressed surprise. After adjusting her hair, she looked at Violet and Emma standing there, then at Henrik. "What just happened?" she asked, an unnatural naivete in her voice.

"Only a test, don't worry, I'm as curious as you. If you're going to work here, I must run a diagnostic. Our work is sensitive, and the bunker need not be involved. Either Simon has lent you to us, or he hasn't."

"How do you know Simon?" Cassy said, nervously.

Henrik looked at her. *Well played. Excellent behavior but too emotional — we will see where the rogue programming comes from.*

The two women and Cassy walked out into the garden. Henrik didn't join them, despite Violet's invitation and prodding. He observed from the window instead. They strolled, talked and at one point laughed, clustering in a bunch. Cassy looked natural enough, he thought. He stood gazing at her, knowing he was in the room's shadow, that the glare on the glass would hide him. He stared intensely. Eventually, she did look around, and her interest in the conversation paused. She looked straight in his direction through the glass, then away. *Could a synth possibly sense my gaze?*

Chapter 37

Most weekday evenings, Bruno Emerson liked to frequent a gym after work. Even if he didn't feel like working out, he still went. It was a posh gym, complete with a restaurant and lounges. He could always just hit the pool for a few laps and sit in the sauna, he thought. And afterwards eat dinner. Since his wife had passed, he abhorred spending much time in his home on Montpelier Villas, but this evening he was there, not wanting to go out. Bruno was contemplating the events of the past week.

The restaurant staff and press demanded to know where Keller Mod had disappeared to and while at first he found it easy to deflect the questions, now things were getting intense. Numerous people wanted a search put out and while the Police claimed to be looking, Keller wasn't considered entirely missing nor wanted. Originally Bruno had stepped in to say Keller had taken a leave of absence to handle personal matters. This didn't wash. While Bruno excelled in the public eye, he now fell short, and people wanted answers. That evening, Stacey had called to notify him she had submitted her resignation as a result of the fiasco. Lurch as well. Both refused to work at a restaurant, where staff could go missing. Stacey was an opinion leader and Lurch well liked. More would follow.

He strode back and forth in his living room a while after he had received the news. He then settled into a downstairs rec room, turned on his gas fireplace and poured himself a glass of wine, tossed it back and decided he might go for a walk. What followed was a surprising, hollow, wooden knock. Bruno sat up and listened until he had to admit, it came from the door. *There is a doorbell for that.*

Half expecting a delivery, or a pop-over by the neighbor who usually rang the bell, Bruno didn't check the camera. He simply walked up to the door and opened it—Keller stood there and nodded. Bruno clearly shrank back, frowning upon recognition, then composed himself and demanded to know what he was doing here. Keller said that he needed to talk. Following a forced exchange of pleasantries, Bruno invited him in. After all, he had told Keller to contact him if he ever needed, but did admit that now was not a good time. Keller asked him why, to which he replied, "Things have been hectic."

"They've been hectic for me too, Bruno. I wonder why. You wanna let me in on what's going on?"

"You have a job to do," Bruno replied, as if an agreement had been arrived at. "And if you don't do it, I can't explain what'll happen."

"All right Bruno, I have two questions. One. The package sitting on your desk with the Morpheus logo, addressed to you, did you happen to open it? Are you supplying the Jolly More clinic with prison micro-chips?" Keller rifled.

"The Jolly More isn't a prison. I'm simply investing in the future—it's a solution for prisoners and offenders on parole alike. Does wonders for keeping people in line."

"Might be an excellent solution for the restaurant too, then."

"The restaurant doesn't employ criminals either."

"Now it does," Keller said, crossing his arms.

Bruno shook his head. "What's the second thing?"

"Have you met with Ed?"

"No. But I've recently met with the Chief of Police and the agreement is that I call him directly, any time I wish. *Especially* regarding you." He pulled out his cell and searched for the number. "Anything you do is on cam, goes straight to a cloud," he added, coolly.

"Bruno, you turned your back on me as I walked in the door. I caught the faint slice mark on the back of your neck. I'd say one of those has been installed in you too, a few weeks ago, judging by the look of it."

Bruno stopped searching. "What are you doing here and what do you want, Keller?"

"Answers. Tell me who Ed is and I leave. When this is all done, you can buy my share of the restaurant. For cheap. Won't bother you again."

"And if I don't? I can arrange it so you don't work anywhere, for the rest of your life. During or after this stint."

Keller simply looked at him. He appeared to not have an answer, nor care.

"Keller, you must leave. I was asked not to respond if you tried to contact me, you remember, you were a wanted man some days ago. I found the murder hard to believe, but the evidence against—"

"What evidence? Asked by whom? She's fine Bruno, alive and well. Do you want to see a photo?"

"Images can be manipulated these days, have been for a long time."

"Who is he Bruno?" Keller said in a gentler voice, calmly standing his ground.

Bruno paused, exhaled through bulging cheeks and, "I don't know, I've never met him. He contacted me a while back. I can't tell you any more except that he isn't a man to mess with—well connected within the Ministry of Defense and obviously the Police Department. Keller, just drop it and go back."

"He put one in me, too," Keller said, patting the back of his neck.

"Your father was a psychopath and you, as his son, must pay. He misled people to think it's possible to infuse a clone with a human. I've put a lot of money into this and now I can die like a bum. Penniless. On a bloody ti—"

"Misled?"

Bruno said nothing, as his vision tunneled to Keller and intense anger percolated upward, seeking any excuse to erupt.

"What the hell were you thinking, believing in this? Killing people along the way? My father had his theories, but he kept them to himself. If you resurrected him into some sort of evolutionary god, so be it. Don't blame me. Immortality is theoretically impossible, the food of cults. All of his research was buried deep in a bunker, most of it lost in an explosion. He did his testing on synthetics, *not people*."

"Deep in a bunker. Same place I got dragged down and chipped, by your synth friend. Or is she your girlfriend now? Shagging a droid, I wouldn't put it past you Mod."

"What? You realize, nothing I do here would stop me from returning to the Jolly More," Keller said, lowering his arms, stepping forward.

"Ask her yourself. It was in an old tunnel hospital. I was taken there in a van, sedated, half unconscious. She took me down a lift and popped it in. When Ed found out, he went berserk. That's when Henrik got a hold of you and—"

"Got a hold of me and what? Framed me for murder so that you could live out your fantasy of immortality? There are some sick people in this world, Bruno, and you're one of them," Keller said, losing steam.

Feeling Keller back off, Bruno laid in. Face contorted, spittle flying from lips, his mouth ejected a string of obscenities describing their apparently failing partnership. The more he yelled, the more he could see that Keller was not going to rebuke him, an expression of concern forming instead. Sensing pity, Bruno began bursting at the seams. *I have nothing more to lose, except my life, which is this man's hands.* The gruesome face faded, and Bruno stood as he was, ending off with an additional threat to call the Chief of Police. Though his features were still flushed purple red, the blood was slowly draining out.

"Call him, doesn't bother me. Prison might be the right solution. And a good, solid hearing where you can tell them all that you told me," said Keller.

Bruno, a tall man who kept in shape and had a youthful manner about him despite pushing 60, was hunched now. Wild-eyed and bitter.

"Unlike you, Keller, I'm married to the project. Till death do us part."

"What does that even mean?"

"The timer was set for two months. Can't be undone and I don't look forward to testing it. Or attempting to infuse a clone. Like skydiving with a handkerchief."

"Timer? On what day was that?"

"My anniversary will be this Sunday. I'm due to arrive the day after tomorrow, so I hope you're ready."

"Don't worry, I am. You won't die, not by my hand," Keller said, chill.

Bruno's face softened, the hate in his brow melted. "You figured out how to do this?"

"No, not yet. But the timer and chip I can get around."

Chapter 38

The train to the Ferry port took under 2 hours. It was half empty and void of Gouyen. The lights of passing villages and towns sparkled in the night amongst shadows denoting trees and tall hedges. The open fields flowed with subtle radiance, slashed by luminescent paths and roads.

That Henrik was no longer a merciless killer and subscribed to little else which transpired at the Jolly More was a relief. Keller had also left Bruno somewhat in his place, and the concept of Gouyen opened up many possibilities. The hallucinations were most likely not hallucinations at all and were not a result of insanity. There was a tiny sliver of a chance that his father had developed something workable. Tom had undoubtedly dreamt a dream, and his theories held some water through a perception of the paranormal. And perception meant something could be detected concretely. *As in look, there it is, see?*

Had father ever tried to tell anyone about his discovery, he would have been locked up then and there. And yet someone had known, agreed, seen the possibilities, and had gone to great lengths to secure Henrik against his will. All the Jolly More staff, for that matter. The mansion would have cost millions to buy and renovate. Last I heard the asking price was over £6. Then the clout in the police force, the Ministry of Defense, and the ministry's bunkers. It required quite a man, or woman, to fit those able shoes and be clever enough to not leave a trace. Management teetered on condemning Tom as a lunatic; who is this patron?

Keller boarded a ferry which crossed over to the Isle of Wight at 4am. The darkness was slowly dissolving to morning glow, an expanse of gradient sky leaving the strait a moody, silver-grey. A light fog lay suspended, diluting distant borders with blurry wash. Keller loved the smell of the sea air, the sight of defiant waves, and the night chill. Together it sparkled and invited his mind to do the same, if only by inciting mystery.

So he took stock of the situation. Gouyen appeared genuine to him — there was nothing more to think or say here. Except her motives for intervening or giving him the flower in the first place. *She said she tried to get into father's head and per the letter she may have succeeded.* Keller reached into his pocket and pulled out the letter from his father.

'*The pressure to perform was immense, from forces I can't explain. Even voices in my head, which, if we ever talk again, I'm hoping you might shed light on. Gouyen she calls herself, or perhaps that's just another name for insanity.*'

Then he imagined Gouyen and her kind walking he earth once more as humans, synthetic ones — a testament to never forgetting. *The preciousness of life is lost when you can live forever dead.*

Or perhaps that's just another meaning for insanity.

After inhaling a microwaved hamburger and fries at the onboard restaurant, Keller wandered outside onto the deck. He leaned on the railing, looking down at the wake and up at the dawn horizon. On the starboard side, he witnessed a man standing by the lifeboats, one hand clutching a rope. He was soaking wet and purveyed a vacant yet dazed expression on his blue-grey, bloated face. He noticed Keller looking, gazed back and slowly faded out, a perverse grin emerging.

A slight tremble pervading his torso, Keller looked out at sea, then again at where the man had stood — it's not normal to see that, he thought, his plummeting nerves grasping for a solid ledge to cling to. *But if Gouyen is legit, why not this guy? People consider you a psychic, you don't have to choose one side of the fence. You can have both — believe in the dead so fully they come alive and celebrate the living so much they never die.*

Keller kidded himself he was slipping into a vivid, 6K world with hallucinogenic add-ons. Cassy had shielded him from the lab; she understood more than she let on. In place of the microchip she removed, she may have installed a drug dispenser or a chemical converter which took substances from his body and catalyzed them into something poisonous. *That's not it. No time for paranoia. But why chip Bruno? How could that help unless Cassy worked for Ed, who then pretended to go berserk? Unless he wasn't acting, and Cassy worked for someone else... or, if Tom really was around.*

Let's say Tom was on to something big. After all, I was a child when the lab blew, and my father might not have told me everything. In fact, he didn't — he gave up enough to rouse interest. And then Keller's focus was deflected to when he kissed Cassy in the tunnel. *She didn't push me back like a stranger might...*

The blast of a bullhorn from another ship snapped him back. As her synth lips dissipated, Keller found it odd that he was always doubting his father. The one person on this earth who had believed him about the blossom and his story about Gouyen. His mother never had, as if he would grow out of it. *Take a look at me now.*

But Katrina, she didn't need to die. See, the preciousness of life is already lost here. And if that's you, father, stuck in a tin can fifty stories underground, is it all worth it?

Chapter 39

After arriving back at the port town of Fishbourne, Keller took a cab. He had his fill of fresh air, fishy air, vague memories and compelling visions. Now he craved his cottage and bed. *Cottage, how lovely. What a quaint existence we span at the Jolly More. The way erudite killers and Frankensteinian scientists usually don't — a drug-infested hotel should have been it. Or a dark lab in a bleak, abandoned warehouse shithole. With thick plastic stripping instead of doors, the kind meat lockers use. The kind in my walk-in freezer.*

When Keller finally reached his place, he lay down on his bed, looked out his window and captured the grey-amber filter coating the fields and sky. He fell asleep, realizing he was no longer afraid.

What felt like an instant but turned out to be 3 hours later, Keller awoke to the sound of someone or something beating his wooden bed frame. He imagined a tall bird had entered the room and pecked at the footboard with its giant beak. He awoke further to find Henrik standing in between him and the window beyond, open, a sheer swaying in the cool morning breeze. The moody, silken fields of a moment ago were bright and sharp. Henrik held a pen in his hand, poised to make another loud tap on the hardwood.

"Where were you?" he asked.

"Brighton. And Ipsworth."

"I know."

"So why do you ask?"

"Keller, we're under a lot of pressure here; your time is almost up. What were you doing?"

"Sitting in a park with a gun in my lap getting shitfaced, thinking if —."

"You look kind of rough," Henrik said, pocketing the pen.

"I was doing some research. I met an old friend."

"Who?"

"Gouyen. I bet you've met."

"How classic. No more joking, what the hell happened to you?"

"I'm telling you. She pops by here from time to time; just you might not know it directly. Henrik, the paranormal activity."

Henrik pursed his lips. "Violet will be our next subject; Ed is pissed."

"Fine. Let's do it. I think we actually have a chance with her."

Henrik looked at him, brow crinkling. "What makes you so sure?"

Keller explained that Violet had been dead 3 times before and that she was a survivor who knew how to hang in and how long. "That last prank you pulled on her should have killed her, but it didn't," Keller added.

"If you had answered your phone, it might not have come to that."

"Bullshit. You were pushing her past any sane limit. And then you were going to dump her at my place, dead. She simply jumped the gun."

"We had an unexpected turn of events, I suggested we go, and she didn't make it."

"I figured you weren't behind it, but my answering the phone? No, I was still staying clear of you."

Both men stood silent.

"I also checked in on August's ex-wife."

Henrik flashed a startled look and continued to caress the edges of his pockets. He glanced around as if someone else might be there.

"I met August too. You have my gratitude; thanks, Henrik; I thought we were really lost."

"Yeah, well, I'm not a killer. Early on, I learned that Ed means business, so I had to find ways to cover my tracks. If he finds out—"

"He won't. Not from me. Do you know who Ed is?"

"No."

"Give me something, Henrik; I'm on your side. We've had our differences but now's not the time. This guy can kill us both."

Henrik swallowed, turned, and glanced out the window. "I've never met Ed. I did prison time for a crime I didn't commit; whether or not you agree, that's how I see it. I'm not sure who set me up for that explosion, but it was proof enough to stop further investigation."

"Did you see this proof?"

"It was video footage of me going in late Friday night, plus the log showing I had used my fingerprint to enter. Further, evidence showed someone had tampered with the centrifuge. That's where the blast came from, according to forensics. Nitroglycerine was used, something you could easily make with stuff around the lab. Old style. Then it looked like a welding tank was emptied—a few were sitting next door in the droid lab. The resultant blast basically incinerated everything."

"But no cams."

"That's the way Tom wanted it. There was nothing to show what happened inside, just theories. It could have been a droid working at night, in conjunction with someone who knew the territory and gave it precise instructions. That also points to me."

"So, they could have used gas to knock them out, then detonate, and erase the droid's memory afterwards," Keller added.

"I could have done all of that too," Henrik chuckled. "Then later, this Ed guy calls, gets me out. Wants me to open a new lab, continue the work, mainly Tom's. Wants to be immortal. A real psycho, says he'll put me back in prison with additional evidence if I don't comply."

"Did you see that additional evidence?"

"No. He's connected, knows people, screws them. Hacks them. I felt I had no choice but to agree. My reputation is poor, and the Cradle sounded fascinating. I was always a big fan of your father so—."

"He was a big fan of you too."

"Sure." Henrik paused, then continued, "Later, I get chipped to further seal the agreement. Felt locked in after the first zap. I got suspicious since he seemed to know my life story. Little details would pop up I didn't think were on file anywhere."

"So, it's someone you know."

"Perhaps. Believe me, I've racked my old head over this. His own clone is ready, but as you know, that's not how he looks. Don't know where the DNA came from, not in any records we have or can get into. And that's a load of records. At this point he's just pushing the whole thing along, desperate. Wants to get in his clone, doesn't want to be first. He figures as long as we're all chipped, he holds the cards. Bruno is his lunch ticket, has a collection of rich, potential clients. Some have signed up. Bruno's chip is on a timer and that wasn't supposed to happen. Claims it was Cassy and so I'm very surprised she's here."

"Bruno can claim things out of convenience, I'm not sure I trust him. He's become foolhardy. Are you running tests on her?"

"Have to."

"Why?"

"She's behaving oddly, yet her programming is sound. I need to dig deeper, Ed is insisting. I've stalled, but he'll ask for an update soon. He wants to know why she acts like she does, he said—." Henrik rolled his eyes just a touch.

"What?" *He just buried something.*

"She doesn't say much, behaving as if she's just your guest—could be they're both playing us. Something's going on you and I don't know about."

"It is, yeah. Do you realize she can remove your chip?" said Keller.

"Yes! Of course I do." Henrik was getting nervous.

"So where is she?"

"Can't tell you that, Keller."

"I see. How many years have you been working with this guy? And you don't have a clue who he is?"

"I said no. Maybe even Bruno. Or Cassy herself, wouldn't surprise me. Now she's here for the final kill."

"I doubt it."

"She's locked up, but if there's a layer in her I don't know about, she might be watching us now. I'm old school, remember? It's not so straightforward, Ed is a voice, not traceable, which doesn't engage, ever. And even if you knew, what would you do?"

"Kill him. There's no other cure."

"And what if you're bugged here in this room?"

"Room's not bugged, plus it doesn't matter. He's a coward. He can't do anything to me, he's laid out all his cards, whether or not he knows it. Bugs won't help him. Nor can you."

Keller watched Henrik nod and leave the cottage. He might as well have been translucent, yet the sun defined him starkly against the shadow of the wood near the path. His grey hair shimmered on one side, as did the edge of his glasses. It was eerie to compare him from back then to now, united by his gait.

Go back to work, Henrik, take a hit.

Chapter 40

"So why doesn't Keller simply try it himself if the signs are so good. He could take Francine's body and be her for a while. Or August or even me. Then heat himself back up and be himself again," Violet said, sitting at her dressing table, doing her hair and chatting with Ed through her smartphone perched on a stand. Violet wore a loose-fitting robe, her shoulders swathed in moist hair.

"Clever. You sound like Henrik," Ed replied.

"Oh Henrik, he's such a bore that man."

"Indeed. But you are still the best one for the job," he said in a tone she had rarely heard, almost human.

"You promised me that after the hospital gig, I would have plenty of time to rest. It almost killed me; that wasn't part of the deal."

"Deals change."

"Not an honest one, and I do take you for a man, a real man."

There was a pause at the other end of the line. While she had her video feed turned on, his was off. *A black box where his marauding little visage should have been.* Violet had called him having learned from Henrik that she was next in line to attempt the infusion. 'Simply infuse it with your grace,' Henrik had said, probably high. *Addict.*

"Just play it through; what would you want to make this more bearable?" Ed asked.

"I don't want Henrik present; he appears out of kilter, to put it mildly. Nor that droid, Cassy, she's been acting up lately, very emotional. Last night I watched her wandering about the property like a fugitive. Somebody should shoot the programmer for that mess."

"Cassy, emotional? Where was she going?"

"Around the cottages, maybe visited the falconer—she told me she had never seen such a bird and wanted to see it up close. Probably to visit her lover," Violet said, applying lip-gloss.

"Keller?"

"Or, the falconer. As you know, Keller wasn't around. By the way, will he brief me, or shall I just show up in the lab tomorrow? I realize that time is tight," she said letting off a tiny grin.

Another pause. Violet intended to toss a few cards upward and see where they all landed. Ed could pick and choose his own outcome. "And what about his bloody eyes? Are they giving him trouble?" she blurted out, sounding impatient now, stopping to stare into the phone cam.

"I'll check on his eyesight; I'm curious myself."

"He may be having visions, so that's a good thing. Unless they're hallucinations or fantasies," Violet said continuing with a little make-up, but keeping au naturelle.

"The droid wandering around after being locked up, how fascinating. Did Henrik let her out?"

"You're asking the wrong person, honey."

"Very well, I'll—"

She cut in, asserting he had little to say. "Do you think Keller can even pull this off? I mean, the closest so far has been Henrik with his fitness boy. My life may be completely worthless to you, but I still value it." At this point, Violet stood up and let the robe fall from her shoulders as she took it off. She turned away from the phone, and walked off to the bathroom, "Excuse me just a second, I'm dressing. I can still hear you, though."

Ed continued to pause and sighed through his nose. Violet heard the slight sound and smiled to herself. *Aha, you were checking me out. Couldn't miss it I suppose.*

Then Ed spoke up, "I believe he can. If you latch onto him once you're flatlining, Keller will help you make the shift — I trust him that way."

"Easy for you to say."

"My dear, I yearn for the moment I will get the very chance to do the same."

"Why, are you terminal? Disfigured?"

"Ha, no. Old."

"Huh. You don't sound old," Violet said on a positive note.

"I am having fun."

"Killing people and threatening them with their lives is fun for you?"

"No. But making an advance in evolution is. The idea of immortality is inspiring to me. I realize sacrifices must be made. But I always offer something better in return."

"People don't always agree with your methods."

"Up to them."

"This all sounds very simple. And I know from experience how things could roll. You know that," she said, returning to the living room wearing only underwear and fluffing her hair. "But I need another few weeks to rest. Surely you can find someone else? You understand I would like nothing better than to wake up 20 years younger and even healthier than I was back then. It's every actor's dream, every woman's too." She wiggled into a pair of jeans, leaving the fly open and waist unbuttoned, having moved quite close to her phone, the chair conveniently out of sights way.

Another pause. Followed by a sigh. "Tell you what. I'm always up for a game," Ed's voice ebbed. "So, I am thinking, since Bruno is our star client, on a bit of a time crunch, we should just go ahead and do this thing on him. We're at the bottom of the 9th, Keller has already had two strikes. This needs to be, as you Americans say, a homer."

"Oh, how delightful," Violet said, swallowing quickly. *An English baseball fan?*

"And if he fails, that will be his last chance. For you, we will get someone else. Or give Henrik another shot. After all, as you say, he was the closest. Mind you, he also kills off the old bodies, no returns with him."

"Ah, is that not a little harsh? Inspiring, I suppose."

"Yes, and after you, come I."

"Right. And you still prefer Henrik? I'm tired of being a sacrificial lamb, Ed. Best go with the safest bet, and that's Keller." Violet felt that the man at the other end of the line, the mighty Ed, was pathetic. *How did he get to control us? How does he influence so many important, key people? Vanity. You tell someone they can live an extra 50 years and be young again; boom, you'll have some takers.* Violet thought of Bruno, who must arrive shortly. Good-looking, clever, how had he let himself be caught up in this? She would indeed find out.

"You may be right, my dear. But let's not let him think so."

"I won't. And what plans do you have for Bruno after he transfers?"

"Business. He is a necessary guinea pig, a warm bowl of soup and hopefully much, much more. Rest then and let me mull things over. If Keller is ready, I'll let him at Bruno. You are valuable to me, Violet; I am sorry how things have been. I will make it up to you but be patient." Without waiting for a reply, he hung up.

After seeing a little flesh, he turned 180 degrees. And if he believes he can transfer into a new, youthful, solid male body, he might also think he can have me someday. What a royal jackass.

Chapter 41

At early dawn, a few minutes before 4am, a falcon circled the field nearby Keller's cottage. The peregrine swooped close, revealing a warm white chest patterned with dark stripes. Wings spread wide to slow down, it landed on the nearby stone wall, its bright yellow, taloned feet holding fast. The large dark eyes, surrounded by yellow goggles, checked their surroundings as the bluish beak opened momentarily to release a piercing tone, repeatedly culminating in a high screech.

Keller awoke, swung his legs over the side of the bed, and looked over to the window, the sound echoing in his mind like a distant dream. He continued to wake up as he looked outside, searching the landscape and sky. The bird, which he thought he had heard, was not there. Instead, partially hidden from view by brush, Keller noted a figure, which waved. *Cassy.*

He pulled on his trousers and a jumper, but by the time he made it out the front door, she had vanished. Keller, pretending to be out for a stroll, a cup of stale coffee in hand, walked by the wood, subtly scanning it for any motion. A hand signaled from behind a giant tree. Keller walked off in another direction but circled back to find Cassy waiting.

"I thought you were locked up somewhere. I tried to—" he began.

"Never mind, it's a room off of a tunnel coming out from the basement, out past the incinerator. You wouldn't know of it. It was used in WW2 or something and looks sealed. I'm tired of tunnels. Henrik shut me down," she spoke nervously, racing to get things out.

"Ok." *He did?*

"I was getting too emotional, so he locked me up; my bad. He ran some tests but not serious ones. He hasn't found out anything. Not that there's anything to find. But I wanted to reach you first; I have something to tell you. If he does a wipe, it can really screw me up."

This droid is genuinely remarkable. Keller decided to listen; it was early, and no one was out. The guards weren't up yet. Watching her expression and the sincerity in it, Keller felt for her. *It.*

"So tell me, how did you manage to wake yourself up?"

"I have a fail-safe he doesn't know about. Yet. I can circumvent. I don't have access to many things, but I'm functional as you can see," Cassy let go a shy grin.

Despite her worried face and beckoning eyes, Keller steeled himself. "I thought you called about August; he's alive, it turns out."

Cassy's lips parted, her eyes wide. "Wow, had me fooled. I guess Henrik isn't as bad as we thought. And you know, he could be using the tunnel I was stuck in to get them out. There's a lab with a hospital bed and everything he would need to keep someone critical, alive. Greased the guards, maybe."

"Could be. You'll have to show me. I also visited Bruno."

Cassy stiffened.

"Cassy, did you chip him?" Keller asked, anger tingling. "I mean, do you work for Ed and is this being locked up, is this a farce?"

"Keller, no, I did chip him yes, it wasn't for Ed."

"And you sedated me so I couldn't see Tom's lab; what the hell was that about? Makes sense if Ed has taken it over. Am I being severely played or what?"

"No! Keller, please, let me explain—"

"If I lock you up, there will be no fail-safe. I can guarantee you that," Keller said, purveying nastiness.

Next, the machine's face looked more human than Keller had ever seen. It contorted into a look of pain and sorrow; if it could shed a tear, it would have at this very instant, he was sure of it. Her voice erupted as a sequence of hushed electronic sound distortions, twangy, synthesized and then choked altogether. "I only came to tell you the truth," it finally spat out. "I can't take this anymore; please take me back. Trash me if you want, but not here."

Keller looked at her, studied her like a dying insect which no doubt was in agony, at least appeared so, but beyond any help he could deliver despite the parallels to a human form. She was a machine and no more salvageable than a croaking beetle by him. But her following words made him livid with burning anger.

"Keller, *I am Katrina*," she said, ceasing her emotions as she looked at him.

He was mute for the next few seconds, scheming to disable the machine altogether, here and now. The synth, looking at him, stepped back, bent its knees and slumped to the ground, its back against a tree. Its hand was in a pocket and came out now, holding something. It was a pressed flower, a Forget-Me-Not. She held it up to him. Keller took it. As he looked at it, the world around suddenly slowed. With a flick, it would break in half and with another, it would disappear into the foliage.

"Only one other person knows our story, and that is you. There's no way it could have been programmed into me, and you know it. The one about Corfe Castle," she said in a deep tone, like she meant it.

Keller flash-backed to the boy who had arrived in England 22 years previous. His father had taken him, along with Alexey and his daughter Katrina, on a trip to the sea. They stopped at

Corfe Castle and while the men stood, enjoying a beer in the shade, he and Katrina rolled down a hill by the ruins, seeing if they could roll right to the moat. Keller noticed little flowers abounding there like weeds, the same as the ones the antler woman had planted in the desert behind his backyard in Vegas. Feeling elated, he grabbed a bunch of the Scorpion Grass and yanked them out, roots and all. He presented the bunch to his Queen, Katrina. Her grubby, dirty hands grabbed them, and they both laughed.

In the next second, he focused on the tiny, flat blossom in his hand; before he could toss it, she spoke again.

"You want me to tell it, or are you? I received a bunch of these, roots included, from a boy who claimed I was his Queen. Kind of cool, huh? Forget-Me-Not, he said."

Keller gave the flower back. His mind spun and raced like a roulette wheel, knowing the answer would be a guess, a stroke of luck or ill fate. The wager was her life, her existence, electronic consciousness stream, or whatever it might be called.

"Keller!" she said, seeing he was off somewhere. "Help me up." He clutched the lifeless, chilly hand until the machine stood, and they could look into each other's eyes. The roulette wheel spun, and the little ball hit a slot. The numbers were all blank. Keller stepped back. *So the letter was not a joke. Can that be?*

"All right. I mean, how the hell did you get in there?"

The synth smiled, yet Keller imagined her wiping a tear from her cheek. There was none there. His own emotions began to erupt. He looked up into the sky, hoping to see the falcon and find that this was all hallucination, a tale played by some brittle faction in his mind. But when he looked back, she was still there.

"Your father was successful. He had developed the thing he called the *Cradle,* and he had installed a few in some of the droids. He said he told you about it. I'm not sure how the explosion came about; he won't tell me for now, said it was an accident. We could smell garlic; your father feared acetylene, but the exit was jammed, malfunctioning. A whir rose from the centrifuge and a moment later, the room was filled with intense fire. We died almost instantly; the heat was horrific."

Cassy stopped for a second, to swallow and hold herself as if cold. Keller could feel his lips twitching, his eyes riveted to hers.

"But a second later, I looked into the flames and could see my body burning to a crisp. Tom was next to me and grabbed me; I'm not sure how exactly, but he did, and we fled to the droid lab next door. Well, through the wall, it was natural. You remember how it looks in there—he pointed to one of the droids and said, 'Take this one but do it now. Now Cassy, get inside! Don't think!' It sounded like he was yelling. We were ghosts Keller, and later I realized he was worried I might just float away or disappear. He seemed to know of such a volatile existence."

"It looks to me like you're not kidding. But I don't—." Keller felt cold in his resoluteness. *No memory transfer.*

"No, I'm not. I can give you more details, but that's the essence. Gives you something to think about. I'm not expecting you to believe me right away."

"Believe you? A machine, you're nuts, seriously."

Their eyes locked once again. A few seconds passed, and Keller looked away.

"You could never stare me down either, Keller."

He turned back, perplexed. "This would be so like Tom to pull something like this off. You're saying he's in a synth too?"

"Ah, yeah." They stood looking at one another.

"The miner... that freak sitting at the desk..."

Cassy put a hand on Keller, he shrugged it off.

"The androids back then weren't nearly so lifelike. What's up with that? With how you look?" Keller asked, looking inward to his memories.

"We've been transferring ourselves to newer models over the years. I stopped. This one was a real killer a few years ago, but now I make myself useful to Simon, I want to be kept in the bunker, you know, near to Tom. This is terrifying for me, Keller, and if you doubt me, it will really suck. Look at me!"

He did.

"I remember when Arnold caught us in the artillery room—we were stealing bullets, just so we could break them open and get the gunpowder out. You said it would be fun to burn. He slapped me in the face, and you jumped on him. Arnold eventually pinned you down, but you tried. For me."

"Ok, I'll always remember that. Right now, I need more proof, something tangible."

"Life's not always tangible; it's not a fricking medical experiment. Or a hamburger."

"I know, I get it. And you should get back before Henrik discovers you're out. I imagine he does a morning round, knowing him," Keller said, wanting to be away from her. Wanting to wake up from this.

Intricate programming? I can almost feel her. See her if I tried. This whole thing is a farce. No wonder Tom appeared crazy, he was. Her last story might have been lifted from Arnold's report, except that he didn't file a report. And he didn't dare tell Alexey he had smacked his daughter. Or tell mine I had tackled him. Tom would have laughed, and Alexey would have beaten him senseless. So, not a farce.

Keller walked a circle, letting out a long breath. *I need to let this sink in.*

"My turn to say something crazy. If you work for Ed, I don't care," Keller began on a fresh note.

"Keller I—. Shoot. Both guns ablaze," she said, imitating an American accent. Texas, Keller guessed. Katrina was always good with accents, to the point he thought she was a spy in training. In the bunker, everything was possible to a boy.

"I can perceive ghosts. Spirits. I mean, I can see them again."

"Well, if it ain't Clairvoyant Keller."

"Yeah, Medium Mod." They both chuckled.

"You haven't gone batshit after all, huh?"

"No. Even if I don't see it, I can still tell if it's there. I mean, it's a lot more obvious than before."

"I'm not exactly a robot now, am I?" she said, stepping closer.

Keller stood, silent. *I guess not.*

"Tom told me that given your psychic abilities you're able to receive the treatment. Not all people are—give one man those eyes, he'll swear he's hallucinating and drive it away with medication. Or get exorcised. Give it to another, like you, he'll look closer. You see, he wasn't insane, he was a *visionary*."

"Hilarious."

"Keller—"

"Why did you chip Bruno? Who made you?" he changed course again, to get it over with.

"Your father insisted. He's been observing the clinic since Henrik got out of jail. He recognized the anti-aging as a facade but couldn't understand what his own research had to do with anything. While he's not much of a hacker, he's learning. Ed tried to track Tom down but never could. Pretty slick, huh? So he lurks around the peripherals but can't get into their system."

"And since it's disconnected..." Keller added.

"But Ed is deeply hooked into the Ministry. In a roundabout way, we discovered that Henrik and some of the other staff had been chipped. Others disappeared when word got out. The chips must be registered to work and, even if hacked, can be found."

"And you traced them."

"It made Tom furious. He retaliated and sent me out to fetch Bruno. And I did, and I regret it. The repercussion was that it pissed Ed, whom we haven't identified. Once he heard you had some success with corpses, he came after you. Fluked really. Keller, at that point, we still didn't know what was going on. I swear it. They wouldn't let me in or ask questions. Henrik recognized I was a synth and could ID me from a distance."

"But you got in this time, for a prolonged visit."

"Thanks to you, Ed smells something," Cassy said, distantly.

"And Ed doesn't want to lose touch, so he lets you lurk. Now more than ever. Not saying a word."

"He watches and waits. Smart in a way."

"Henrik plays along. We both do, granting the devil his wishes," Keller said, relief dawning on him.

"It's funny because my memory of Henrik is terribly vague, not much more than what's left from childhood. He's probably been wiped from my machine memory aside from a few basic records, yet he can manipulate me with verbal code and he seems to suspect something. It's complicated, Keller, don't leave me like this. I've been taken apart before, and it's a nightmare, unlike any you can imagine." Her voice turned to a synthesized mess again, and Keller stepped closer still and drew her in. They stood a while embracing each other.

"You should go back now," he said, giving her a gentle shake, "Before Henrik does his morning rounds. Violet also suspects you of odd behavior and has seen you walking around. She's been acting weird lately and can blab it to Ed. Get back there, and don't give anyone any reason to rip you apart. I'll come up with something, promise."

"And wipe the back left woods cam if you can. I doubt anyone will notice at this hour, but just in case."

"Yeah, I'll have a look." Keller turned and parted, surprised at his own vacancy. Cassy stood a while and watched him go.

Chapter 42

Violet had insisted upon a particular corner room, not long after she had arrived back from her Brighton hospital escapade. She was weak, yes, but kept working on the orderly until the orderly mentioned it to Emma, who finally didn't mind. Even in her half-comatose state, she knew she needed every advantage, and a room with a view for a person who was all but bed-bound was one of them. And over a week later, aside from short walks outside in the garden, she was still stuck there.

Her room faced south-east as well as north-east. She overlooked the front, the fountain and could see the gate and lane too. She was quite content with this arrangement when Bruno Emerson arrived early afternoon on Wednesday, May something. *He's here to stay and leave his old self behind. Sounds like we're part of a religious cult or something.* While past his prime, Violet decided he was quite handsome and fit. When his wife was crippled in a skiing accident, she needed a new body, and while this was a common statement amongst those in her predicament, Bruno had gone all out to find a solution. Ultimately his wife had passed under mysterious conditions, and Violet didn't doubt Ed had somehow been involved as Bruno was a key investor.

What kind of man searches the dark web to help his wife? You've done the same thing to help yourself, Violet. She had hated the usual result from plastic surgery, the frozen look. The bizarre-looking faces with the veiny old hands. Those were always a giveaway and Violet, to humor herself that there really was nothing else despite the risk involved, had dared to visit the Jolly More. She ended up playing the role of her life and it was scary, to say the least.

The arrival of Bruno Emerson eased her mind yet didn't. He was a notable businessman in the United Kingdom and if he had bought into this, the entire island was in for it. Whole body anti-ageing as Henrik liked to put it, might sound good to the elderly or ill, but it sure as hell lead to problems if it fell in the wrong hands, especially a fruit cake infusion like Ed.

Did Ed sincerely care for her or was it a fake advance? Or a divulgence his sense of macabre humor, allowed? *Take a wild guess.* It wasn't even humor—Ed was simply an all-out psychopath acting out his delusion. He would achieve immortality, no matter the cost. That kind usually got what they wanted, one way or another.

Mod was no match; he was far too decent. And the droid, that was a wild card. She had removed Emma's chip and perhaps the receptionist's too, who then disappeared. Perhaps a Russian spy, returning to the mother ship Ed, Violet chuckled to herself. *Get your act together and tough this one out. You're not over the hill yet. In a darkened bar you could probably lure Mod in. But Emerson, easily in broad daylight and Ed, would be happy with your corpse.*

A man with a death chip in him about to get killed so he could venture on to a better life in a new body was pretty extreme. He had guts, even if he was being coerced at the same time. Violet liked that, liked his looks and liked him on YouTube. And now he was here.

The entourage, consisting of a security guy, Emma, Keller and Henrik, met Bruno at the car. As it pulled away, the group headed inside and Violet got ready to go downstairs and, if nothing else, to observe from afar. It couldn't hurt and knowing her own past, such observances usually led to something interesting. She knew how to pick them. So she fixed her hair, put on a clean hospital gown and a neat cardigan over top. It made her look girlish. 'Feigning feeble' she would throw in as a garnish at appropriate intervals.

Through her open window, she heard Keller's voice along with another man's. She walked over to it and looked out. Just the two of them, walking and talking. Keller looked civilized and curt; Bruno looked at ease. The electricity must have been released in an earlier conversation; she was glad they had made a truce.

Violet pulled herself back as Keller looked up towards her window. He had a way about him. His eyesight had not worsened — he could see things others missed or didn't see at all. *Or have I become too obvious?*

Bruno was speaking rather intensely as they walked along the wood. He spotted the Kid playing from a distance and stopped. Keller, gently took him by the arm and led him in a perpendicular direction. *Not that Bruno doesn't already know, he simply doesn't need to know more, three days before his own transfer. Nicely played Keller.*

In the next few minutes, Violet took the lift down, and was relieved to discover the receptionist was indeed gone and hadn't been replaced. She walked through an empty reception hall and headed outdoors. *By this point the conversation will be waning, Keller will spot and introduce me.*

The two men, noticing Violet exit the front entrance and make her way to the fountain, strolled over. What Violet had hoped for was unmistakably surpassed. It was love at first sight — in the traditional, modern, and animal sense.

Violet was an actor, though past her prime, was still very attractive. Bruno noticed her and after they were introduced, recounted some of her movie roles. Add on to that she had survived an atrocity and was recuperating, well, that just drove him nuts. *A woman in distress is precisely what he needs — ah, and he keeps darting a glance at the bit of tat he can see. Naughty boy Bruno, did you see it all in the hospital?*

And Violet needed a man she could lean on, someone who would lean on her later and would need taking care of himself. After all, he was older and would no doubt retain his frame of mind, even after their infusions. It took the edge off the *unknown* aspect for Bruno and the risk — meeting another 'patient' had its advantages. Violet was alive after being dead, was what mattered. Mod had pulled it off and would do it again, despite the complications.

Keller eventually left them to it, wearing a quizzical expression. Violet insisted she would be alright in Bruno's capable hands and would show him around.

"After all, I've been here longer than you, dear," she said to Keller, taking Bruno's elbow as they walked on.

"I understand he visited your summer house in Maine," Bruno began.

"He did. I think it was important he do so. It introduced him to me, who I really was, what the clinic was and so forth. And it got him out of the country until the confusion died down. You created such a drama."

"Wasn't quite how I imagined it, I actually didn't know who you were and that it was you who — "

"Never mind that now. If he showed up here, Sussex Police may have followed. How did you convince them of his guilt, so quickly?"

"You'd have to ask Ed that."

"Poor planning on your part Bruno, but nevertheless, all ended well," Violet bulldozed on, knowing he liked it. They walked and talked for another hour and then dined together.

Keller headed back to the Mansion. The moment of truth would take place tomorrow, leaving a day's grace before the chip was set to 'expire' its host. He stared at the ceiling above his bed, absent mindedly following the cracks in the plaster to a patch which looked like water damage.

That Bruno stood on the side-lines as Violet's body was replaced by a dead clone and she herself shipped back to the Jolly More, was probably known to her. If anything, he was in her debt. *She'll probably collect whether or not he knows it.*

He thought of Cassy and wondered if she was awake, wondered if what she had told him was true. It angered him to think a droid who worked for a man like Ed had reached such a state of simulated consciousness—that she could outsmart him and convince him she was a close childhood friend who had died most viciously. Yet he also had to admit she had a way about her, her personality, her way of teasing. *Just like Katrina.* Plus, the facts—her stories were real. If someone had approached Alexey or even tortured him to procure stories linking Keller to Katrina, it was doubtful these would come up. Corfe may be, though not about the flowers—Katrina was a tomboy and would never admit to it. The artillery room, she also wouldn't say, for fear of what might happen.

Tomorrow was Keller's last chance. If things went astray, he would be off to prison. Yet Keller failed to understand how this unknown 'Ed' fellow carried so much clout. Yes, probably a hacker, crème de la crème. If Neufeld Bunker knew nothing about him, that was a sign. The Neufeld knew everyone they decided to know. It meant that maybe it wasn't a person at all… and then the mining droid popped into his mind, sitting there like it were another day at work. *Is that you Tom, seriously?*

Chapter 43

This was the day Keller would infuse Clone Bruno with Bruno himself. *A true vegetable infusion.* Somewhat convinced that it could be a success, Keller made his way to the mansion along the wooded path, to prepare the lab—his mind in a twilight zone.

Familiar squawking crescendos from a low pitch to high, tipped with screechy, crass melodic ornaments, greeted him along the way. Skyward, the falcon soared in a wide circle. Suddenly it dove, plummeting faster than a rock, propelling itself downward like a lethal projectile. Keller watched, fascinated at first, trying to understand its trajectory. A second later he deduced it was heading straight for him! As the bird pulled out of its high-speed dive, talons downward for the kill, Keller cringed, stumbled backwards, and tripped on a root. A classic moment which left him winded on his back, looking upward at pines framing the view. Keller rolled over, got to his knees, and searched for the bird. No trace, no sound. Instead, 3 or so meters away and leaning on a tree trunk, Gouyen stood, a serious smirk on her deathly face.

"Was that inspired by you?" Keller asked.

"What do *you* think? You look shaken considering I don't exist, Keller. I'd say damn near fretful. Scared even. The great Keller Mod afraid of a non-existent spirit."

"What's this about? I'm about to attempt another infusion in case you missed that."

"Why do you bother if you don't believe in the world of spirits? In that which you plainly behold with your own eyes and mind."

"I'm not the believing type. And what I perceive can be twisted by the likes of you, whatever you are," he said, not giving in.

"You had more balls when you were a child."

Keller didn't respond. *When she sees fit, she'll go. Always does.*

"You know, she could vanish into thin air, if she wanted," Gouyen added.

"Who?"

"Perhaps you'll understand when it's too late." With that, Gouyen was gone.

Keller brushed himself off and continued to the mansion. *Funny that you'd show up right at this moment, right when I need my wits about me.* It was a deadly game he played, one without rules and little foresight. Prison could be his next step; at this point, he didn't think any lawyer would even consider taking such a case. They would insist he plead insanity and then get locked up in an excellent psychiatric facility. Like the plastic surgeon had, and if truly lucky, Ed would have a fresh chip sewn in for good measure. Similar guards probably—callous ex-criminals who liked the work and enjoyed the pay. And had a curiosity about the mentally very ill. He could live out his life there, with visits by Gouyen too, and talk out loud to her. Some of the other patients would no doubt believe in her existence and even see her.

As the fountain came into view, Keller entered more deeply into the twilight of his mind's unexplored dark side. The glimpse into the afterlife which he had learned to decipher, and the people who appeared there—this was all grade school compared to what lay forth.

A congregation of figures had convened, socializing and circulating. Keller was surprised until he realized they were not living, at which point a panic tickled his spine, running up and down like a feather. He sucked in a breath then exhaled and continued walking. The murmur of the crowd bubbled along with the gurgling water in the fountain. Most wore black, black suits and black dresses. Some eyed Keller and sent him an uplift of the jaw or a nod. As if *he* were the man. He received a half smile from whom he definitely remembered as an aunt. *Is she even dead?*

It was becoming tough for Keller to understand how none of the others, the living, noticed or felt the phenomenon. It reminded him of some gathering he had been to but couldn't quite connect to the crowd. *Déjà vu. Looks like they haven't seen each other for ages.*

Keller watched them, amused, feeling they came to witness the result of the clone infusion and pass judgement; hoping for a day when science proved ghosts were real, as if anyone cared for such proof. *Hoping for the day they can return to the living and be seen. A get out of jail free card.*

Morbid exultation nibbled his blunted nerves when he heard a single solitary scream plume from the lab side of the house, an open window there. It was followed by excited yelling, a begging of sorts. He chuckled at first and then doubled over laughing as he continued to walk. *Now this! All of this! New day, new insanity!* He bathed in glee. *I'm not going in there now, sounds unnecessary.*

Keller mingled instead, nodding to a few of the ladies, shaking hands with some of the men. Probably thanks to Gouyen, they knew of Jolly More and what took place there. Their eerie forms looked placid—a giant illusion with no beginning and no end. Liable to split off, disperse or congeal harder as it bent out of shape and broke the rules of reality. *Those stuck between life and 'whatever came next' had convened in numbers and Keller perceived each and every one mainly because he knew he could, if he wanted to. A conundrum.*

A few minutes later, the burly guard arrived from the security hub, oblivious to the festivities and was radioing reception for an update. Keller heard the orderly's serious response, which fueled his gleeful mood. The orderly had appointed himself part-time to reception since the receptionist had fled. Glee led to laughter once more and Keller exited the macabre gathering for a patch of grass all his own and descended to his knees, his hands reaching out to the dewy blades.

"What are you on?" the guard asked. "Sounds like Emma screaming, I'll take a look."

Keller studied the grass for a few moments, which was rather long and healthy. "Sure, go for it."

A ladybug crept up on the end of a moist blade, then popped into flight and was gone. Sobered by how tiny the little dotted creature had been, Keller took another big gulp of air and exhaled. Yet when it's back had opened up to reveal wings and it kicked off, there was distinction in its departure. *You couldn't catch me even if you tried, you giant bastard.*

Chapter 44

Henrik tended to the clones every morning. He personally loved each one like an exotic pet. He fussed over their diets, monitored their growth, studied samples taken from all over their bodies and saw to it, they were healthy. As growth was rapid, many times that of a usual human, a mistake one day, might lead to tragedy the next.

While the synthetic people he had pioneered in his youth were extremely fascinating, they also made sense. The intricate development of organic life forms was so complex and miraculous, he had no idea how it came about. None, as far as Henrik was concerned. There were theories, of course. One of gods, and there were dozens of them if not hundreds, who may have divinely intervened and tipped the scale from mud to man. But that didn't quite add up. There was an intervention, yes, but Henrik saw no sign that it was a god. He did see life, and he felt it. The bodies were simply missing their lodgers. 'There's no light on, no one at home,' as Tom used to say, regarding the droids.

Henrik respected Keller, the boy who had become a man. Today the next step in evolution would be confirmed, Henrik felt it in his bones. Here at the Jolly More. Keller was ready and though he had a greyish cast about him, fringed with reddish tones, the man who talked to the dead would prevail. There was no other way for this all to end.

Yet he also knew Keller to be in a tough place. He wanted to stay alive like the rest of them and had to buy time to do so. It was moments like these amongst his creations in the clone hall that Henrik thought of Keller and how much he cared for him. If he could persuade Cassy to remove his own chip, the search to locate Ed and kill him would be sped up. They needed each other. The insane were often hard to contain and most unpredictable—this one was the kingpin.

The body Ed had designed for himself, insisting on the reckless reprogramming of DNA, reflected egotism. He designed a tall, ravishing man, good build, large chest cavity to sustain a healthy set of lungs, muscles which toned well, and gave it horse-like teeth, a Roman nose, brow, almost pointed ears, a streamlined skull, and large feet, to complete the apparency of what he thought was greatness. Henrik knew that true greatness came from within. Many amazing people, for instance, were short and mediocre looking. A fierce-looking synthetic could be programmed to be superior in its class. An eminent human, well, that depended on other things.

He donned scuba gear, climbed a ladder, and sat down on the edge of the aquarium housing Clone Bruno, and swung his legs into the fluid. With him, he had a thick, streamlined jacket made of chain mail armor—loops of enmeshed steel covered by a layer of neoprene. It was heavy. The armor on his shoulder, he grasped the edge of the tank and slid into the fluid, sinking quickly in a cloud of bubbles. The splash and tumble didn't bother the clone, it swayed from the currents instead, feral in its repose.

Henrik hauled the armored jacket onto Clone Bruno, and it buckled under the new load. In seconds, it clumsily reacted and stood straight. After that, Henrik pulled out a remote and opened an app, which controlled oxygen levels and the exercise regimen itself. It initiated instructions programmed into memories supplied to the brain.

A cloud of bubbles swirled around as Henrik remained in the tank, helping the clone if it fell, got confused, or lost its bearing. After an hour, Henrik warmed the beast down.

A ghoulish performance on the one hand, a feat of harmony on the other — the clone had no idea what it was doing. *No sense even talking to you, chappy.* Clone Bruno was as fit and healthy as could be expected doing underwater workouts wearing ancient style armor. Keller had agreed after running physical tests himself. *Keller Mod, who had thought the mischievous boy would never grow out of it. Or was it his gravitation towards trouble which led him to see the dead and persist down that path?* Henrik was ashamed for having given him up to Ed, it was a moment of drugged confusion which plagued him often, a chilling, indestructible reality.

In these golden mornings he felt better, of hopeful mind. After Clone Bruno's exercise, his metal jacket was removed, and the string of exercise memories terminated. Henrik waited a while as the heartbeat settled to low and returned the clone to its trance-like state.

After climbing out, Henrik cleaned himself up, and it was during a sip of cold coffee he was alerted by the speaker phone — he could hear it scratching and screeching from the lab. Something was amiss, Ed seethed. *Oh, for heaven's sake, what now man?*

No sooner had Henrik entered the lab when he noticed Emma, grey, awash with concern. She pointed to the speaker, with an intense 'where have you been' look on her face.

"I was feeding and exercising our key man," he said, a tone of the morning's good mood in his speech. Perhaps it was that tinge of happiness which set off Ed, persuading him to teach a lesson, Henrik thought, as an intense stream of electricity clutched his body. His bones felt like they were cracking as his teeth clamped with a horrifying seizure. He fell to his knees, a ravaged squeak emanating from his chest. Emma's eyes opened wide, she sat frozen for the first moment in disbelief, "What are you doing? Stop!" she said, her voice alarmed. "You'll kill him!" she wailed, the sound morphing to a scream which spread through the house and out its windows. Emma ran to Henrik and knelt over him, confusion stumping her efforts to help.

"As he did me. Why did my clone keel over and die?" Ed asked, not phased. "I checked its vitals on my app, and they express death. The video feed shows it to be fallen, its face smushed against the glass."

Henrik could not answer, he had just seen Ed's clone. It was strong and healthy, he thought, above the pain.

"Wait, I'll check. The internet feed could be disconnected. The clones are all fine, I assure you, especially yours," Emma said, shaking, having run her hands over Henrik's body, which felt like a rock. The seizure gripped him, then seemed to soften, so she got to her feet and ran into the Clone Hall. Moments later, she yelled, "It's fine, it's alive, they are all healthy. Please stop! I've taken a photo, let me show you," she said, tearing up.

In the next moment, the burly guard and orderly entered the lab, their gazes fixed on Henrik and the foam exiting his mouth. Before he could speak, the burly man also crumpled to the ground, screaming in agony.

"No entry to the lab, for you," Ed rasped then chuckled.

"We heard the screams and were concerned," the orderly said, watching as the burly man stopped twitching.

"Emma is here to help Henrik. Now get lost," Ed surged, distorting the filter. The burly man crawled dizzily out to reception as the orderly followed, looking bewildered, muttering words of assistance.

"When will my clone be ready?" Ed asked.

"He's ready now," Henrik hissed in agony, thankful for the diversion. "You just need to show up." Emma knelt on the floor next to him. She leveraged his head and shoulders into her lap, wiping the foam from his mouth.

Pause on the other end. "You know, Henrik, I don't have to kill you. I can make life a living hell, but so that you can still function. Note our friend, the plastic surgeon. Seen him lately?" The next zap arrived. Henrik seized once more, froth squeezing from between his clenched teeth. Emma screamed, "Stop! I'll kill your bloody clone for real if you don't stop!"

There was another pause and a rough tapping of plastic.

"Ah, I see where this newfound courage comes from. You seem to be disconnected, Emma. That can also be fixed. And I'll fix that bloody droid so that it never performs another operation!"

Emma didn't answer, as she tended to Henrik. Once again, the seizure softened while sounds continued to issue from the speakerphone—a pen scribbled on paper then a spoon rubbed and tinkled against china.

"And as for that droid, Violet tells me she's been running around and acting quite human, is it true?" Ed continued, no change in tone. "We agreed her humanity was a joke."

"Emotional is one thing, but 'human' sounds a little far-fetched, don't you think?" Emma answered as Henrik sat up, profusely sweating.

"But it was Tom's intention was it not, for this to be possible. I mean, it's what we're doing here isn't it?"

"Tom was insane," Henrik mumbled.

"Keep her locked up and make sure she can't leave. For a real joke, try the memory scan, even if it kills her or ruptures her programming. Tell Keller she won't be released until Bruno's transfer is a proven success. If it's not a success, then we will mail her piece by piece to his prison cell. Or, we'll set her up in a cell next to him, dead. Yet live enough so that she can follow her new programming and satisfy the men. I'm sure they'd enjoy a pretty droid, warm or not. And take my man for a run. I'll be over there soon, to meet him myself."

"You're coming here?" Henrik said to no one in particular.

"Yes, and I will bring a new chip for Emma, if she's around or not." The line went dead.

Ed often threatened to pay a visit. Odd, Henrik thought, to not be able to see your own creations. He was exhausted now, his eyes slowly closed, but not before an echo passed within his mind, a tiny signal crossing his determination to black out and give in. 'I know that voice' it said, take off the synthesizer and there he is. No class, knowledge or insight. A simple little man who has made himself sadistically at home in my world. *I know that man, but who is he?*

Chapter 45

At a few minutes past 11pm, Henrik awoke. Confused as to what room he occupied, he swung his feet over the bedside and gingerly stood up. Wobbly, he walked over to the window, parting the sheers as he got close.

It was a black, moonless night. He peered out over the grounds in front of the building. Layered darkness, the glow of the outdoor spots spilling onto the terrace and the hum of silence soaked his senses. The fountain lay still, its glassy pool reflecting the blackness around it and shimmering spots. He wanted to be in that pool, to cool off and wash away the weight of being a prisoner of his own life, Ed's gruesome voice still lingering in his memory.

This mustn't happen again. I can die, it's not worth it to go out quietly, paralyzed on the floor.

Then he thought of Cassy locked up in the tunnel. He had to talk to her. He would ask her to take out his chip. The time of day didn't matter to a droid, she had long since reached her charge. He on the other hand, felt dizzy. The faintness passed, and he drank water. A queasy feeling remained, but he pressed on. It was as good a time as any and dawn might be too late.

He made his way down the elegant stairwell, not worrying about cameras anymore. It made no difference. Still in bare feet he could feel the sponginess of the lavish carpeting. As he came to the reception area, the tall windows stood glowing, he could make out little bugs flying in the spotlight beams, frazzled looking, circulating non-stop as if battling the light rays for right of way. Perhaps it was their sensory perception, which was set off balance by the stark light, surrounded by darkness. Or their navigational systems breached once they found themselves gargantuan in front of a tiny sun in a dark universe hemmed by trees.

Henrik paused in the center of the room, feeling the space melt into shadow above him, the cathedral ceiling hardly visible. He had erased many of the records Cassy had of him yet understood she did in fact remember some things. She was wary of him, he could sense it. Odd for a synth, he thought, and pondered how many security levels it had. How artificial minds were rigged these days. Henrik felt out of date on present matters and hated his craving for cocaine. Walking to his cottage would be a waste of time. If he got to it, he might not return until morning. Instead, Henrik made his way to the lower stairwell, avoiding the rattle of the lift.

Down in the basement, he followed a hall lined with stone and brick to the furnace room, which housed a large cremation oven, doubling as an incinerator. Two meters to the right of it was a doorway which had evidently been sealed with brick and mortar. Henrik searched one area of the right edge for a tiny hole. He procured a ball-point pen from his pocket and pressed the little indent.

Seconds later the entire segment heaved open, swung inward, and Henrik entered an old tunnel which ultimately led away from the house. About 20 meters in, he came to a much newer doorway, inset, made of metal. Next to it was a security lock, activated by print or code. Henrik added his thumb, the door clicked as it unlocked. Inside he flicked on a ceiling light. A prison cell no doubt, from a bygone era, refitted as a lab with basic equipment including an earlier prototype of the memory machine. Cassy lay on an operating table. She did not move when he entered, yet a tiny dim light slowly pulsed at the base of her jaw indicating the charge was complete.

Cassy perplexed him because he knew that his contemporaries who were building the brightest and the best synths no longer worked in Neufeld. The operation had been moved to a secluded location above ground, in Northern Wales. The Cassandra V23 was considered passée, yet Cassy behaved as if she were human—emotional, irrational at times, defiant, as if someone had gone rogue and did their best to program a *believable* individual. As far as Henrik knew, this had never been done. Not to such a compassionate extent.

Henrik searched gently behind her left ear until he found a tiny lump. That he pressed until she stirred. Next, he spoke a string of code and her machine consciousness became alert.

"Who are you?" he asked.

"I'd like to ask you the same thing. I have records of everyone at Neufeld; my file on you seems to be missing," Cassy replied, tension welling.

"Yet you know of me, I can tell. Who says I'm from the Bunker?"

"Tom's files mention you, I assume—"

"You assume? Humans assume, make mistakes without knowing. Vagueness over fact. Cassandra V23 is not a new model. Such subtlety or 'humanity' as some call it, is not part of your programming. And yet you installed a chip in Bruno. Also, *assuming* he needed one?"

"Droids make mistakes in that they can't *assume* unless it's programmed. Like a train which is heading for a mountainside with no tunnel. If it is programmed so, it will just crash. Balking is not an option, though it could be addressed with some very simple calculations. C'mon, you've seen it. *Mistakes.* I've had updates but I can't override certain things which are asked of me, at proper security levels."

"That makes little sense. Is Ed playing us from both sides?"

"I don't know. Henrik, you don't look so good," she said, a gentleness entering her voice.

"I know, I got zapped, hard. Who asked you to install a microchip in Bruno?"

"That's been erased."

"Surely someone as complex as you has various fail safes. Access one."

"Make me."

"Fair enough. Listen, this is not why I came down here. Ed has asked me to run some diagnostics, memory scans amongst others and then shut you down terminatedly. Cassy, he doesn't give a crap. He wishes you absent from the picture."

"And you care because?"

"I simply do. And, I'm just a little stuck."

"Unstick yourself then. Memory scans are for human consciousness, it will be futile in my case. As you know, there is nothing in my head for it to pick up. Bluntly put," she smiled wryly.

"No harm in trying then, right?" At the instant of saying so, Henrik noticed a minute tick on her lip. "Unless of course someone is actually in there, in which case it could be living hell."

"What is it you want, Henrik? You didn't come down here to tell me I might get hurt, did you?"

"In a way, I did. But yes, I had a reason. I'd like you to take out my chip. If you do, I'll do everything in my power to keep you from machine dissection. I simply won't allow it."

"I'd be happy to take it out, but I can't."

"Why? I'll bring you back to full capacity," he said, noticing his voice getting louder.

"Trust factor aside, you're important. If I take it out, when he presses the button, you won't react properly. You need to tough it out for now until Bruno's transfer is complete."

"And if it doesn't get completed, he blissfully hits the switch all the way. If you're human at all, I'm asking for compassion."

"Wait just another day. We can't even track down his identity, and believe me, I can track down anyone," Cassy said, matter-of-factly.

"You can't track me despite the fact I'm standing in front of you. Who's we?"

"That's confidential. I'm sorry Henrik, your chip must stay intact for now. If Ed realizes it's out, he could really cause problems for all of us."

"That's ludicrous! I haven't been able to trace him either but you're pissing me off now. The only person who has taken a life is Keller. As for Ed, he could be on his way now."

Before Cassy could say much more, Henrik muttered a pile of code. It left her immobile. He could see she was still struggling inwardly when he groped for the little nodule behind her ear and pressed. She shut off completely, and he lay her down, letting her head drop onto the table. Henrik stared at her a moment, brushed aside the lock of hair which had fallen over her face. He straightened her out, clothing too, as if preparing for a presentation. The final switch he located in her mouth, set in a wisdom tooth, using a sickle probe. "Not so young as I thought," he muttered, pressing it for 15 seconds. She was off, yet Henrik felt unsure. Unlike Keller, he didn't act on any inner voice. If something remained which could bypass the switches without touching them, then so be it. Henrik enjoyed a good loose end, even in a moment of darkness.

But he made up for it in his next action—he used straps to fix her to the table. Arms, hands, legs, feet, hips, and torso. Half expecting her to wake up, he hurried along. Her eyes remained shut, but her muscles kept limber. Odd, he thought. Should be stiff, hard to move. Henrik continued along until the bands were all fixed. *There's no way unless she simply bursts them open. This is not the bloody Hulk.*

Keller would no doubt come down on him, but he had to find her first. Time remained for things to turn around, he thought, a twang of guilt pulsing through.

Cassy felt disheartened and alone. The big shutdown was incomplete, she was still there, she could still circumvent what had just occurred, though it would take a while. She kept still while Henrik strapped her down, being careful not to move her eyelids — emotions ran rampant and if he caught any movement whatsoever, he might resort to something more extreme.

For a while, she didn't care. The code Henrik had muttered was most alarming and effective. She decided it must be how a dog felt, one who was tied to a post and left behind or outside for the night to guard a house. Except a dog was allowed to move. She remembered such dogs from her distant childhood in Russia. They spent their entire life outside, barked and attacked anyone who tried to come close and were overall miserable, vicious and hungry. *Who is Henrik?* Cassy had memories of him but very vague, like a person with no name or identity. *I thought I knew him a few days ago.*

The exit clinked as the lock engaged. She imagined Henrik glancing back through the little window in the door before he left. Cassy remained still. Then she heard his receding footsteps and relaxed. She didn't like him around; he was too far gone with his addictions.

Her eyes wouldn't open. Ironic, she couldn't move anything, not a finger! *Humph.* She cared little about that either, she'd handle it after a while. If Keller didn't believe what she had told him, there was not much point to this existence, she thought. There weren't many people with his sense of perception, and meeting another was doubtful. She would be deprogrammed, grossly dissected, and eventually she would leave.

Cassy felt creepy. Like on that first day, right after the explosion and during the intense fire. While the rooms were partitioned with thick stone, half a meter, the smoke found its way inside. Probably through the door. She remembered seeing it but not smelling, not being bothered. Just an emptiness, like now, where she was surrounded by alloys, teflons, silicones and couldn't move. Like a bad dream which became reality, as there was nothing to wake up from.

Chapter 46

The new agenda for Clone Bruno's infusion was simple—Bruno himself would be pushed into a corner where he had to make a choice: fight to live or join the dead. Survival would be the bait. While both Clone Francine and Clone August had heartbeats, were breathing air and sat next to their counterparts quite alive, Bruno's clone would come to the theatre lying submerged in the amniotic-like fluid it lived in and hooked up to an umbilical cord. Alive, but not independently.

Though Keller doubted himself to be a barometer for the spiritual world, Clones Francine and August had seemed to have had lights on even though no one was home. *Expecting someone. A minimal glow.* Once removed from the fluid, a birth of sorts occurred where they were mechanically resuscitated while fully unconscious—the cloned bodies then breathed on their own. Since they resembled living entities, humanoid look-alikes, Keller anticipated this was where the fear lay. These were the monsters both Francine and August saw and ran from. *Right or wrong, it was something they felt.* The 'light on' theory wasn't exclusively his to perceive.

In Bruno's case, he would be given a chance to be reborn on his own, literally. He would be resuscitated like a drowning victim if it looked like he *wanted* to live. The trigger, somewhat similar to that which makes a newborn fill its lungs and breathe for the first time, would be set off once the fluids were drained from the bath—the lungs would engage and empty themselves. The comparatively large lung capacity meant Bruno would have to fight for his life. Keller, Emma, and Henrik would help.

Cassy remained locked up, and Henrik insisted she stay put, Ed's orders. Everyone was eager to move forward, Keller noted, Bruno included. *I'm curious to see how this plays out, how dark.*

Violet was nowhere to be seen.

A swarm of spirits socialized around the outside of the house once more. The group had returned in what appeared to be a gathering of friends and family. Once again everyone wore black. Keller moved through the crowd solemnly this time, nodding to the guests. Some nodded back, some smiled, a few even hailed a cheer. *They've been here for two days, yet anticipation is running strong. What are they up to?*

The entire property was charged. Emma felt it too, a sense of being immersed in crisp, dense, ionized air. She claimed it was good for her hair, so the more, the merrier she told Keller, though he wasn't sure if she even believed him.

After he lay down, Bruno was sedated, yet remained conscious. His gaze meandered to the door which led to the Clone Hall. What he had told no one, aside from Keller and Violet, was that he in fact wanted a new body. He had rounded up investors who wanted to see him pull it off, and if he did, the future could be bright on many levels. What had happened to Myron was spooking the investors and Bruno would fix this. Then he would deal with Ed. No more chips under any circumstances, it was his promise.

The door to the Clone Hall opened. While Bruno expected to see his clone rolled in, he didn't. Instead, a long rectangular container sitting on a lowered trolley was wheeled in and positioned next to him. He could hear the fluid inside lightly lapping against the sides, much like a bath.

"What's that?" he asked.

"You. When you come back, it will be like being born. You'll have to fight for your first breath and cough up anything your lungs can't absorb. They are full of liquid."

Bruno sank back into the padding as if he was about to suffer a car crash. "Playing a drowned victim was not part of the deal — this is no doubt Ed's idea…" he grumbled awkwardly. Bruno tested his wrists and legs. They held fast. His heart rate shot up. Bruno trembled, shook, was struggling to speak more but the anesthetic now prevented him. He grew more tired and sleepy instead.

Bruno seized as his memories spun out of control, flicking by at an alarming rate on screen just a few feet away. Henrik had ramped up the speed parallel to the anesthetic taking effect. Simultaneously Keller and Emma initiated the cooling, setting it to coincide with the memory machine. At the targeted time, Bruno would flatline, and the memory transfer to his clone would be complete.

Keller noted again Violet had not appeared. Henrik shrugged. *It's not like her to no show. Bad timing for cold feet. He'd surely attempt the jump for Violet, if nothing else.*

Bruno slipped out of consciousness as his vitals continued to flatten. Henrik shrugged again. It was too early to die, the memory transfer wasn't done. Then Keller picked up a scalpel he had strategically placed out of view. Without much ado, he held it against Bruno's jugular vein, pressing gently. "Slow down the memories. I want to see the last two years."

"Keller, that could take hours," Henrik responded, nervously.

"Just put in one parameter. Have it slowed down when he's talking to someone, that's all."

"Keller, you're still talking a long time. I can get zapped for this and if he dies and disappears, I die too. You go to jail. Think this through."

"Slow it down or he dies *now*."

Emma cringed. "Keller, honey, I have to agree with Henrik, think it over."

"Time is wasting, slow it down!" Keller said, letting the blade press more against the skin of the neck, all but cutting into it.

Emma reacted first. "Henrik, do it. Let's have a look. I'll slow the cooling."

"How convenient for you both," he said, slowing the memory transfer so that individual pictures, blurred and vague as they were, could be momentarily distinguished. What had appeared a pulsating, flowing stream now looked like an old, damaged film being played at breakneck speed. Views of a bed, window, business meetings, hospitals, doctors, nurses, driving, wife, dog, neighbor, street views, café, dog, window, TV, wife, friend, street views. The apparently mundane life of a publicly visible entrepreneur showed his dog more than it did his office at Lucy's. *Ah, and an affair.*

Running much faster than life itself, it was a comedy of simplicity. Bruno liked to swim with his eyes open and go to bed late. He liked to stare out into his backyard for a while in the mornings, study the trees over the neighboring yard, look at the clouds. His wife's smile made him draw her close. A finger in the rear-view mirror showed he didn't like tailgaters. Summed and cross-sectioned, Bruno had a good life. In the speed of it all, his wife visibly deteriorated and while he met many people, they tended to repeat. There was nothing out of the ordinary—the places where the footage slowed were average conversations. Wife, mailman, plumber, secretary, nurse, doctor, barista, and so on.

"Can you add in his heart rate as a parameter, when it was unusually high?"

"I suppose," Henrik responded, typing, his own interest growing. "High heart rate shots. Nervous in general. Conversation." The view of slowed spots changed. Threats could be seen, people angry, his wife crying, shouting at him. A man in the street yelling. A car accident. His mother dead. His dog dead. Wife dying and dead. Cassy meeting him.

"Slow!" Keller shouted and Henrik turned it way down. "For all we know, Cassy could be our man too," he said, regretting his words. There was nothing much said between her and Bruno, the sound conveyed ill-defined small talk.

Following were more of the usual high heart rate incidents, driving, arguing, visiting lawyer, funeral parlor and so on. But at one point Keller watched his phone pass into view, answering a call, then passing by and up to his ear.

"Here, slow for the sound." While it was fuzzy, what came in was the electric synthesized scraping of Ed's voice. No doubts. Keller glanced at Emma, who expressed with her eyes, 'See, not him.' Then she flicked a glance at Henrik.

Feeling her unease, Keller glanced at Henrik too and saw that sweat had appeared on his shirt under the lab coat. Henrik glimpsed the speakerphone, then seared Keller with loathing in his eyes. He reached into his pocket and pulled out a few pills, swallowed them dry. "It's not him, let's wrap it up," Henrik said.

"Relax, the speaker's shut off and the video feed shows us setting up—there's a one-hour delay. I can swap it out at any time and, well, I doubt he'll catch the blip. If he asks, let me answer for it, I'll deal with him."

"You mother f—, I can literally die for this. If he tries to connect... was it you who put in the dead clone footage? Was that you?"

"No, c'mon, I'm not sick, Henrik. You are. All I'm trying to do is identify Ed. At least now we know it's not Bruno."

Henrik sped up the machine, getting closer and closer to the present. Memories from inside the Bunker might have revealed something, but Keller noticed Bruno's vitals were worsening at a steady rate. Knowing the man could die sooner rather than later, Keller signaled Henrik to return to flat out speed. The vague images returned to a blurred flow.

Emma breathed with relief as Keller swapped out the delayed security cam footage for real-time. The speakerphone volume got turned up. They listened. Nothing. No crackle, fingers thumping or breathing—no sound. Ed wasn't on.

Henrik joined Keller in the control room.

"Yesterday he mentioned coming here, so he could be on his way," Henrik spoke nervously.

"What?"

"He's threatened before and has never shown. Besides, he can probably imagine we might try to kill him, he would probably bring backups. God knows. He's pretty obsessed with that clone of his, you know."

"Yeah, I gathered when he zapped you yesterday."

"Anyway, probably a false alarm."

"Let's hope so. Mind you, if he wants a safe and pleasant infusion, he'll have to behave, be a little friendlier. Showing up wouldn't hurt either."

Then Bruno flatlined.

Moments later, Keller perceived Bruno's translucence materialize next to his own dead body. He was standing, a worried look on his face. Bruno looked behind Keller and then off to the side. For a moment, Keller marveled at the beauty of him, the energy field. *What's he looking at?* Keller spun around, there was nothing there. Yet he could sense an auspicious magnetism.

Keller looked back at Bruno to see panic and defeat in his eyes as he again stared somewhere beyond. "Get in!" Keller appealed. "It's your life, like you wanted it." Bruno moved towards the clone, still focused on a point elsewhere.

Keller glanced backwards. His lips parted as he turned to look. The room was full of translucent figures—spirits, souls, ghosts. The party had apparently moved inside, though more solemn now. A familiarity shrouded the space. An organ started to play, gentle, melodic high notes—the scene before him made sense now, emotions rushing in, wildly sloshing into gaps and crevices of mourning. The picture held firm—it was his father's and Katrina's funeral! Out of the corner of his eye he saw a figure standing away from the crowd. Bruno's wife perhaps, a benevolent smile on her face. He didn't care. *Let him have her dead soul if he wants.*

Keller began walking towards the coffins, the high notes morphing into a dark requiem thrashing his ears, his mind. He wanted to be up close, touch them. He wanted to rip open the lids and peer inside. He wanted to know for sure that Katrina and his father were inside.

Emma suddenly caught him by the arm. "Where are you going? He's ready, I saw him move a little, and shudder. We need to resuscitate."

"Not yet," Keller said, his own voice sounding meek above the resonating organ pipes.

He wanted to put his hand on the coffins, which continued to beckon relentlessly. Keller beheld the woman who reminded him of his Aunt — she was his Aunt. Then he recognized cousins, an uncle, friends of his father's and standing up front, Alexey. Alexey? He's not dead. None of them are. He spoke out to them, asking what they were doing there. The music blasted louder still, churning ominous chords.

"Keller, he moved! Who the fuck are you talking to? Keller!" implored Emma's distant voice.

Henrik pulled the plug on the bath. Next, he disconnected the umbilical cord, and as the body was triggered to seek oxygen via its lungs, it writhed in desperation, floundering, breathless. Clone Bruno was drowning, unable to cough up the liquid. Emma produced a suction catheter and Henrik shoved it down Clone Bruno's throat, into the trachea.

As Keller listened to Emma's fading pleas, he walked towards the coffins and the crowd. They smartly receded and then evaporated, as did the music. Dazed, Keller turned back to see Henrik and Emma preparing to resuscitate Clone Bruno struggling in the tub. *Bruno, had he made it?* Glancing back one last time, he saw Gouyen, at the door to the lounge. He nodded to her. She smiled, darted a glance in the direction of the action behind him.

"Looks to me like someone has made a choice," Gouyen said, satisfied.

"Yeah, I suppose," Keller replied, still foggy.

Gouyen dropped the smile and receded behind the closing door.

Something is off.

"Keller!" Emma continued, guessing what might be transpiring. "Help us, he's trying to breathe!"

Keller turned again; the clone was writhing in the tub while Henrik applied CPR. Emma readied a syringe with one hand, the other holding the suction tube. Confused, Keller joined them, replacing Henrik with the chest compressions. Henrik suctioned the water from Bruno's lungs, yet the heart rate of the clone was diminishing. It was truly drowning.

"Hold on dear chap, those nasty fluids are being evacuated," Henrik said, excitement lacing his attitude. No sooner had Henrik spoken, he yanked the tube out. The clone convulsed in a brutal heave, sending the remaining liquids out of his mouth in a torrent. Choking, coughing, sputtering, it clenched the edge of the bath and hurled more. And after a pause, hanging over the side, he stiffened once again, headfirst, shoulders following, in a great, garglesome gasp of air! Keller, Henrik, and Emma stood back, hypnotized by the human-looking thing, battling to breathe. It coughed some more, spit, shook and every once in a while sucked air inwards—a raspy, bubbling hiss suggesting turmoil. Then it wailed, the kind of low rumble one makes when they are struggling and angry. The clone was incoherent *but alive*.

"You look like you've seen a ghost, Keller," Emma commented. "But well done."

"I was losing my mind, thanks for snapping me out of it. I thought I saw something, yes. Well done to you too," Keller said, putting a tight arm around her shoulders. He shook Henrik's hand.

"Never mind that now. So far, so good. Let him struggle, he'll make it," Henrik commented, trying to calm Clone Bruno down. When Henrik lay a hand on him, Bruno's eyes opened momentarily. They were wrought with agony, bewitched. Instead of screaming, Bruno slumped back slowly, looking at the ceiling, his shoulders at the back wall of the bath now, head propped up. His lids got heavy, the agony dissipating. He passed out.

"OK, let's dry him off and move him to a proper bed. And then keep our fingers crossed for when he wakes up," was all Keller could think of saying. It was a bittersweet feeling of success—something incredible had just occurred, just not for any good reason. He noticed Henrik slip out to the lounge.

"What do we do with the old Bruno?" Emma asked, wiping the clone with a towel.

Keller wanted to laugh again, gleefully mull over what Emma had said, as if Bruno were an unwanted doll. "Make sure he's dead. Do an injection if you must, I'd hate for someone else to take it."

"Excuse me?"

"Nothing. You're right, let's just keep him in the morgue until his funeral. Or whatever they have in mind. He has children?" Keller asked.

"None that I know of."

"Relatives?"

"Probably, must be someone."

"Or not. No wonder Ed chose him. Loaded, no people of his own. Wife mysteriously dies. Did he leave any instructions?"

Emma and Keller looked at each other and concurrently bubbled over with suppressed laughter. The glee swelled and warmed the room. Henrik returned, his fatigued eyes gratified — a new sprig of energy crossing his manner. "I would actually toss him in the incinerator and forget he was here." The three of them cracked up as stress discharged into the air, neutralized.

"What did you do with Myron?"

"Incinerator."

"Doesn't anyone ever come looking?"

"Nope. A real family type probably wouldn't find himself here. Not natural. I mean, say Bruno's wife was alive, what would she say?" Henrik commented.

"The idea was they both would be alive together," Emma answered.

"And suddenly show up in society, 30 years younger?"

"Well, now he can do it with his new girlfriend."

"Where is Violet anyway?" Henrik looked around. "She wasn't in the lounge either."

"I'll check when we are done here, as long as she's around when he wakes up," Emma said.

"Back to the two Brunos, Henrik, seriously, what do you suggest?" Keller asked.

"Get rid of him. There can't be 2 Brunos, no way," Henrik was adamant, "If anything were to happen, and despite any contract he may have signed, this will all look too unbelievable. Well, wacko. There is no point in holding on to the old body."

"What if the new one doesn't live?"

"Myron did, so will he. Now imagine if Myron's old body was around? What would the wife say?" Henrik continued.

"I don't know. I mean, what could she say?" Keller deliberated jokingly.

"My experience with Violet, when the whole thing got out of control and we tossed her clone into the mix, was quite unnerving. The police didn't have a choice but to believe and luckily everything got solved before anyone pried further. This is different."

"You mean the killer was caught?" Keller asked, suddenly serious.

Henrik looked at him but didn't answer.

Chapter 47

Keller watched as Henrik dropped the temperature of Bruno further and administered one more injection, a lethal one. Gouyen's facial expression haunted his immediate thoughts and while no more spirits occupied the lab, Keller felt something was not quite right. Her expression had been foreign to him, and she had been eager to leave. *She likes to exit once she's done something. When a task is finished. She must have orchestrated the funeral. Why?*

Violet remained absent. Keller thought of going upstairs himself to check on her; he texted, and she didn't answer. While her behavior of late was bizarre, she was flirting with both Ed and Bruno—that could only be strategy. But she definitely needed to be present when Bruno woke up. *Bruno needs all the help he can get, we don't need another Kid.*

"Emma, things look pretty stable here, can you go check on Violet?" Keller spoke up.

"Yeah, sure. I'm as surprised as you are." Emma finished what she was doing, organized herself and walked out.

Moments later, the speakerphone quietly crackled and hissed. Unusual for it to do so, as was an added distant throbbing sound which cut in from time to time.

"News gentlemen, any good news?" the unmistakably awkward voice of Ed resonated through the room.

Keller nodded to Henrik. "Good news sir, Bruno made the jump. He's in a coma but his vitals are good," Henrik reported, relief surging.

"Yes, I can see that, excellent! I pray for his rapid return. Congratulations gentlemen, you have just altered evolution itself." For the first time Ed sounded satisfied and eager. "I think the line may have been down for a while, perhaps on my end, but I did catch some of it. Very nice, much like we thought things might go, Henrik?"

"Yes, indeed. Keller suggested we run the memories concurrently despite what it does to the brain. It seemed to work. As did the staged birth slash drowning resuscitation. I guess we'll know when he wakes up." Henrik wiped his sweaty brow and mustered a smile.

Keller wanted to see the face of the coward behind the voice. *You simple little bastard, happy now, closer to what you wish to achieve for yourself? Henrik down at your feet, all but a shell of a man, eager to please.* Then he composed himself. "What about Cassy? How about we unlock her?"

"Either of you touches her, Henrik dies. Let Bruno wake up first, I want to see him sitting and hear his voice. Besides, she is to *sleep* a little while longer. I will be over there in the near future. After my own successful transfer, she will be released, not before. Why are you so interested in an old droid?"

Keller looked at Henrik, who stared back at him. *This guy is tiresome.*

"I promised to return her in one piece. Those synths are valuable, and she has a specific function in the bunker. And with her — ."

Suddenly, the door to the lounge flew open as Emma rushed in, eyes ablaze with pain. Since Henrik and Keller faced the speakerphone, she all but bit her tongue, "Violet's ah, please, come quick," she said targeting Keller and strode to the crash cart for supplies, "Lots of blood," Emma whispered, barely containing herself, holding back tears, flushed red.

Keller, noting the intensity in her plea, helped her grab the crucial items and rushed off with her, bounding across the lounge, into reception and up the ornate, carpeted staircase fearing the lift was too slow.

"Good for keeping your mouth shut. What happened?"

"Someone sliced her throat," Emma whispered audibly, face quivering.

Keller didn't answer as he made haste. The orderly who was not present at reception flashed through his mind, as did the security guys, one by one. A severed jugular meant the killer had nerve. A seasoned pro was more likely than a newbie. *Interesting, don't overthink it – the orderly is still a contender.*

Back in the lab, Henrik sat dazed, striving to make small talk with Ed who pretended he didn't mind something was wrong with Violet. "She was an odd one, don't you think?" Ed continued.

"Yes, she was. Quite likeable though," Henrik admitted.

"I agree. I hope it's not too serious. She has a new body awaiting her in the Hall..."

"Yes," Henrik replied, monotone. "Are you on your way then?"

The speakerphone beeped off, the distant throbbing subsided with it, and the room was quiet aside from the usual hospital-like sounds of the monitors. Bruno lay peacefully, his breathing shallow, a little craggy but rhythmic, his heart normal. Henrik looked out the window and debated whether to run upstairs. He didn't need to witness what occurred, by the look on Emma's face Violet could be dead. With Keller having left, Ed had dropped the line. Henrik noted the fake courteousness in Ed's voice—he was up to something. That simple little man was on the move.

Upon arriving at Violet's room, Keller found the door open. A large pool of blood had coagulated around her head on the floor, her strawberry blonde hair immersed in places, messily straggled. She was much paler than usual and undeniably dead. Keller checked her pulse and breathing. There was nothing to show any light was on, note left, or that she was in the room at all.

"She's gone," he announced. Tears streamed down Emma's cheeks. She momentarily brushed them away.

"I'll call the orderly to mop this up," she fumbled for her phone.

"Did you see him around today?"

"Keller, I don't know, he was at reception yesterday, last I recall. But if you think he did this, you're wrong. I assure you, he's no killer. The security team, that's another matter."

Keller nodded. "Fine, but I'll clean it up. Please get Henrik to help me lift her."

"Get him yourself. You put him at significant risk earlier on, why?"

"We all needed to know."

"There are other ways. You can check the memory backups, for example," Emma said with a hardened look. "Henrik has paid his dues, more than you can imagine. Don't think you have Ed's favor, he favors no one. Besides, you were off in dreamland during most of the procedure."

Chapter 48

Emma hummed a gentle melody while cleaning up Violet, washing her hair, and changing her clothes. She chose a pastel-colored floral dress, refusing to mourn, and did her hair in braids. When she finished, she also stopped humming. She called Henrik and Keller both to take Violet to the basement.

After arriving, they transferred her to a cart, rode down the lift to reception, wheeled her on through the lounge and lab to an anti-chamber fitted with a utility lift. Its doors parted and the two men and stretcher neatly fit inside. The trip took 3 seconds when the doors parted again. The ensuing scene was characteristic of the mansion—the old stonework and broad beams brushing against modern décor and technology. Minus any cams.

They wheeled the cart out of the lift, its rubberized wheels running silently on the smooth, painted concrete floor. As a low, stone arch drew near, the view suggested a state-of-the-art wine cellar lay beyond. It wasn't to be. Dusty bottles of rare vintages, tastings and jubilant anecdotes were supplanted by a cremation oven, a morgue trolley, the stench of disinfectant and the silent weeps of the dead.

Keller steered towards the contemporary refrigeration system. He chose the top fridge door in the middle and pulled its stainless handle. As the door swung open, a waft of cool air hinting stale flesh coalesced with antiseptic and stagnant must.

Keller hated these fridges for the traces they left behind. Then he thought of Nora, and how she probably saw him as a monster by now. He was tired of being alone in this world. Even Henrik's dignified pompousness had become welcome, Emma's candid manner, and he saw a friend in the kidding orderly. *What is his name?*

Henrik, as if seizing the moment in an area of the house unhooked from surveillance, spoke up. "You're pretty good with planting fake footage in the system. Nice work."

Keller turned to look at him before they heaved the body onto the retractable shelf. "I had to do something. I needed to look at his memories without anyone freaking out. I didn't want to wait until later, in case something glitched. Henrik I—"

"Did you also create the footage of the dead clone?"

"You know I didn't. Let's get her in. Grab the other side," Keller said sliding his hands under the stiffening body of Violet, one under her back, the other under her right thigh.

"I kind of like it down here," Henrik said, amused. "You realize that footage could have killed me so it's in my interest to find out exactly how it got there. I'm no saint Keller, but that was a dirty trick."

"I don't trick, don't need to. I doubt Emma had anything to do with it either."

"Correct. I doubt it was Emma too. But it also wasn't the orderly, the vanished receptionist or our unsavvy security team," he squeezed out the words.

"And when were you going to tell me the murderer was found?" Keller rebuked.

"Makes no difference. The killer is Ed, and that clone was never alive. He just needed some guys to plant it and someone to take the fall."

"I was the fall guy first and could have been again. You should have told me. As for the footage, he's probably bluffing about it, though he sounded pretty peeved," Keller's anger diminished.

"He's sadistic," Henrik continued in a lowered, stressed voice. "But I've been talking to him for years—what's real and what's false can often be the exact inverse. And with you on the verge of success…"

"That's crap and you know it." Keller was losing his patience. *He's missing the big picture. Grossly off-kilter, anguished.*

"The footage wouldn't have been too hard to create."

"So then maybe you did it. It doesn't matter now, he'll soon see his damn clone. Henrik, I don't set people up to die or feel pain. It's me, Keller!"

"Matters to me," Henrik said as they lifted Violet up onto the platform and solemnly rolled her into the refrigerator. Keller could perceive that Henrik cared for her, bitterness filled his eyes and the neat wrinkles on a face flickered strain, edging towards desperation.

"If you're worried about being zapped to death, then get Cassy to take it out. Set her free first. I'll talk to her and—"

"Nonsense! She's worried it'll tip Ed off. He's already noticed Emma and unchipping me might *unleash the wrath*. Prissy. And I doubt it's really that—probably thinks I don't deserve to live, thanks to you," self-pity clawed at Henrik's words.

As Keller turned to push the stretcher back to the lift, he heard an unexpected clicking sound, nevertheless, one he knew well. It was metallic, bold yet quiet, a ratcheting noise topped with a click. *His mother's smiling face flashed before him, scarfed and drenched in the desert sun.*

He looked back blithely—Henrik was holding a pistol. A dark grey, hefty piece. Glock 19. Keller knew it fairly well. *He and his mother were both laughing after she made one target, a beer bottle, with her eyes closed. Probably the far eye squinted, he thought.*

"Now that you've saved the day, where does it leave me?" Henrik's droning brought Keller back.

"Henrik Poole, a man of surprises. It leaves you in your shitty life, the one you've always had and wanted," Keller continued, now looking into his eyes. "Seriously?"

"Despite your ill viewpoint of me, I don't plan on dying. Not yet. The work on Bruno was as much to do with me, as you."

"I'd say it was all you. Where did you get that?" Keller said, pointing with his chin.

"Oh, this? It used to be Myron's. Must have been some badass or just paranoid."

"The original Myron, maybe, but you lost him, remember?"

"Still a miracle."

"And what about her?" Keller said, nodding to the fridge. "Who took the fall for the clone's murder? Who's locked up?" he continued, slowly stepping towards Henrik.

"That's an elaborate story Keller, not sure if you want to hear it."

"Lay it on."

"It was our previous surgeon. Talented man."

"You forced him to make a prosthetic face of me, to fit his own..."

"Someone who might be mistaken for you at a distance, in poor lighting or on security footage. The mechanics of the situation are what you think they are. He was pulled out of the psych hospital, filmed by surveillance cams around the area, and returned. In his state he was willing to do absolutely anything for a few hours of peace — what you heard about his chip is true. And surprise, there's a pause button."

"Then you turned him in after I agreed to come here," Keller said.

"It was simply a matter of tipping off the right people and planting the face."

"My how connected our good friend is."

"Like a parasite to a brain," Henrik muttered, his gaze unwavering.

"This is ridiculous. Put that thing away and let's get Cassy out."

"Sure, guess it doesn't matter what we do with her at this point, might as well power her up. Ever thought she might work for him?" he said, letting the gun fall to his side.

"I did. So let's ask her. But first, it's Bruno's turn to go into the oven."

"You're really into this, aren't you?"

"Gotta clean up the mess," Keller said, walking over to Bruno's body.

"You're just as sick as I am, Keller."

Chapter 49

Something's going on in the mansion today, the Kid thought to himself. He had been let out that morning to play, had returned for lunch, found none made, and helped himself—he knew where all the good stuff was and ate tortilla chips, cucumber slices and ice cream. No one noticed him, and he liked it that way. The ratty receptionist had gone off somewhere; at least he hadn't seen her in a few days and now the orderly was away too. Emma had probably forgotten he was not back in his room or else she would have come looking.

Instead, they were all on one side of the house, where the lab was. The Kid was told to stay clear of the lab and what lay beyond. He wasn't sure exactly, but he had once caught a glimpse of tall aquariums with people in them, asleep standing up. He felt the tanks looked familiar but couldn't understand or remember why. He was confused because another man's memories were in his head—some of them had to do with the tanks. A guy called Myron. And whenever Henrik came to see him, he was always trying to find out where Myron had gone, as if he, The Kid, knew anything about that.

Back outside he looked up to the skies and beheld the falcon circling. It was elegant and dangerous at once and the Kid loved him for it. He wanted to look through its eyes and feel how it was to soar high above, spot a mouse in a field, dive down and have it for a snack. The Kid reflected on how a mouse might taste and imagined he liked it but only if cooked in the oven. Like if the cook made it with BBQ sauce, burned a little, sticky. Then he thought if he might like eating the eyes and decided no. No eyes, claws, ears or noses. The fur would have to come off, he had seen it done in a movie.

"You would know where Myron is, wouldn't you?" he whispered to the falcon under his breath. "You really need to let Henrik and the rest of them know, even the man on the speakerphone, the grumpy one. If only you could talk." The Kid peeled his eyes away from the sky and saw one of the security guys in the distance looking at him. He pretended not to notice and moved towards the house as if going back. He didn't like playing with the guards, they were rough with him. Though they did teach him to fight. One even showed him how to use his pistol. They shot at rocks in the next field but were heavily reprimanded by Henrik.

Once near the house, the Kid simply made his way along the side as if going to the back entrance and disappeared out of view.

"Is he still supposed to be out?" Vernon asked the burly man, beer in one hand, pointing a thumb back in the direction of the mansion. Vernon wore his dark blue uniform and with greying unkempt hair looked chivalrous in a shopping mall kind of way. The burly man, also holding a beer, shrugged. He was a touch portly and his musculature defiant, though his saturated tattoos suggested shrinkage. The two of them looked childish, circulating around the little house, drinking, burping, farting. They kept a good eye on things, even though there was not much to look at aside from Emma, they felt, now that Cassy was locked up.

"I don't know, looks like he's been out all day. He's a good kid, let him be," Vernon concluded.

"Yeah, never known him to run off; should be fine I guess." They clinked bottles absent-mindedly, and each took a sip. "Boss is coming looks like," the burly man said.

"He says that once every few months or so, but never does. I'll believe it when it happens. Why, is there something you're worried about? The place is in decent order, just people missing," Vernon chuckled.

"Yeah but he can't blame us for that, I didn't hire them. And after the blackout in Violet's room, Emma said not to worry, Violet got moved and the cleaner accidentally bumped the cams, getting the cobwebs. They'll hook it back up themselves."

"Sounds a little strange to me, but whatever, she's a strange gal," Vernon said, burping.

"That she is. Strange in all the right places."

"Relax, Henrik's got dibs on her."

"Henrik as a certified coo-coo bird."

"Yeah, and you're a certified everything else." They sniggered. "That I am, that I am," the burly man added. They stood a while, each shifting his gaze in no particular direction, then Vernon staring off as if in thought, "Besides, the boss told us to stay put. No one is to leave the premises until he arrives."

"We live here Vernon, aside from weekends sometimes. Half of them have already left. There's something going on, I can smell it. We need to get a cam in the lab. What kind of security guards are we supposed to be if we can't see the entire building?"

"I don't even want to know what they do in there. The pay is good, my parole officer is satisfied, I can get shit-faced during my shift, and I even have a small apartment. Only it's shared with you and that my friend, must change."

"Well, you talk to Ed. That guy's another bucket of nuts and bolts that just don't match."

"I know mate, I hear ya loud and clear," Vernon clanked the burly man's bottle.

As far as the Kid was concerned, he had lost his tail. He moved around the garden like the devil on waves of smoke, ducking, weaving, rolling, his imaginary pistol always upright. He hid behind a tree, dropped to his chest and slithered past a bush. He headed for the wood, a little alcove with a heap of stone at the back of it. To him, it was HQ and his superiors were waiting for him there. After watching a bee inspecting a leaf for a few seconds and admiring how it was able to scratch its back with what appeared to be its forearms, the Kid sprang to his feet yet kept low. He peered over the bush and, seeing no one else in the garden, sprinted for the crumbling stone alcove. The musty smell of perpetual shade greeted him as he swept past the heap and dove behind it, his face and chest hugging the rocks. He enjoyed the cool roughness on his cheek and next beckoned for someone to open the hatch. He was about to imagine a circular door spiraling open when something caught his eye. It was beyond the rubble down below — a hollow space. At the bottom, a pool of water reflected light seepage from the cracks and spaces.

Before he knew it, his hands were pulling rocks out of the way, he needed to get to the pool, it was a discovery. In a matter of minutes, he cleared the loose stones which seemed to be blocking an opening, a passage for someone short. He peered inside and as his eyes adjusted, the Kid made out what looked like rough steps. He stepped inside and sat down, taking stock. There were seven steps to the water. He threw a stone in and it landed on a floor, an inch or so beneath the surface. Not to worry about drowning. He followed the dark ripples to the other side where a rectangular shape appeared, a proper door!

The Kid moved forward, gingerly testing the water, then boldly crossing it to the door. This is just what I need for my headquarters, he thought, hardly believing his luck. He paused a moment to hold his breath and listen if anyone was in the garden above. Just the usual bird chirps and bug noises answered his breathing.

Next, he tested the door. It was wooden and ancient. And rotten. Yet it gave way when he turned the newish looking latch. This was adventure, discovery! He pulled the door open and as he did, the top hinge came apart, crumbling with rust. As he dragged the door further, he thought of how he might fix the rot. He looked at a memory now, of his own hands, callous and strong, operating an electric handsaw. They weren't actually his hands, and certainly not his memories, but there the picture was. He could even feel the weight of it, the smooth plastic grip and the trigger he pulled to make it work. That's not so bad, he decided.

Once inside, he could barely make out the empty space. And then, as his eyes adjusted further, he distinguished a glow perhaps 5 meters away—it appeared past a bend in a tunnel made of stone with an arched ceiling. Still in shock at his finding, the Kid stepped forward, towards the glow, emulating a favorite movie character moving towards an alien ship. His mind raced as he groped for where the tunnel might lead. He made his breathing shallow, his steps barely audible.

As he neared the bend, strip lighting became apparent, both along the bottom and the top. The stretch of tunnel past the bend was dry and repaired in places. The first thing which caught his eye was a lock system, next to a metal door a few meters away. As the Kid came up to it, he noticed it had a little window, like his own room. He stuck his face close and peered inside. He made out what looked like a lab to him, dimly lit, metallic reflections describing lab stuff. Then he spotted a figure on the table, sleeping. It was Cassy!

From what the Kid could remember of her, after snooping around, was that she charged, sitting up and even standing. He thought of her as a bird because she didn't fall over when she did so and also didn't move. And her head seemed to settle on her shoulders and though she hadn't feathers which puffed up, he imagined them doing so. It was far-fetched, but the Kid didn't mind. Now he began drumming on the door, it was almost evening, and she should get up. Cassy didn't move.

Next he made his way further down the tunnel, to what looked like a blocked passageway and heard muffled voices coming from the other side. The words were hard to make out, but it was an argument. Two men sounding like Henrik and Keller. What were they doing there? Yes, strange things were going on that day.

He tried once more to get the sleeping Cassy's attention, but to no avail. After, he made his way back out the wet stairwell. He liked the musty smell of the ancient stones crusted with moss and wondered who else at the house knew about this place—he wasn't the first to tamper with the stones, they were easy to clear. Next time he would bring a torch and while he didn't mind snakes, meeting one without seeing it was perilous.

Back out in the Garden the kid inspected his shirt. It was wet and quite stained. He didn't care, shirts could be changed. But who to ask about the entrance? He would hint to one of the guards he was curious about the house. Maybe that would lead to an explanation.

The Kid stood facing the wood and tossed stones, aiming at tree trunks. After a few lobs, he walked back into the garden and decided it was best to get a fresh shirt and then visit guards. The Kid would have simply gone inside if it weren't for his intense interest in all things that flew in the air.

In the distance, at least a mile away, a helicopter appeared and looked as if it were coming closer. The Kid had only seen one before, the inside too. When Myron arrived. He reflected once more on how him seeing that was even possible. Yet he had, clear as day. Then he thought of Gouyen and how he liked to hang around her when she came to visit. But then was different to now—it was as though he had become Myron.

The Kid looked back up at the helicopter and indeed, it was nearing, the beat of the blades barely audible above the engine. He stayed under the cover of the trees, keeping close to the trunks as he positioned himself for a better view. He wasn't allowed to wander into the woods, but he had to see. Two treasures in one day—the Kid suddenly had to pee from excitement and did so on yet another tree, out of view of the house. Henrik had taught him, just in case.

The chopper landed in the next field and the Kid sensed it meant trouble. Four men got out, formally dressed. One looked old, but the other three were young and sturdy looking, like himself. Well, Myron. The Kid had always thought himself just a skinny lad, fair skin, big eyes and knobby knees. When he looked in the mirror, it surprised him to find a James Bond type looking back. Whatever, he could live with it. His plan was simple. First, he would break out Cassy.

Chapter 50

From 9000 feet, the sheep down below reminded Ed of magots, scourging a beautiful strip of green. The sleek, dark grey utility chopper he and his men had boarded at an airstrip just outside of Ironsmith, had surprised him in its outward simplicity. Yet when given a quick tour, he saw that it was well armed and contained plenty of cargo space. It suited his Plan B for the Jolly More perfectly.

Soon they descended rapidly, more quietly than expected from such a monster, and landed in a field behind a wood flanking the mansion from the west. From what Ed could see, the magots had barely noticed. *Nor did any of the sheep in the mansion I presume.*

There were two pilots aboard, three synths which were highly efficient soldiers dressed in plain clothes and Ed himself who wore a long dark coat, black jeans, and leather boots. Very apropos he considered. His neat, white, balding head sat perched atop a pedestal like black turtleneck leading down to a tall bony old body.

Ed called the shots. Despite his age, he lightly dropped from the chopper's cargo door. Three synths followed him, and the pilots stayed put. They were to stay aboard until further notice as the party would be leaving soon — the visit was to be short and effective.

Ed, accompanied by one synth, headed in the direction of the security hub gate house. The other two had been given instructions to apprehend the Cassandra V23 who lay in a tunnel which could be accessed via the back garden.

Agilely making his way through the dusky wood, the old man approached the security house within minutes. The two guards there, having cleaned up their own party upon hearing the helicopter's arrival, came out to meet him.

"You're both drunk," Ed said as he neared.

"Finally nice to meet you, sir. Not drunk. We are done with our shifts, just hung around, as you asked. It's a pleasure," said Vernon.

As the burly man put out his hand, Ed didn't move, keeping his distance. "Round up whoever is in the house, all of them. I wish to see you all in the lounge. The Kid and Violet too. Everyone. Use force if you must," Ed said.

"No need for that, I'm sure they'll agree. Been a little weird around here today. Emma screamed again; Keller called to say she found a rat," said Vernon, the burly man nodding.

"I know what took place today. The main point is that you don't intervene, ever, regardless of how things look."

"We never do. I mean, we really need to see what goes on in the lab if you want us to protect the house properly," Vernon said, glancing at the burly man.

"No," the controller said with finality. Meeting the guards in real life made him nervous. Then, after a pause, "Where are they all?"

"The orderly and the receptionist split, haven't seen them for a day or two. Keller and Henrik carted someone through the lounge, probably heading to the basement. Violet's room is blacked out and Keller said he'd rehook the cam himself, to not bother 'cause Violet's sleeping. Emma's probably in the lab, but we can't—."

"Basement?" Ed asked, distantly. "Why do you think that?"

"You have a morgue down there, remember?" the burly man said this time.

"Violet's dead?" Ed's tone wavered, concern creeping in. He recalled Emma rushing into the lab, shouting Violet's name. *Had she looked upset?*

"Dunno, couldn't see the head. It was covered—." The burly man stopped talking.

"Go and fetch them, then. And whoever's on that cart."

"It'll be a cinch, but I don't think anyone's ever met you, sir," said Vernon.

"We'll see about that. Now go." His voice was plain, aged, and carried little weight. The two guards glanced at Ed's partner, no doubt armed, and obliged—they realized one or both of them also held a control app for their chips.

When Vernon reached the reception along with the burly man and checked the screens there, to his surprise, the lab showed up. *Someone's hooked in more feeds.* Emma could be seen and the new guy, Bruno, was asleep in a hospital bed—simple but shaped, set in a minimalist setting hemmed by white and stainless. Vernon scratched his Adam's apple and exchanged glances with the burly man.

They both apprehensively continued through reception and entered the lounge, which was vacant. Several steps later they stood at the lab entrance. Neither guard had the code, the proper finger or iris needed.

"He said to use force if necessary," Vernon began.

"On the staff, not the door. I don't want to get zapped again," the burly man retorted.

Vernon knocked. *The door slid open.*

"My, how smart you are," the burly man muttered.

They walked into the lab and found Bruno alone, sleeping. The control room was empty too. The screens were turned off and as Vernon reached for the mouse, the burly man held him back. "Don't intervene the man said. You've seen what I've seen, which is plenty. More people come into this place, than leave."

Shrugging, Vernon stepped back. "What's through the door over there? My guess is, should be a hall."

"We don't need to check in there just yet. C'mon, there's lift there in the anti-chamber," the burly man added.

"How do you know?"

"Don't ask."

The two men stepped aboard, and the burly man touched the button for Lower.

Emma had retreated to the Clone Hall when she noticed the guards arrive. She opened the lab door remotely, so they wouldn't make a ruckus and stood out of sight behind the aquariums, in a blind spot, watching the security feed on Henrik's waterproof aquarium phone. Her eye kept fixing on the old man coming up to reception now, followed by what looked like a younger man, neat, fit. The old one looked cynical, and awkward. His aged head was very round, set off by the turtleneck much like an albino cabbage variant sitting on a darkly cloaked pedestal. *First prize for vegetable at a farm fair, no doubt.*

Then she watched and listened as the security guards passed by the Clone Hall entrance, stopped a few seconds to chat, and continued to the antechamber where they entered the lift. The doors closed. Seconds later, entirely new footsteps arrived, ones she had never heard — stealthy and evenly timed. Emma looked back at her phone and watched as the cabbage-headed man came into the lab, a protégé or something following him. The old man walked to the foot end of Bruno's bed and stopped there. The protégé remained at the door.

"Congratulations on making the transfer, Bruno. I gather you are alive and hopefully well. That is very, very good. Now you just need to wake up and tell me you're OK. Then we will go from there, me old china," he muttered. Emma heard the hollow words from the entrance to the Clone Hall as she paused there. After almost two years of hearing his voice filtered through a synthesizer, she could hear little similarity. Yet there was something about *how* he spoke — the tempo, the emphasis, which convinced her this was the man. This was Ed.

"So you've arrived," she said, mustering a nonchalant persona and straightening out a few things as she approached the side of the bed. He didn't turn to face her, she noted from the corner of her eye. Bound by secrecy, the moment was awkward. "And I see you've brought a friend, how charming."

"How is he?" Ed asked.

"Coma. Vitals are good but as far as brain damage goes, we don't know. The Kid isn't exactly Myron, but this time was certainly different. I am confident Keller has — "

"Fine. Is Violet all right? You sounded shaken earlier," he commented, patience evidently waning.

Emma didn't answer. She continued to straighten out the bed and surroundings as she might in light housekeeping and headed back towards the doorway to the Clone Hall. While her mind spun, strain surfaced on her face in brief twitches, a flare of the nostrils, and her eyes glassed over. *I can't answer him, I lose no matter what.*

"Please stay," the old man said.

"I usually feed he clones about this time," Emma mustered.

"Just stay, please. Was Violet taken to the morgue?" he said in an overly gentle tone.

Emma, her composure cracking, bolted for the clone hall. As she neared the doorway still open and beckoning, a snap of fingers bit the air followed by a menacing yet muted blast which blended with an excruciatingly hot, paralyzing pain in her side. *Fucker shot me.* Emma, propelled further, slammed into the aquarium ahead, bounced and crumpled to the ground. In her curled position she could see her crème colored, pressed tunic develop a crimson splotch, just above the pleats. The young, neat looking man loomed over her — he was getting blurry and dim. Emma blacked out.

"Don't kill her. It's not meant to be a slaughter. Come back in here, I'm sure our guests and staff will arrive soon," said Ed.

The man walked back into the lab, casually leaving Emma to bleed. "Whatever you want. I have eyes on the entire house, remember, I logged in when we got here. No one upstairs, the blacked room I can make out from the hall, the door is open. Have seen no movement there. One man is outside hiding in the wood, the basement appears vacant, yet per floor plans there should be more rooms — we'll have to remedy that for the future. And a few people next door at the falconry, minding their own business despite the landing of a military helicopter. Why exactly did we bring it?"

"I want it for its versatility and speed. We need to relocate a few things to the Bunker. Closer to home," Ed said.

"A truck would have sufficed."

Ed looked at the groomed synth with distaste. "Where was I?" he said, walking back to Bruno. "If anyone is still around, they should have heard the shot and are running to see," he commented, leaning on the bed now. "I'm surprised you haven't woken, Bruno. But I will ensure there is a treat for you when you do."

Ed began inspecting the IV system and monitors. He opened the cupboards one by one and then stopped when he saw a multitude of medications to scrutinize. He picked out a vial of propofol from the flat of them, giving Bruno a smirk. "It will be on standby. I'm only telling you because they say that people in comas can see and hear everything. Let's just say, hear. A head start is always good, makes the game more interesting for those of us unawares," Ed sniggered.

Waiting in the shadow of the wood for a while, the Kid observed what was transpiring around him. The old man with a cabbage for a head, dressed for winter, had gone to the gatehouse and apparently was ratting out the guards. He had Mr Perfect along with him who looked effective yet shorter than golf-ball head.

The other contingent, two more perfect-looking men of unknown race, was heading towards his new-found headquarters in the wood. These the Kid considered Mr Perfect 2 and Perfect 3. P3 carried what looked like a metal tool chest as if it were a little girl's purse — lightly. They must know about the entrance, he thought. Then a plan struck him, he would do his best. Cassy was sleeping, and these guys looked daffy enough to be one of her kind.

The Kid wandered out into the grassy area ahead of him, between the mansion and the cove. He approached his football, which he hadn't touched since morning. He quickened his pace to a run, synced his step with the ball, and came in for a hard kick, sharp to the left. The Kid often practiced with the guards and the gardener too. At this moment the ball sailed high into the air, arced beautifully, and came crashing down but 2 meters from P2 and P3 as they approached the alcove. The ball bounced off a rock and P2 moved quickly to kick it back. His aim was terrible, and the ball deflected sideways into the wood. He moved to get it, but by then the Kid was behind the alcove, out of sight and an instant later lunged on P3 unexpectedly. Classic tackle. Both the Kid and Mr P3 went crashing down, the latter slamming down on rocks embedded in the earth. The Kid lay on him, having embraced the man from behind. He could feel he was not human, reminded him of Cassy when she allowed him to touch her arm — the Kid had squeezed with all his might and Cassy had just chuckled.

But seconds later P2 was upon him, and the cuff he felt on the side of his head sent him to disorienting depths of darkness.

P2 and 3 entered the tunnel, dragging the Kid with them. When they arrived at Cassy's chamber, P2 made quick work of the security lock and proceeded inside with P3 close behind. The Kid was left in a corner, still out cold, scratched and bruised.

"Funny, she doesn't look human. At all. The Cassandra V23 is a piece of junk," said P2.

"C'mon, she's kind of cute I'd say," P3 pretended.

"She was designed that way," said P2, not impressed as he ran a scanner across her bodice. "She's human only in her glitches. Naughty bitch."

"She let herself get caught in this nut house by a drug addict. The code he used is quite crude, and shouldn't have worked. Compassion is such a mistake."

P2 and P3 proceeded to back-up Cassy's memory, on all levels, to prepare for the laborious disassembly ahead. They knew she was designed to withstand warfare, her limbs and body were not prone to be taken apart. Beneath her skin sheaths of aramid wove through her body, covering mechanisms of alloys and synthetic resins for which there was no heart. Instead, its impregnable core housed an empty space beyond gravity, in which were suspended a billion tiny sensors, each created and maintained by a simple, minute AI covered in its own armor.

"Just remember, the head and upper torso are to remain intact," P3 muttered to P2.

"Ya, well, there's something in the middle of this piece of junk I've never scanned before."

"That's because there's *nothing* there." They both laughed.

Chapter 51

Having pushed Bruno into the cremation oven, Henrik stood listening, adjusting the flue of the chimney to the open position as he did so.

Keller had remained by the fridge to see who else might be in there aside from Violet's body. *Here you go again. I'm not pulling you out this time. You made your choice.* He slammed the door next to hers, shut.

"Be quiet," Henrik made a loud whisper.

"What?"

"Chopper, listen. A big son of a—"

Keller stopped and listened. Indeed, the distant beating grew louder until it sounded like it was not very far away at all. Being in a stone basement suggested that the noise was much louder upstairs. *It's nearby.*

"Yeah, sounds like a twin-rotor. Something nasty, has that high-pitched hum. Must be *him*." The lines on Henrik's haggard face magnified, any poise he had left vanished.

"Ok, so let's double them up, help me get Violet in there. I don't need that psychopath getting creative again."

"He's always got something in mind, rarely if ever called for."

They pulled Violet from the fridge and shoved her on top of Bruno, crudely jamming her in. Henrik slammed the oven shut, started it and set the flames to full blast. Keller couldn't help but look through the little blackened window and watch the fury envelop them. *Their macabre romance sprouted explosively, so probably don't mind the double cremation.*

Keller took a few steps back from the oven and leaned against the trolley. Henrik paused too and pulled out a cigarette. They stood in silence for a few minutes. Keller noted a tremor in Henrik's hands.

"Hey, listen, we'll deal with him. You've done a lot of great work here."

"Keller, he had more respect for Violet than for me. Albeit probably fell for her. It's not about great work. I have created live bodies for the man, which aren't savages. That is epic."

"You did, and it is. Violet certainly worked on him, just not sure what angle."

"Our interests in mind, indubitably."

"I won't abandon you, nor will Emma."

"God dammit, what's going on?" Henrik said, turning.

"What now?"

They could hear the lift doors open, close and the two sets of footsteps walking towards the morgue, talking, "The light's on in there," one of them said.

"Give me the gun!" Keller hissed. "Give it here Henrik."

"You even know how to shoot that thing?"

"Taught by the best."

"Belinda..."

Henrik handed him the gun and cartridges just as the double doors swung open. Standing there was Vernon and the burly man whose smug composures strayed to oafish surprise as they were met with a wild-eyed Keller holding the square no-nonsense simplicity of a Glock 19, pointed their way.

"Hey, easy now. We just came down to tell you that the boss has arrived," Vernon said, slowly raising his hands. The burly man began to move behind him.

"Get back out where I can see you," Keller said, calmly. His head tilted back a little and eyes widened.

"Take it easy. What are you on Keller? You look strung out. There's no need to—" At that moment a shot came from upstairs, again muffled by the distance through the stonework, yet distinct enough to be clear what it was.

Keller heard it and didn't hesitate. Not hesitate was what he often did, so adjusting to a morgue scene holding a gun was bumpy but doable. "Shut up and stand apart! So I can see you both." Vernon was sweating now, but the burly man didn't move.

Seeing that speech was futile, the words *drop in the bucket* from his boyhood rang in his mind as the front sight dot dropped into the basin of the rear sight, and they lined up with the gallbladder of Vernon. In the next instant, Keller squeezed. The impact shoved Vernon back and the burly man had little choice but to catch him. "You shot him!" he yelped as Vernon screamed.

"Yeah, I did," Keller yelled, losing it now, laying in to fierceness, "I once counted how many people get messed up from guys like you every day. Can you imagine how many that is in a year, can you count that high?! Pull the gun out and drop it on the floor, stop wasting my time!"

The burly guard obliged, letting Vernon slide to the floor. Henrik promptly picked it up, checked it over, and unlocked the safety. "Leave him there and let Henrik search you. Vernon'll survive." Tense moments passed as Henrik did so, Keller resolutely eyeing the burly man. "Now get on the shelf," Keller said, brutally opening a fridge door and pulling one out. While Vernon wheezed on the floor, the burly man looked at the shelf and then back at Keller.

"You've got to be joking," the burly man said.

"Hop on. Unless you need some help, a better reason." Keller pointed the gun at his head.

"No, no, I'm getting on. What did I ever do to anyone?"

"It's what you didn't do."

Over the next few minutes, the man was heavily dosed with anesthesia, strapped down and rolled into the fridge on a tray. The temp was turned up, but not much. *Likes to wear shorts in the winter, no doubt.*

Vernon was bandaged, given morphine on top of anesthetic and pushed into a separate fridge without constraints. He could move if he needed to. Keller slammed the door shut and noticed Henrik smiling wryly at the burly man's muted yelps.

"What do you think's going on upstairs?"

"Don't know. We'll soon find out," Keller spoke hurriedly. "Ed can zap you anytime. I'll go upstairs alone, he doesn't need to see you yet. Or ever, really. You go and fetch Cassy. Start her up and get her to take out your chip. No excuses."

Henrik hefted the gun, bit his tongue and moved towards an old sealed up exit in the wall near the furnace. Once again he pulled out a ballpoint pen, searched for the tiny indent and pressed. It gave way easily. "Surgeon's design, balanced like a charm," Henrik commented. Keller flattened his lips and lifted a brow as Henrik disappeared inside the tunnel.

Keller took the stairs instead of the lift, thus avoiding the lab where he guessed the shot had come from. They were dark, musty, and had seen little use in the last century. Halfway up he stopped, realizing he was still holding the gun. He tucked it in his left side, handle forward, under the lab coat. Safety off. Keller continued up the stairs and gingerly opened the exit door to reception, bated breath.

Reception was quiet. In a few strides, he made it to behind the desk and checked the security feeds there. In an instant, his gaze zeroed in on an older man standing in the lab. He knew that stance, the partial profile, he had watched the man from hiding many times in the distant past. Arnold! Keller let out a hiss of breath and leaned back against the wall. Arnold's face from the recent visit to the Bunker flashed by. Then his face after the explosion all those years ago. Ed was Arnold. The one who had turned people to hideous acts of crime and degraded them to indifference was Arnold.

Keller all but gasped, suddenly standing straight. Arnold had turned to face the camera. *That little crooked smirk, how comforting.* Keller scanned the room to see what might have triggered Arnold to look at the cam. There in the control room, another man was also staring back at him. An immaculate man, looking awfully precise. Keller smelled army synth. Newer than Cassy, no doubt. *Clever act Arnold, but you should have remained in hiding. Not a big favorite in these parts.*

Chapter 52

As he crossed the lounge and approached the lab entrance, Keller rid himself of all emotion and thought—he was a big fan of simplicity. *If you do it, do it deliberately, no doubts. Until you drop to the floor, dead, you're still Keller.*

The tall windows told of a dark, moonless night to come, it was overcast, and evening had set in. Silhouetted trees not too distant swayed silently, testament to the oblivious peace which lay outside. The sliding door to the lab was two meters away, then one, then Keller opened it and strode in. Arnold stood by the bed fiddling with IV tubes and clamps. He was trying to rig something, something to put Bruno out, Keller guessed.

"What are you doing? Leave those alone. You're not much of a doctor the last I checked."

"Hello Keller, your father thought me not much of anything. Yet here we are, having altered evolution in my house," Arnold said as he turned. Closer and in real life, Keller was surprised to note it was actually him. Gone was the feigned Alzheimer's, the look that his life was over.

"Have you ever been in this place?" Keller asked.

"Better check on Emma, if you know how, she's bleeding out. One of the guards shot her."

"You sure it wasn't your guy there in the control room?" Keller said, grabbing bandages, morphine, scissors, scalpels, stapler, syringes and such. His arms were loaded. At that moment, still thoughtless, Keller darted his right hand into his lab coat. The man from the control room walked into the lab, evidently humored at the mad attempt to save the nurse he had recently gunned down. In the next instant, Keller tripped and fell headlong towards him. The droid's face pulsed fake surprise as he tried to catch the assortment things flying his way and glanced to the side, anticipating a collision with a nearby trolley. *Good boy.* Gun in hand now, Keller began to fire as he fell, knowing it wouldn't be the hot desert sand that met him.

Keller crashed to the floor hard, pumping 9 rounds into the immaculate man's chest and head as rapidly as he could, keeping him off balance. Most of the shots mattered little, but number seven hit a sweet spot—a soft area beneath his chin where it penetrated a channel to a secondary control center in the head. The main one being behind armor in the chest, Keller reckoned.

Disoriented, the man grabbed hold of his own pistol and simultaneously prepared to land a blow with his foot as Keller squeezed off another shot. The blow never arrived, the grip on the pistol loosened. The machine slowed and became incoherent. Keller jumped up behind him now and put round 12 into the droid's cranium at the top of the synthetic spine-like structure but let 13 sail past, hitting Arnold, who was just about to fire, in the chest. Arnold was winded and fell back. *Got a vest on Arnold?*

Keller moved forward now, in the fresh pause. *Squeeze just before the dot reaches the target, so that by the time you pull the trigger, it's spot on, Belinda giggled.* As memories began seeping into his head, Keller blocked them out. He shot Arnold in the thigh. And then, coming in closer, in the hand which fumbled with his gun. The pistol spun away as Arnold made the remaining distance to the floor wheezing, coughing and pitifully shrieking.

Keller turned back to the droid, shoved the gun in his mouth and let numbers 14 and 15 off. 16 he forced down his throat, and the machine appeared to shut down. Keller put the barrel to the droid's eye and fired for good measure. *How do these things die?* *'They don't,' he recalled Alexey saying.*

Keller ejected the clip and inserted a fresh one. He turned to Arnold. "Give me an excuse to shoot you, and I gladly will. We both know your time to die has arrived. There's no other way."

"Always a way, Keller, always a solution. For one, I can give the order to free Cassy," Arnold mumbled through a layer of gob and froth.

Keller ignored him. "Hey, ever seen your clone close up, in the flesh?"

"No, Keller I—"

"Give me a minute, I'll take you there." Keller tucked his pistol away and scrambled to pick up some of the things he had dropped. Afterwards, he attacked the cupboards and trolley again for fresh supplies and disappeared into the Clone Hall. He skidded to the floor next to Emma and detected instantly she was alive. He clipped her uniform away, noting the bullet had exited the back—it was a clean shot. He abated the bleeding, administered morphine and roughly bandaged her.

Keller ran back to the lab where his new friends were laying, quietly. Arnold had also nodded off, his chest still heaved gently beneath the long coat. The spittle on his lips had built to a white, gummy slime and the puffy, dried-up apple face had deflated somewhat. *Good.*

Keller returned to Emma and peeled back the bandages. Next, he stapled. This woke her up but barely. As he told her to relax and that she would make it, Emma's eyes rolled back, and she fell unconscious once again. After finishing, Keller left her there on the floor to rest awhile. He looked up at the clones, unconscious, a shiver running down his spine and a sick feeling welling in his stomach. He glanced at the darkened tank.

Arnold is Ed. Keller sat down. He had to be smart now, on how this all ended. No Court of Law would ever believe what had transpired, yet some specialists in the field, might. Henrik had, after all, used an already developed technology for growing the bodies. Somewhere out there was Vasiliev. Henrik wouldn't say where, but with Ed gone, his chip removed and with a little drug rehab, he might talk.

Keller made his way back to the door and looked without entering. Arnold had propped himself up and had slithered over to a bundle of gauze; was wrapping the shot arm. He winced but took the pain quite well, Keller thought. The droid hadn't moved. Another chill ran down Keller's spine as it occurred to him the horror which had taken place. He thought of Cassy and Henrik, and realized he had to move. *Where are they?* He wanted to patch Arnold up, nurse him back to good health, despite all. That was impossible now. *Suddenly loving everyone, are you?*

He walked over to Arnold, an ebbing heap of animate bone trying to fix itself. Keller administered a shot of morphine and helped him with the bandages.

"We can negotiate Keller, come to an agreement," Arnold said, wheezing. "And Cassy is free to go, I'll notify my men, or else—."

"I didn't think it was you, Arnold, such a *nice* guy. *Loved my mother to death.*"

Arnold looked at him for a second, concerned, his eyes tinged with grief.

"Let's have a look at your super-clone, shall we?" Keller fetched a wheelchair from a closet, unfolded it, and rolled it over. He hoisted Arnold to a sitting position, then lifted him up from behind and sat him in the chair. He made a quick search for any remaining weapons. Arnold managed a new, tickled smile. "There is nothing there. I'm usually not armed. Just things need to get done."

Keller didn't reply, instead walking over and giving the droid a long look. *Did it twitch? No, your brain must have. When Henrik returns, he'll check it over.*

Keller rolled Arnold through the entrance to the Clone Hall and past Emma. Arnold's clone was there, up font and center. Keller could feel Arnold recognized it. Not far away was Violet's, August's, Francine's—each one stuck in a sleepy moment. A label for passers-by might simply read 'Human male and Human Female' followed by a brief synopsis on how it survived, its history. Eating habits etc. 'Prone to create societies, tribal.'

Keller rolled the wheelchair in front of Arnold's Super-C. They had jokingly named it that because of its height and athletic appearance. Keller gave Arnold another shot of morphine and roughly bandaged his thigh, so he wouldn't bleed out just yet. The stage was set, and the audience had arrived.

Chapter 53

As the orderly drove by St John's Church on his way through Wroxall, the large blue clock up on the steeple showed almost 9. It had grown dusky. The orderly didn't like moving about by day since he didn't want to meet any police, not that they were looking for him. The events at the clinic had gone over the top, and so he had departed. He was not chipped, not yet, and wanted to avoid it. That was no way to live. The image of the burly man's expression while being zapped was etched into his brain along with Henrik lying on the floor, tormented.

But as he passed by the church and came to the next street, he could see some of the fields to the north and glimpsed a stream of smoke rising up from where Jolly More Mansion sat. *They must be burning stuff. That's my job... Judging by the thickness of the stream, it's on full blast. Dangerous to be left on like that for too long. That thing is old.*

The orderly had loved his job and liked the quirky atmosphere. The big boss was a strange one and the experimentation on humans probably wasn't legal, but who knew. Many things done on humans in this world were dangerous, yet still considered lawful and even necessary. He drove on thinking about the young man who had purchased a joint on the esplanade in Shanklin and after smoking it, proceeded to scale the cliff lift building. Arms outstretched he dove from it convinced he would land in the ocean 60 m away. *Not lawful and not necessary, but the dealer got off on a warning.*

As he reached the edge of town, he slowed down and parked in a clearing at the side of the road. He had planned to go hunting, but the stream of smoke bothered him. It was far heavier than usual. He tried to call the front reception, just to see if anyone was there—he could test the waters regarding his disappearance. The phone rang, but no one answered.

He started up the car once more and continued on to the wood where he hunted. The season for deer had ended in April, now all he could hunt were hares and rabbits. He rarely shot them unless one passed along. It was something about the large brown glassy eyes and the cute fur. He could shoot at a target, some bottles perhaps, but he also didn't want to attract anyone, especially the game warden.

The orderly pondered some more, checking his coffee cup, which was empty. Then he heard the beating of a helicopter. He searched the skies and spotted nothing. Then suddenly it appeared. It was longer and sleeker that any he had seen, a black, evil smudge low in the darkening skies. Twin rotors, no running lights. It was heading for the general area of the clinic, yes, to a field behind it. *Must be a VIP patient. Myron had arrived in one, but much smaller. The big boss might be arriving...*

The orderly decided he wanted to be at work after all. He could still make a good enough excuse and if they chipped him, so be it. This was too crazy to miss out on and working as a janitor somewhere and shooting at bottles for the rest of his life wasn't interesting.

He started up the engine yet again and drove off to the Jolly More. He wound through the calm countryside, the falling dusk adding a brassy glow, accented by the cooing of a dove here and there along the way. In minutes, he pulled up to the gate, but no one came out of the guardhouse. The orderly parked over to the side and got out. He knew how to unlock the pedestrian side to let himself in. Afterwards, he walked straight up to the entrance of the guardhouse. He knocked, and when no one answered, he tried the handle. The door swung open, and then he strode inside, offering a loud hello as he did. The guards were absent. *Odd to leave the door unlocked for the night.* As a reflex, he went over to the monitors and cast an eye over the property and the rooms of the house. The chopper sat still, with two pilots inside. The incineration room he couldn't see, no feed—the orderly knew what was down there.

With interest, his gaze stopped at the lounge—the door to the lab was open. *Weird, it's never open.* Since there was no feed for the lab either, the orderly adjusted Lounge Central Cam B to point at the door. Next he zoomed.

Bruno appeared to be sleeping, but a heap on the floor was stirring. The man looked well dressed to the orderly, yet severely battered. He studied his head. It was blown apart, strips of synthetic skin were hanging, torn—he was not human. This did not phase the orderly. Nothing surprised him about this place, yet the armed chopper had come close.

Knowing things weren't right, especially with a shot-up synth lying in the lab, the orderly trotted towards the house, a high-powered shotgun slung over his shoulder. The reception cams would reveal all, he had to investigate. Although the surrounding countryside and mansion grounds were peaceful, he kept a watchful eye for any movement. This was the biggest hunt of his life. He carefully eyed the windows but perceived nothing unusual, not that he could see inside.

Reception was deserted. *Where the hell are they?* Shuffling around to behind the desk, he noticed Keller in the Clone Hall accompanying an old man in a wheelchair. *How nice.* He was showing him a clone. *Boss? Bloodied up and bandaged?* The orderly searched the other rooms to find them empty. *Where is Henrik, Emma, Violet and the Kid? The guards?* Then his eye returned to the busted-up human looking droid, on its knees now, inspecting itself. It was armed. Then he flipped back to the Clone Hall cams and noticed another heap of a human. Her clothing had been cut open—she was bloodied, bandaged but didn't move. *Emma!*

"This pistol has 17 rounds in it, fresh cartridge," Keller explained, placing the barrel up flat against the glass of the tank with a clink. "I'm sure one of them will make it through, if not the first. The glass is thick, but is it armored?"

"Of course it's armored. It would be a shame if you did fire, and it ricocheted and hit you smack in the forehead. Truly would," Arnold was biding time, forcing a nervous snigger.

"Did you blow up my father's lab, with him and Katrina in it?"

"No. My theory is, he did it himself. He was hardcore, Keller. Why do you think I have remained loyal to his work, even though he scorned me?" Arnold said with a note of melancholy.

"He didn't scorn you. He simply kept things to himself. You and my mother liked to party it up in your office sometimes. Don't think I didn't know. And the quaint little meetings in town. They may have looked innocent to me back then, but I know now, they weren't."

"Your mother was lonely. Do you even know what an exciting life she had led before your father? And then to leave Las Vegas for a sleepy English town?"

"She chose him. And he was lucky to be taken on by the British."

"Thanks to Henrik and his foresight."

"So why do you think he did it himself?" Keller could detect Arnold was stalling but wanted to hear how he responded.

"He jumped I think. To the *Cradle* in the droid, he rarely mentioned. Yes, your mother and I weren't the only ones drinking. He joined us sometimes. Probably hated me for the fun I created, a little oasis in the gloomy tunnels. But alcohol can loosen the tongue, and I can read between the lines, even your father's."

"You say he killed himself along with Katrina?" Keller asked, attentive now, Arnold looking back at him.

"No," Arnold replied slowly, "The explosion was premature, perhaps by days. It's just a theory, Keller."

"And what happened to my mother? Was she another theory?"

"Drug overdose. Not directly, but she did like her uppers, downers, and everything in between."

"After eloping with you, she came back different. Depressed."

"Drugs can do that Keller, c'mon, you know better," Arnold's tone turned cynical.

"Did you perform the first memory capture experiments on her? I mean considering her past, it would have been like going to the movies."

Arnold was clearly taken aback. He paused before speaking and for Keller, that was answer enough.

"Keller, I loved your mother…"

"So much that you'd fix electrodes to her head and sucked the life out of her," Keller said as he walked to the other side of the tank.

"Where are you going?"

"I thought you might want to see him run. You know, you zapped Henrik pretty good, he really suffered. This will prove that your clone is alive and well. Aren't you worried he may be dead, standing up? I mean, he doesn't really look alive, does he?"

"I can see his vitals are good—sure, make the bastard run," Arnold said, uneasy.

Keller ran the memory and fed the clone all the information it needed. While doing so, he looked at young Violet, standing lightly with eyes closed, moving ever so slightly with the stream in the circulation system.

"Come, I want to show you something, Keller," Arnold said as the clone began a light, jog. Without the ballast on his bodice, he moved awkwardly, suspended, the liquid in the tank swirling.

Keller walked over to the phone in Arnold's outstretched, good hand. The screen showed a POV shot of Cassy being disassembled. Her face and chest were open. Limbs partially missing. "It's getting quite serious at this point," he said with concern in his eyes, the kind a headmistress gone awry might have before brutally beating a child. "I told them to leave head and chest intact, but something has caught their interest. I hope they don't bugger the central system. Arms and legs are details, the head too really. Shooting my man in the eye was not of great consequence, I'm afraid."

"Go ahead, keep her." Keller grabbed the phone and threw it, letting it smash against a tank wall. Arnold paid little attention.

"Hmm. See, I have suspected something. Cassy has always been an odd one and I feel her traits have carried on from previous models, though they had no reason to. She wasn't programmed that way. Perhaps just a hunch, but as you know, those are usually less wrong than right. I'm glad I allowed her to visit. We must keep Simon out of this, don't you agree?"

"Bruno's alive. The deal was you let her go after he wakes up. Then you said she would be set free after your own transfer. Now your men are busily taking her apart. Not much left in you I can trust, Arnold." Keller pushed the wheelchair right up to the glass and left him.

"So, you *are* interested," Arnold said, blankly.

"Not in the least."

"Don't you wish to behold what is in the blacked-out one?" he asked, seeing Keller circumvent the aquarium. They could barely see each other through the bubbles, the clone had reached a good running pace.

"Not really," Keller answered, matching the distaste.

"Here, just a quick look." Arnold spun the wheelchair with his good hand and wiggled his way over to the monitors. He used his thumb print to open a new console—it slid out quietly from the counter. He punched in a code, hand shaking, then turned back to Keller. He nodded to indicate something behind him. Keller turned and beheld what was in the last aquarium, he could see it normally now, like the others. *Inside was his mother.* A normal, healthy-looking Belinda, ever so slightly moving with the current.

"That's..." Keller said, turning back, strained. He lifted his gun back up to the glass in front of him.

"Yes, as I said, I loved her. While I'm alive to log into my system back in the Bunker, everything you see here keeps working. If I don't make it back well, it will eventually become an open book to the Ministry of Defense I'm afraid. The footage of you at work might look a touch dubious, I hate to say. Stay with me Keller—I'll create a clone for you as well in case you ever need it, and anyone else you wish."

Keller looked at Belinda again.

"Here's one you already know sweetpea: If it looks too good to be true then it's probably not," she said tousling his hair. Keller had wanted to keep a sidewinder as a pet, saying there was tons of them in the desert and that he'd be actually happy to catch 3.

Then he suddenly snapped back to Arnold. *This isn't happening, not today. No stray paths.* "Instead of Belinda joining you, how about you paying her a visit instead?" he said, tapping the aquarium with his pistol.

"Don't you dare," Arnold mumbled. "Keller!" he yelled, hands shaking, the bloodied one raised now too. Arnold's voice morphed from despair to anger. "Of course I blew your father up, along with that pesky girl. No one ever suspected that an idiot such as I might pull such a thing off!"

Keller stared at him, not moving. "I agree; I don't believe you."

"And your mother squealed like a pig when I first put the electrodes on her head. She had been expecting breakfast in bed," he squeaked disdainfully. "And when I was done, she didn't remember a thing!"

Keller began squeezing the trigger. The tank, under tremendous pressure from its contents, exploded as he continued to fire. The running clone was abruptly flung loose and kept running as the current swept it over Arnold. It fell with the snap of a bone and the thud of heavy flesh pummeling marble. Keller was flung against the next tank, Clone August's, as tonnages of liquid and glass, blasted him. The safety glass, though not sharp, lacerated his clothing and skin leaving a mottled pattern of bruises and cuts. The aromatic fluid bearing the wreckage, gushed over all, including Emma who hadn't stirred in the commotion. Her body might have been a cadaver awash, limbs flailing indifferently.

From the lab entrance, a horrific figure had emerged, its head and neck severely destroyed, clothing littered with holes, wet and tattered. It unleashed gunfire. Keller rolled to the side but as the other tanks were punctured and burst apart, the entire clone hall became a turmoil of glass, amniotic fluid, and bodies. While Keller choked on the liquid, his thoughts were of Emma. *She could drown.* As he flicked the fluid from his face and eyed the gunman, he saw it was the synth. *Do they ever stop?* It was functional after all and stood against the flow of liquid and glass, hardly staggering to remain standing. It searched the carnage and then raised his pistol towards Keller.

The synth began firing once more, but in no particular direction as its half-torn head was simultaneously gouged by a separate blast. Next, the hand firing the gun viciously flopped over, hinging listless at the wrist, letting the weapon drop. Then more shots were fired from what sounded like something evil, Keller believed, hunkering down, ears deafened. The mutilated synth keeled forward into the flood. Behind him stood the orderly. *You're late for work.* Keller got to his knees now, desperately trying to avoid the larger pieces of furniture, monitors, metal, and glass surging around him.

In seconds, the orderly made his way through the flotsam and gore after a thumbs up from Keller, who heaved a breath, spit, and staggered to his feet. He was soaked in blood and gunk but happy to be whole. A bullet had grazed his arm, the glass and metal shrapnel had cut him in dozens of places and though the blood streamed out, he knew none of it was deep. Adrenaline had kicked into overdrive as he moved on and considered what had just occurred.

Keller checked on Arnold, who lay face down in the slime. He callously flipped him over and felt for a pulse. Arnold's eyes opened. "Help me up, please," he said, calm yet distant. Keller pondered over him a moment, old memories flashing by. His mind stopped dead at one, of a nurse who took care of his mom: *'Belinda liked to talk about her life as a spy and that her memories were backed-up safely,' the nurse said.*

Any notions of compassion dissipated then and there. He asked the orderly for his shotgun, positioned it a foot from Arnold's face. Keller's vision grew blurry from the tears flooding his eyes, and his hands grew numb clutching the metal. He squeezed the trigger. At such a close range, the shotgun was beyond powerful. Keller's ears rang, hands shook, and he felt a dullness pervade his very core.

Sorry, no more backups.

The orderly stared, his hands raised to cup his ears. As the slop on the floor lapped at the disfigured, cratered heap which used to be a man's face, he and Keller both paused for a moment.

"Did you see anyone else around, on your way here?" Keller began.

"Nope."

Keller repeated the gory chore with the Clone Arnold, who had risen to its knees nearby, anguishing brutally for his first breath, unable to get up further. The shot slapped him vigorously in the side of the head in sequence with a spray of bone bits and brains. The giant humanoid fell sideways, eyes dull, with a heavy splash and an eerie, hollow knock of its skull against the smooth, stone floor.

Still dazed, Keller scoped the Clone Hall for the ghost of Arnold himself. Nothing projected itself. *Probably doesn't have a ghost.*

"Wasn't Ed supposed to go on trial or something?" the orderly began.

"We already had the trial. He's guilty," Keller said, void of any emotion.

"I'll pack him in the oven then. Who's in there now?" the orderly asked, catching his breath.

"Bruno and Violet. We had to be quick about it."

"That explains the extra smoke. I noted the stream was thicker than normal."

Keller smiled for the first time in days, not including any insane glee. "Yeah, I guess it would be. Henrik let her rip."

The two of them retreated to the lab, helping Emma along, who had woken up gagging severely. While the orderly helped her up to an operating table and carefully dried her off, Bruno stirred.

At first, his vitals became notably stronger, and the monitor showed more energy. Finally, his eyes opened. *Bruno has woken.* Keller stood at the edge of the bed and said nothing. Bruno looked at him and closed his eyes again, lips trembling. "I'm thirsty," he said. Keller smiled for the second time in the last few days, his eyes dampening. *Bruno is alive, the infusion was a success… yet the question remains…* "Who are you?"

Bruno paused; eyes open again searching Keller's. "For heaven's sake Keller, Bruno," he whispered. "Why are you wet and bloody? What the hell is going on in the Clone Hall?" he asked as a sufferer of lockjaw might. While Clone Bruno had indeed woken, it had a smooth, mannequin quality to it which, when rippled with human expression, tingled the nerves.

"Ok, so you're really there," Keller swallowed.

"I'm here, yeah. Are you there? You look pretty messed up. I'll call an ambulance."

"No Bruno, just rest."

"Were you gonna shoot me?" he asked, nodding to the shotgun.

"I thought about it."

"Keep him alive long enough to run some tests at least," Emma interrupted, sitting up on the operating table a few meters away, doing her best to brew a smile. "It worked Keller, I heard him."

"Of course, you heard me. You're not deaf, Emma."

The three of them just looked at Bruno.

"Better go check on Cassy. She's in a tunnel which branches out from the morgue. Two men are taking her apart," Emma said, looking at Henrik's phone.

"How do you know?" Keller asked.

"Henrik has his own cams, not important now. With Arnold dead, they may stand down."

"I doubt it. Depends on what they were told. Henrik already went to check."

"Keller!"

"Ok, I'm going. But get Clone Violet ready, if she's alive. If not, try Francine."

"What if Francine is dead too, try August? I mean, what are you going to do?" Emma asked. "I thought you don't believe anyone's inside Cassy. She's just a synth."

"Maybe, maybe not." Keller walked out of the lab, throwing the gun back to the orderly. The orderly looked at Emma as she winked. "Glad you're back, luv," she said.

Chapter 54

"It's burning too hot, this whole place could blow. The oven's old and someone hooked up gas to it." the orderly said, bent over the controls. He peered inside, "They are gone and so are most of the ashes."

"The bones you mean," Keller said, impatient to move on. "It's them you want left over."

"No bones. So what about family?"

"No family."

"Seriously?"

"Yeah. Besides, explaining what happened might be risky."

"Crazy you mean."

"And Bruno, well, he's alive and we can't have two. Let people wonder about his age if they want. C'mon, we gotta go."

The orderly nodded thoughtfully as he turned the gas off and flicked the panel door shut. When he heard someone yelling from inside the fridges, he paled, wide-eyed, and looked at Keller.

"We'll get them later," Keller said starkly.

Keller passed through the tunnel entrance first and the orderly followed, toting his Berretta 130 with one large cartridge in the chamber and 9 on deck. He had another 20 on his belt under a light windbreaker. In the next minute, they arrived at the chamber door. It was closed, but the sound of pneumatic tools humming and popping escaped and rattled the tunnel.

Keller investigated the little window, and the orderly joined him. The view was not hectic. Two droids stood over a body on an operating table—quickly, carefully, and precisely working to take it apart. Two human-looking guys working on an inhuman, alloy, silicone, aramid, and nylon cadaver. Keller spotted the Kid lying on the floor nearby, unconscious. Henrik as well, bloodied. Keller recalled what he had told him and now recognized that at least he had tried. *Still alive. Both.*

The Kid stirred but then froze. He carefully looked sideways and then noticed Keller in the little window, who was shaking his head and motioning down. *Stay down.*

Instead, the Kid continued to scan the room and in the next instant rolled over to a trolley, leapt to his feet and grabbed a pistol. *He's behaving like he has nothing to lose. Like he's in a fricking video game.*

The Kid began firing into the back of P2 who stiffened, dropping his pneumatic tool, then slowly slumped over onto Cassy.

The reaction of P3 was momentary, a blur. In the next instant his outstretched hand had already fired the piece it held, the charge slamming the Kid smack in the chest. It shoved him backwards against the trolley, where he leaned a second before crumpling to the floor.

By this time, Keller had grabbed the shotgun and pumped numerous rounds into the window at close range, to no avail. The orderly cussed as lead pellets flew around the tunnel, a few catching him on the leg.

Next P3 aimed at the little window himself, fired, and the glass blew right out if its frame, pulverized. Both Keller and the orderly had jumped to the side, enduring the heat and glass powder as they did.

P3 came to the window, peered out at the two, turned and walked back to Cassy. He shoved P3 off of her and continue his work. "If I see that barrel come anywhere near the window, I kill you both. Promise. And don't go near the hall cam."

Keller was about to reply when Gouyen arrived. She leaned on the platform where the remains of Cassy were clamped. "You in there?" she asked. "Time to hustle. You can't stay. I mean, you can, but there's no point. Katrina?"

Keller saw nothing more, felt nothing. Only the synth, oblivious, kept on working while Gouyen waited patiently. When Keller made to speak, Gouyen glared him down.

"You can live in my world, child. You don't ever have to forget what happened to you and what will follow," she said, her eyes softening.

While there was no physical answer, soon Keller caught the idea that something had changed. That there was movement from within the droid's carcass.

P3 continued his display of diligence, ramming a pneumatic chisel at Cassy's chest armor. The orderly stared at Keller, shifting from foot to foot, obviously about to speak, yet didn't.

"It's your time to live Katrina, remember what you've survived. We must make haste. Mayhem has unleashed on this house, and we know not what follows," Gouyen continued.

Keller gasped. Katrina momentarily projected a vague shell of her old self sitting up. She glanced vacantly at Keller then away, swinging her feet over the side of the operating table and hopping down, easily, silently. Without looking back, she followed Gouyen across the room and disappeared through the wall. *She's still 12!*

Keller turned to the orderly, "Forget Cassy. We need to get Henrik, and that's all. The Kid can wait."

"What's left of him can wait, yeah. Were you, ah, having a moment?"

"Something like that."

P3 continued working. Keller quietly knocked on the door. "Hey."

The droid spun around, bounded up to the entrance in a few steps, and suddenly pulled it wide open. "Now you're pissing me off," he said, holding the barrel of his pistol up to Keller's head. P3 up close was a harrowing sight. His smooth skin, even with its imperfections, was perfect. The nice, thick hair and glassy dead eyes made him look extremely sick. Borderline evil.

"Take it easy, Arnold's dead," Keller said, remaining calm.

"All the more reason for me to pull the trigger."

"Let me take Henrik, he's hurt but alive. You can scan my retina and you'll see there's no order to kill me. If you violate your programming, you'll end up like her. There will always be someone newer and faster."

P3 scanned Keller's retina, paused to receive data, and then jammed the barrel right against his temple. "I'm keeping her. I know what went on up there, but I have my orders."

"Go right ahead. I doubt you'll find anything out of the ordinary. You realize Arnold was crazy. Crazy and rogue."

"I'm obviously not worried about him. But Cassy's coming along, she belongs in the Bunker, not outside. Take Henrik if you want. Do anything weird and I shoot. Don't trust you guys anymore. Not after that meathead terminated my partner."

My partner. Keller reflected for a moment. *The droid computed that the body of Cassy holds the answers to her behavior.*

"So why are you taking her apart?"

"Orders."

"Who's?"

The droid turned, continued his work and did not answer.

The orderly fetched a gurney from the morgue while Keller tended to Henrik. Upon stirring, Keller helped him up. "C'mon, we're not welcome here right now."

"What the hell, I was out cold. That damn machine," he murmured. "Christ, she's almost all gone. Beautiful work, mind you," Henrik said, noting the heap of technology on the surgery table as he limped out, clinging to Keller.

"She's gone completely. You did what you could, let them have her," Keller said with a grave note.

"Yeah, sure," Henrik said, distress tugging at the corners of his mouth.

"It was Arnold, by the way."

Henrik looked at him, stunned, then shook his head. "You killed him?"

"Yeah."

"Bloody right."

Chapter 55

Out in front of the house, Katrina stood by the fountain, beckoning the water to flow. None did. She sat down on the curled edge of the basin and marveled at the spiders skating on the surface, not leaving a ripple as they glided along. The sculpture of a little boy playing the flute on a log next to a mermaid sat quietly over the pool. The mermaid lay against him, eyes blissfully shut, a slight smile emerging. A lone vine embraced the walls of the basin, its flowers budding and blossoming. Katrina looked at the spiders, then at the horizon. Then the trees.

For 12 years I was Katrina. For 19 years, a synth. Now I'm something, not anything. Yet here I am.

She heard the entrance to the mansion open and looked to see who it was. Keller stepped out onto the terrace, paused, and stood there. She decided to be invisible, not to project herself. After all, she was drained. Katrina found that a faint, transparent image of herself showed when her emotions ran wild. It faded out when she was melancholy or calm. It required energy and when she didn't feel like it, she didn't have it.

Keller can tell I'm here… Katrina felt her non-extant heart rate rise, and her invisible cheeks turn warm. He walked out a few more steps and stopped to look in her direction. Some of the blood on his clothes had turned brownish, other parts glistening red. *He's still bleeding all over. Dying bit by bit. Keller…*

•　　•　　•　　•　　•

Somewhere in the distance, she lay on her back, dizzy with mirth, staring at the sky above. A boy appeared over her, grass cuttings and leaves stuck to his shirt, wild-eyed and puffing. He was saying something and handing her a ragged bunch of blossoms, some dirt from the roots falling on her dress. She didn't care. He continued to speak, there was no sound. She only knew she felt like smiling, laughing.

•　　•　　•　　•　　•

What would it take to reach you now?

"You ok?" Keller finally said, a tremble in his rough worn voice. "Katrina, I can see you."

"Is that somehow important?" she said.

"Yeah, it is. I'm sorry if I doubted you and I'm sorry what you've been through."

How embarrassing, he can see me, all 12 years old of me. "You have no idea what I've survived, you can't possibly comprehend such a fate. I don't care what you think you see, I don't need your apologies." *I just want to run to you… but I can tell you're not here for me.*

"I get it. But you must move on. I don't believe in your fate. You chose to listen to my father and get into a droid and live a life of hell. Look at him now. Brilliant, sure, but at what cost? And to what end?"

"So, you're telling me to screw off?"

"And look at the Kid, he has Myron's memories. Who needs that?"

"I love you, Keller…"

"I love you too, always have. Probably always will," he said and paused. "You can't imagine what it was like to watch the lift hut go up in smoke..."

They were standing close now and soaked each other in for a while. *He saw Cassy as a woman, he sees me as a kid. I'm the same one...*

Keller spoke up first. "But now you need to go—no droid bodies, no clones, no hanging around and haunting people. Or not haunting them. I don't think it's what you want. You need to wipe the slate. Clean. The cycle of life is precious, let's keep it that way."

"That's bullshit, Keller," she declared and turned to walk away.

"It was Arnold all along. He tried to take a walk in my father's shoes," Keller said, raising his voice, beckoning.

Katrina spun, squinting her eyes in spite. "Arnold?"

"Yeah."

"That creepy little fuck," she said.

They both stood again as Keller rummaged through his pockets. "This is my keepsake from Corfe Castle," he said, pulling out a worn, bloodied, folded photo of Katrina in which was nestled a dried forget-me-not blossom. Holding the little stem in his fingers, he gently spun it back and forth before snapping it in half and tossing it to the breeze. "But all stories have their place. I'm not going to dwell. You want a clone? Violet's body is still alive. But you don't want to be part of this nightmare."

"So then come with me, if you love me," she said, stumbling a little, her smile not coming out right.

Keller made as if to speak, then said nothing. He just looked at her. Katrina turned away, not caring if he could see her or not. She faded. All she knew was that a vast emptiness overtook her and that she felt tired of it all.

Keller searched out the fields and beyond for a while. She was gone, trading places with the breeze. He turned and trudged back inside, wobbly, trailing blood as he sauntered through reception.

The synth from the basement chamber was busy hauling Cassy and her parts to the chopper. He had neutralized her and then some. His partner, P2, sat lifeless, propped against the reception desk, waiting to be picked up. Keller walked into the lounge and settled on a sofa after collecting first aid supplies from a cupboard. The floor was flooded there too. He didn't mind. As he sat, fatigue settled in as his nerves received the signal that he would live another day after all. He began bandaging his wounds, where he could reach them, not bothering with disinfectant.

Katrina followed a path which led to a stone wall. She had noticed it when arriving at the Jolly More but had never made the time to investigate further. She did so now, giving in to a magnetic pull in the path's direction, a fascination. *I'm dead, let it pull me.*

"The poor souls that come by me, following the light, thinking there must be something better, reflecting how pitiful their life has been — they're missing the fact that they themselves are what makes it anything at all. You are the better, or the worse. It's all up to you. You can follow a thousand paths, lights, fantasies, it will not help," Gouyen spoke up from behind.

"So what?" Katrina retorted.

"Most of us aren't happy living in between lives."

"Why do you do it?"

"It began as revenge, and then I got hooked, like an old maiden, I suppose. *You* can still go back. Try at least. It will be much harder once you've gone this path, the path of the haunted, the lost, the desperate to be what they once were but never will again."

"What's in it for you if I make it?" Katrina countered.

Gouyen just looked back at her.

Gotcha. "I mean what are the choices?"

"Confusing isn't it. But your situation is unique, and I feel you hold the wild card. It would be a shame, considering Leonard and Bruno succeeded, not to give it a go. I mean, if you want to of course."

"Ahem, why don't you try it?"

"Perhaps I will, when the time is right. Child, you've just completed the impossible and I must say, you're in great shape," said Gouyen with an air of mischief.

"Ah ha. Well, I care little for Bruno. But I liked the Kid."

"I realize that. But the Kid is dead and gone. I'm not sure where, they don't always linger," Gouyen added with an air of misfortune."

"I gathered, he tried to save me. Valiant boy."

"Yes, he is. And an excellent friend."

At that moment, Katrina looked up at the circling falcon and watched as he landed on a pine branch. "So, you know the Kid. How about the bird?"

"Yes, it was and still is a very smart bird. Peregrine. Douglass is his name."

"Hey Doug."

Keller sat in the lounge, staring out of the windows from across the room. It was over. He had killed Ed. Ed who had been Arnold. He had lost Katrina. Katrina who had been Cassy who hadn't lied. He closed his weary eyes but then opened them when the faint cry of a falcon trickled in. It appeared in the distance, high up, circling. Keller got up, slowly, tipping a vial of morphine yet keeping his gaze on the bird as he walked towards the window. A bloodied bandage roll slipped from his fingers, dropping to the floor, unravelling. *What does that damn bird want now?*

The peregrine continued to circle. Down below on the path along the stone fence, a woman in a period dress stood talking to a skinny girl dressed in jeans and a t-shirt. They both looked up at the falcon and watched it land on a pine branch. The falcon took off again and swooped lower to settle on the stone wall behind them. Katrina turned back to look at it and then her gaze wandered toward the mansion.

Chapter 56

Keller and the orderly stood outside in the back garden and watched as P3 lugged the remains of P1 through the wood and into the clearing beyond where the military chopper lay waiting. It was his last trip and while P3 worked in silence, he gave a chin up and a snort to signal what Keller guessed was a parting. Keller nodded in response. In minutes, the twin rotors were spinning and with a quiet roar, topped with a whine, the featureless beast melted into the dark skies, accelerating in an arc upwards until it was barely visible, at which point it moved away to the North.

"I'm surprised the police haven't arrived," the orderly began.

"Why?"

"Shooting, smashing glass, it's a real mess in there."

"This is one of the most solid mansions I've ever been in. The walls are thick, made of stone," Keller said, slurring.

"Right, so we can continue killing each other and no one will ever notice," the orderly speculated.

"I suppose. Arnold was careful of the staff he appointed. Do you have any relatives, ah..."

"Grey. The name is Grey Mahoney."

"Any relatives, Grey? Or anyone who would check on you if you didn't come home tonight?"

"No, not really. But forget about my relatives Keller, you look bad. We need to get you to a hospital. You and Henrik and Emma. This DIY shit isn't funny."

"No. Emma is a fine nurse. It's nothing a little first aid can't handle," Keller said, feeling dizzy.

Grey took Keller by the arm, and they walked back into the house, through the rear entrance, and into the lab. A plumber had been called to take care of the emergency flood and though he expressed his concern over the contents of the aquariums which were nowhere to be seen, he didn't ask many questions. He was on triple overtime and pretended not to care, despite his eyes which popped out naturally as they were and darted about to the jolts of shot nerves.

Keller visited Bruno, who was in and out of slumber and riddled by nightmares, but in good spirits once awake. Henrik was also quite satisfied after a double dose of morphine—Emma was finishing up cleaning his wounds.

"Hang on hon, you're next. You could use a few touch-ups, Keller."

"Thank you. Never felt better, in some ways."

The clone of Violet lay on the table, umbilical cord disconnected and breathing on her own. *Emma and Henrik must have resuscitated.* Her tattoo peeked from beneath the hospital gown, and she too had been bandaged in places. Keller stared at her for a few seconds. *Who does a tattoo on a body which appears to be in a coma?* He scanned for a 'Be back soon' sign. There was none and just a very dim light on—she was technically alive— her heartbeat was strong enough though fluctuating, oxygen level good. *Did she twitch?* Keller turned away, shaking his head. *I need a drink; I'm getting delusional again.*

He walked out of the lab, into the lounge and stumbled to the fridge using one hand to stabilize himself along the counter. *Thirsty, very thirsty... pray there be a bottle of vodka in the freezer.* He felt a blackout coming on and grasped the fridge door handle, wishing for a drink before it arrived. It's a long way down, he thought as his knees, numb, failed to buckle. Keller fell sideways; a board teetering over and hitting the floor full on with arms barely out to cushion the fall. As his eyes closed, he could see something blurry approach. In seconds the bare feet were near his face. He glanced up and saw a swimming image of Gouyen looking down. "Get up," she said. Then blackness. Silence.

The orderly, Grey, continued burning the bodies. After the Arnold + Clone Arnold duo followed August and Francine. The Kid was last, whose ashes would be collected in an urn, he decided. *I'll do the scattering myself.* After slamming the door shut and having a smoke, Grey went outside and walked to the gate house. The last he remembered he had left it open. When he was but 50 meters or so away, a car pulled in and stopped, leaving its headlights on. Though blinded, Grey could make out the outline of a light bar on its roof. *Don't mind if I am a touch psychic.*

When a policeman got out of the cruiser, Grey recognized his silhouette too. "Hey Neil," he began, "Lemme just get the gate for you. Guards aren't on duty and the intercom's been disconnected. Sorry for the wait."

"Hey Grey, no problem. I didn't know you worked here."

"I take care of the place. Renovations going on, again," Grey mustered a nervous chuckle.

"Who's up there now?"

"One of the doctors is working late, wants to make sure it all gets set up right."

"It's a little warm out to be running the furnace so hard, isn't it?" he said, nodding to the back chimney and the dark cloud looming above.

"I was just burning some garbage."

"At this time? Remember, no more than 50kg an hour or you'll need a permit."

"Nope, nothing like that, it's just a one off," he said as the vision of a snugly fitting Arnold together with his large, totally unlike him twin, flitted by.

"I haven't noticed any tradesmen coming this way, nor has anyone in town mentioned renovations here."

"Well, it's more about the equipment. There are a couple specialists who visit the site from out of town, the mainland actually. We'll have a local trades guy come in to do finishing touches. Neil, was there a reason you came out here tonight?"

"I have a report from someone on the edge of town saying they witnessed a UFO taking off from behind the mansion without any running lights. In the back field there. I know that's pretty far-fetched, but did you see anything which might explain it?"

"That was a helicopter, dropping off stuff and picking up old stuff."

"Helicopter."

"Yup. Army grade. Nothing to worry about, the lights were on all right."

"You must be pretty high end," Neil carried on, trying to generate interest.

"We are," Grey replied flatly.

"Well, I guess it's nothing then. Let me know if you have any problems."

"Will do. Good night Neil."

"Goodnight." The officer walked back to his cruiser, got in and drove off.

Grey remained by the gatehouse. It was dark. The crickets chirped and somewhere a frog throated. Dew glossed the grass and bushes. *I could get used to this place. Probably some game in the wood and adjoining fields too.* Grey walked inside, flooded with relief he still had a job and most likely wasn't going to prison. *Actually, I damn near love it.*

Then he cast an eye over the monitors, his eye naturally gravitating to the only point of interest. Lounge cam 3. The plumber and an agitated Emma were over top Keller who was lying on the lounge floor next to an open fridge, apparently unconscious. Grey felt for the car keys in his pocket as he bound out the door.

Chapter 57

In late August, a woman boarded a train at Paddington Station in London. The train took her to the city of Bath, where she arrived an hour and twenty-six minutes later and got off. The ride had been uneventful, yet the trip itself was a journey into the known unknown. A friend had offered to drive her, but she had refused. She wanted to take the train by herself and while this was no remarkable event for the average almost 30-year-old, it was for *her*.

She put her foot on the platform and gingerly stepped out. She proceeded to the center, hiking her bag higher onto her shoulder and paused there to collect her thoughts. People were eager to leave the station, so she joined the stream.

Get in a cab and stop killing time, she said to herself. Her phone was in her purse, but she decided not to use it quite yet. *Maybe one will just show up, they always hang around stations.* Sure enough, three were sitting and waiting for a fare. She walked by them and onward down what looked like the main street. She had been on it as a child numerous times but couldn't remember what it was called. If she continued, it should take her to a historic bridge across the River Avon. *I'm not ready to see him.*

After a few blocks, her legs were sore. All over. Joints, muscles, and even veins. While she had been undergoing physio for over three months, the going was still rough, and this was her first trip outside of London.

The town was as she had remembered it—neat, tidy, light yellow stone buildings, smooth and aesthetic. She walked a couple more blocks, ignoring the searing pain in her legs. She stopped in front of a café near the river and debated whether to go in. The woman worried about sounding weird, out of her skin, saying something awkward. She looked at the pavement until a dizzy spell passed. Then upon looking up, she saw the reflection of a strange person—smooth, healthy, V-shaped face, strawberry blonde hair, green eyes bright yet foreign, nice build—on the slight side but fine. She was wearing a summer dress with short sleeves. A tattoo narrated from her left sleeve—a captain at the wheel of a vintage ship. *Oh christ, it's me. Stop staring. There's probably someone sitting at a table right inside, somewhere.*

The woman turned and continued walking to the river and the historic bridge. *I'll stop and sit down in the park. No. This is ludicrous. Get in the next cab, which comes by.* A block or so further, she did. Minutes later the cab arrived at a house on Warminster Rd, in the south of Bath. On the driveway stood a huge black shiny RAM pickup with an extra-large cab and a short bed. It was jacked up, and the tires had a heavy tread. *Yep, this is the place.*

She got out, walked up the drive towards the gate, and noted a figure move beyond a curtained window to the right of the front door. *He's in the kitchen.* She couldn't make out who it was yet knew by the stance and mannerisms. The woman wasn't stopping now, she had reached the point of no return. She strode straight for the door and knocked. A man opened it, and before introducing himself, he stared for a second, pushing himself to speak. "Hi, you must be here to see me. I'm Alexey."

"Yes, hi, I know," she said, stretching out her hand. He shook it.

"And your name, miss? I didn't catch it."

"I'm sure you'll be able to guess it before long."

Alexey paused and looked at her, vexed. "You wanted to talk to me."

"Yes," she said, smiling, looking sideways at a planter for an instant.

They stood a moment, glancing at each other.

"How rude of me, c'mon in," he finally said.

She followed him through a narrow hall which ended in a few steps going up — from there the route split, a doorway led to the left and one to the right. They took the one to the left and the room beyond opened up to a considerable space with a tall bay window and skylights. The décor begged to be cottage-like but wasn't. *Same old, same old.* A large ornate gold lamp was lit, tassels hanging from the shade. Graceful patterns adorned the area rug on the floor, reflecting another on the wall. Three high-back chairs occupied the living room along with an ornate sofa. The woman blinked at the blue and mustard walls and noticed the cupboards bursting with put-away things. She walked to the bay and peered out into the garden, another conundrum of overgrown plants, tall shady trees and patches of stonework. *He's no gardener, never was. But I like this place.*

"You caught me off guard since you remind me of the woman who got killed a few months ago, molested by, well, first they thought it was Keller Mod and then it turns out, some surgeon slash patient from that psychiatric long stay place, down in ah — ."

"Newport, Isle of Wight. Except that I'm much younger, she must have been in her fifties."

"Yes, of course. You definitely look *young*. With TV it's sometimes hard to tell, they only show a quick glimpse."

"Yeah, sure do," she said, her eyes and lips suggesting more words to follow.

Alexey looked at her another moment and offered her a seat on the sofa. He sat down on a high back himself and soon made as if to get up. "Would you like a glass of juice or some coffee? I have beer too. Wine?"

"I'll have some water, please."

He made his way to the kitchen across the narrow hall. She stood and climbed upstairs to the bathroom. Alexey returned with a glass of water for her and a beer for himself. He looked around and heard the toilet flush. He sat down, squinting his eyes, slightly nodding his head. He took a sip of beer.

"I had to use the toilet, I hope you don't mind."

"No, of course not. Glad you found it ok."

She blushed slightly and took a seat in front of the glass, picked it up, and drank most of the water.

They sat in silence for a few seconds, then Alexey spoke, "So I'm glad you came over. Was there a reason for your visit, I mean…"

"Ah, yeah, I know that you and Keller are close, so I wanted to tell you that he's ok."

Alexey moved to the edge of his seat. "Let's be honest with each other, you look like Violet, even have her tattoo. I imagine if you know Keller and are making a mystery visit, you're from the mansion, am I right?"

"The Jolly More Mansion as well, yes."

"How else do you know him? And what the hell happened out there?"

"A lot happened," she said faintly, glancing down.

"Are you ok? I mean you drank that water pretty fast, maybe have some more? I can—"

"I'm fine," she said, looking back up, the drama fading. "I know Keller from his childhood."

"That's impossible, He's what, 30? I'd give you 20, 25 tops."

"28. I'm going by 28. It's the skin, it's new."

Alexey's eyes widened, and he sat up straighter, wiping the palms of his hands on his thighs. "Then you're literally from the mansion, a patient? Had like an epidermic graft?"

She mustered a shy smile. "Yes, I had the works you might say."

"The works. Must have taken a while."

"No, not too long. I just happened by and —."

She reached over and pulled her purse closer to herself. In her bag was a wallet and from that she produced a tiny blue blossom with a thin stem and sliver of a leaf. A dried Forget-Me-Not. She passed it towards him. "I remember Keller from Corfe Castle, he gave me this there, well, a whole pile of them."

It was Alexey's turn to grey. A second later, he flushed red. "Is this a joke? My daughter Katrina was at the Corfe with Keller. I drove them, along with Tom. We had a day trip. I don't recall you being there. And he certainly didn't give *you* any flowers. Nor her."

The woman remained quiet, taking a sip of water, except the glass was empty. Alexey took a big glug of beer, then caught his breath. He looked out the window as if expecting someone at the door. There was no one there, simply a car reaching the dead end and turning around. *He must think I'm a nutcase.*

"Keller told me the story about the antler woman whom he saw as a child. Do you believe him?" she asked.

"Antler woman? Oh, yeah, I vaguely remember that. The little tyke saw a ghost back in Nevada. Tom certainly believed him, pretty much based his research on that — the idea that some children can perceive ghosts until they get older and lose their ability," he said with relief.

"The antler woman told him that the Forget-Me-Not, Scorpion Grass as she called it, represents the human soul in a way. Beautiful, fragile yet tough enough to survive almost anywhere as long as it had a little water. In some places, it abounds like a weed. Like at Corfe."

"I get the idea, is there a point to all of this? I mean, a youngish woman claims to know my daughter with whom I was very close. I don't remember you, I'm sorry. Better tell me about the mansion, providing that's why you're here," he stumbled on.

"What do you want to know?"

"Last I heard, Keller was in the hospital, badly hurt. Then I lost touch. What happened?"

"It was Arnold."

"Arnold?"

"The guy behind it all. The voice. Ed."

"You don't say. Huh, never liked the bastard. Caretaker slash scientist was trying to inch his way in on Tom's work. Called himself a hacker. I call him a hack. Bones, skin, and add water," Alexey released a stiff chuckle.

"A hack or hacked, I'm not sure. But it was him. Anyway, in the end there was some shooting and the tanks shattered, Keller was badly cut up, lacerated. He lost a lot of blood. Made it to a hospital barely in time, so I was told."

"And as a patient, you saw all of this?"

"I saw him at a distance. The rest I heard from Henrik."

"Right," he said with a leery undertone.

The woman stopped and glanced at him, then continued, "And since Arnold has gone missing, presumed dead by one of the droids who accompanied him, all three were Xi7s, but Keller and the orderly took one out and the Kid, another. So, since Arnold is missing, the RAF police are investigating. I mean, it's hard to tell what exactly they're doing, but they suspect something since the wreckage at the mansion was quite bizarre, yet no technology was found. Ah, really bizarre, as someone like you can imagine."

"Xi7? You are aware of droid models? Secret, Ministry of Defense models?"

She said nothing. They both paused. Neither looked at the other. While Alexey took another gulp of beer, the woman eyed her empty glass and then him. She pursed her lips.

"I can get you some more," he began.

"No, thanks."

"Did Keller tell you the story about Corfe Castle?"

She didn't answer but gave him a serious expression, one suggesting she was upset. "You always supported Tom, why?" she said instead.

Alexey spoke calmly now, "He is a genius, and I thought highly of him."

"And?"

"He was on to something big."

"So?"

"So, I think he was right, I believed in the man."

"And if someone walked up to you and said they had been *transferred*, like a human to a droid or a human to a clone, would you believe in them?"

"Maybe. It's a touchy question. In theory…"

"So, you wouldn't."

"I didn't say that."

"But even though you respect him, the idea of transferring a human to a droid body might sound good theoretically, or in a bar, but in life there's just no way. Am I correct?"

"This conversation is impossible. Did you come here to challenge the integrity of my ability to assess a rather risky scientific theory? The last time I had one like this was with my—." Alexey stopped talking, wrinkles of perplexity drawing on his face.

They both took a breath, talked a while about the Isle of Wight itself and speculated on how Arnold might have risen to where he did and managed to involve Bruno in the scheme. As the woman talked, Alexey looked at her observingly, searching to find something he missed, in her face.

The afternoon wore on and eventually, she made an excuse that it was time to leave. She stood up. Alexey rose as well, apprehensive. They stood a meter apart.

"What else did Keller not tell you?" he said.

"You mean like about when you and your daughter, Katrina, first came here from Russia," she paused to swallow and then continued slowly in Russian, "and didn't know a soul. Her mother had died, your wife, the one who called her Pupsik?" she smiled a little nervous slant.

Alexey paled again, his head floated back, aghast. I know those eyes. Impossible. Yet I know them. She would never have told a boy such a funny nickname, Keller would have made fun, he rarely had an edge on her. Wait, she spoke Russian…

"Do you want me to sing the lullaby that—" she swallowed again and stopped talking.

"No. Enough. How did it happen? I mean you said you happened by, like it was a fluke…"

Tears flooded her eyes, her stance wavered. "If I could get into a cold tin can, then a warm body was simple…" She stiffly flopped back down on the sofa and wiped her tears.

Alexey knelt in front of her. "Katrina," he said, choked, embracing her knees, thighs, sides, tears randomly dribbling over his face, the wrinkles having smoothed themselves,

"Papa…" she whispered, running her hand through his hair, the other pulling his shoulder closer. "I had to test you. It's been such a long time that I wasn't sure myself who I am."

"I understand. This will all take some getting used to. I'm speechless, I…"

"Don't talk papa. We will talk again, and again," she blurted a laugh. "After all, I could be an imposter, trying to get an inheritance."

"Ah, yes, an imposter who looks like someone who got murdered by Keller but actually set up by Arnold," he chuckled. "I see," he said, pensive. "So is Tom around too?"

"Yes, lying low."

"Lying low… this is insane…"

"Yup. You're telling me."

Chapter 58

The jet that flew Keller from Bristol in the west of England to Bangor International Airport in Maine, USA, was military. What Keller couldn't understand was why he was being flown there, or out of the country at all, considering his situation. He looked down at the tracker on his ankle, half expecting it to sever the foot from his leg, 40 or 50 seconds after take-off. But even halfway across the Atlantic, it failed to do so.

After waking up in a hospital on the Isle of Wight, Keller found the Military Police waiting for him patiently, ready to escort him to Neufeld Bunker. In the following months his life consisted of recuperating and sporadic interrogations. The investigation was led by Simon Evstrom, the security boss. Instead of fighting the situation, Keller went with the current—it was rather strong but would eventually spit him out, he hoped. He just didn't know where and now over the Atlantic, he wondered.

The landing in Bangor, Maine, was smooth, but instead of taxiing to the main airport building, the plane headed to a separate hangar off to the north. The planes they passed on the way were not commercial, the dull grey fuselages void of portholes suggested refueling planes for jet fighters.

Their own plane stopped in front of the furthest hangar and cut its engines. Silence ensued. Aside from two trainees and a flight attendant, the plane was empty. The attendant, a comely woman with an appetite for chit-chat and nosiness, buzzed about, tidying up. This one has no light on to begin with, Keller thought. She approached him now and told him he was free to leave, glancing at the place where his tracker was hidden by his trousers, then at him, and smiled nervously. "Just watch your step on your way down, it's a windy day."

Keller nodded and headed out. *Really, that's it?*

"Someone will meet you in the hangar Mr Mod," she said after him. "And good luck with it all."

Keller negotiated the steps and promptly headed towards the massive hangar door. And there, standing by the edge of the impossibly tall, narrow opening, not moving but facing him, was a figure. A woman, hands by her sides, dressed in pants, cardigan and t-shirt, hair flowing and ruffled by the breeze. Keller slowed his pace. *She reminds me of someone.* From a telltale stance through to posture, and by the oval face and inset eyes, dark behind sunglasses. She smiled and waved at him. *Someone here to pick me up, who knows me or is pretending to be a delightful host or something. That smile looks damn real, the nerve of these people.* Keller was aware of the tracker with each step. *Probably has a remote in her pocket.*

Keller scanned the hangar for any MP types and saw none. A few maintenances crew worked away servicing an ambulance plane. He slowed 10 meters from the woman.

"Hi Keller."

"Hi," he played along. *Gouyen?*

"I'm here to meet you of course, and be your escort," she continued to beam, radiate. The smile was as real as any smile Keller had ever seen in his life. Laced with flirt.

"What's going on?" he said to the woman.

"Seriously?" She took off her sunglasses.

Keller was suddenly shocked ashore by a large, soft, bubbly wave of recognition. *What the heck, Nora?*

"You look so different without the lab coat and stuff, you got me. Your hairs, ah, out."

"Yeah, it is."

"Escort? Are we going somewhere?"

"Yeah, we are."

He strode towards her now, and they embraced. "Thanks for meeting me, it's been hell."

"So I hear," she said, her voice melting the doubt.

"Got this thing on my ankle still."

"Relax, I actually have something for that."

"I figured I'd scared you off."

"Not yet," she said, turning and leading the way into the hangar.

"How did you know about all of this?" Keller asked.

"For one, I visited Lucy's, thinking I might find you there. Your phone had been off a long time," Nora began, emotion filtering in. "They told me you disappeared, basically. After the news story, I didn't know what to believe. You didn't strike me as the rape and murder type but then, the world's pretty messed up."

"Yeah, I wanted to—"

"Then I happened to talk to Lurch. I mean he basically hit on me until he realized who I was, ahm, then he suggested we visit your place, said he had a key, so we did. And of course, Tarzana was curious too. You have quite the collection of friends."

"Lucky me."

"No, I mean I really like them," she said, looking him in the eye, unwavering.

"K. And how did you know to pick me up?"

"Bruno. He said he was your partner. And that he heard from Lurch I was worried about you. I mean, I guess I was. He was basically checking me out. Thankful that I helped save Violet although I hear she's dead again. I'm sorry," she said pausing to look in his eyes.

"Well, it is what it is, she did it herself."

Nora made a lip shrug but Keller could see her eyes still smiled. "Then Bruno said if I wanted to see you, he would arrange it, so I took a chance you might want to see me too. And that eventually led me here. Bruno's quite a guy," she said, nervously laughing.

"Unpredictable," Keller added.

"He seems very youthful to me. Just stiff or something, peculiar."

"Nothing a bit of physio can't fix."

They had come to the back of the hangar where a car awaited just outside.

"Well, we have a drive ahead of us so you can tell me your version of what really happened, Ghostmaster."

Keller shot her a nervous, thin smile as they got in. Then he noticed the driver, the fragment of a face in the rear-view mirror.

"He's Ok, he's with us," she said.

"Who's us?"

"You'll see, it's a surprise. You've been there before."

"What? No..."

"Yeah. It's Ok. And we'll get that bracelet off you in no time."

As they drove on, the route came back to him, much like witnessing a nightmare reflected in life. Minus the edge of being tracked and hunted. The healthy young greens of spring had darkened, some even changing color. A sense of timelessness touched the trees and fields along the way—oaks, maples, beaches, and pines casting their usual shadows. One followed the stream of the prevailing winds, another grew straight up with maybe a thing for the south.

By the time they pulled into the dark lane walled by tall trees, the white Victorian shining further on, Keller finally felt the nightmare of Jolly More Mansion give way to hope. The quaint streetlamp still waited for its time to come on. The smell of the sea beyond the house and the whoosh of the waves permeated the car as they opened the doors and got out. Keller wanted to say, 'Home sweet home,' but a light hysteria supplanted the thought. They walked up the old, worn yet freshly painted steps to the veranda. It looked as when he had last seen the place, yet he could sense someone foreign stirring inside. It wasn't the Uncle, though Keller was prepared not to be surprised if it was. *Bruno?*

The last time Keller had entered the house was under armed supervision. This seemed similar yet wasn't at all. Bruno appeared youthful, vigorous, and in good spirits. They embraced.

"How do you feel, Bruno?"

"Been better, years ago. Sore, and everything aches but I appreciate this new phase in my life. It's very exciting."

Nora giggled a sudden slight burst. More like a girl than a Pathologist who spent her days working on dead bodies. *She is truly amazing. Or has she been planted?*

Keller stood looking out of the window at the sea. The view of the deep blue-turquoise waters, frothy, set against a dramatically clouded ultramarine sky, brought with it a momentary lucidity he now drew upon. The gulls bounced and lofted about, and so could he. *Find out what you're able and stay neutral. If Bruno can override the military police, he is to be reckoned with.*

In the next instant, a waft of fatigue swept over Keller—he attributed it to the fresh sea air. He turned, walked over to a chair and sat down just in time to see a third person exiting the kitchen with coffee and tea. *Cassy!* Keller glanced at Nora, who blushed a little and smiled. *God, she can smile. What's going on?*

Keller took a coffee and noted the droid did not try to recognize him.

"It's time you fill me in. This is all so tiresome, with the flight and all. Literally."

"Yes, I agree Keller. Let me start with Cassy. Just a droid, no Katrina in there."

Keller looked at Cassy, half expecting a subtle, sarcastic response. None followed.

"Cassy, can you take care of his tracker?" Bruno asked.

"Yes, no problem," she said as Keller lifted his pant leg. Her voice was a matter of fact and entailed no emotion. *One less complication.*

"And Simon agreed with this?" Keller asked, cautiously.

"You're here, aren't you?"

"Yeah. So must be off the record."

"Yes, and we'll figure it out. Besides, Henrik's back at the Jolly More, courtesy of Simon, helping with the investigation enough to make sure the Military Police find nothing of importance. It would be such a waste and who knows who might get a hold of it. What is Tom's, must remain with us."

"Simon wants it for himself?"

"He does, but he really has no clue."

"Let's hope he doesn't dream of continuing where Arnold left off," Keller said, sitting back.

"Henrik is watching him, and we have help."

"Who?"

For a moment the room was quiet. Nora's smile melted and Bruno frowned. "Tom. I think."

"You think."

"Yes. For now, Simon probably wants to get to understand more without spilling the story up-lines. But if anyone else gets curious, it could easily become messy. So, Tom has asked not to be contacted for now. He'll let us know. And when you're ready, he'd like to talk to you."

Once again Keller was reminded that Cassy—Katrina, had told him the truth. The vision of her 12-year-old self, walking away and fading, played for a second.

The room was silent again while Keller took a breath. "And how is it you chose Violet's place to hang out in, Bruno? I mean, did she mention you in her will, or just checking up on it?"

Nora stiffened now, biting her lip and suppressed an upward surge of air. A throaty grunt popped out.

"Keller, you're a decent man," said Bruno. "What did you do with my uncle's body?"

Keller registered the question, massaged his forehead and then looked for answers in the cracks of the wooden floor. He swung his head up and gave Bruno a stare as Nora laughed out loud.

"You burned him out there on the beach, I take it? The wheelbarrow had been washed but had an ashy residue," Bruno said, keeping a straight face.

"Yeah. Ah, I built a pyre and set him on fire at night. That's what I gathered he wanted, based on the stories he told. Besides, I couldn't leave a trace of him, not considering the situation." Keller paused, the scene in the lab right before Bruno's transfer rushed back to him. Gouyen at the door, then leaving. "Violet?" he asked, concerned brow contrasting a slight grin.

Bruno smiled, "Took you long enough. Nice bod, huh?"

"Not my first choice for you, but not bad I suppose — gives you a whole new role to play," Keller dribbled.

"I have the perfect costume and voice. And a vast collection of memories to draw from. Doesn't matter what I say, people believe it. A touch of make-up adds a little age though I must say I do keep my distance. What was he thinking?"

"He wanted to score young again," Nora said.

"Have you seen him, Keller? Has he, ah, reached out to you?"

Keller broke out of a trance, "I suspected something that very afternoon. The place was suddenly flooded with souls, and I think he got overwhelmed. Maybe saw his wife in there. I don't know after that; hasn't reached out, no."

"Next question is, do you want to go off the grid? You won't be very functional from prison, let alone in military prison. And I can't keep you out here forever with that tracker on. Simon or no Simon."

"Francine and Arnold are dead because of me," Keller mustered to say.

"You made decisions which allowed the rest of us to live, not just yourself. Arnold had it coming and there was no way he'd let Francine walk this earth. We all did our part, but you were the common thread. You solved an impossible problem and that kept things going. There is not much chance that either a Judge or anyone in the court will understand what went on. Even military, never mind civil. No matter what you, or any of us say. Transfers to clones, Keller? Infusions? Prison or not, you'll have to carry a dark secret around with you regardless of what happens."

"Sounds like a dead end. Get me out," Keller said, looking at Bruno, Cassy then Nora.

"Fair enough. Let's do it," Bruno said, nodding to Cassy. When Keller began to stare at Cassy, Nora spoke, "It's not her. She would have made a crack by now."

"You've met?"

"Yeah."

"Like, which one?"

"Katrina, I mean, she looks different now."

Chapter 59

What followed for Keller was bliss. No tracker, no chip, and no severe threats or investigations. They were done for now. Keller experienced a breezy ocean caress as he stepped across the threshold and onto the front veranda. A second later the old wooden, screened storm door bounced shut behind him, the little latch rattling along. From the peeling rail to the crow which took flight from a pine branch high up — it all resonated through him as he trod to the sun-warmed steps and down. Grains of sand stuck to his feet, having found their way everywhere — blessed and carefree. Nora was a few yards ahead as she made an elegant half-turn to make sure he was following. Like a child might — the swirl of her summer dress completed all the sun touched and shaded.

When the conversation had steered itself back to Neufeld Bunker, Nora insisted they go outside for a walk and Keller obliged. The discussion had turned to Tom and whether it was he who substituted the fake footage of Arnold's clone keeling over. Keller insisted they probably just needed to ask him, noting Bruno's eagerness to visit the tunnels. *For Violet, not knowing something juicy, is a tragedy...*

Getting a grip on the fact that Bruno's clone was inhabited by Violet, enthralled Keller. At times, it looked as though Bruno was wholeheartedly playing the role of Violet with absolutely no slip-ups. *No wonder she was so into that guy, the woman had a plan.*

The sand and the cool water felt good under his city feet. Nora walked next to him; they didn't speak for the first while. Eventually, her hand made it into his—small, cool, and dry. Keller glanced at her and caught the slight lengthening of her lips, corners up. It was in her eyes and his too.

"Do you miss your father?" she began.

"Not until a little while ago—when I was returning to the Jolly More from London."

"I see."

"Before that, he died, and that's all. I was afraid to miss him, in case it was him behind everything, an insane man."

"Then he didn't blow himself up along with Katrina?"

"Either way, doesn't bother me anymore—I'm sure it wasn't planned like that. But even if I could get a chance to see him today, I wouldn't go. Not now," he confessed.

"So, about Katrina..."

"What?"

"She came back. She took Violet's clone," Nora said with gentle directness.

Keller remained quiet. *Stubborn.*

"I met her when she checked up on you. She's quite pretty. Tall, fit, just a little stiff maybe."

"Violet was an actress. Makes sense. Katrina was a tomboy and also pretty. What difference does it make?" Keller asked, teasing.

"I just thought maybe—"

They strolled a while in silence. The gulls had noticed and made up for it, diving, and clamoring. Out on the sea, windsurfers had ventured from the bay. A lobster boat cruised by, and a tanker loomed in the distance.

"Nora, do you really want to know who I missed?"

"Not really."

"It was you," Keller said, shooting glances her way.

She smiled and nodded, the words written on her face in light blush. The wind caught her hair and scattered it over her eyes just then—she brushed it away.

"I'm surprised you have a stomach for all this. I had thought you'd keep your distance," he continued. "I mean, regardless of what you do for a living."

"You definitely take my top rating for weird Keller Mod. But there's something about you that tells me it's all true, what happened."

Keller turned and stepped in front of Nora facing her now. She glanced at the sea, then looked back into his eyes. His gaze met hers and he noted a plot germinating, reflecting his own. His hands coaxed her hips, gently pulling forward. A moment later, he kissed her. Then she kissed him back, wrapping her arms around his neck. They stood like that a while.

"I'm glad you showed up here," he finally said.

"Yeah, me too."

They turned and kept walking, as the waves gently shushed the sand.

"A good friend recently told me that we created Evolution ourselves so that we could be together. Instead of being lonely spirits cast out in the middle of space," Keller said with a shrug. "Let's face it, we briefly met 2000 miles away and now here we are."

"The Ghostmaster has spoken. Tell me more enlightened one," Nora said, scrunching her nose with a smile.

He grabbed her by the arm and pulled her along into the water, the frothy surf winding around their legs. A ribbon of seaweed bobbed nearby, a castaway.

"So, this is where you cooked the guy?" Nora grinned through strands of hair.

"I panicked, big time."

"Understandable I suppose, considering the situation."

"Let's go swimming…"

"You wanna drown me?" she asked, pulling her dress off and throwing it back on shore.

"Maybe," he said popping a smile, taking off his shirt and shorts.

"Would you consider me a natural selection or unnatural?"

"You look all right," Keller said, realizing the lameness as the words left his mouth.

"All right?"

"Ok, you're naturally super attractive and I'm having trouble keeping my jaw up and I fell for you the moment I entered the morgue." *Also weird.*

"Am I supposed to believe that?" she said, taking her glasses off and tossing them on her dress.

"You seem to believe all the other stuff…"

"Hey, can your dad fix me up? I'm tired of these things, I hate contacts, don't want laser and I'd love to see what you see in this twisted world of ours."

"How did you know about all that?" Keller asked pausing.

Nora made a comical laugh.

"He's only fifty stories underground, hidden within an abandoned military installation, but I'll see if I can make an appointment," he said, splashing her as they walked back into the water.

"Keller, how did you find out about your perceptions in the first place?" She splashed him back.

"Gouyen."

"Who's Gouyen?"

"I saw her when I was a boy, she was planting Scorpion Grass in the desert."

"Like Forget-me-nots? Forget-me-not Keller Mod," she said with a mischievous giggle.

Keller stopped and looked into her eyes, plunging into their depths. Then he took her hand and gently pulled her deeper in. Nora took a couple steps, dove past him and Keller dove in after her. They surfaced, spitting water and laughing. The gulls circled, chattering, deliberating whether to join in. It was another lovely August afternoon by the sea, in Maine.

Acknowledgements

Writing this book has been an adventure and as my first, quite ominous. It's one thing to dream plots and scribble notes and quite another to nail it all down on the page.

So first off thanks to Reagan Rothe and his team at Black Rose Writing for being my publisher. My sincerest gratitude. Thank you also to Leah Chalmers, an early reader (an editor by trade) who gave me much valuable advice that allowed me to turn a newbie attempt at writing and channel it into something resembling a book.

Thanks to Dr Sameer Zaman for his advice on medical procedures and his ideas on things that could go wrong yet remain credible. Thank you to Fay Collins for reading, and for the pointers which I referred to many times and still do.

Thanks also to Elizabeth Bailey, author, for her kind advice. And finally, thanks to my wife for beta reading—she read each version—and for giving me a nod to say, "It's ok for you to do something crazy, I don't mind, just get it finished." I'll always be grateful for this.

Author's Note

The book takes place in locations inspired by Appuldurcombe House on the Isle of Wight, the city of Brighton, Brighton Pier, the military tunnels in Corsham, the city of Bath, parts of Nevada, and the coast of Maine. I have taken artistic license with flair, from altering a few details to adding in entire entities.

Anna Bågenholm* and Audrey Shoeman** are two examples of people whose heart and breathing have stopped during lengthy periods of hypothermia lasting many hours, and who survived. There have been many more such incidents, but it is not the purpose of the book to give credence to any methods it describes nor draw parallels to the above-mentioned cases.

About the Author

Peter Kiesners grew up in Canada during that golden period between the first color TV and the beginning of Internet—a time when fuel for dreams overflowed. A creative at heart, he went on to study the arts and worked at over 30 jobs varying from chef, portrait artist, and designer, through to photographer and videographer. He has lived in numerous places including Mississauga, Toronto, Manhattan, Muskoka, the Rockies, Latvia, and finally settling in an English village with his wife and daughter, and on a career in writing where those dreams take on a life of their own.

Note from Peter Kiesners

Word-of-mouth is crucial for any author to succeed. If you enjoyed *Scorpion Grass*, please leave a review online—anywhere you are able. Even if it's just a sentence or two. It would make all the difference and would be very much appreciated.

Thanks!
Peter Kiesners

We hope you enjoyed reading this title from:

www.blackrosewriting.com

Subscribe to our mailing list – *The Rosevine* – and receive **FREE** books, daily
deals, and stay current with news about upcoming
releases and our hottest authors.
Scan the QR code below to sign up.

Already a subscriber? Please accept a sincere thank you for being a fan of
Black Rose Writing authors.

View other Black Rose Writing titles at
www.blackrosewriting.com/books and use promo code
PRINT to receive a **20% discount** when purchasing.